Choice, Set Free
Book 7

The Tae'anaryn

& the

Voyage of
Imagination's Dawn

by Dr Joseph Ireland, PhD. "Dr Joe"

The Tae'anaryn *and the* Voyage of Imagination's Dawn

Copyright © Dr Joe Ireland, 2022 www.drjoe.id.au

Cover design and internal art by Dr Joseph Ireland, with the drawings of Toni/Oum by Karlie Ireland.

Published by Creating Science www.CreatingScience.Org

Minor editing changes 3 October 2024

National Library of Australia Cataloguing-in-Publication entry

Author:	Ireland, Joe.
Title:	The Tae'anaryn and Voyage of the Imagination's Dawn
Series:	Choice, set free. Book 7.
Imprint:	Dr Joe
ISBN:	978-0-6484941-9-5 and 9780648494195
Date:	30th April 2022
Pages:	308
Size:	140mm x 216 mm (5.5 x 8.5 in)
Spine Width:	16.383 mm = 0.645 inches
Weight:	359.692 gm = 0.793 lb
Target Audience:	Primary school age. "Middle fiction".
Subjects:	Individuality—Juvenile fiction.
BISAC:	YAF000000 Young adult fiction
Dewey Number:	A823.4 F IRE
Lexile Number:	750

About the author

I like writing books, I really do. I like it much more than reading books, which I can barely stand. Which, I suppose, is a bit of a curious thing for a man 14 novels deep into his own storytelling, but that is me.

I'm currently training up as a Positive Behavioural Specialist, which is a bit of a surprise. I'm left wondering what to make of my now 'hobbies', of doing the occasional science show and lecturing in *Teaching Science* at the University – a total treat to be sure! All this does not help to answer the question, 'who am I?', but it does highlight the problem I have in answering that question just at this time. Maybe it's all just 'meant to be', because I find it all very wonderful and vastly more palatable than being a tyrannical monster of authority that my community, the parents, and the children themselves expect me to be when I'm being a … *teacher*. <shudders>.

Hopefully those days are behind me now, which begs the question of why I'd even want to lecture, since adults can be the very worst of students. With kids, it's never personal until you make it. Adults will try to destroy you when you fail their expectations, and they will feel entirely justified in doing so, which is so, so very sad. Why do we wait till boiling point to mention something is upsetting to us, far beyond the point where something constructive could be done about it? Will we all one day learn to use reason, and perhaps some courage? But now I'm just whinging, and you did not come here for that.

I don't know why I write this story, but I MUST.

Sincerely,

Dr Joe.

Dedicated to:

Karlie, whose first picture of the 'boy' not only ensured this book be written, but whose last picture is the capstone of it.

20,91,5,9 1,8 55,6 32,4,3,32,2,8,3 2,16 26,1,16,6

Contents

Table of Images

Characters

Kialessa's Immediate circle

Kialessa – the innocent child of an archdemon and a thief, she is trying to protect her King, whom she loves dearly, from a cruel assassin's knife.

Darrix – Her good friend, the prayerful warrior or 'paladin', and a full-blooded human. He wields the legendary blade Defender.

Posk – Another good friend, the half troll prince of exceptional physical strength and much-less-than-exceptional wisdom.

Piex – The part star dragon wizarding prodigy, a good friend who needs Kialessa's encouragement and wisdom often.

Allastassia – A not-so-good-but-always-there-for-you-friend, a talented and very ambitious part dryad enchantress.

Senior students also on the voyage

Aolith – Only daughter of a royal family; while not in line for the throne, Aolith is still a human princess. She trains hard and is known as an educated and honest judge.

Natasha – A cervitaur (half human, half deer), who is on exchange in order to learn the ways of the humans, from her people who live in the far north of Lenmer'el. She struggles with some cultural norms, such as wearing dresses, but is known as a kind and creative individual.

Marchan – A capable human wizarding student of Lenmer'el. Piex speaks poorly of him, but Marchan is known for his cunning, wit, and ability to wipe the floor over everyone else on trivia night.

Federach – A powerful dwarven priestess of the earth goddess Mya, she is known for being forthright and overly blunt at times. She is expected to head back to her nation by the end of next year.

Dale – The son of an aspiring noble human family, Dale makes a particular study of siege equipment and large weaponry. He is one of a few names on Kialessa's 'do not like: is a big bully' list.

Boats

Gap's Edge "The Edge"

The nation's only heavy military ocean going vessel. Staffed by fifty, she often brings another fifty soldiers of the fleet. Her armament includes thirty heavy crossbows, a flaming catapult set foremast, and a submerged alumium ram. She is a three masted galley with a compliment of thirty oars for when there is no wind to sail by, or when great haste is needed.

Sea's Bounty "The Bounty"

A large four masted sailing ship, a hulk to be exact. She carries most of the trading materials and supplies, and one hundred sailors as well. She is broad and wide, with plenty of well stocked cargo space. She is well built, and young, commissioned in 301CY (3 years ago).

Imagination's Dawn "The Dawn"

A carrack, with a large mainsail in the centre, a hind sail on the back next to the till, which is used for steering, and a foresail at the front. There is also a bowsprit, which is a small sail at the front used for steering that lies almost parallel to the sea.

She is the oldest, most magical boat in the nation, perhaps indeed in the entire great Kingdom. Three interchangeable interdimensional rooms in the same space host a spacious King's cabin (where at least one of his bodyguards is at all times), a storage room/wizard study, and a small chamber that includes the priestess shrine/general's quarters/steward's station. The mass of all three rooms adds to the ships total mass and must always be accounted for. The three levels on the ship are the main deck, with all the rigging (ropes) and sails; the crew quarters below deck, where the servants and sailors relax and sleep in bunk beds; and the cargo hold, which is quite large, and has room for several extra beds and the large amount of cargo the small ship carries.

Adversaries

Truevine

A powerful elven archdruidess who suffered an unnamed tragedy years ago at the hands of her fellow elves. In bitter vengeance she slew them all, some in front of their families, and is now a wanted criminal hiding from the elf Queen's judgement.

Tobiuus – An extremely capable master of wizardry, the archmage was a wanted criminal for many years due to his open use of necromancy, and apparent disregard for the sanctity of both life and the afterlife. He was captured by the sagemaster Coure De'Feur of Lenmer'el last year at the battle of the Far Keep. He is related to Piex as his grandfather's brother, though they usually refer to him as Uncle Tobiuus. He is a half star dragon, though far crueller.

Brandish "The Slayer" – A physically powerful half giant who revels in battle and slaughter. Once a paid mercenary, he frequently overstepped his quarry for the sheer delight of battle. He was eventually poisoned and captured, and has spent the last five years in prison at Emerel.

Jerik "The Dog", assassin of Kings – Rumoured to be linked to at least a dozen deaths amidst the nobility of Emerel in as many years, the Dog failed three times last year to slay the good King Dunnkan of Lenmer'el, mostly due to the imposition of the royal protector Baroness Kialessa Winterhaven of Lenmer'el, a tae'anaryn. Jerik displays a wide variety of powers and abilities, including shape shifting into a greyhound and a sand form, inhuman speed and balance, and a high resistance to magical effects; in short, almost nothing is known about this powerful and enigmatic, individual. And while his title may refer to him as an assassin of Kings, it is not known if he has ever actually succeeded at that quest.

Venues

Emerel – The capital city and name of the nation that rules over a loose confederacy of seventeen other countries known as the Great Kingdom, of which Lenmer'el is one. It is also the name of its first King, Emerel, crowned after the defeat of the troll hoards around three hundred years ago.

Lenmer'el – the youngest and smallest nation of the Great Kingdom, though one of the largest in terms of sheer land size. Most of the land is undeveloped wilderness lying with the Elven Wyldwolds to the north, Troll lands to the west and south, and the Bounteous Shallowsea to the east. Kialessa and her immediate friends are all from this region.

Treedawn – a small town to the north of the docks of Lenmer'el. It has good hunting grounds and is known for its excellent fishing. A regular migration of trees nearby makes further development inland unwise.

Cairnhold – a small settlement to the north of Treedawn, primarily the settlement of a single Baron Lord Cairn. The superb views and excellent fishing are mitigated by the difficulty in accessing the keep far up on a steep embarkment, though locals swear they wouldn't have it any other way.

Dae Montol – the ruins of one of the satellite citadels of the ancients. The golden streets are long since plundered from well before the settlement of Lenmer'el.

New allies

Anaesu – the youngest son of the Merking and his second wife, the young Anaesu is known as a sweet and gentle soul with a tendency to let his curiosity get the better of him.

Toni/Oum – The only known survivor of the most powerful race of humanoids the gods ever made. Known as 'the ancients', it is said they made a city of pure gold, and once brought peace to the warring primordial gods. Toni has an insatiable curiosity, coupled with unparalleled power, wisdom, and creativity. He also has four arms, four eyes, and two minds.

Wanderer – a unique fey dragon created by Oum, Wanderer can teleport and enter the dream world at will. She appears to form a bond with Kialessa when they visit the forest Oum created and has defended for the past three hundred years.

Darissius – the eldest son of the Merking and a captain in the King's army, he is expected to take the throne one day. He is a loyal son, and like most merkin, he loathes Karnissis.

Karnissis – the sworn and divinely appointed protector of the Merking. He is some form of octopus cervitaur, but most assume his condition is a curse caused by his evil and seditious nature. Nevertheless, he serves the Merking's interests with dark pragmatism and a loyal devotion to rival even the Merking's most ardent supporters.

Harrowbar Minerson – Darrix's father, and a powerful merchant in Lenmer'el, even more so since recent events. He is a very motivated, practical human man, commonly in the company of the King; his wife (Darrix's mother) is rarely seen in public.

Anaxarides – prince royal of the King of the sharkmen, he has assumed the duties of the throne ever since his father's mysterious illness. He is admired for his cunning and ability to dish out revenge served cold. He is considered a just ruler, though his laws are often far harsher than his father's.

Leonidis – champion to the King of the sharkmen, he is usually seen in the service of the acting King, Anaxarides. Leonidis is known for his

brute force and direct tactics, but has shown a rather devastating cunning since coming to work with Anaxarides on a more regular basis.

Glossary

Anemone – a squishy sort of sea creature

Condescension – speaking in simpler terms to someone less informed

Diatribe – a 'rant', an angry speech

Dissipating – spreading out and getting thinner

Elucidate – to clarify

Errant – wrong, or slightly wrong

Eructation – a loud, sudden sound, like a burp

Erudite – clear and informative

Fervid – intense desire, passionate

Heinous – really, really terrible

Indefatigable – undefeatable enthusiasm

Inevitable – totally unavoidable, often predestined

Maw – a mouth, usually round one with lots of teeth

Miasma – a haze or cloud

Monologue – a long speech or play, sometimes a very boring one

Necrotise – to kill, usually due to disease or illness

Obecience – a movement of respect or deference

Simulacrum – an image or representation, usually of a person

Titbit – a small piece of useful information

Transcendent – above all others

Theorems – a thought that can be proven logically correct if the underlying theories are taken to be true

Unequivocally – in such a way as to leave no doubt

Unperturbed – still, silent

Zephyr – a light breeze

Every Day

Thank you, my friends. And remember; you don't only live once;
you live every day. So choose life.
Toni, cited in Recollections of the Tae'anaryl.

Jerik, the Dog, "Assassin of Kings", crouched silently, his eyes upon the pool of still water at his feet. Images within the water swirled into being at his command: the docks, the sailors. The boats being loaded.

'How long you gonna be doing that for, man?' a gruff voice demanded. It was Brandish, the Slayer, recently escaped from prison at the capital of Emerel under very mysterious circumstances.

Jerik hushed him to silence. He stared carefully before replying. 'Three boats? I would have expected more. And only two hundred soldiers disguised as sailors? This all seems a little beneath you, doesn't it, King Dunnkan?'

'Perhaps he really does think so little of you,' a woman's voice teased. She was Truevine, an elven dark druidess wanted for a hundred counts of murder, yet still not brought to justice in as many years.

Jerik scoffed, his breath upsetting the waters and thus, upsetting him. There was no detail he wished to miss. 'More likely he underestimates the amount of danger we bring to him.'

Jerik looked at the images. It was not the sailing ships that had him worried, or the soldiers. It was not even the King's personal bodyguard, or the rod of his authority, which had called down the terrible curse that itched and burned the left side of his face every waking hour. No, it was the dozen or so children the king had thought to bring with him. Jerik watched them closely, memorising their body movements, studying each of their faces in turn.

'Pathetic, using children as a human shield,' Truevine mocked. 'Does he really think Serros the Sun will guard his cause simply because he has brought some youth to die along with him?'

'More blood,' Brandish shrugged. 'Fine by me.'

Jerik scoffed. He knew all too well that their foe knew exactly what he was doing. He watched fervently, till at last his eyes caught on the one he sought: the little twelve-year-old child of prophecy. She had red skin, and horns. She had a prehensile tail, and eyes that glowed red when she was angry. And she was, by far, the most powerful, most dangerous, and most innocent obstacle in the way of his vital quest at this time.

'She really got you rattled,' Truevine continued her mockery.

Jerik snarled; he could not help it. He was a dog in form and in heart. But there would be no mercy this time. She had removed the only obstacle keeping her safe, and now she was the only real obstacle keeping her king safe. If he chose to hide behind her red skin and horns, she would have her only wish and die protecting him.

But he did not have a chance to reply before the wizard cut him off. 'Oh, don't worry about the child. She has no idea of the suffering she has secured for herself, and her King,' Tobiuus, the archmage, informed them with cold murder in his eyes. 'For the Destiny's Maw awaits them both …'

16

Setting Out

You are amazing, you are wonderful!
You can do things no one else can do!
Wherever you are, the world is much better!
Wherever you're not, we're missing one you!
Humdug, dwarf scholar, in a private letter to his uncle's son.

Bright bells sung out, startling the seabirds from their late winter rookeries. The dock was alive with activity, heavy set sailors swearing as they tussled to and fro, bearing stock and rope as they loaded them into the enormous sailing ships. The burning face of Serros lit the sky, warming away the frosty morning chill. If she'd had the courage, Kialessa would have squealed with delight.

Darrix, one of her best friends in the world, walked up beside her. He had been starting some sort of adolescent growth spurt, and was now as tall and broad as almost any human adult, though the bad teenage acne gave away his true age. 'They're nearly done.'

'Is that why you're not helping out anymore?' she teased him.

He grinned; it was hard to offend the paladin's squire. 'The sailors aren't keen on having me below deck during the packing, and I really don't know what these here above deck need. The King wants us hauling anchor before mid-morning, so they don't have time for my ignorance of sailing ships.'

'Haven't you been on several before?' she asked. His father was a rich gem merchant, and while the older man took another boat, he was coming on this voyage as well. Surely Darrix had been sailing before.

'Two, actually. Short voyages to the city Cairnhold and Treedawn up north. I was eight; I wasn't allowed to touch anything.'

'But now you're fourteen you have to act like a man!' Allastassia chided him from over her shoulder. The part dryad enchantress was helping several strong sailors haul up some ornate luggage, covered in twisting vine runes and locked with interwoven liana – probably nothing more than her personal makeup kit. The sailors struggled under the load, and though she didn't lift a finger to help, she spoke encouraging words. Kialessa had come to recognise the magic in the enchantress's words. She was helping them find strength and competence in her own magical way.

'You'll be grateful for the interdimensional spaces on this magical boat,' Darrix replied, looking like he really would have liked to help if there was any possible way on the small gang plank.

Allastassia huffed. Her family was not coming on this trip; they were staying to help the Queen run the Kingdom in the absence of its King. Allastassia was used to having a room to herself, with two servants and a closet of dresses larger than most people's houses. Now she would be sharing with all the other student girls on this voyage. The sailing ship was huge, but Allastassia would still need some kind of personal space on this voyage. They all would. People scurried to get out of their way, and as if that wasn't enough, one of the ship's cats ran past and almost tripped her up. 'Oops! Bah, not enough room to swing a cat,' she muttered.

Another voice spoke up: 'While your enchantments often defy logical explanation, I cannot understand why you would want to harm a feline by rotating it in a circular motion.' It was Piex, the number one apprentice to the greatest wizard in the land. Piex was a wizarding prodigy, with a near perfect memory and intense love of books. But he could sometimes miss the subtle things; like whether or not people were just using an old saying, or making up jokes about cats, apparently.

'I'm pretty sure it's just a figure of speech,' Kialessa informed him.

Piex look surprised, but nodded.

'So, you ready for your first sea voyage?' she asked him.

Piex breathed in heavily, and patted the boat with as much courage as his eleven-year-old hands had. 'I have researched everything we require regarding this voyage. The Bounteous Shallowsea will be a nine-week journey if all goes well. We're going the long way – it is quite a wonder we don't teleport there.'

He glanced at her. Everyone knew there was a very important and very dangerous reason why they were taking the "long" way. A deadly assassin was trying to kill their King and ruin their Kingdom, and she was the reason that assassin had failed at it last year, at least once. Even so, he'd come very close to succeeding, and so the King had decided this was their chance to draw out their enemy, and deal with the problem once and for all.

'It will be worth it,' she grinned. The King was here, with his four most powerful bodyguards. They held the rod of the King, within; the promise of everyone in their nation to protect him. It might seem they were vulnerable, riding out away from his castle and onto the sea, away toward the council of Kings to which he was called, taking with him the best students at his college and best treasures of his Kingdom to impress the council at Emerel. But Kialessa knew it was just a feint. They were going to win this one, and she would never have to look that strange and dangerous dog/man/assassin in his hateful eyes ever again.

Piex nodded, never much one for words unless raw information was involved – in which case he might speak for hours. He cleared his throat. 'I have a small supply of wormwood and ginger, and have written several prayers to Waaglah, goddess of the oceans. While most creatures are afflicted with nausea from the constant motion of the boat, I do not think it will affect me. My mind has too many important things to consider.'

'Like how to burn up a small army?' she teased. He'd been trying to master *mage's fiery conflagration* for several weeks now, with no success.

He nodded, and would have said more, but the rumbling sound of someone climbing up the boat from the outside reached their ears.

It was Posk, the irrepressible half-blood troll prince, gifted with inhuman strength, rapid healing, a mystical power of being able to heal other people's bones, and a pair of steel gauntlets that helped him smash things. He clambered up the side of the ship like an enormous ape, effortlessly leaping right over the balustrade. 'Someone say Piex is ready to burn up an army yet!' he grinned.

Darrix spoke. 'We didn't say, "Yet".'

Posk pouted. 'I'm ready to see a giant sky ball of fire! Do it, do it now Piex! We can wave the people goodbye with your sky fire!'

Piex looked like he was ready to try, but then shook his head nervously. 'The … people are too close, and I am not ready.'

'Move aside!' Allastassia demanded, making sure her sailors had access to the hold. 'You smell, Posk,' she added.

'Like this,' he replied, breathing in through his nostrils. 'See, good smelling. Ooh, smells like sea!'

Allastassia didn't even bother arguing with that, and Posk laughed like he'd won a point or something.

'Kialessa,' Allastassia said, pointing to a lock of her errant burgundy hair that had gotten in front of her eyes. It had been harder to keep it tied back since Flameheart, another tae'anaryn had set her unburnable hair on fire, but that was all a story for last year. Now the wind was having its own way with her fringe.

Kialessa tutted, and put her hair in place. She needed to look her best; this was a voyage for the King, the most important in the past four years, perhaps the most important in her entire life. Not only would they have the chance to trade magic and information with the sixteen other Kingdoms in the Great Kingdom, but they might also have a chance to free themselves from the threat of fear. This was worth living for. This was worth fighting for.

Then there was a small hubbub as the entire continent of senior students, all five of them including the cervitaur Natasha, clambered on. Their unofficial leader princess Aolith, a close relative of the king, gave her a quick grin. But they were a busy, noisy lot. And they were all armed. Everyone was expecting a fight on this voyage, but that was why the king brought gifted teenagers; all the better for gaining the Sun god's favour. Plus they'd all proven their worth against the troll horde last year. And with several hundred of the king's best soldiers, they would make a force the best assassins in history would have to consider carefully.

Posk scuttled over, imposing himself between herself and Piex so they had to move away, or hug him. He was often like that.

'At least you're not late this time,' Allastassia finally shouted back at him.

Posk tapped the magical headband he'd "borrowed" from Piex ever since last year. 'Hey, I always knew what day it was before Piex gave me this thing and made me normal smart!'

Allastassia's reply was lost as she disappeared into the hold, bossing around sailors.

Posk turned back, openly admiring the crane they were using to help load the back of the boat. 'Epic,' he muttered.

'Levered counterweight,' Piex explained. 'The load arm is four times the length of the effort arm, so the latter must be four times as heavy.'

'Eeeeepiiiiiic,' Posk agreed, sounding like he'd actually understood what the wizard was saying. He watched some more, then tapped the banister with his steel covered fists. He fell silent, looking concerned.

Kialessa looked at her friend. 'Is something the matter?'

Posk was quiet for a moment more, and when he spoke, it was softly. 'She's old, this traveller on water. Very old.'

Darrix nodded. 'Yes. A new coat of paint doesn't hide the fact that she's almost a hundred years old.'

Posk glanced at them, looking more worried than Kialessa wanted anyone to be on this hunting and trading trip.

'But she's a magical sailing ship, Posk,' Kialessa said to encourage him. 'You'll see. Magical. Some say she can move forwards even when there is no wind!'

Posk looked around, unsure. It seemed he had other misgivings, but was not able to put them in words just yet. He struggled with that sort of thing a lot.

Darrix helped out. 'She was built in our King's grandfather's day, Posk. So, yes, she's over eighty years old, already more than most boats can achieve. But this is elven lightwood, blessed by a priestess of the goddess of the water. It will carry us sure; it can do nothing else.'

Posk didn't seem convinced, 'Yes, but don't those priestesses curse things as well?'

A moment later, Allastassia arrived, wiping her spotless hands on her magical hanky that never got dirty. She walked over to join them. 'Let us hope it does not come to that,' she replied, watching the seabirds with great interest.

Piex offered his support. 'Of the three boats in this company, I am the most secure upon this one,' he said. 'See that four masted sailing ship over there? That carries most of the trading materials and supplies, and one hundred sailors as well. She is well built, and but young. "Sea's Bounty" they name her, though I think it unfortunate.'

'Why's that?' Posk inquired.

'I think I'd rather keep the bounty all to ourselves.' Piex grinned at his pun.

Darrix chuckled. 'And what of "Gap's Edge", the three masted galley over there?'

Piex replied, 'The nation's only heavy military ocean going vessel, the Edge has survived two gales, outrun a leviathan, and driven off an attack by a colossal squid that was preying on fishing ships. Staffed by fifty, she brings another fifty soldiers to our company. Her armament includes thirty heavy crossbows, a flaming ballista set foremast, and a submerged alumium ram that has never been used.'

'Best boat in the fleet?' Posk inquired.

Piex shook his head. 'This boat, "Imagination's Dawn", bears the King. It is the oldest, most magical boat in this nation, perhaps indeed in the entire great Kingdom. It has born the King's father, and his father's father. Never, not once, in its entire unnaturally long life has the staff been lowered at this boat.'

'The who been what-ed?' Posk asked.

Allastassia tutted, always first to educate the half troll. 'The staff *lowered*. It's a ritual of the priestesses of the sea goddess, Waaglah. Whenever a boat is launched, a priestess or priest of the sea goddess may be seen at the cliffs. If they hold their staff upright, the boat will return to harbour safe. If they lower their staff to the waves, the trip is cursed. Most boats will return straight to harbour if the priestess lowers their staff.'

'Sounds wise,' Posk admitted. 'Who's the priestess?' he said, looking out.

'A curiosity I have already noticed. We don't appear to have one today,' Piex said.

'All the better,' Allastassia replied. 'We already know we're sailing into death and danger. No need to spook the crew further.'

'Gonna catch the Dog?' Posk asked.

'We'll do much more than that, if we can!' Kialessa celebrated grimly.

For a moment no one spoke.

'I never thought I'd die on the water,' Allastassia suddenly confessed.

'No one's going to hurt you,' Posk disagreed, a little too quickly, and moved to cling to the banister Allastassia was calmly sitting on. Kialessa grinner to herself – he had a huge crush on Allastassia, who hated him.

'They harm our King, they harm our Kingdom,' Darrix told them. 'His life is bound up in the nation, and it may crumble if he is slain. This is a very brave thing the King is doing. Very brave.'

'Good we get to help,' Posk nodded, looking positively indefatigable.

They agreed. Sailors began to remove all but one of the gang planks, lining it with red carpet in preparation for the arrival of their King.

'*I'm* not yet ready to die,' Kialessa responded to Allastassia's worries.

1 The boat

'That is good,' she agreed. 'You have something to live for.'

'Live,' Posk agreed. 'I like living.'

Trumpets sounded as a bright sleigh, pulled by four furry posks, arrived over the muddy snow that remained of the edge of winter. A moment later, King Dunnkan stepped out, golden sword in his hilt. Four individuals flanked him on each quarter. Lord Grudon, the part fey steward to the King, and holder of the Rod of Lenmer'el, watched the crowd with his shrewd, purple eyes. Beside him, High Captain Bon Sure'e stalked, wearing at least a dozen axes. He returned his soldiers' smart salutes with a lazy gesture or two of his own. Behind him, shuffling with librarian grace, Piex's tutor the elven sagemaster hurried along. He seemed an unassuming old elf in a blue cloak, but none in all the land dared challenge his arcane prowess. And to his right, the dwarven high priestess Lady Jacinthia Stonehall walked at a steady, dependable pace. Her faith alone had stopped a plague many years ago; Kialessa thought it a great encouragement to have her along on this voyage.

The crowd cheered as the King took to the plank, and made his way onto the ship they stood on. He turned to wave, his red cloak billowing around him in the morning air. He nodded to the steward, who, raising the glowing rod, commanded the entire city to silence. When the King spoke, his voice sounded across the entire scene; it was likely to be heard across the entire country.

'The future is unknown to all of us, though we like to guess our journey. We might all wish for strong sails and calm winds, only to find our journey surrounded by storm and savage sea. But a life lived in fear is no life at all! I take this journey, *we* take this journey, on behalf of you all! To represent our proud and honest nation to the best of the world! To live despite threat of storm or sea or cruel assassin's hand!' He glanced at Kialessa then, but turned to the crowd as they shouted their encouragement. He held up his hands for silence, and they gently obliged him. 'For what is the purpose of life, but to serve those we love?'

The people seemed profoundly touched by his words; some even shed tears. He was deeply loved, and despite the very public threat on his own life, he risked it openly to protect them all.

But those words stuck in Kialessa's heart. What was the purpose of life? Did it have a purpose at all? It was something she'd never considered. She'd wondered what her life was for, but what about life in general? Was it not, "To serve the gods"? But then what did that mean, when each and every god had a very different interpretation of what that meant?

'What *is* the purpose of life?' she wondered aloud, and all her four best friends turned to stare at her. But if they had answers, it was soon drowned out by the peeling of the harbour bells and cheering of the crowd as they prepared to leave.

Then a sailor started to sing. He was a huge, dark-skinned man with a distinct Sanmarellian accent.

Attend the sails, oh windlass true,
We're heading o'er the sea!
Come sing a song for me and you,
Though wild the tempest be!

Then, without any signal, the entire crew joined in what must have been to them a well-known chorus. They timed it to their tasks, hauling rope and unfurling sails along with the beat.

King Dunnkan just stood there, beaming.

Hey, Ho, away we go!
We're heading o'er the sea!
Come hail or sun, till we be done,
The goddess hear our plea!

Again, the song leader sang in his powerful bass voice,

Sing hai, hun, till the rising sun,
And a dawn on Emerel's shore!
Though cruel assassin's blade we wait,
We'll pay him back twice more!

People cheered and again the chorus sung, only this time there were some high tenor parts that really sung out above the regular melody. It almost seemed to Kialessa that singing was an unspoken requirement of being a sailor on this ship, but as she watched not everyone sung. Some held to the rhythm or beat out the meter by stomping with their boots.

Then it appeared it was Allastassia's turn to improvise a verse. No one told her to sing, but they all knew when it was her turn:

Though gale and storm, past safer shore,
We risk it to be free!
For no fear holds our noble King,
And it has no hold on me!

Another chorus, then the song leader pointed at her. Kialessa shook her head, fiercely. She had no music for this!

Thankfully Darrix stepped in and saved her. She wasn't sure what she was more grateful for: the chance to not have to sing, or the chance to hear him. She really was fond of his singing voice.

Though dark leviathan's rank breath,
Might darken brighter days,
We'll cut it up and make some soup,
And welcome morning's rays!

People cheered, and none louder than she.

The chorus rang out again, and then the chorus master sung,

Our precious cargo be a King,
Against which fate must leer,
But the cargo of our greatest love,
Are the hearts we each hold dear!

The chorus rang out, and the song master pointed at Posk.

Posk looked around, beaming. He was loving the music and clearly desperately wanted to be a part of it. With a grin he thumped the deck in time to the song, but when it was his turn to lead he simply chanted, 'Music, music, music, MUSIC!'

Everyone roared with laughter, and the song was done. Complex improvised lyrics were never Posk's strong suit. But Kialessa had to grin as they tried to work his lyrics into a new verse. She knew they'd be singing it for weeks.

She laughed as the winds filled the mainsail and the boat took speed, but a moment later a strange movement caught her eye. She looked up, finding her gaze drawn towards the cliffs at the edge of the harbour. A single tall human stood, silhouetted against the morning sky and wearing weathered brown sailor's clothes. In her hand she held a long rod, hooked, for fishing. It was similar to the staffs the priests of Waaglah, goddess of the oceans would use.

Actually, if Kialessa didn't know any better, it looked *exactly* like a staff of the goddess. There was something deeply unsettling about her presence to Kialessa, and she found she could smile no longer.

And then, without a word or sound, the individual slowly lowered her staff until it lay horizontal to the silent, calm waters of the sheltered bay.

Three Days

The two most important days of your life is the day you are born,
and the day you find out why.
Arbagoa, Hamadryad stagewrite and adventurer

Piex hung off the edge of the boat; he'd been that way for three whole days. His poultice he'd thrown away in disgust before the end of day one, his ginger and wormwood he'd consumed entirely by the end of day two. By now, he had nothing left to throw up, and sat there, looking noticeably green, even for a part star dragon like he was. Green and miserable.

Kialessa went up to comfort him again, 'Hey soldier, you still keeping watch?'

Piex huffed, and glanced at her with a frail smile behind his tired eyes. 'I don't understand, why won't it go away? Nothing helps!'

'Not even reciting the times tables?' she asked. He loved the times tables.

'Not even the sevens, which are my very, very favourites,' he replied miserably, and wretched some more.

A moment later, a neatly dressed officer walked down the steps to stand beside them. He had a broad hat, and thick woollen gloves and coat for the cold winter air. Kialessa recognised him as the admiral of the fleet and commander of Imagination's Dawn, and a good friend of the King, though she'd spoken to neither of them thus far on this voyage. He looked down at the young wizard – who glared back at him – and laughed. 'You'll get your sea legs soon enough!' the admiral promised him. 'Go see the priestess, no need to be proud.'

Piex looked at Kialessa. He'd been trying to wizard his way out of sea sickness. Seeing the priestess was an admission of weakness, in his mind. But he nodded, looking like he was going to get up, but then sitting back down quickly. 'Soon, yes.'

Just then, one of the ship's cats strolled casually past. There were two cats on board: a grumpy old ginger tabby, and this black one. It was a sleek black with white feet, as though it was wearing socks or something. And as the admiral bent down to bump foreheads with the creature, Kialessa suddenly realised she recognised that cat.

'Hey!' She was surprised. 'I've seen that cat at the castle of Lenmer'el!'

This, of course, was not strictly accurate. She'd actually seen him strolling about in much the same, confident way – except it was in the mysterious shadow realm that existed coterminous with the castle at Lenmer'el. How he was able to pop between dimensions was a mystery to her! But she was sure of it; if not for his little white socks, then most certainly for the confident, almost arrogant way he carried himself.

The admiral patted the cat affectionately, 'Aww, li'l Socks here! Found 'im padding about in the streets, and he just up and follows me here. Might have been the bacon I kept feeding 'im!' the admiral said with a grin as he ruffled up Sock's scruff. 'Ships like these need a cat or two, though most people make the mistake of thinking it's just to keep those rats at bay.'

Kialessa wondered what cats *were* for then.

'Good luck …' Piex tried to explain, but seemed too sick and had to take a breath. 'That, and companionship, I suppose.'

'Right you are, young wizard, though there is also-'

Before the admiral could continue a voice proudly shouted, 'All attention, King on deck!'

'Oh, stop that Grudon!' the King shouted. 'As you were, all of you! For goodness sake, we have a long journey. As you were at all times!'

'But my liege, you must-' the steward protested.

'Enough, Grudon,' the King demanded, and that was sure to be the end of it.

Kialessa pushed passed the admiral, but as soon as the King saw her, he walked on over and opened his arms to hug her.

She jumped up and hugged him, which was a special privilege only she and the royal grandchildren seemed to have. 'Where have you been!?' she demanded.

King Dunnkan sighed, seeming to shake aside worries in his heart. 'I suppose I was hoping to have certain business matters sorted out by this time.'

'Those matters,' the steward muttered, 'were never going to be sorted out by this time.'

King Dunnkan nodded, and stepped over by the balcony, holding her hand. He patted Piex on his head. 'As you were,' he offered his encouragement, and Piex looked a little better.

King Dunnkan sighed, looking out at the waves, and then glancing at Piex noted, 'Have we a sheltered cove nearby we can weather the lunch hour in? I think a pause will do us good.'

The admiral nodded, whistling to the sailor at the till and making a gesture she did not know.

'I had supposed,' the steward argued with a diplomatic apology, 'with our visits to the cities Treedawn yesterday and Cairnhold the day before, that you might have liked to get our voyage underway?'

'The King chooses well,' the admiral disagreed. 'The Weather's Shelter rides up on our stern in the next hour. It's a sheltered cove renowned for its clear waters and calm bay.'

'And I think it might do the children good to learn how to swim,' the King informed them.

Kialessa gulped. During her preparations for going on a sea voyage, she'd realised she might need to learn how to swim. Many sailors never learnt, but she didn't doubt her King intended for her to master the water as well. But she'd supposed she'd have a little more time to prepare.

The steward gazed in the rod. 'I sense no danger.' Then, curiously, he held the rod out to her – the only other person apart from the King who had ever touched that rod without coming to harm. 'What do you think, Maid Winterhaven?'

She had not been expecting the request. She was arguably the King's backup or extra protector, but what that meant no one knew, as there was only ever one protector of the King. Perhaps this was just the steward trying to figure this out as well. She stepped forward, looking in the small crystal ball at the end of the black wood rod. She touched it, in case that helped. 'I see nothing,' she confessed after a moment.

'Hmm,' the steward muttered, looking pleased with himself.

The King grinned, then Piex moaned.

'Come, young wizard,' the King said. 'Let's get you in the water. It will do you some good.'

Piex didn't look impressed, but he didn't dare disagree with his King.

The boat swung about as the wind caught the waxed linen sails, heading closer towards the shore. Kialessa had already decided she liked the Bounteous Shallowsea. It was full of life, and fish were very common. She and Allastassia had spent every spare minute of the first three days looking, looking for all they were worth, to see if they could sight a mermaid. They apparently rarely came this far south. The lookout had called one at day two, but she was never sure if that was just to tease them. They had seen nothing. But such moments were rare, for it was clear the king intended for them to learn all they could on this voyage. It was like being at the college on the sea! She'd already mastered every knot they'd given her, they were a little impressed with that.

'Well, off with you then,' the steward shoed her away. 'You need to be dressed for swimming.'

Kialessa was momentarily surprised. 'We have swimming clothing?'

The steward rolled his eyes, and the King and admiral laughed.

'Go see honoured young Allastassia. She brought them in her magical vine chests,' the steward huffed, and shoved her away.

She was tempted to think it rude, but then remembered a year ago he didn't even dare touch her. So, it was kind of a compliment, really. She grabbed Piex's hand, and he slowly stood.

'Swimming clothes!' she squealed unintentionally, or maybe intentionally, and dragged him away.

***

The water was cold, *icy cold*, as Allastassia splashed down and several drips landed on Kialessa. But it only took the enchantress's breath away for a moment. 'Fresh,' she muttered.

Kialessa looked down on the still water. It was crystal blue, with white sand covered in grey streaks clearly visible underneath. Small, spiked, brown anemone clambered slowly along the sea bottom, pulled about by tenacious currents. Clumps of green seaweed clung steadfastly to the rocks nearer the shore. They kept Imagination's Dawn safe in the deeper water. The Edge and the Bounty remained further out, no one on board seeming to want to indulge in the King's little side quest of teaching them how to swim.

The crew had lowered a jollyboat into the water, with several rags, flotation bladders, and a stout looking sailor. Darrix was already in the water, swimming laps around the entire boat, 'Just to warm up'.

Piex was still in the ship.

Kialessa looked at the bright water, wondering why it was so difficult simply to jump right in like the enchantress. It was *only water*.

But she'd never been in water over her head before. The cups of water during the weekly bath didn't count.

Allastassia swished her hands forwards and backwards, seeming quite at ease and not sinking at all. 'Jump in, Kia. It's fine.'

Kialessa twirled the edge of the blue chequered swimming gown they'd given her. It was cute, but a little heavy. She knew it wouldn't drag her down like her dagger and armour would, but would it hold her up?

'Just push the water down,' Allastassia instructed. 'Long, steady strokes, just like this.'

Darrix arrived. Throwing his head back, he breathed in heavily. 'Fresh,' he stated, accidentally agreeing.

Allastassia splashed his face, and with a laugh he splashed her back.

Kialessa did not want to deny herself some fun.

So, she jumped in.

They had lied; the water was *bitterly cold*. Frigid beyond belief. Kialessa feared she could only live a few moments in water like this. Desperately, she pushed the water down, trying to get back to the surface. It took an agonisingly long time to get there, and she felt herself panicking. Her chest ached and her limbs trembled. She heaved against the water up to the surface and took a desperate breath, surprised and dismayed to feel her entire body immediately sink right under the water again. She thrashed helplessly. It didn't seem she was getting any higher.

Suddenly, a firm hand lunged down and grabbed her arm. The sailor pulled her up and helped her cling to the edge of the jollyboat. She was trembling all over.

Darrix and Allastassia were by her side in a moment.

'You all right?' Allastassia asked.

Her teeth chattered a nonsensical reply.

Darrix rubbed her shoulder. 'You get used to it. Come, keep moving, it'll chase away the cold.'

She glared at him, but he was smiling too confidently to be making things up. He showed her how to tread the water, and how to paddle against it. She tried again, and again. It seemed she was slowly getting it.

Then there was a huge splash.

'Posk is here,' Allastassia explained.

A moment later he surfaced, raging against the water. The sailor had to save him too. Darrix showed Posk, yet in only a few moments he was swimming like he was *made* to do it. She looked at him bitterly, yet with a big grin and a huge breath, Posk dived under, and with a wide sweep of his arms, shot out under the entire ship.

'Well, that's very daring,' Darrix said.

'He's good,' Allastassia admitted to herself.

Darrix took a deep breath and went to join Posk on the other side of the boat.

'Come, like this, like this,' Allastassia explained calmly, sweeping her arms side to side with her palms on a downwards angle. 'It's called treading water. You can do this.'

She seemed so very calm and confident, Kialessa just had to give it a go. Soon, to her delight, it was clearly working. She was trembling with the cold and with joy.

Allastassia looked up. 'Come, wizard, join us!'

Kialessa looked up at the young wizard, who looked doubtful. He began to climb cautiously down the rope ladder and into the jollyboat. He was wearing the chequered shirt and pants of the boys, but seemed to also be wearing a seashell for good luck or something. 'Join you I must,' he seemed to be muttering, 'but I fear I will not be any good at it.'

The boat rocked as he stepped in, and he sat down quickly. The sailor grinned, and looked like he wanted to toss the timid wizard in right there and then.

A moment later there was a squeal from above, as several other people leapt over the railing to land right in the water. They were the senior students: young princess Aolith; Federach, the harsh priestess of the earth; the cervitaur Natasha, who spent most of her time with the beasts in the storage deck. There was also Marchan, the apprentice wizard, and Dale, the jerk. To be fair, Dale was the son of a powerful duke, and he specialised in light artillery with a skill that put most soldiers to shame. But he was bossy to the point of unkindness, and Kialessa simply hadn't forgiven him for it.

And without any care in the world, the five of them jumped right over the little boat. They hit the water with a squeal to rival a dragon, making more splash than Kialessa should have thought possible. It left her gasping for air and spitting out salt water.

Allastassia was dutifully complaining with a grin. The five senior students swam around with great skill – even Marchan the wizard. *Humans are really rather impressive at times,* Kialessa thought to herself.

Natasha swam up, kicking her four legs with great skill. She wore nothing but a bra, but no one mentioned it – the culture of the cervitaurs, who were half deer/half humans, was very different to the rest of the Kingdom of Lenmer'el. Natasha hated dresses, and sleeping indoors, and lying down. And wo betide any who tried to ride her back without her express permission! But she was honest, and kind, and strong. She had been sent by her tribe to help them understand the humans better. 'Maid Winterhaven, why dally you by this little boat, trembling so?'

''Tis cold,' Kialessa replied through chattering teeth.

'She is a fire tainted tae'anaryn,' Piex explained, wiping himself down with the rags. 'She's vulnerable to the cold.'

'Nay,' Natasha protested. ''Tis because she is so slight, and thinks she can keep warm while not moving! Come, little one, take hold of my mane. Let us swim.'

Kialessa did as she was told. She didn't think Natasha had much of a mane, but it would do. Her body was very warm, but Kialessa knew better than to try and climb aboard. Natasha swam around a bit, and they chatted.

Kialessa slowly found herself getting more and more confident, and soon was treading water for a few moments at a time. Soon Natasha swam away and Kialessa pushed herself back towards the boat.

By this time, Piex had lowered himself into the water, finger widths at a time in order to "acclimatise" to the cold.

Or simply drag out the torture! Kialessa trembled as she reached the boat.

'You lack courage, wizard!' Natasha informed him as she floated past.

He ignored her and looked at Kialessa, seeming concerned. 'You're getting pale.'

'Agreed,' the sailor muttered. 'Time to get out, little one.'

'I'm fine,' Kialessa muttered, but then noticed how much her muscles ached. 'Oh, all right.'

She could barely rise, and needed to be carried out. The sailor wrapped her in bundles, and then her body took to shivering uncontrollably. She began to wonder if there was some truth to Piex's words.

She watched the humans and others swim around for ten moments or so. They seemed to be having such a good time. Aolith was so fit; she kept on going, and beat everyone, including Darrix and Dale, in a swimming race around the ship. No one seemed bothered by the cold; even Piex shivered quietly the whole time, while learning nothing more than how to tread water. He was not very enthusiastic, and Kialessa found herself so cold she had no will to join in again.

'Summon me the Maid Winterhaven,' a voice said from above.

Kialessa looked up. It was the dwarven high priestess Jacinthia Stonehall.

The sailor helped unwrap Kialessa, and she climbed up with hands so cold they had trouble holding the rungs of the ladder. But she was warm enough not to tremble too much now. She soon stood before the aging dwarf, high priestess and great judge of all the land.

The old woman looked at her with dwarven sternness. 'It will not do to have you shudder away this opportunity our King gives you.' She raised her holy symbol, and it burst into white fire. 'Kialessa Winterhaven, this day the Eternal grants you freedom from all weariness and cold!'

Immediately the chill was gone as though it had never been there, and her muscles felt like she had only just woken up from a good night's sleep. She grinned at the old woman, who nodded back.

With a squeal, Kialessa ran and leapt off the side of the boat, diving down into the water with considerably less grace than Darrix and Posk during their competition. Only when she surfaced did she remember to thank the kind God who'd made this possible, turning around and muttering out a prayer of thanks far too quickly.

She shouted to the other students, and Natasha and Aolith swam over to get her. It was exhilarating to be with them this time. Darrix taught her to hold her breath for a long time, filling her lungs from her stomach, and Aolith finally taught her to swim properly – she didn't look tired either. Best of all, Marchan taught her how to lie on her back and simply float there for as long as she wanted.

Soon, someone suggested they check out the lagoon nearby, and so off she swam with the others. The waters there were crystal blue; dark grey fishes with orange stripes the size of her hand swam by underneath them, little blue guppies darted in and out of the sparse seaweeds. A huge turtle the size of a chariot swam across their path, and Posk dared swim down and touch it. It appeared to ignore him.

She splashed with the others for some time, till eventually they climbed up on some sand polished rocks to rest. But Kialessa wasn't tired or cold at all. So, she lay on her back in the water and enjoyed watching the sun, letting the current take her into the sheltered bay where it would eventually take her out again, or so Aolith had promised.

A sudden movement caught her eye. Kialessa turned and saw another huge sea turtle struggling up the thin beach of the outermost cliffs of the bay. It was only a baby, but even the babies of this monstrous species were bigger than a handcart. It occurred to her immediately that the young creature was probably heading the wrong way. She wondered what it might be doing, and then it slipped and fell on its back. She watched it struggle pathetically to right itself.

'Poor creature,' she muttered. Without wasting another moment, she swam lazily over there, being sure to not startle the monster, but hoping also it might right itself.

It did not.

She stepped up onto the sand. It was nothing like the sand of the docks at Lenmer'el. It was pure white, and soft like powdered glass, almost warm. It squeaked as she stepped it down, squishing wonderfully between her toes. She looked to see if she'd startled the sea turtle baby, but it seemed to have too many of its own problems to worry about right now.

She walked up to it, watching over its purple scaly skin. Its huge eyes regarded her with alarm, its giant flippers trying desperately to get a grip on the sand.

'Poor creature,' she muttered again. She climbed up to one side, kneeling down to right it, her shoulders the same height as its armoured underbelly. It tried to swipe at her, but she'd already been quite careful to stay out of its reach. She gripped it thoroughly and hauled. It was so incredibly heavy she wondered how the sea carried it at all. She adjusted her grip and tried again.

Thankfully, it seemed the enormous baby turtle figured out what she was trying to do, and lifting its flipper out of the way, helped her roll it over.

'Over there,' she said, pointing at the sea.

It seemed to nod, and slithered on over, crashing down into the water where it belonged, and Kialessa wondered how it had gotten stuck here at all.

Then she looked up, and her eyes locked with another's. It was a boy, about her age, watching her while peering out from some nearby rocks. He had a touch of green to his pinkish skin, and deep aqua eyes. He had ornaments of shells and seaweed in his hair, and his hands were webbed. His waist, tapering down from his hips, ended in a tail. His scales glittered in the sunlight, and he stared at her with panic in his eyes.

He was watching carefully from on top of some rocks about twenty paces away, on the other side to where the turtle had lain. He would have seen everything. An instant later, he threw himself into the water and disappeared with almost no splash.

It all happened so quickly she hardly had a moment to realise what had just happened. She'd seen a merman, a merboy in fact! They were famously shy around land dwellers, but protected their lands fiercely. What had he been doing here, so far from home?

Finally, her thoughts found her voice, and Kialessa squealed with delight. 'A merboy! I just saw a merboy! Where did you go? Come back merboy! Let us talk!'

But there was no answer from the unsleeping waves.

She didn't wait for the current, but threw herself into the water and swam back frantically to see the others. She was glad to have the advantage of the prayer about her; she would have drowned by now without it. The others saw her approaching and drew near.

'A merboy, I just saw a merboy!' she squeaked.

They looked around, quickly deciding that there was no point trying to find him now.

'I wonder what he was doing so far away from his Kingdom?' Aolith asked.

'I wondered the same thing,' Kialessa confessed.

'Are you sure you saw a merman?' Marchan asked.

'Mmm, ha,' she nodded, treading the water with a little more grace now.

Dale looked worried. 'Did you see any more? Was he armed?'

'Their territory doth change with the seasons,' Natasha replied, 'But I know not that it does extend here. This is far too south.'

'Perhaps there is some trouble?' Allastassia supposed.

'More likely part of a raiding or hunting group,' Federach guessed. 'Did you see any more?'

'Nuh-uh,' she admitted.

'Weird,' Federach muttered.

'Well,' Dale said, treading water with respectable skill, 'at least it wasn't a sharkman. Those bloodthirsty brigands are all kinds of trouble.'

Everyone agreed.

Just then, a dark shape swelled up in the water underneath them. Something grabbed Kialessa's ankle fiercely with a cold, metallic grip, and she squealed involuntarily. Just at the same moment, Allastassia let out a cry of surprise herself.

An instant later Posk burst up, laughing loudly. 'Ha! Got you both!'

Everyone started laughing. Aolith had her sword out already. He'd frightened them all, sneaking up under water like that.

'Posk, one day, I'm going to turn you into a snake!' Allastassia said angrily, splashing water at him. The reeds up underneath them were already stretching out, brushing up now against their toes.

'Good!' Posk retorted, 'then I can finally sneak onto your pillow and give you a *real* fright!'

'Posk!' she shouted in frustration. Arcane energies swam around her, but with a laugh and a powerful thrust of his arms, he was under water in an instant, rocketing away and out of their sight. He was truly an amazing natural at swimming.

A moment later, Allastassia looked over towards the boats. 'Oh, hello, Piex.'

Kialessa was momentarily surprised to hear Piex was swimming about … only to find he wasn't. He had cast some kind of levitation magic, and was floating above the water in his full wizard robes. He was trailing a thin rope, but had apparently been pushing himself along the water with a small paddle. He was completely dry, and stood there floating about a half pace above the water like it was something he did every day.

'Seriously, levitating, Piex?' Marchan, the second-best wizard in the college, protested.

Piex didn't answer him at all. 'The captain bids you return to prepare for the evening meal. We rest this night in the cove and set out at first light tomorrow.'

They started back immediately.

'Party time over?' Posk asked, approaching them.

Piex nodded, using his rope to pull himself back. 'The King says we have spent too much time worrying, and expects us to all return to our studies immediately.'

'Already!' Dale protested. 'But college isn't back till next week!'

'Oh, shut it,' Aolith told him. 'Some study will do your idle mind some good.'

'Testing those military ballistae on the Edge is what'll do me some good!'

'I'm sure it can be arranged,' Piex muttered, sounding like he hoped the loud and bossy Dale might spend the rest of the voyage over there.

'Kialessa saw a merman child, a boy,' Darrix told Piex, paddling his arms slowly as they returned.

'This far south?' Piex wondered. Hand over hand, he slowly made his way back, no faster than anyone swimming.

'That's what I wondered,' Aolith stated.

'Curious,' Piex replied.

Wizards

Pray as you will, you cannot be more than the destiny that claims you. The purpose of your life is to serve the gods, the one who chooses you, whether you like it or not. You are made to be a certain way; act like it.

Tomin, Archpaladin of Serros, 313 CY.

They took their evening meal below deck as usual. Naturally the King ate without them, in his room, with Aolith and his councillors. Everyone else ate with the sailors, so it was a very casual affair. Everyone seemed delighted to hear Kialessa tell them again about the merboy; it was a very good omen to see one, apparently.

After dinner, Piex and Marchan arose, as they usually did, to attend to their wizardly studies.

Kialessa was just preparing herself to help wash the dishes once again when there was a tap on her shoulder. Marchan was there, grinning broadly. He indicated she should follow him out. Not knowing what to think, she handed Darrix her plate and rag, and followed him. Darrix gave her an encouraging grin and started washing the dishes immediately.

She stood on the cool deck, a gentle salt breeze toying with her hair. No one else were there apart from Piex and the wizard, sagemaster De'Feur.

The wizard spoke softly. 'Maid Winterhaven,' he said to her. 'Piex has been telling me about your accomplishments at the Sanctum Brumae, and your assistance at the Far Keep. Would you like to learn some more wizardry on this journey here? I think you might be ready for it.'

Her mouth fell agape in surprise. 'Wizardry … How … How much?' It was required to pay a wizard for their tutelage.

He laughed, then seemed to get an idea. 'A small contribution from your shadow trove would be more than adequate, I think. Come, the King has asked me to teach you. Would you like to learn correctly the science of wizardry?'

'I would like that very much.'

He grinned. 'Good, good! Come with me to the King's cabin.'

Piex was grinning politely, and she jumped up and down with glee.

The wizard put a stern hand on her arm, and looked at her very severely. 'Now, young Maid Winterhaven. Wizardry is very serious.' It seemed true; he was always very serious. 'You must promise again to keep sacred anything you learn here. You must… many secrets. Keep them close, do you understand?'

'Yes.' She understood.

He gave her a gentle smile. 'Come.'

Piex and Marchan walked behind them, and if she could have dared, she would have shoved that slow moving wizard right on his behind and gotten him into the cabin with all haste!

They walked in, and she found the room completely different to what she had expected. The King's room was outfitted like a wizard's study, or more likely magically transformed somehow. There was stuffed bedding and storage crates in the corners, but the main table was given over entirely to wizardry tomes and alchemical materials.

To her great surprise, there was Aolith, and two other adults as well, both dressed like sailors. She had seen them around the boat but hadn't given them a second thought, nor had they ever attempted to speak to her. Aolith was carefully measuring out reagents into a highly calibrated set of scales, with another woman's help.

'Hey, Maid Winterhaven,' Aolith greeted her informally.

Kialessa was too amazed to reply. Since when did Aolith know wizardry?

'Many secrets,' the sagemaster muttered with a grin.

Piex stood beside her while Marchan went to help Aolith, and the wizard dealt with some paperwork the other sailor handed him. Kialessa took the chance to whisper to her friend her now burning question. 'Is Aolith a wizard?'

Piex nodded, 'And a rather capable one too, I must admit. Often the equal to Marchan, who claims to nothing else.'

Kialessa was amazed. She'd never once seen Aolith perform wizardry. 'How?'

Piex looked serious, 'She studies in secret. I did not even know till last year.'

'No,' Kialessa admitted. 'I mean, *when* does she learn?'

'She learns with us, the other wizarding students,' Marchan said with a grin as he carried some clean bottles past them.

Aolith stared carefully at her bubbling reagents, not looking at her as she spoke. 'It's to help deal with any … future trouble.'

Kialessa still wasn't sure what that meant.

The sagemaster took it upon himself to explain. 'The young princess is far more capable of defending herself than any assassins or ruffians might expect, and fully versed in arcane law in the event of those who might use magic to upset her future rule.'

'Everyone thinks I can only use a sword,' Aolith explained.

'What a surprise when she reveals their secrets with *mage sight*, or turns herself *invisible*,' Marchan boasted.

Kialessa was impressed. 'You can turn yourself invisible!'

'Practice it every day,' Aolith boasted.

'She's actually the one who worked it out,' Marchan confessed with an admiring grin.

'Can you turn yourself invisible yet?' Kialessa asked Piex with a cheeky smile. He'd been working on that spell for a year.

He mumbled his answer so quietly, she took it as a no.

Marchan and Aolith laughed.

'Can you levitate yourself?' he retorted.

'I'm… getting closer…' Marchan boasted, and Aolith scoffed. He protested, and she made him help her grind some moss. They laughed as they talked, which looked a lot like flirting, but Kialessa knew it couldn't be, because she was royalty, and he was merely a rich family's son. But they really did get along *very* well. The other two older sailors were working on their own projects, and essentially ignored them all.

'Where did all these wizards come from?' Kialessa asked.

Aolith took it upon herself to answer; it seemed she was the second in command here, though not the oldest by any means. Perhaps it was her nobility that allowed her to speak over everyone else here, even the sagemaster wizard. 'Welcome to the council of wizards, young Maid Winterhaven. You now know one of our nation's greatest secrets of defence and, indeed, trade.'

'There are wizards everywhere?' Kialessa asked.

That made them laugh. The sagemaster answered, 'With half a dozen students every year, I have trained over three hundred capable wizards in my time at the service of King Dunnkan. Most serve in the military, or constabulary, as city defence or support to a town guard somewhere. We have at least one wizard in every major town and city, though it's not commonly known. They support the town guards in their work, or help to protect the nobility in matters arcane. Pure wizards such as myself, Piex, and Marchan are rare, but we are around, you will see.'

'I would have never guessed,' Kialessa admitted.

Piex added, 'The council meets yearly through magical means to discuss matters and share research. We answer to the sagemaster here; it is his most important duty to the King.'

The wizard nodded sincerely. Soon he finished what he was organising and sat down. 'Now, young Maid Winterhaven. Let us attend to the matter of your own education in the more subtle sciences of the arcane. As you have already taken an oath of silence to revere our secrets to Piex at the Far Keep–'

She almost interrupted him with her surprise, but remembered just in time. Everyone was so busy they didn't even seem to notice. But she'd never actually taken an oath, or met with any binding magic to keep such secrets. She'd just told them she would, and let it be that. It was one of the core tenants of her faith in the Eternal. Should she tell the sagemaster? He was already deeply into his speech.

'–and as you are already committed to the people by the Rod of the King of Lenmer'el–'

She'd never done that either, she realised.

'–I feel under no obligation to bind you under any further oaths. But remember, this knowledge is not for everyone; it is too complex, and the raw powers that construct reality are not to be trifled with. You understand? But we'd best get you properly prepared, if you would be so kind as to acquire your spell book?'

She wondered what he meant for a moment. Then she remembered they had taken her magical chest filled with all her possessions, and magical shadow weave, on this boat with them. She almost ran out to get it from the hold, then remembered she didn't need to. She reached through the shadowrealm and into the magical chest; grabbing the largest book in there, she pulled it out.

Aolith and Marchan looked really impressed.

'*Praesedium eronocrux* and a fourth dimensional pairing,' Marchan announced.

'Spatial recurve,' Aolith decided. 'The shadow weave is clearly visible at the iris interface.'

'Yes, yes, not bad,' the wizard said in a voice that dismissed their attempts at impressing him, or figuring out the magic for themselves. Then he leant forward, speaking only to Kialessa. 'We will also need the scroll of *mage sight* Piex made for you last year. I think that would be a good start; since you have already read the standard work of Academicleas, and have enough grounding for a *stone on fire* spell, I think we can skip most of the basics and get right to work. If I may borrow your key, please, Kialessa?'

Without asking why, she took the little silver key she kept on her necklace next to the sacred symbol Darrix had made for her – the key opened her chest, though she rarely if ever used it – and handed it to him.

He held it in his hand, and worked a simple wizardry she'd not seen before. It was clearly some kind of shadow magic, and a clear disc of black energy, written with glowing black runes of power, sprang into existence. Kialessa immediately recognised it as similar, if not exactly the same, as the one her half-sister the wizard Raynah had used to help them plan their escape from her late father's fortress last year.

The wizard put his hand into the shadowrealm, fumbled around for a moment, and pulled out a piece of parchment. Kialessa recognised it as her plea for help that had never been necessary. 'Not that one.'

He returned it, fumbled around, and retrieved her scroll. It still had the broken wax seal Piex had made on it.

Everyone looked really impressed.

'Epic,' Marchan wowed.

'He makes it look so easy,' Aolith muttered.

'Paramount proficiency,' Piex praised his master.

Kialessa was too impressed for words, but her expression must have said enough. Then she was a little worried that he'd just shown her that her secret treasure chest was actually very easy for someone to break into if they knew where it was, had the right spell, and held her little silver key. 'You did make that look easy,' she admitted.

He seemed to guess her thoughts, and handing back her key he left her to consider this revelation without saying more.

Aolith finished what she was doing, and walked up to Kialessa. 'Time to get you into a new outfit,' she told her, indicating towards a screened off section.

'New?' Kialessa marvelled. She half expected someone to be amused at her wonder, and Aolith certainly was.

The sagemaster spoke. 'You will find that wielding arcane powers requires clothing of highly specific make and virtue: practical, yet powerful, and unencumbering to the powerful magic we must work. Aolith will show you,' and he kept on reading her scroll.

Once they were hidden from the boys, behind a folding petition, more or less, Aolith held out her hand. 'May I see your sash?' she asked.

Kialessa had expected it, but was still wary. Apart from baths and swimming, and one or two formal events, she had not taken off the magical sash the King had given her for saving his life in almost a year. Magical clothes were self-cleaning and self-repairing; they changed to fit their wearer's mood and personality, and never need ironing. The sash contained clothes to work, study and rest in. There was simply no point to parting with it. But she removed it, leaving her with nothing on, so she was thankful that the gently swaying cabin was nicely warmed.

Aolith wasn't bothered in the slightest. She rolled out the sash, and admired the runes that marked Kialessa's three outfits. Then she pulled out a scroll. 'The master himself wrote this, determined to make an item of power. This algorithm … program, sorry, spell … Which word do you prefer? Anyway, this spell will convert the materials of one outfit of clothing into a pure, raw form of information, a complex symbol that you see in the other three outfits. I imagine you'll need a key word to activate it; dragon speech would be *magicae*, do you like that? We can use any word you like.'

'*Magicae*,' Kialessa nodded; it would be easy to remember.

Aolith smiled to herself, rummaging through a chest of clothing. 'Anyone wearing that sash and saying that word will be dressed in your clothes, whether they suit them or not! Magic can be very weird at times; however, it might … Oh, here it is!'

She pulled out an enormous, glorious wizardry gown, deep blue, and very long. 'Nope.'

Kialessa watched in disappointment as Aolith put it away. Then she pulled out a deep brown corset, with cream coloured skirt that seemed to fit on using metal rings. 'You're an *action wizard*; you need to move. The skirt is absolutely vital for dissipating magical energies, the cuffs help you form rune signs using your own body. The corset is actually more a vest for concealing powerful reagents and such. And it has a scroll case on your hip here to help you carry things, safe even against immersion in most liquids. Besides, you'll look *fabulous*.'

Kialessa couldn't disagree; it was clearly a dress of masterwork creation, with flawless needlework and mysterious patterns bespeaking a work destined for magic. It came with dark pants and some fashionable felt boots. It would look great.

She helped Kialessa dress in the outfit, and even trimmed her fringe. 'Does no one cut your hair?' she muttered, careful to keep every last strand.

'Be careful to keep every last strand,' Piex shouted at them through the flimsy partition.

'I do, dracoling!' she told Piex quite forcefully. Seemed she was still not to be intimidated by the part dragon prodigy. 'Aside from reagents, we think your hair might be able to make fireproof gloves, or a mat, perhaps. If one day you feel like experimenting?'

Kialessa didn't know what to say. She'd honestly never thought of that.

'That, and evil sorcerers can use strands of your hair to try and take control of your spirit. There is that too.'

She already knew that, but in all her years, no one had ever successfully set her hair on fire, except Flameheart. Kialessa wondered what had happened to all the strands her mother had cut away – were they still around somewhere? They used to throw it into the backyard. 'I imagine there are a few fireproof nests for the birds in my valley,' she admitted.

Aolith glared at her, and then burst out laughing. 'Fireproof nests! Now there's a thought!'

'I imagine this does not impart fire proofness to the eggs within,' Piex ensaged.

'Does that mean we can make a flexible fireproof frying pan?' Marchan asked out loud.

Hmm, Kialessa pondered, *It is probably quite possible, if it could also be watertight.*

'Hmm,' Aolith muttered. 'If we could perhaps make it watertight.'

'Return to your tasks,' the wizard huffed.

Kialessa smiled. She was going to like hanging out with the wizards.

Once Aolith was satisfied that the outfit looked satisfactory, she gave a nod. Then she pointed at Kialessa's necklace that Darrix gave her.

'Oh,' Kialessa agreed; she didn't want that to become a part of the outfit. She had already removed the enchanted scarf Allastassia had given her for her birthday at the end of last year at the midwinter festival. But she swished the dress. It was nice to wear dresses.

'Don't let the wizard catch you doing that,' Aolith threatened with a grin, whispering though the constant creaking of the sailing ship hid most noises. 'He'll remind you it's "not a toy".'

'He's very serious, isn't he?' Kialessa said.

Aolith looked dark, then grinned and bent down to whisper, 'He's one of the silliest creatures I know, actually. You just take some time to get to know him. An absolute treat. Definitely a nice guy; you'll like him. He's very random though, can get a bit hard to follow. Can't tell if he's joking or being wise sometimes. Thankfully you have Marchan and me to help you make sense; Piex is so next level it's frustrating.'

Kialessa nodded. This kind of thing about people and relationships was important information.

Aolith smoothed out the scarf, patted Kialessa on the shoulder, and unfurled the scroll. Then, with a wry grin, she enacted some kind of simple wizardry and the scroll floated in the air on its own, highlighted with golden flecks of magic.

Kialessa barely resisted the urge to say, 'Oooooh.'

Aolith allowed her a glance at the scroll. It was a careful program, she could tell. Quite specific. There was the *Ecce,* and the *Et num,* and a bunch of numbers too. But she didn't get much of a read before the entire scroll evaporated and became the magic of the spell as Aolith activated it with a, *'Magicae ad induendum!'*

Kialessa's clothes disappeared in sparkles, swirling into a bright vortex that dissolved into the scarf, leaving a glowing golden rune circle thereon. Now there were four such ornate symbols.

Aolith tied it around her waist.

'Magicae,' Kialessa said, and the outfit folded out around her again. It fit even better this time, and was comfortable and flexible. She slipped on her necklace, and when she wrapped on her scarf it immediately changed into a deep burgundy to suit the outfit.

Aolith pushed her out, and the others clapped their approval.

'I was thinking the blue robe?' the wizard asked.

'She needs to move,' Aolith said without apology, which seemed a very rude way to speak to a creature who was her tutor, three hundred years older than her, and the most powerful wizard in the country.

To his credit, he took her decision in his stride. 'As you wish.'

Piex looked impressed. 'Cuffs! Ingenious. And the hardy material fulfils wizardry requirements without overly inhibiting movement. Yes, yes, very practical.'

Aolith nodded. 'Glad you like it.'

But Piex was not about to give away free compliments. 'But brown? It seems very dour.'

Aolith replied without a pause: 'She has no need of gaining any more attention than her horns and skin already grant her.'

Piex simply nodded, not pressing the point.

'And now,' the sagemaster said, putting down his reading. 'Piex, I believe it is your turn?'

Piex grinned, did a little excited jump, and then looked very nervous.

Kialessa walked up to the table, *almost* managing to resist the urge to swish her skirt. No one seemed to mind.

Piex took out an ornate box from the crowded shelves. It was carved with beautiful symbols, and bore the markings of magic about it. He placed it on the table. It had no lock or latch, so he opened it with words of magic. Inside, a pretty gold-coloured bronze headband, inlaid with a deep sapphire of some impressive value lay.

Piex was grinning, 'This is for your birthday, Kialessa!'

She looked up at him with a half grin, 'Seriously, Piex? All right, thank you. This is very kind of you!'

He smiled, 'It's a headband of wizardry!'

Now she gasped.

Marchan rolled his eyes. 'He keeps giving them away, yet insists *I* make my own,' he muttered.

'You're not an apprentice, we feel,' Piex said, 'and I thought this gift befitting.'

'That's worth over sixteen thousand gold coins,' the wizard

mentioned.

Now *that* was a fortune. How could Piex have gotten even the raw materials? How did he find the time? And was he really that good that he could make a fully empowered wizardry headband at only eleven years? She knew he was good, but *that* good?

'That's very good,' she admitted, wishing for wiser words to say.

He didn't seem to mind. 'You deserve it. Thank you so much for standing by me … and believing in me. So here you go, your very own headband of wizardry.'

He held the box up to her and allowed her to see it.

'Well, try it on!' Marchan offered.

Kialessa was deeply touched. This was another Kingly gift. The others were smiling at her, and she wondered if they'd already tried it. Or, at least, they knew what to expect. They all had wizardry headbands on, it was obvious to her now.

Holding her breath, she picked it up. It was cool and light, feeling almost delicate, yet twingling with potential and power. She placed it on her head.

Immediately she felt a little dizzy, then things snapped back into focus. All her thoughts seemed … really well organised now. Thoughts and events from years ago flitted through her mind as though summoned there by will. Suddenly, entire tomes of mathematical equations opened up to her understanding. She felt like a genius. '*Je sais tellement! Oh mon dieux, je peux parler elfique!*' Kialessa shouted in pure elven.

They laughed, then the sagemaster stated in elven as well, his very clear native accent shining through, 'I elucidated the protocols for elven language myself a generation ago. I trust they will serve you well.'

'Now we can keep secrets from the others!' Marchan grinned, speaking pure elven.

'I hope you like it,' Piex grinned. Then he switched from Elven to dragon speech, but she understood every word. 'I trust these additions will aid in your studies of magic.'

'You …' she wondered, secretly hoping everyone could have one of these miraculous gifts one day. 'You just spoke in dragon speech and so am I and … Wait a moment.' Her mind slipped back to the first conversation she'd ever had with Piex. '"*Panton said in oratio draco sanus profundus,*" and that meant,' and here she switched back to Emerellian, '"Everything said in dragon speech seems profound"? Was that joke, Piex!?'

He laughed. 'We weren't very good friends yet … I'm sorry. Yes, that was what I said!'

They all laughed. Dragon speech and elven? All without study or effort! She rubbed her hands together with glee – she was ready to learn wizardry!

With the sagemaster correcting some scroll work Aolith had been working on, and Piex still trying to crunch the numbers for his *fiery conflagration*, the task of explaining the *mage sight* spell was left to Marchan. Kialessa was initially concerned that he would be too difficult to understand, but truly he had a masterful grasp of what it meant to learn wizardry from the basics. With a mind enhancing device to assist, she understood it all in moments, constantly skipping ahead. He kept joking she'd be giving Piex a run for his genius, but she didn't really believe it.

There was a whole section on using something called trigonometry to calculate the triangulation between her eyes, the target, and the local intrusion point of something called *Lumos's light*. It was simply fascinating: a whole new branch of reality accessible only by the mind, and the strange ideas the wizards used to explain it all, called 'theories'.

They began to tire around midnight, and soon the sagemaster insisted they all tuck in. The night watch was swapping out, and the captain of the King's Guard came in to guard the King's room, though Kialessa had still seen no sign of the actual King. She had to wonder if he was sleeping in some kind of interdimensional space, perhaps. Either way, as tired as she was, her mind was filled with light and knowledge and questions, and she wondered if she'd ever get to sleep again.

She skipped with Piex to the ship's upper hold, and no one asked where she'd been. With nothing more than a magical word, she slipped into her favourite magical dressing gown and threw herself happily onto her bunk, her head so full of equations and words and languages she'd never worked on learning.

Briefly she wished she could have had one of these headbands when she'd started learning to read last year. But this would do; it was a gift she truly appreciated, and would put to good use! She wondered how she would ever get to sleep, but her new headband seemed to realise what the plan was, and appeared to go into some kind of downtime mode, falling quickly to a soft, muted wonder of dancing, sleeping thoughts. It was a miracle beyond reckoning to the happy tae'anaryn.

Too happy, she forgot to brush her teeth, and she forgot to wash her face and hands. And the simple task she would often regret skipping most of all: she forgot to say 'thank you', and to pray for safety and protection each day for herself and all she loved, from the Source that made all miracles possible …

2 Kialessa, Wizardess

The Squid

The purpose of life is to discover your gift.

The work of life is to develop it.

The meaning of life is to give your gift away.

Words of the goddess of the waters. Spoken by Drou Negerthaal, half-twarnae priestess

'Where did that come from?' Allastassia squealed.

The sky was still dark with dawn. A solider was ringing an alarm bell furiously; sailors ran to and fro, tying down sails or bearing weapons. Kialessa had barely risen herself, and now dodged between them to see what had the lookout shouting and pointing.

Water bulged in a surging heap only a couple of hundred paces behind them; something powerful was rushing to attack the Dawn. The Edge was trying desperately to catch up, running full sails, and all oars as well. But it would not be enough to catch the monster before it caught up the Dawn.

'Oh,' Piex stated with a bored voice he liked to use when something genuinely bothered him. 'A thirty tonne giant squid is bearing down on us.'

'Full sails!' the admiral roared. 'Keep it astern! We don't want it to catch up with us for even a moment!'

Days had passed in peace and silence, broken only by the daily chores of running the ship, and welcomed wizardry study. There had been no warning of an attack.

They gazed out at the enormous creature's wake as it ploughed along, seeming without effort, through the sea.

'I say we turn sail and take it with the ballistae,' Dale shouted.

'You'll not have much luck,' the admiral replied, though soldiers were arming the ballistae already. 'It can dive in a heart's beat below where the bolts will not have any effect. No; I fear it'll tear off our rudder.'

'Can a beast so do such?' Federach asked.

'Aye,' the admiral replied. 'Especially if driven beyond their nature. I do not think this is a natural hunt.'

Everyone turned to look at Allastassia and Natasha, the most fey creatures aboard. Natasha nodded. 'She trails us directly, as though a dark spirit drives her to rage. There be much very unnatural about her.'

The admiral mumbled words that were hard to hear: 'I would have thought the assassin would have attacked long before, and now he sends this? It is a strange play.'

'One to test our strength, and resolve,' high priestess Jacinthia muttered, securing her armour. It seemed her prayers had already failed to turn the beast.

'No mercy!' the captain of the King's guard roared above the chaos. 'If it's a fight the monster wants, it'll be a fight it gets!'

Natasha didn't look pleased, yet the beast surged rapidly on.

Kialessa was startled as the high priestess took the moment to call Darrix, another sailor, and herself to join her at the back of the ship. 'Come, ye faithful.' She took them to the stern. 'Look to the horizon; tell me what you see.'

Kialessa did as she was told, but saw nothing but the swelling waters and darkening sky. She turned to face Darrix and the sailor, who was probably some hidden priestess as well. They both looked with steadfast determination to the horizon.

Kialessa sighed, and looked harder. This was not a trick *mage sight* could help her with. She tried to look with her feelings, and suddenly sensed a deep fear lingering there. It was no surprise; a giant squid was bearing down on them. But this felt different, something that it should not be … It was deeply unsettling.

'When securely anchored on faith, evil hides no fear that can best us,' the priestess ensaged.

Darrix spoke: 'I see a large serpent … or eel, perhaps? It rides with many soldiers upon it, or within it. I don't understand how this can be.'

The sailor spoke: 'She is uncomfortable in these waters; they do not suit her. But she is driven to pursue our destruction, this I am sure of.'

'Good, good, well done,' the priestess nodded. 'Seersight must be honed to be developed. Can you see more?'

They looked for a moment more, but Kialessa could see nothing of which they spoke. And yet the priestess spoke as if she'd seen it all already.

The sailor spoke again: 'The serpent will not attack today; this is but a test.'

Darrix replied, 'But the monster does bring death.'

The priestess nodded. 'Good. That is right. Now, to your stations!'

They ran, but Kialessa kept waiting, wishing to see what Darrix and the others so easily saw. But that was not her gift, and she did not think the wizards would ever work out a spell to imitate this power, because they'd already had centuries to try. 'How?' She asked the priestess, before she'd remembered her manners. 'I'm sorry, your eminence.'

'Say on,' the priestess gave her leave.

'How do they … I mean, how does one …' She was lost for words.

'See?' The priestess nodded. 'It is a gift, a blessing. One granted by virtues and faith, but honed by hard work and skill.' She looked down at Kialessa, and must have been moved by her concerned look. 'Do not worry, the serpent that pursues us is only an ally to our enemy. But until this moment, I have not been able to see her either, for in attempting us harm they are revealed, as is natural law. Yet the authority that darkens even my sight must be great indeed.'

Kialessa pondered those words, but the surging swell moved closer and closer.

'I don't think we will outrun it,' Kialessa observed.

The admiral seemed to hear her. 'Furl the sails! Open the mizzenmast and prepare to drop the starboard anchor! We turn, hard!'

Sailors ran to obey. Dale laughed out loudly, and ran towards the largest ballista at foreship.

'My liege, what are you doing?' the steward shouted, running out of the inner chamber, the King right behind him.

'So, a little diversion? If it's a fight he wants, a fight he gets,' the King demanded, and Kialessa felt her own soul steel with resolve at her King's words. People stopped shouting in chaos and focused on their work.

The steward took his first look at the monster as the boat slowly turned. Then he gulped. 'My liege, perhaps it would be best for you to weather this little zephyr below deck?'

In response, the King drew his sword. 'And miss the adventure? For our nation and our people!' he shouted, and everyone took up the cry.

'Prepare to turn starboard!' the admiral ordered, and people began to grip the edges of the boat, or to tie themselves on. 'Young master Dale, you get *one shot.*'

The beast surged nearer, and this time Kialessa felt as if she could feel the boat lunge about in the monster's wake. She turned, and saw deep underwater an enormous black eye staring out at them malevolently. She honestly felt that if this beast had been driven to evil, it had not needed to be driven very far.

'Now!' the admiral shouted.

Chains clinked as the enormous starboard anchor fell. A moment later it caught hard on the sandy seafloor. The boat, already tilting right from the action of the sails, turned intensely. The beast saw its opportunity and surged towards them.

'Now!' Dale shouted, but his words were a half breath too late. The beast was partway under the boat by the time the first bolts hit the water, it was so incredibly fast. Barely a bolt would have hit it.

The Dawn lilted as the monster swam under them, then tilted noticeably as the beast took hold. Giant tentacles began to work their way up the ropes and towards the mast in the morning light.

'Don't give it a moment!' the admiral roared.

Sailors hacked at the appendages with spears and axes, but the monster's hide was incredibly thick and flexible. Ropes snapped as it tugged at them, trying to pull itself up and towards the mizzenmast – the largest mast at the centre of the boat. Several *magus spherae* from the wizards aboard tried to discourage it, but the monster kept rising up from the waters.

'Turn her!' the admiral roared. 'Turn her portside west!'

Kialessa dimly wondered how the sailors were going to achieve that, with a thirty-tonne monster trying to climb onto the boat. But she didn't have long to think about it, as then the creatures huge eye appeared. Several sailors hurled weapons at it, and it blinked just in time and pulled back with a shouting screech.

'Now!' the admiral roared, and sailors surged towards it.

Kialessa watched with fascination, wondering how on earth she was going to be of much help. She called her acid dagger, thinking it might be of some use. She was about to charge, when she stopped. This was just like battle training, everyone running around and shouting. This was the time when it was usually smarter to stop, and look.

The beast was holding its own in the dim light, the splashing of its battle slowly extinguishing the lights on board. They would need light again soon. Indeed, perhaps it was vulnerable to light, and that was why it had attacked now. Somehow it was effectively defending itself, battering down sailors with a tentacle or two while several other tentacles tried to rip down the sails and rigging.

But then she noticed a greater concern: a dozen other tentacles, and she began to wonder just how many it had, had snuck their way around the sides of the boat, and were preparing to snatch up sailors, warriors, and wizards from all over.

'Behind you!' Kialessa squealed, and everyone looked at her. Just in time, the people noticed the dark tendrils sneaking up on them, and the monster lost its advantage. Indeed, with a hateful screech, it lost several tentacles as well, hacked off by frantic sailors.

Kialessa was just beginning to think how clever she was, how good she'd been in saving what must have been a dozen lives, when a black slithering appendage wrapped around her waist. With a dismal squeal, she lost her grip on even her favourite dagger, and could do nothing as it slipped from her grasp. She screamed.

Several axes hit the tentacle, but it was one of the big ones. Even the captain couldn't get close enough. Kialessa tried to shadowstep out of the monster's grasp, but found she was either too panicked, or the thick ichor of the beast was somehow preventing her. It dragged her towards its face, lifting it up to show her a deadly snapping beak. Kialessa struggled against the crushing tentacle but found herself quite stuck in its vice-like grip.

A moment later, she was enveloped in a spherical forcefield of pearlesque light, and she fell from the monster's grasp. She looked up to find the King was holding the rod out towards her, granting her his protection. In a hideous display of disrespect, the steward ripped it from his grasp and turned the rod to protect the King again. She fell from the air, but still landed on her feet.

Time paused, as Kialessa realised what might have just happened. The King himself had transferred his protection to her. Even for just a breath, that was a terrible risk. Without that protection, he could have been shot, cursed, or torn in half. It was a dreadful decision, and one he should have never made.

But he looked at her as though he really cared about her much more.

She said no more, but stood up to fight.

The creature reached out towards the mast, and Kialessa again felt it was not accident that it crushed or quenched every light and lantern along its way. The wizards began to summon small glowing orbs that flew around the monster, highlighting it, but the monster reached on.

'No!' the captain of the King's guard shouted. He leapt down from the deck he was standing on to land right before the monster, the entire boat somehow shaking at his footfall. With movement almost too fast to see, he cut up two tentacles in a single powerful blow, freeing the sailors within. He flung an axe, hitting the beast in its eye. The monster screeched in pain; the axe bounced away, but left a notable cut.

Rising up, the creature focused all its attacks on the captain. He swung about with raw battle fervour, slashing and hacking with prescient might. Sailors stood back to let him fight. The giant squid responded by attacking him with ten tentacles at once, ploughing into him from the same direction. He blocked them with crossed axes as they pushed him back to the other side of the boat. He battled on. Step by step he advanced on the creature, and it pulled back from every battle just to concentrate on him.

Kialessa grinned. She knew the monster could not win against this champion.

Just then, the captain slipped. A tentacle had lashed out, and covered in water spray and monster blood, the floor of the Dawn had betrayed the captain. He fell hard. A tentacle gripped his ankle, but he sundered it in a moment. Even so, Kialessa saw one of the huge tentacles had taken the distraction. Raised high, it was going to crush him right into the floor, and probably leave his broken body bleeding below deck.

He was about to twist sideways when the entire boat lit up with a blinding white light. The priestess held up her symbol. Battle stopped.

'Abate, now!' she commanded.

The beast seemed unwilling, or unable, to attack. But it did not flee. Instead, it roared.

'I had that,' the captain protested. He held out his hand and a man at arms threw him his legendary bow, *Hera Lira*. Kialessa knew this would be the end of the combat. 'You needn't hold it for my final blow.'

'This was not for you,' she grinned.

Suddenly the monster screeched in mortal agony, and the Imagination's Dawn was pushed violently away. Even so, the beast seemed stuck now on the boat completely.

Kialessa heard cheering from behind the monster's head.

The Edge had arrived and, apparently, had finally put its untested ram to its intended use.

The captain grinned, and burst into laughter.

The monster flailed helplessly. Stuck between two ships and impaled on a metal rod, it could do nothing. Tentacles twitched painfully.

'Here, let me help you,' the captain grinned. He ran up to the upper deck, taking position where the monster was pinned. He aimed his bow.

His aim was flawless.

The King stood by the captain of his guard as the sailors helped the fallen, and tried to decide what to do with several tonnes of dead sea creature.

Suddenly the sailors began to sing again as they worked.

What shall we do with a mighty monster?
What shall we do with a mighty monster?
What shall we do with a mighty monster?
In the darkening sky?

And the singer replied,

Cut him all up and make him supper!

Then everyone joined in.

Cut him all up and make him supper!
Cut him all up and make him supper!
In the darkening sky!

Everyone cheered, but the noise was cut short. 'Bon Sure'e!' the King announced.

The captain knelt at his feet. 'My liege.'

The King drew his sword, and placed it on the younger man's shoulder. 'You are hereby promoted to General and Commander of all the military forces of Lenmer'el. Rise, General Bon Sure'e!'

The captain – sorry, general – looked startled. But he nodded and saluted. 'An unexpected honour, your majesty!'

'Too much?' the King was grinning.

'Never!' General Bon Sure'e grinned, and turned to quickly help organise the sailors.

The battle had been sore; two sailors had not survived, and a dozen more needed to be transferred to the Edge for healing. Kialessa herself had almost died, but it was not all a waste. They had saved the King, and they had fought together. And Kialessa had to admit – giant squid tasted delicious.

Every Hope, Every Prayer

*She nodded. No other battle would test her father more, and no
other battle would make him stronger. He had to face this – alone;
with all her love and prayers, but alone.*

Kialessa, 314 CY, cited in the Year in Jail

That night, Kialessa had the unrivalled privilege of eating dinner with
the King. He sat at the head of the table, opposite the steward, and she to
the steward's left hand. The high priestess, sagemaster, the newly
promoted general, and Aolith ate with them. It was a slow, subdued meal,
and the steward spent most of his time glaring at his King.

They were well into the second course of red meat and salad when the
King finally spoke up. 'I don't know what's got you so bothered, Grudon.'

Kialessa glanced at the steward. Everyone did.

He ground his teeth, but after a moment spoke with impeccable
manners. 'My liege. You are King. And all we have is yours … but today,
you were most unwise!'

Kialessa almost gasped, but one glare from Aolith silenced her.

The King looked more than just a little angry himself. He took his
napkin, wiped his mouth, and handed it to a servant. Kialessa recognised
her as one of the royal staff that usually served at the castle, and briefly
wondered if she was a wizard too, or if not, what secrets she may hold, or
have overheard in her service. It was very brave of her to be on this ship,

or did she even have a choice? She'd been nowhere during the battle. Who was she?

The King cleared his throat. 'Well said, well said, honoured Lord Grudon. Perhaps you will forgive my rashness? Had it been you, I assure you I would have acted no differently.'

3 Dinner with the King

The steward, honoured Lord Grudon Fletcherson, sighed exasperatedly, and the priestess glared at him. 'Our lives are your own, and your life is most precious to us all, yes, yes indeed. But I fear-'

'You fear,' the wizard interrupted, 'that in saving Maid Winterhaven's life, the King has unwittingly shown a weakness our enemy is likely to exploit?'

'With all due respect,' the general muttered, 'this is not news to any of us.'

The priestess sighed. Everyone looked at her. She waited until the King gave her leave to speak. '*Impenetrabilis* is one of the greater powers of the rod of Lenmer'el. To have you, my King, leave its sanctuary for even an instant is a dread risk.'

That seemed to upset the King. Tears actually began to stir at the edge of his eyes.

Kialessa's heart stung. Was she in trouble? Was her King to be chastened by his bodyguard and closest friends for her? Suddenly, dinner did not taste so fair anymore.

The King looked out the small windows at the rising sea. 'The purpose of my life is to make life richer for everyone. I will not be the King of a dead nation.'

No one argued.

Kialessa set her fork down, and felt like bursting into tears right there and then. But she did not.

Aolith reached out and held Kialessa's hand, and the steward glanced at them. He spoke again: 'He is clever, this assassin. My suspicion is that if he now knows you are willing to use *Impenetrabilis* to protect your people, my kind King, he will expect us not to use it again.'

The general laid down the mug he was sipping at and almost shouted, 'What?'

The wizard leaned forward. 'But what if, in knowing we are aware of his knowing we have used this power rashly, he may expect us to indeed use it again in the future?'

The general groaned, and the King hid his smile.

'With a foe such as this,' the priestess ensaged, 'both are reasonable suppositions. In either event, the protective powers of the rod are greater than any other nation of the seventeen. We cannot afford to use it. Not ever.'

'Agreed,' the wizard said.

The King was silent a moment, and they all looked at him. 'I do not regret my action. Indeed, if it gives our foe a false sense of prediction regarding us ...'

Jacinthia, the high priestess, continued: 'Our foe will rightly expect that you will use that power again, against our better judgement, if it is to save the lives of those you most treasure.'

To that, everyone agreed, which to Kialessa was very curious. Perhaps, then, this was just a reminder to her to never try and rely on salvation from that source again. For to trade her life for the King's was simply not an option, to any of them. His very life was bound up the in Kingdom. All knew the binding powers of the rod and the land; if the King died of anything other than natural causes, or at the hand of the gods, the land could well be expected to die with him, and its people be scattered and homeless. This was a dire threat indeed, and one worth risking a daring voyage.

Either way, it seemed she was not, directly, to be chastened any further.

'Even so,' the steward continued to ponder, 'the squid was clearly just a test of our resolve, and study of our tactics.'

The general's voice growled, 'I wish this demon would just come out into the light. I'd slay him right now if I knew where to strike!'

Jacinthia laid a warning hand on his hand, and the steward spoke. 'Your time will come, Bon Sure'e.' It seemed they had a sort of system sorted out already for calming down the ever-eager general.

Kialessa did not know what to think. Had she done something wrong? A dozen lives had probably been spared in that moment, though she'd forgotten to look after her own. Did her one life mean that much to the King?

King Dunnkan looked at her and then, glancing at the steward, nodded in her direction.

Honoured Lord Grudon turned to face her, the rest of the people at the table, expect perhaps Aolith, caught up in some conversation the King was making. The steward held out the rod to Kialessa.

It was black, made of some form of polished ebon wood. Levitating at one end was a diamond sphere, mystically engraved with the coat of arms of the nation. Invisible within, every promise of the people to protect the King, and their country.

Then the steward held it nearer to her, indicating she should take it.

Without fear, but perhaps a little nervous about holding the most potent magical device in the nation, she took hold. There was no thunder, no lightning. Not even a twingling to indicate it was anything other than a pretty stick. She turned it in her hands, admiring its weight, thinking it might make a rather convenient mace if someone needed a nice clubbing upside their head one day.

The steward grinned. 'Maid Baroness Winterhaven, I am glad I can finally share the burden of wielding this rod with someone else. You've seen what it can do, but that is only a taste of its true power. *Veridictus*, the power to lay an oath and strict punishment on those condemned, and *Impenetrabilis*, you already know. But there are over thirty powers in this rod, perhaps even more. We have not yet seen the day when it is to come into its full reckoning.'

She looked at him in shock. *Thirty powers?* Few magical items held more than one, and she'd only ever heard tell of a handful with two or more. Thirty was beyond belief. It was extreme.

He nodded sincerely. 'Come, I think we should show you. Look into the sphere. Gaze into it with intent. Tell me what you see.'

She peered into the crystal ball. There was … nothing.

'No,' he chided her. '*Respicio*, see *them*. The people. Look inside for the citizens of Lenmer'el.'

Even as he spoke the key word, the visions erupted on her mind. She knew she was sitting in the Imagination's Dawn; she could feel the gentle rocking of the chair within the boat. But suddenly she could see, as within a dream, lives. Thousands of lives. Hundreds of thousands. Millions. Not just humans and their allies. There were … trees. And insects … grasses …

70

'Does the King govern all this?' she wondered.

She felt the steward's erudite mind guiding her sight, his own intelligence a fortress of privacy. 'Indeed, the right given by Mya at the birth of the first race, the ancients, and passed on to their creations the humans, elves, dwarves, trolls, and all the others. To govern a nation is to become a steward, a servant, of all living within. It is to own and be owned by the land herself.'

As he spoke, she could feel what he meant. She saw the authority of her King reaching deep into the earth, right to its very heart. She saw him answer to the air above the nation, and have his wishes behoven and answered by the waters that flowed.

She almost felt like she could see the entire country, but there was too much to take in in one moment. The castle at Lenmer'el was a beacon, a blazing fire of light. There was the distant Far Keep, now a lighthouse of his authority. But there were hidden places as well, much that she felt she knew existed but could not find. Then her late father's old fortress came into her view, the Sanctum Brumae, and the soldiers that nervously guarded it like paper dolls.

The steward grunted, as though he was hard put to the challenge of keeping up with her young, curious mind. 'The rod struggles to represent every life and authority, at times. But this is a road map, an outline, of all within King Dunnkan's authority. Note how the places that grant him a deeper allegiance are more easily discerned.'

She let her mind take him to the place he was 'pointing' to – her mother's old inn. The foundation was there, cleared by gnome stonemasons. They were preparing to build the new inn when winter was done. Her parents were camped out in a travelling caravan they'd purchased. Her mother was out hanging the washing, her adopted brother Kiel was picking late winterberries. Her father, she was ashamed to see, was again testing the new mead he was brewing for potential customers.

She looked at her old man, the man the gods had adopted her to as a true father. She saw his old and weathered face, his greying hair. The shame within his eyes at the undying control alcohol still held on him. She felt within her a stirring; a hatred, and a pity. She felt the magic swell, and knew she had the power to force him, to make the alcohol become a poison to him, till he could taste it no more without being sick.

But then she felt a wisdom of more than a hundred years echoing in the rod. She saw that forcing him to change was no lasting solution. He would find another way to serve his demons, she was sure of this. There was only one lasting solution – he had to do it himself. He had to win this battle, and despite her all love, she could not fight it for him. She could only love him.

She felt a hand on her face, and realised the steward was wiping away a tear from her eyes. She sniffed, and tried to clean her face.

'You see so quickly,' he muttered.

She nodded. No other battle would test her father more, and no other battle would, in the end, make him stronger. He had to face this alone; with all her love and prayers, but alone.

She looked up, and noticed the stalwart steward blinking away his own tears. He spoke; 'Two hundred thousand citizens … Every life a story, and every story the same: overcoming. How your King bears it, I may never know.'

Kialessa pondered, 'Perhaps it is his battle? The King's, I mean. No other would bring out his strength, and no other would test him more.'

She looked at her mighty King, new understanding weighing on a young heart. To know and feel the wisdom of every King and Queen who had ever held the rod was an enormous power, one she didn't even know was possible. And yet the Kingdom was vast. So many people, so many life forms! 'If only… I could save them all.'

The steward coughed. 'You see so quickly!' He sat back, removing the rod from her tentative grasp, ending the visions. 'Perhaps this is good, very good.'

'Why do you show me this?'

He did not answer directly. 'The powers of the rod are many. You would think, wouldn't you, that seeing into the minds and hearts of every citizen, that it would be a light thing to find our assassin. We try, every day, but we don't see him.'

'Could it be he is outside the nation?'

The steward grinned. 'You can scry there, too, if they have sworn alliance to this Kingdom. But no, he is veiled from our view somehow. We not only know not how to find him; we don't even know where to look.' He sighed and sat back. 'It takes great skill and focus to see each life. I think you have to actually *care* without feeling a need to *force* them into a particular course of action. Some of the most rich and powerful are invisible to my sight, I think, because I really *do not* like them.'

She pondered that. It seemed a strange thing to admit. Why did he need her to know this?

He held out the rod again. 'Draw into it the people's power. Their rage at the offense of having their King's life threatened.'

She reached out and touched the rod he was holding. At first, she strained, then found the power flowing effortlessly into her. She had to stop trying in order for it to happen. There was a great rage, and an indignity, riding upon an undercurrent of fear and power.

'Stay yourself,' the steward counselled, holding the rod a little away. 'This power, *Gratos*, is used to empower our warriors in battle. With this, a hundred could face down a thousand warriors. It does not guarantee victory, nor guarantee freedom from suffering and wounds. But it takes the strength and will of the nation and grants it to those willing to fight for her. It makes warriors of common strength and skill reach far beyond, to acts of impossible heroism and, well, luck. We used this at the battle of the hill when the troll hordes of Ki Tieri first attempted to invade the nation last year. We two hundred stood against ten times that number for long enough, till the sky dragons intervened. We would not have prevailed, but it would have cost them the same to deny us that day as to conquer the rest of the country. And rightly so; for if we had fallen, the rest of the country was lost anyway. So, you see, *Gratos* does not grant any power or prayer beyond what the good people already hold, but it can concentrate it, making normal people heroic, and heroic people legendary.'

She nodded, feeling the power twingling up her arms. She realised it would respond to her commands even as it guided her actions. The will of everyone, she could use it to empower her shadow weaving, her combat prowess, even her own prayers for healing and faith.

And it was not entirely unfamiliar to her – she had felt its effects before, when facing down the assassin on the day he'd set fire to the throne room, or cleaning up all the shadow weave in the entire country. It was a free ticket to power. No, not free; it was paid for by everyone who loved and cared within their whole entire country. And while she held the rod, she could feel it.

If only she was wise enough to know what to do with it! She handed the power back to the steward. She felt so small against such might and responsibility. She looked at him. Why *was* he teaching her all this?

The high priestess was looking at her, 'There has only, ever, been one protector of the King. In all nations, in all of history. Only one.'

Kialessa nodded, she already knew this. Then her heart suddenly pricked with fear. She gasped, and turned to the steward even as the whole room fell to sudden silence. 'You think you are going to die on this voyage, don't you?'

The room fell silent, and they all turned to look at her.

'I sincerely hope not.' The steward shrugged as though he hadn't a care in the world, and went back to eating his dinner.

The Peninsula

*Being alive **is** the meaning! Life is wonderful and fascinating*
even without a purpose. Sense it, experience it, feel pain and joy and
failure. Sentience is a wonderful privilege denied to most.
Toni, 314CY, cited in 'Recollections of the Tae'anaryl'

A week slid by. Piex still wasn't fully well, and the steward took no further opportunity to tell Kialessa more about the rod. So Kialessa studied with the wizards. She had mastered *mage sight* by this time, and was starting to learn *magus spherae*, which seemed to be a kind of rite of passage to any 'real' wizard. It was dangerous, reckless wizardry, but fascinating! One would pack as much instable matter into as small a space as possible and throw it at an enemy. She had to define a target, and calculate the radius cubed, divided by three, multiplied by four times the circulan ratio. She could do it all by hand on paper, but the headband made it easy.

They gave her and the other students little to do on the ship, so she had plenty of time to practice. Piex was happy to help out; it seemed to push back the nausea.

Around midway through the new week, Kialessa noticed the ship was heading back in towards the shore, which was interesting. She noticed Allastassia at the foremast; the part dryad practiced her enchantments so much there that the entire area was covered in grasses and moss. There wasn't much space to dance, but she still made the most of it. Though right now she was mediating quietly, sitting cross legged in the air, conjured butterflies fluttering around her head.

This was probably not a great time to chat, but then again, it might be.

'We're changing course,' Kialessa whispered to her, in case Allastassia was too busy.

The blond enchantress' eyes flung open, and she looked around. Then she stood up gracefully like some kind of picture brought to life. 'Hey, bosun!' she shouted to the second in command. 'What brings us about?'

The old man shrugged, but the admiral was there in moments. 'Your King bids us veer shoreward. There's a nick in the rudder we want to get righted, and we head for a sheltered cove there.'

Kialessa looked at his face as he spoke; it was stern, unquestioning, professional. But there was something in his voice she could not place … Was it nervousness? Something about the rod had made her wiser. 'You have doubts?' she asked.

Allastassia turned back to listen intently.

The admiral grinned, then laughed. 'They speak true that say the King's pet demon is cunning indeed! Please, I mean no offense. And the King, he speaks for the gods … but I shall be honest with you young maids, as future leaders of a good man's Kingdom – there is a place near the cove that will make the sailors mighty nervous.'

Piex approached, his voice excited. 'You mean the ruins of Dae Montol? I have always hoped to see them!'

Allastassia gasped. 'An ancient city! Yes, I felt it. I knew I was feeling it.'

The admiral looked impressed. 'Indeed, m'lady. Dae Montol is a citadel of Civit Aurea, it is believed. Small, 'n' well plundered by now. But I suspect he will have you young ones explor'n' it, as he is want to expand on your education, 'n' all.'

Sure enough, within moments the King emerged. She had not seen him in a week, but that was perhaps wise for his safety. Sailors on deck scurried to salute or to clean things up.

'As you were,' he laughed. He seemed to be in a good mood. She almost didn't wait for his invitation for a hug, though the other's stood back. Within moments all the students were on deck, awaiting his instructions. Had they been called? The rod could surely do such a thing, or had they simply known of themselves?

'Within the hour, we disembark,' the King announced. 'The sailors have some repairs to make and we have some time to explore. Senior students, you will head to the abandoned citadel of *Dae Montol*, and explore it most carefully for any relics or items of magic and power that may be there. Take any equipment you need. Are you ready?'

Aolith stood forward, 'Thank you, good King. We will bring you a report before nightfall.'

He nodded. 'And you, junior students. We have a task for you as well.'

Kialessa noticed a sly grin on the steward's face, but could not guess what the apparent joke was about.

The King continued, 'There is a veil of power located high up on the ridge, by the edge of the bluff. You are to go there, see if you can pierce the veil, then return and report to me. Understood?'

'Ah, good King,' Allastassia muttered. He gave her leave to speak. 'What if, perchance, we are able to piece the veil?'

The King smiled, and the steward laughed. The steward spoke. 'Go through and tell us what you find on the other side. Failing all else, we will meet you in three days on the other side of the peninsula, understood?'

'Yes, good King,' Allastassia said with a bow, but Kialessa knew her friend well enough to know that she did not like this assignment. Three days of walking through virgin wilderness was not something the enchantress was accustomed to; her magic was typically employed in large groups of humans clustered in cities.

Piex was probably about to die of exhaustion – the supplies alone would weigh more than he did. But she knew he was a loyalist. He would never openly question the King's express request.

Kialessa knew this was going to be an interesting three days.

***

Shimmering sparkles of light twinkled under Kialessa's fingertips. The veil rose up high among the trees, invisible unless touched. It felt soft, but electrical, and she knew there was no way that she could possibly force herself through it.

'Impassable,' Piex announced.

Kialessa was inclined to agree.

'Look,' Allastassia pointed, 'the creatures of the forest pass as though the veil didn't exist.' And as they watched, a slow-moving lizard crossed the barrier without harm or impediment in any way.

Kialessa looked over at the enchantress. She had been impressed at how quickly Allastassia had made it through the forest, till she'd remembered she was part dryad. Allastassia LOVED nature, and would probably sleep naked under the trees without a second thought if someone didn't make a rule against it. She was fit, too, and was always dancing. Only Piex had struggled up the hill in his wizard vest and satchel, till Posk had insisted on carrying him. It had made no difference to Posk's pace at all.

'I wonder who made it?' Kialessa pondered as she continued to run the veil under her fingers.

Allastassia pointed back down the mountain. 'The senior students are currently exploring the *exciting* ruins of an *ancient* city, and you wonder? I think it no surprise.'

Darrix disagreed. 'Their city is in ruin, yet their veil is intact? No, there is something alive maintaining this.'

Allastassia ran her hand over the veil again, conjuring sparks to test the field, but it did not yield.

Piex had sat down; he still looked exhausted. 'I, for one, was really hoping to explore the citadel of Dae Montol. I was praying for the privilege. Now we find ourselves at the most boring and least informative of all venues? Why did the King send us here!?'

'You question his judgement?' Allastassia teased him.

Piex, of course, didn't realise she was just provoking him. 'No, no, I promise!' he almost begged. 'But … oh. I did so want to see the ruins.'

'Yeah,' Kialessa agreed. Perhaps it had simply been a hike to stretch their legs?

Darrix looked up at the veil. 'I do not think our King would have sent us all the way up here without expecting something. There must be a way in …'

Allastassia stood back. 'All right, stand away,' she commanded.

They all leapt backwards. A moment later she summoned a bolt of lightning from the sky and threw it at the barrier. It shuddered, but did not yield.

'Wow, you're really gett'n' good at that,' Posk congratulated her.

She did not reply.

'I have been studying the magical radiance,' Piex claimed. 'And while I consider it unlikely, I think we might be able to open it with the magic key spell wizards often use.' He took a moment to make the mental calculations, then touched the shimmering wall. It did not budge.

Piex was visibly disappointed.

'Here, let me try,' Posk replied, and stalking up pounded on the wall of light. Ripples of energy flowed up the veil. 'Hey!' he shouted, 'You let us in!?'

Nothing happened.

They turned to her, but she had nothing to add. 'Perhaps just getting here was the quest.'

'There is something alive in there,' Darrix added, and Allastassia scoffed.

Posk grunted, the troll way of agreeing. 'Shiny tells it right. There is some Master of the forest beyond, and he does not want to be disturbed. I guess we enjoy the view and get away from here. My heart speaks a warning; this is not a place for us.'

Kialessa thought it uncharacteristically shy of Posk to say that, but he was a wild, nature sort of young boy. Sometimes he seemed to sense things no one else did.

Piex sighed. 'I can't believe he'd send us all the way up here to fail.'

Allastassia turned to face the ships, still visible in the sheltered cove far below. 'I'm with Kialessa. The test was simply to get here. Why would the King want us somewhere that he cannot follow? I think we should leave. We have made enough noise already.'

Piex looked at the forcefield sadly. 'If I had more time …'

Posk offered the wizard his arm, but Piex declined. 'I'll be all right on the way down.'

'Well, I liked the view,' Allastassia said, stepping onto a tree branch and allowing it to lower her gracefully to the ground below. 'Darrix, you coming?'

He was still gazing at the veil of light. For a moment Kialessa thought he might give up his watch, but then she noticed he was still simply staring. She moved to see his face, sober and intense. The way he got when he had found something he did not ever intend to give up on.

'Darrix?' she asked.

He looked up at the light. 'Please, hidden Master of the forest beyond the veil. If you will, may we pass?'

For a moment the forest seemed to hold its breath. Then, suddenly and with the sound of shattering fragile glass, the veil split down the centre.

Darrix looked at her, surprise and excitement written all over his face.

She must have looked just as surprised.

Without another pause, Darrix stepped forward and seemed to turn invisible in the forest.

'Darrix, what are you … Darrix, wait!' Allastassia screamed, scrambling up to join them.

Posk grabbed Piex around his petite waist and charged towards them.

Kialessa looked up at the parting in the curtain of light.

'What do we … Ooh, Darrix! You …' Allastassia sounded frustrated.

'Shiny got us in!' Posk sounded impressed. He rushed forwards, and Piex struggled from his grasp.

Allastassia was already heading in. 'Darrix! We can't see you! Darrix …' her voice began to fade as she turned invisible.

'Fun!' Posk said, and charged in. He must have run straight into Allastassia because Kialessa could hear her chiding him.

'I guess we go in?' she suggested.

Piex looked pale.

'I suppose,' he muttered. Not willing to be last, he walked right ahead.

She followed immediately behind with a bit of a grin. *We got in! I guess we will have news for our King after all!*

The Master of the Forest

Tobiuus snarled. 'You are all so precious. There are no "gods", just those powerful enough to impose their wanton whims on others. We may once have been a creation of the gods, but we are left to ourselves, occasionally getting their help when we amuse them enough. But life and fate are our own … at least, for those who are willing to admit that truth.'

Tobiuus, archmage and prisoner of Emerel. Cited by Coure De'Feur, according to the castle records CY 314

Kialessa grinned. Piex was still complaining about the small, biting insects.

'But you really do,' Allastassia argued. 'You just *ask* them, Piex. That's all you do.'

'I tried, yet they bite!' he protested.

'You should just cover yourself in mud, that's what I do,' Posk replied.

'That's disgusting,' Allastassia protested.

Without another word, Posk rolled off his branch and plunged chest first into a nearby bog. Rolling around, he was covered in moments. 'See, no insects!' he bragged.

'Better check yourself for leaches,' Darrix pointed out.

Posk shrugged, 'Everyone gotta eat.'

'Eww, Posk, that's disgusting!' Allastassia protested.

Kialessa and Darrix were sitting quite close to Allastassia in the trees, hoping to shield themselves in her protective aura. They had been walking the rest of the day in the quickly fading light. Piex was despondent; no fire could be kindled in the woods. It was clear the Master of the forest did not allow it. Piex lived by fire, studied by it. Hid in his tent from the insects with it. But there was no flat ground anywhere to be found for tents either.

Again Allastassia chided him. 'Climb up here, wizard! There is no safety in pride. This is the forest, for Winter's sake! If you want to survive to see the dawn, we have to huddle. There is no other way.'

Piex did not look comfortable – there was no way this sort of physical proximity was permissible in the college, at home, or even in the town. But this was a military excursion into untamed wilderness, and they'd been trained for this very sort of thing. Huddling together all night for pure survival was one of those things.

'Come, wizard,' Darrix agreed, squishing up between Allastassia and Kialessa. 'And you too, Posk.'

Allastassia groaned, 'You sure?'

Darrix nodded, taking off his breastplate and grieves. They were icy cold in the thick evening air. He could not rest with them here.

Branches began to fold around the 'nest' that Allastassia was building, or requesting, from the forest. Thick, dark leaves made a roof.

Posk climbed up in a moment. He shook the mud from him fiercely, like a dog shaking water from its back. It was actually surprisingly successful.

'Don't you dare touch me, troll,' Allastassia demanded.

'Hey, no worries,' he agreed, snuggling between Kialessa and Darrix. 'Coming, wizard?'

'Well, if I must.' Piex then levitated himself up, mist trailing behind him like the failing shreds of his dignity.

The insects fled visibly from him as he climbed into the nest. Allastassia patted him on the head. He tried to snuggle down, but he had to sort of press his back against Allastassia. She was grinning, and he looked very embarrassed.

'Nice, wizard,' she teased, patting him on the head again.

He was silent moment, 'Thank you for the sanctuary,' he replied.

'No problem.'

'Yes, thank you,' Kialessa said.

'Agreed,' Darrix replied. 'Thank you.'

There was silence.

Posk farted.

The entire nest almost exploded apart. Allastassia sat up and shrieked at him, cuddled between Kialessa and Darrix at the far end, 'If you dare do that again – !!'

Posk burst out laughing, 'Sorry, sorry! Yes, yes, no, thank you, fair enchantress. May your haven keep us warm and safe this evening.'

Allastassia lay down, still simmering. 'I swear, Posk, I will drop you from this nest and you can sleep in the mud like you always wanted.'

Thankfully, Posk didn't seem willing to pick another fight by bragging about how much he loved mud. He was quiet for a moment, then said, 'Thank you, Allastassia. Piex would freeze to death without this.'

No one argued; it was quite true.

'You all need *me* to keep warm anyway,' Posk said with a yawn, sounding like he was just stating a fact. Kialessa wasn't sure it was true, but it certainly made it easier. She was sure Darrix would be warm, but Posk was simply warmer. And with her magical night gown, she didn't really have an excuse to cuddle up to anyone in particular. Allastassia seemed to prefer hugging Piex, like a plushy little wizard toy.

'Darrix, will you offer devotions?' Allastassia asked.

'Seems more your thing, given the situation,' Darrix replied.

'No,' she said, like it was something she'd given some thought to.

Darrix then sung an evening hymn, Allastassia softly harmonising an improvised countermelody to the second chorus without effort. He then said the night-time prayer, but Kialessa was never sure if she heard the end of it. She was asleep in moments.

***

Kialessa awoke next morning feeling quite well rested, curious dreams flittering away with the shuddering of her eyelids. It felt like it had been a busy night, but she had not awoken once, and the forest has stayed silent. There had been dreams – the eye with two irises, one surrounding the other. It was a strange vision that fled as soon as she tried to recall it.

She found herself still in their cramped little nest, but noticed that it had been big enough. Then she realised Posk must have stepped out at some point, meaning the strong arm around her was Darrix's. She grinned to herself, and waited until everyone else woke up.

Dawn was just creeping over the horizon. Darrix stretched out painfully, and Allastassia didn't seem too comfortable either. Piex slept on.

Darrix climbed down, and she followed. They took the time to set their morning meal, far simpler without fire to warm things. He blessed the waters, and after Piex woke up, he made him warm the waters till the soup was quite toasty. In all, Kialessa thought it a delightful feast.

It summoned Posk in short order. He'd somehow managed to catch some furry critters that looked a little like ferrets. Allastassia made him release one because they had no fire to cook it. He didn't release the other, but ate it raw after bleeding it. He tried to offer the meat to them, but not even Kialessa could bring herself to eat raw meat. Posk, on the other hand, wasted very little of his morning catch. He even used the fur to make a toilet, which Kialessa thought was actually quite thoughtful and practical of him.

She wished she had more to offer, but the Master would not allow her *stone on fire* wizardry, not even her *finger fire*. They had no wisdom that could explain this power.

'Who do you suppose this Master is?' Kialessa asked them during their quiet morning preparations.

'I felt him near in the night,' Allastassia said.

'Do you think he is any danger?' Piex asked, looking small.

Allastassia shook her head. 'Dangerous, yes, but dangerous to us? Not really. More curious, I think.'

'I feel his eyes often on me, always,' Posk said, softly.

Kialessa knew what he meant. There was a presence in this forest, constant and vigilant. 'Is he an ancient tree?' she asked.

Again Allastassia disagreed. 'No, I don't think so … though the old trees govern many forests like these.'

'A dragon, I think,' Piex ensaged.

Allastassia wasn't convinced.

'He tells me,' Darrix announced, 'that he intends the innocent no harm, but I'm not sure he has declared us innocent as yet. I think he intends to test us, even if he doesn't know that himself yet.'

Kialessa nodded. That felt about right. Even the forest seemed to agree. A sudden breeze moved the trees, and Allastassia and Posk both looked up sharply.

'As much as I am curious about such a being,' Darrix said, 'we need to make it across the peninsula in three days. It would be a simple task, if not for the thickness of this unknown forest.'

'I know which direction to go in,' Allastassia said, and pointed.

No one argued with the part dryad. They made ready to leave.

'Maybe he is a spirit?' Piex informed them. 'It might explain some things, and the access to ancient technologies.'

A strange sound echoed through the forest from nearby.

Darrix looked on, holding the pommel of his sword.

'I don't think we'll need that,' Allastassia told Darrix.

'Actually, I think it's exactly what we'll need,' Darrix replied.

Posk nodded, picking up a small log that he could wield as a club. 'Not so sure about this,' he admitted, falling in line behind "Shiny".

Allastassia pushed Piex forward in front of her, and walked on, making sure Kialessa was keeping up the rear. 'I guess we find out,' she said.

They did not get a dozen paces before a creature attacked. A shuddering screech rent the air, and Kialessa covered her ears reflexively. Piex fell over, even Posk seemed stuck to the ground. Only Darrix and Allastassia stood tall to face the threat.

There was a laboured creak as a huge, winged beast alighted on a wide branch of an overhanging tree. It had a head like an axe, with dragon wings, and sparse, tattered red feathers running down its chest. It screeched at them again, but did not attack.

Darrix stepped back a pace or two in order to confer with the others as they recovered. 'It must be guarding what it considers its territory.'

'Yet I feel we must go that way,' Allastassia said.

Posk was back up. 'We can take it.'

'No,' Darrix and Allastassia agreed.

'I have my bow,' Darrix said, 'but we do not know this creature's purpose, or its powers.'

'Though Kialessa does have that whip,' Allastassia reminded them.

Kialessa looked down at her whip, *Man'yifikanse's gift*, pretending to be a belt as usual. It was dim tan coloured, not at all the blinding white it liked to be when its powers were called upon to face great evil. Kialessa had to assume the unicorn's gift did not consider this creature evil, and that meant that if she used it, she would be left to her own skill and powers. She shook her head at Allastassia. If the gift did not want to fight, she thought it wisest if she did not either.

Posk moved back, seeking to cover Allastassia. 'Sing it, Alli. See if you can charm our way past.'

Allastassia nodded, and gently moved him aside.

She took two paces forwards until the monster growled. It had razor sharp fangs and its eyes betrayed a deep, bestial intelligence. Kialessa looked it over. Its wings were short and powerful, just right for moving quickly though a crowded forest it would know perfectly well. This was not a battle that would go their way if it had to happen.

Allastassia started to sing, a lively sonnet to Spring.

The creature growled.

Allastassia tried again, a lullaby.

It screeched in rage.

She huffed, and tried something the trolls had taught her, with movement and energy.

Throwing back its head, the monster let out such a powerful wail it would have been heard from the Imagination's Dawn and back again. Allastassia was forced to cover her ears.

Then the creature, incredibly, began to weave an enchantment. It seemed to dance, striking its claws against the tree with arrhythmic percussions. There was a mystical order to the song, a primal power. Kialessa immediately knew it was dangerous.

'Allastassia, get back!' she shouted.

Nobody moved.

'It's attempting to mesmerise us!' Piex panicked from behind her.

Kialessa leapt forward, screaming for all she was worth tried to shatter apart the magic of the dance with her own voice. It worked. Allastassia stumbled back, and Darrix and Posk raised their weapons. Kialessa dragged them back as quickly as she could.

The creature just looked at them, dark intelligence it its eyes. Then, it spoke. 'Everyone got to eat …' and, with that, it flew away.

They breathed a sigh of relief.

'What was that creature?' Allastassia asked.

'One I care not to face again,' Piex said.

Darrix sheathed his sword. 'We stood together, and thus we stand still. Good work, folks!'

Posk patted his armoured shoulder. 'King of birds, I name him. I think it best if we take as little as we can from this forest. Leave nothing but footprints. The danger here is very real.'

They all agreed. Allastassia led the way as they marched further into the forest, convincing vine and brush to lean aside. Walking single file they were trying to head towards the lowlands at the far edge of the peninsula, where it would be easiest to board the Dawn once more. No one wanted to have to jump from the high cliffs at the far edge, but Kialessa prepared her heart for the eventuality just in case.

Hours passed. Soon Posk turned to them and said, 'I grow hungry.'

Darrix stretched out his shoulders. Kialessa didn't know how he was able to manage his strength holding out a sword and shield for hours on end, but he did. 'Let us look for a clearing.'

Allastassia mocked, 'There is no such thing here! I have never been in a jungle such as this one. The life is so thick!'

'Yes, and did you notice the insects?' Piex asked her.

'No one can ignore them,' she muttered.

'No, see,' he said, walking up to a flowering vine. 'See, they act in a symbiotic relationship to the plant life that I have never before witnessed. Watch!' And with that, the touched the vine. To Kialessa's surprise the flowers actually were the insects; they sprouted wings, and floated up and up into the air. Piex sighed. 'There are species here that have never been described in any textbook, anywhere. Entirely new branches of life living only in the sanctuary of this forest … Gladly would I spend a lifetime studying them.'

Bright sparkles of flying flowers swarmed gently in the air around them, shimmering in the dappled sunlight that rarely made its way to the forest floor.

'Beasts too,' Posk said, pointing to a patch of ground covered in what might have been writing, or simply some scratching tracks. 'I do not know these marks or what could have possibly made them. We passed through some monster's territory a little while ago; I think we can risk a rest now.'

Everyone agreed, and Piex muttered, 'Oh, look!'

They turned to see a clearing dimly lit in the forest. Cautiously they made their way over.

Posk stopped dead, with a disappointed frown, when he saw it. There was a bald hill, treeless and round. 'Stop!' he demanded.

No one challenged him.

Kialessa looked around. There was no fallen tree to indicate why this forest would have a clearing. Just a large, round hill.

Posk picked up a large piece of wood and threw it onto the top of the hill.

Everyone waited. Nothing happened.

He picked up a stone and hefted it right onto the apex of the hill.

They held their breath.

'Oh, well, maybe it is just a–' Posk began.

Suddenly the entire hill lifted up from either edge and snapped shut like a giant mouse trap. Huge, teeth-like spines graced the now clutching maw of some creature. Then it began to rise up.

'Back it up, back up!' Darrix ordered, trying to keep everyone behind his shield in their orderly retreat.

The hill rose up on a tree-like pillar, a giant plant of some kind. It thundered against the ground like some kind of terrakinetic roar. Allastassia almost ran in panic, but they kept together. The plant maw turned to face them.

'Don't you dare!' Posk shouted and threw his club, which hit the plant in its "face", and it trembled.

Then it lunged right toward them. It shattered a tree in its charge. Kialessa jumped out of its way, hoping to get around to the trunk and stop it somehow before it swallowed half the others. It was not a nice thought.

There was a metallic crash, like steel on alumium, and Kialessa turned to see Darrix holding his sacred blade Defender flat, point down, against his miraculous shield of the Eternal. They sent out a wall of blue sparks that formed a brief forcefield of some kind, and the plant monster could not bite him.

Posk cheered. Darrix looked momentarily exhausted, as if the act had taken a great toll on his very spirit to accomplish.

The plant trap monster pulled back, thundering its pain like a roar from the ground. From her vantage point, Kialessa could see the situation quite well. 'Allastassia, now!' Kialessa shouted, praying the part dryad enchantress had some kind of solution to their giant, man-eating plant problem.

Glistening with arcane lights, Allastassia commanded the powers of nature around her. Flowers bloomed and turned to face her enemy. Vines animated, and lashed out at the plant monster, pushing it back. She seemed to be singing, some powerful enchantment of rest and repose.

But the plant monster was not so easily placated. It rose again, pushing back her magic. Rising high up in the air, it opened its maw and shuddered. Kialessa felt the twingle of magic all around her, and the enchantments around Allastassia all died but for those in her arm's reach. All around the plant monster, dread orange blooms sprouted. Dark sparkles of magic opened them, spreading a cloud of pollen so thick it was clearly visible. Whatever they touched began to turn into hardened, dead wood.

Allastassia screamed, a sure sign the magic was besting her. With wide, flowing sweeps of her arms she tried again and again to push back the cloud of pollen death. But it was as if the entire forest was fighting her. On and on it pressed.

Then Piex stood in front of her, and with a wizardry spell she knew fairly well from their combat training, he reprogrammed the air to form a curling wall that pushed the pollen backwards. Within a few breaths, it had crashed back into the man-eating plant that had conjured it, and it turned into wood and fell silent.

Moments later, dark green leaves began to sprout from its trunk.

'Not a permanent solution,' Allastassia announced. 'Come, let us away.'

They retreated till they felt they were safe. Well, safer. The forest was still almost impossibly thick, with great snakes everywhere they looked, and strange, giant, six-legged spiders. But nothing else attacked them, so they rested an hour for lunch. They ate their biscuits and beef rations, and Posk picked up some giant crab pondering slowly along a log he was sitting on.

'You sure that's not poisonous?' Piex asked him.

He nodded. 'No bright colours.'

'That's quite astute of you,' Allastassia complimented him, seeming genuinely impressed.

'Besides, Shiny got me if I start having fits, right Shiny?'

Darrix smiled, and nodded, forgoing the chance to launch into a lecture on religious obligations and the requirements of the gods in healing. But his hand was near his pack of soldier's medical supplies; it always was.

'It would not matter,' Posk said. 'I guarantee there will be some creature or another with the cure here. This forest, I have never seen anything like it.' And with that, he started eating the crab alive, headfirst, his own eyes gazing about the magical forest with great suspicion.

The Toad

*You're all rather precious, don't you think? The purpose of life is to **live**. Life upon life, creating its own kind in form, time and time again. Each together, contributing to the balance that allows all things to live that live upon this world. Your life, of necessity, will be brief; and you will one day be food to those whose lives you once consumed. So if you can find any **joy** in your life, well, then I think you have found a good thing.*

Élu Choisi, sage and counsellor to the Elven Queensage of the North – Sagesse L'aimé. Recollections of the Tae'anaryl.

Soon it was time to press on again. Kialessa found they were heading toward a thicker section of jungle, if it was even possible. Allastassia had to go first, convincing the plants she could to move aside. It was slow going work, but otherwise Darrix would have had to get through with his sword, and they all agreed that was not going to be a good idea. Thick, dark green leaves pressed around them, always wet along the edges and smelling like leather and rain.

They had barely gone an hour when the Piex shouted, 'Look!'

To their left, a dancing fairy light wandered around. It was very rare to see a fairy, so Kialessa stopped.

Allastassia moved forwards. 'Seems odd but … *Yip!*' she squealed in surprise. Something had shot out from the underbrush and snagged the fairy right out of the air.

Allastassia charged forwards, Kialessa following.

There, sitting on a large log, was a big, brown, fat toad – its tummy still visibly glowing from its fairy meal.

'Spit that out! Spit that out right now!' Allastassia demanded.

'Arrgbit!' the toad replied.

Allastassia grabbed it up in both hands, spinning around. 'Spit it, spit it, or I'll eat you too!'

'Arrggbbbb,' the toad protested.

'You want to be fairy cursed forever, stupid toad?' She shook it fiercely. 'A fairy is no meal for you, don't be such a fool.'

Posk stepped up. 'Here, let me.' He grabbed the toad's mouth in his huge troll hands. It struggled fiercely but Allastassia didn't let it go. Somehow Posk managed to get a little finger inside its mouth. With a measure of forceful care, he pried it open.

A moment later a little fairy light flitted out. Kialessa could see its wings and legs, but the fairy fled as soon as it was out – not even pausing a moment to say thank you. If she said anything at all, it sounded like, 'Run, run for your lives!'

Allastassia put the toad down on a log. 'Now, let that be a lesson to you; don't eat things that can speak.'

The toad didn't look impressed.

'You'll be fine,' Darrix told it. 'Plenty of other things in the forest.'

The toad just glared at him.

'Let's on,' Piex said, a quiver in his voice.

'That toad would thank me if it could,' Allastassia bragged.

The toad croaked a protest as she walked away.

'Why, if he didn't know any better,' she continued, 'He would be stone or toadstool by now. Eating fairies, such folly!'

She laughed, but stopped and spun around as the frog barked at her. Not a nice bark either. Loud, like a dog.

'Well, that's unusual,' she admitted.

'I think we best away,' Piex was sounding very worried now.

Then the toad roared. The thunderous eructation blasted from it like a dragon's roar. Allastassia was knocked back on her behind.

The toad began to advance on them.

'Yup, time to leave.' Allastassia scrambled to her feet.

Then the toad sprouted wings.

'Not a toad!' Allastassia said with panic as they all rushed after Darrix. 'Has this forest no rules!?' she protested.

Kialessa made sure the others hastened away first, and as she watched, the toad flapped up on its bat-like wings, its forelegs growing longer and into claws. Its eyes split and divided, like an insect's. It grew larger and its neck extended.

It did more than that, but by now Kialessa was running too. The toad's roaring became louder and deeper as it charged after them.

'To the large tree!' Allastassia shouted, probably hoping for some tactical advantage.

There was a large thud behind them, and then the snapping of a log. Whatever creature the toad now was, it must have been huge.

Kialessa ran with the others to the base of a huge sprawling fig tree. Allastassia was talking to it frantically. Posk and Darrix were armed, and Piex had things ready for a *golden shackles* spell.

Then the monster reached the bare space under the enormous tree. It was a full-blooded dragon made of crystals and earth, with the same colour and angry personality of the toad. 'Foolish mortals,' it chided them. 'You think to take from me my prize? I have hunted that fey for weeks until today. You will pay for your insolence!'

Darrix stood up and saluted. The dragon regarded him cautiously, as tales told they often did of men in steel. 'Mighty dragon, please, forgive us. We have much food to share, if you would like to join us?'

'Join!' the dragon scoffed. 'Stale meat and grains unenchanted? You … insult me with your offer!' and it prowled about dangerously.

Posk spoke next. 'You will still gain more than if you try to destroy us, toad!'

The dragon scowled at him. It was about twice the height of any of them, so not a full-grown adult dragon. Its claws where thick though, and clearly used to piercing hide and stone. Its neck was thin, and its wings broad. It looked like it might struggle in the thick forest. It smelt like soft earth and warm mushrooms. 'I hunger, and claim the little one,' it said, pointing at Piex.

'I am a wizard!' Piex tried to protest.

'All the better,' the dragon replied.

'You want him, you go through us,' Allastassia threated, ice spinning into a shield beside her, and she begun to levitate without even trying.

The dragon scowled. 'So be it!'

It tried to leap forward, but Posk put his hands on the ground and somehow pulled it out from under the dragon's feet. It stumbled. Piex's chains began to form around him, but the dragon's eyes glowed and the chains fell to the ground.

Kialessa had never seen anything like it. She wanted to use her sling, but it was sacred to the goddess whose favourite creatures were the dragons. So she pulled out her whip, a deep rugged tan colour, and looked for a chance to strike. Darrix traded blows with the dragon, trying to subdue it with the flat of his sword, or at least distract it long enough. It looked like it was about to tear Darrix's shield away and go for his neck, so she cracked the whip, and it ducked away just in time.

Suddenly it leant backwards, took a huge breath, and began to breath a choking, caustic acid at them all. But in the next instant, Allastassia was standing there, a sudden vortex of magical fey sparkles engulfing the dragon's deadly breath. It dissipated almost without harm, and though Kialessa's eyes stung painfully, she could see that the dragon was most displeased at Allastassia's enchantment.

'Well done!' Darrix thanked her.

'You'll have to teach me that,' Piex whimpered, whipping spittle from his face.

'Gorgeous ...' Posk mused.

Then with a roar the dragon swung its tail around, trying to trip Darrix, but he jumped the blow. Posk pulled the earth sideways, and the dragon fell. Then, before it could rise, the old willow roots reached out and began to entangle it. Within a breath it was pinned prone. Again the golden shackles spread around it, and this time they paralysed him entirely.

Darrix was on it in a moment, sharp blade pressed against the dragon's thin stone neck. 'Yield,' he commanded.

The dragon was breathing heavily. 'And what, so you can end me without protest? The Master of the forest needs me. He will not be pleased with you if you harm me.'

Darrix relaxed. 'We have no need to harm you. But you will claim nothing of us. Go in peace, vow you will not harm us, and we will let you go.'

The dragon breathed heavily, looking around with wide eyes at them each in turn. 'You claim no treasure? Dragons have great hoards, why do you not demand a price from me?'

'Safe passage would do us well,' Darrix said.

Posk agreed.

The dragon huffed, a sulphurous fire from his nostrils staining the air. 'Our bodies are rare, useful for empowering any spell of wizard or enchantress ... Why not just cut me up? Are you not even curious? A nature dragon's heart of stone will fetch quite a price at Emerel, I am told.'

Something happened to Kialessa's mind. She found herself thinking that, indeed, the price and prestige of a dragon's heart would be quite a prize. If she took that to her King, he would be impressed. Very impressed indeed. He would shower her with thanks, and praise, and–

'Stop it, toad!' Allastassia shouted. 'We'll have none of your pretended treasures! Just grant us our lives, and our freedom. Why did you let us into this forest anyway?'

The dragon laughed, and began to shrink. 'Oh, that wasn't me.' Within a few breaths, the golden chains flowed to the floor to surround a very dark and very ornery looking toad.

Kialessa looked up through the branches. There, far away on a much larger tree, a stone brown dragon sat. It was huge, far larger than the transmuted one they'd just battled. It laughed, just like the toad. Then it began to fly away, its voice speaking in their minds, *I trust, Master, that you feel these younglings have passed your tests?*

But there was no answer.

'A test then,' Darrix said.

'We passed?' Piex asked.

'Was that toad a dragon? Or not?' Posk sounded lost.

Allastassia nodded, allowing her hand to fall from the willow's trunk. She looked exhausted, and it must have taken a large portion of her power to convince the old willow to help them.

For its part, the toad, which might have only ever been a toad, slunk away, none the worse for its apparent misadventure.

'I wonder what he needed to know?' Darrix asked, regarding the Master of the forest, presumably.

'How much we like fairies?' Posk grinned.

'Compassion for our foes,' Piex told them.

'I thought it was greed,' Kialessa guessed.

'All such things,' Darrix said, and sat down to rest.

***

Night fell swiftly in the magical forest; the entire life shifting so dramatically in colour and hue and form it was as if an entirely new forest grew around them. They had hoped to make it further, but decided the large tree was kind enough company for an early rest, and an earlier start in the morning should mean they'd have enough time to make the lowlands before midday, should the King be waiting.

Kialessa was just beginning to dread the thought of another night of dry biscuits and conjured water when a clear thought presented in her mind – the Master would allow fire tonight.

She looked up at the others, knowing they'd had the same thought.

'Woohoo!' Posk shouted. He immediately began to gather sticks.

'I got this,' Kialessa said, picking up a large stone.

'Be careful not to harm the tree,' Allastassia reminded them.

'Piex,' Darrix asked, 'can you levitate the stone? Then, Allastassia, would you mind forming us another nest? I know it's a little cramped–'

'I can fix that,' she promised, already deep in discussion with the tree.

Darrix continued, 'Then we can be warm.'

'We still need a stick to hold the frypan,' Posk confessed.

'I'll show you how to make a frame,' Darrix replied.

'Yeah, Mum does that too. I been meaning to learn. Lead on, Shiny!'

Within moments they were set up comfortably in their sheltered, insect-free hut of warmth. The stone on fire lit the space beautifully, Kialessa's new magical runes floating and purple in the air around them, no longer fragile, until she mentally dismissed them. It was good to be trained by proper wizards now!

They talked for hours; it seemed they were well into breaking their promise of getting an early night. But to Kialessa it was such a special time. She still felt so young, and they had to rely on each other in a dangerous world. But hidden in their magical nest, it seemed a wonderful place. Allastassia had all kinds of "get to know you" games. Posk competed with Piex for telling great stories, and lost decisively. Darrix just listened and laughed, but she got to hear a little more about his family, which was nice. As for herself, Kialessa was just content to listen.

Then they talked about the quest, about the assassin and the danger he brought. They made her tell them about the five times she'd met him so far, more than anyone in the Kingdom, though they already had heard it all. The conversation became dark, wondering what it might be like if the assassin won, or what would become of them all if the Kingdom fell. Only Posk had nothing to lose but friends, and he valued them deeply. Even he did not make fun of Allastassia's concerns.

Soon a crashing noise was heard, calling them to sudden silence. She listened, but whatever creature it was passed on soon. It would have to be huge, perhaps as large as a full-blooded dragon. Thankfully, it did not seek them.

Allastassia spoke in a muted voice. 'Perhaps we best to sleep now.'

Everyone agreed, using their backpacks as pillows, the rest of the equipment at their feet. The nest was small, but comfortable.

'Perhaps Posk can sleep in the middle, as he is warmest,' Allastassia said.

'All right!' Posk agreed.

'If you will,' Darrix suggested, 'I am the tallest, and the nest is largest in the middle.'

'Oh, yeah, good point,' Posk shuffled back.

'That is *fine*, but we two do *not* sleep well together. Posk is just too hot,' the enchantress argued.

'Good point,' Posk shuffled back.

Darrix shrugged.

Piex turned to Allastassia. 'Kialessa has the enchanted robe; I think it best if she sleeps at the edge.'

It annoyed Kialessa, but it was true.

'Come here, plushie!' Posk held out his arm to Piex.

Piex muttered his protest, but Allastassia began to snuggle herself between the boys anyway. Posk was grinning broadly as she put her arm around him for her own comfort. 'Would for my mother's smelling salts right now,' she muttered, ever ready to complain about Posk's personal scent.

Kialessa snuggled down, holding Piex's hand just for convenience, since they were all pressed together anyway. It was cosy.

Darrix said the evening devotions, and Allastassia hummed along an improvised countermelody that spontaneously generated some pretty glowing fey lights to brighten their small nest.

For a long time there was silence.

But Kialessa felt very safe that night.

***

Kialessa stretched. From the glow of light between the cracks in the nest, she could tell that it must be early morning. She looked around. Darrix was already up, and it sounded like he was preparing some breakfast. Piex was snuggled back-to-back with Posk.

She looked up over the half troll's shoulder and there, snuggled right up against him with her hand on his chest, Allastassia lay. Kialessa grinned to herself. Posk seemed to have had his wish; her hair stretched out, flowing across his arm and chest and under his head such that it might have very well covered his pillow. They looked so peaceful together. So happy.

She knew Posk would cop some lightning for this. And he'd consider it well worth it.

As quietly as she could, she rose, and slipped lithely out through some folds in the branches. It was a tight fit, but the tree seemed genuinely willing to help her. She climbed down, taking care not to switch out her nightgown for armour till she was well away from Allastassia's hearing.

She reached the forest floor, admiring the small campfire Darrix had going. He was boiling some water, possibly preparing some broth.

He smiled at her, and together they prepared breakfast in silence.

Just as it looked like it would be time to wake the others, Allastassia gave a contented giggle from the nest, followed by Posk's, 'Morning, Sunshine.'

Allastassia squealed, and the nest exploded with lightning. The tree did not seem too pleased. Allastassia sat there, preening, while Posk laughed so hard he fell off the branch and had to catch himself. Piex was clinging to another branch, white with fright.

Darrix laughed, and since no one seemed hurt, she laughed as well.

They spent a preparing hour resting and chatting. To Kialessa it seemed their minds were quite alert. Perhaps even too much so, but she did not dwell on it – though Darrix was very, very funny when he wanted to be, and Piex took to drawing pictures of all the creatures he could.

'Oh, you need an enchanted quill, Piex. Those pictures are awful,' Allastassia announced.

He sighed. 'It is true. Would that I might keep as many samples … but I feel it unwise. The Master has not yet made his wishes clear.'

They nodded, the forest falling silent again at that title.

Posk poked Piex. 'You should ask him.'

Piex didn't seem to like that idea.

Posk stood up, and cleared his throat. 'Good Master of the forest, on behalf of the Kingdom of Lenmer'el, we thank you for safe passage through your domain, and ask you to reveal yourself as soon as you can, all right? Piex here wants to take some simples. No, samples. Yes, and we'd very like to ask you in person, all right?'

They waited; nothing happened.

'You're such a fool, Posk,' Allastassia protested.

'You try it,' he told her, and sat down happily.

She huffed.

Darrix stood up, and bowed to the trees. 'Master of the Forest, thank you for showing us the power of your work, and depths of your creativity. We beg you for safe passage through your forest, and ask you, if you will, please reveal yourself, for we would thank you in person.'

They waited.

Allastassia laughed. 'You do realise that his creativity has almost killed us on *three* occasions!'

Darrix grinned. 'That we know about.'

'Four,' Piex said.

They looked at him.

'Those insects would have eaten me up.'

Everyone burst out laughing, it seemed so funny.

Allastassia stood up, speaking with exaggerated eloquence. 'Master, as seemeth thee good, this diversion is most entertaining, but we would like to be done now. So if you could just show up, that'd be *so* nice!'

Kialessa almost died with laughter; it was such a disrespectful and comical way to talk to a creature whose near omnipresent power flowed through every tree and flower all around them. But the Master did not present; Kialessa didn't think he would.

'Meh, I tried,' Allastassia shrugged.

'You try, Tauira,' Posk encouraged Kialessa, using his favourite troll term for her which meant 'master'.

She jumped up, and was planning to say something silly, when all thoughts died in her mind – the way they sometimes did when she was praying to the Eternal. Her heart suddenly realised they were actually in quite a lot of danger, and didn't really know how to deal with it. This Master, whoever he was, held their lives in his hands, or claws, as the case may be. She spoke, respectfully, 'Master of the forest.'

Everyone calmed down at the measured pace of her voice.

'Your world is beautiful. Thank you. Please, please keep us safe. And, if you want … we would very much like to meet you. If you'd like.'

There was a thud in the ground, and a whisper seemed to pass through the trees. Then the trees began to move, forming a clear path in a direction further in towards the continent. Gentle leaves fluttered down to the ground, highlighting an arched corridor formed by the trees.

Allastassia arose. '*My word*, you did it!' She patted Kialessa on her shoulder.

Kialessa didn't think it was her. It was the Master, touched by the words of one who had been taught to treat her enemies like her friends. 'Come, let us see the creator of the forest,' she said, and her friends followed.

Stone Words

The more we care for the happiness of others, the greater our own sense of well-being becomes.

Dali Gedzelai, 316CY, cited in 'The Year in Jail.'

Piex ran his hand along the blue stone. Upon the stone, strange words were written. 'Cool, like steel,' he announced.

They had barely walked a moment through the archway, but the magic made it clear they had been teleported somewhere. Piex informed them all that he did not think it was far away, but the forest here was deeper, older; if that was even possible. The trees were immeasurably ancient, gnarled and knotted. But they were healthy, and strong. The ground was soft and dark, but Posk found the tracks of hundreds of different animals, including insects the size of a horse.

They had been taken to a deep ravine where it looked as though the sun had never touched the dark ground, so thick was the canopy of leaves. And there, at the centre of the ravine, a strange egg-shaped vessel lay, split into eight sections. It was made entirely of blue stone, embedded in the soft earth for countless ages. And all about them, even stranger, almost alien life forms, of hue and form beyond imagining, now hobbled or scurried in all directions. It was as if they had stepped into another world. Even the ground slowly tilted and rocked as though it was stuck on the back of some enormous, magical, megalithic tortoise.

'It feels like a shrine, doesn't it?' Darrix asked her.

Kialessa nodded; there was a distinct, powerful, sacred presence here. Old. Older than any of them.

The forest was silent as they walked through the kaleidoscope of strange life and down the soft earth to the fallen stones, and Piex ran his hand along it. 'I know these words. They are ancient.' He tried to pronounce them, and the world suddenly rippled with power.

Allastassia held his arm, and he tried to read no more.

'Look, there's a part of your name here Kialessa – the "lessa".'

He said the word, and something shifted in the air – no, more … in the very reality that surrounded them, and they all took for granted. It was like infinite potential and liberation, but it had no structure, no sentence to give the words their specific purpose for being spoken in this moment.

'There is magic in these words,' Piex informed them.

It was true. No one spoke.

Piex continued, in Emerellian. 'It seems to be instructions of some kind; I can't make sense of them. There are words here, yet they slip from my mind even as I grasp their meaning … I cannot read them.'

A voice replied, speaking to their minds and not their ears. It was a young voice, yet calm, and incomprehensibly powerful: *And it is well you cannot.*

Kialessa turned in fright, and watched an unusual creature levitating down through the air toward them, silhouetted with light behind and within. It had four arms, apparently, with clear webbing between its prehensile toes and fingers. It was tall, much taller than any of them. As it drew nearer, she could see it had four ears, and four eyes on its large head. There were the two irises in each eye, just as she had seen in her dreams. And it felt like it was smiling at them.

Allastassia and Piex threw themselves to the ground and bowed, Posk quickly following. She felt no compulsion to kneel and neither, did it seem, did Darrix. The creature didn't seem to mind either way.

'An ancient!' Allastassia said, her voice filled with honour and fear as though she addressed a king, or a god.

Kialessa felt curious. She had only ever heard tell of the first race of sentient humanoids, created long ago at the dawn of time by the ageless goddess of the universe Lallaellaia. It was said they were so powerful they could stop gods from fighting each other. It was said they were so wise that when they built a city of peace to celebrate all races, it had stood for over a thousand years, and was made of pure gold.

The creature levitated in the air above them, arms forming mystical patterns in the air as it commanded the magic around them with what felt like unfathomable intelligence. Kialessa immediately recognised him as the Master of the forest; the unsleeping double irises were his. He watched them all with a serenity that was deeply tangible. And, if she didn't know any better, she thought he might actually be laughing on the inside.

That's an ancient, she thought. She'd been told they'd all moved on three thousand years ago to a higher plane of existence, but their magic and technology was still to be found all over the world. It was one of the most sought-after prizes of all kings and wizards. They had created, at least by some accounts, all sentience races such as humans, trolls and elves.

He spread his arms, and spoke, his voice a thunder of deep and resonating wisdom within her mind. *What would occur should a wizard of the great Academicum at Emerel combine an octopus with a cow?*

Kialessa wondered what kind of mighty test this could be, what unfathomable riddle to examine their worthiness. The Academicum was the greatest school of wizards and scholars, the only university in the known world.

They all looked at Piex, and he pondered deeply, but could not say.

The ancient spoke: *A visit from the city guard and immediate withdrawal of funding …*

For a moment there was silence.

Then Piex burst out his shallow, nasal laugh.

Allastassia glared at him.

Darrix was grinning, 'It was a joke.'

Kialessa was stunned. *A joke?*

The ancient grinned. *I was hoping it might have gone over a little better than that. I see I will be working on my humour a little more. At least Piex gets it.*

'Immediate withdrawal of funding! He, ha!' Piex chortled.

'I don't get it,' Posk protested.

The ancient glanced at the half troll, and in a moment he grinned as though someone had just explained the joke to him.

A joke? Kialessa pondered why this being would greet them with a joke.

The ancient hovered in the air above them. Allastassia and the others stood as though invited. Kialessa heard his voice again, inside her mind, combined with cascading emotions and images, so that his communication was unequivocally clear. When he spoke, he seemed to speak to them all. *I have waited over three hundred years for the privilege to speak to other living humanoids! What a treat! I have enjoyed your company these past three days, and I am grateful I heard your request to visit me.*

It was almost impossible to misunderstand him, his wisdom in mind and clarity in speech were so transcendent.

Allastassia looked lost for words, and Darrix seemed too impressed, so Kialessa spoke: 'Thank you, kind one. If I may, shall I be so bold as to ask your name?'

He grinned. *I have never been given one, but those here who can, call me Oum.*

The sound resonated through her mind like raw power and intelligence, it was a strange sensation, and a name she was not keen to risk speaking out loud.

'Oum,' Posk pondered out loud, but the name was different, somehow harmless in Posk's voice. 'Well, good to meet you, Master of the forest. We have enjoyed your tests.' Posk spoke with a princely dignity, despite his rough appearance and simple language.

Oum grinned at him. *That makes me glad. I am gladful … grateful, you came to visit.*

'Wait,' Posk pondered. 'Your parents, didn't they name you either?'

They did not, Oum explained. *Nor have I ever met them. I hear their minds from far away, with the others now, always, but they are not here. I suspect they left this sphere some time ago.*

Kialessa almost asked how he'd survived alone without parents for three hundred years, but then thought better of it. The stone egg would have protected him, and he could clearly defend himself if he had to. The entire forest was a sanctuary built for, or by, him.

He nodded in agreement at her thoughts, and levitated down to the ground to join them. He sat cross legged on the earth, barely touching it. It was as if levitating was a normal thing he did. When he spoke again, it was with a touch of sincerity, and concern. *I perceive you are threatened. A mighty hunter pursues your course. He brings three with him; one you know, though you cannot see as yet. The other two are new to your minds. One commands the flow of natural force with vengeful intent, and the last seeks only the thrill of death. Their minds are strange to me most of all. It is as if they wish only to do you harm … but not to consume your remains at all. This is strange to me.*

They were silent for a moment.

'So,' Darrix muttered, 'the assassin's got friends.'

Oum nodded. *Some suns ago, the one of cruel intent forced the greater cephalopod to assault you, blinding it so that it saw no other course but your deaths. I … do not understand this.*

Kialessa felt she knew what he meant, but Allastassia replied, 'They seek us harm for reasons we do not yet fully know. This hunter, this assassin, has tried on many occasions to harm our King. He seeks to profit from his death in some way; we do not know why.'

Yes, the Red King of men, King Dunnkan. I have seen him in your memories.

I would very much like to meet him … I have watched his eyes pass over this land for many seasons; his, and his father's, and his father's father's. From when only the long eared walked these lands on the rarest of occasions. Your assassin seeks to harm your King? To what end? Why is this?

Darrix replied, 'We do not know what profit he gains, but this is not a new thing. We think he serves an even crueller master, whose plans are threatened by our good King.'

Allastassia scoffed. 'There are those among us who seek to do harm for no other cause but the thrill.'

Oum pondered this for a moment. *A drake, once, found his way to this land. He was not like the others, his horns were great, his skin did not burn. He hunted for the sport, as you say. Hunting for the glory of overcoming another life, and nothing more. I slew him, for he did much to upset the balance of life in this forest. I thought him caught up in some disease, or perhaps born with it, so unnatural was his thirst for death. Do you think those that hunt you suffer a similar affliction?*

'Unlikely-' Allastassia began.

'Nope,' Posk interrupted. 'He hunts for power. We don't know why and I don't care. He dies the next time we meet, and we will be free of his threat.'

Oum pondered that. *Your minds are like the dragons; you can use the language, and you have vivid imaginations, and you can make choices based on the wisdom passed down through the language of your ancestors. Thus you have power over your reality. You can change, and so can they. Would death punish them enough to seek change? Is this your only option?*

Posk did not reply, but Darrix sat forwards. 'Perhaps not, but it will bring us peace.'

Oum did not agree. *I have seen worlds where death is permanent. One broke the bonds on this world; I have seen those slain return. I have sought the souls of those that wandered myself, and brought them back to their physical form. Death is but a temporary setback, for some.*

Allastassia agreed. 'Imprisonment, then. The steward has a gem that can seal a prisoner's soul away, perhaps forever.'

You wish to confine them? This is cruel indeed. But perhaps not more so than your own death. Yet I do not understand this. It is as if with your powerful, wonderful minds you can imagine terrible threats, and a death that might only possibly be, and thus fight with all your life for that which might not even exist. Again, I am lost at the irony of all this. And he shook his head.

Darrix chuckled to himself. 'Yeah, it's a bit like that.'

'We each have much to learn,' Piex spoke up.

Oum smiled. *You want to know by what knowledge I built and maintain this forest? By what wisdoms I created these?* he said, holding out his hand to a weird looking stick-but-sort-of-insect, who crawled slowly on and then off again. *Your species does not live long enough for me to teach you all I know.*

'Master,' Piex begged, 'surely one as wise as you can teach me!'

Oum smiled. *Ever so you have implored me since you first entered. There is much I will not share, but I can impart a little, if you like?*

'Yes, please,' Piex said.

Oum began to glow from within, and he seemed to be talking to Piex, like, a lot. As much as was possible, in fact. Dozens of conversations going on, all in one moment in Piex's mind. Kialessa managed to catch some of it: discussions of the ribbon of life, webs of interconnected lifeforms hunting and being hunted, of natural machines too small to be seen flowing through the blood of living beings and keeping them alive. It was extraordinary.

But it could only last a moment before Piex almost fainted. 'Enough, Master! I can take no more.'

Oum smiled, and let the magic end. *Few have tried, and none have ever listened as well as you do, young wizard. I think we will have many conversations as yet.*

Piex grinned happily, but looked more than just a little tired. They chatted for some time, the ancient having many questions and one or two bad attempts at humour. But his restless mind never seemed to cease wanting to know.

This I do not understand, Oum continued his questions. *Why do you so fear death?*

'For that is the end,' Allastassia tried to explain, looking very wise. 'The great resting, when our souls go on, and our power to change this world ends.'

Nothing you have said is true, according to what I have experienced, Oum replied, looking disappointed, while Allastassia looked deflated.

Oum left them to their thoughts for a moment, then looked around at the woods. *Consider it thus: there is no life, or death. Only balance. In this forest, what you call death cannot be without birth, and no birth is achieved without the death of those who sustain it. Change there is, always, but if life bloomed unending, this forest would come to ruin. And if death overtook it all, then all would be dust.*

For every flower that blooms, it must first defeat all that would compete with it to reach the light, including its own siblings, most often. And for every flower that dies, its physical form replenishes nature. Change there is, always, and balance. But of life and death I am poorly convinced. Why would someone hunt you to death for glory or power? I do not understand this – it will not change who you are, nor grant them always the power they now crave.

Kialessa looked at his beautiful world. 'I suppose … I hope you never do experience our lives, so fragile, and find you do understand it.'

He looked at her. *I have a request, if you will hear it?*

She nodded.

Take me with you.

Allastassia gasped, and Darrix frowned.

Allastassia spoke first. 'Master, there is great danger in our world. This hunter, he is not unique. There are many who would harm you if they thought it would bring them fame or money.'

Fame, I understand. The males must often present their prowess to the females if they wish to mate, though in some species this quest is reversed. But what power is gained in the death of one who does not threaten you? Why do you build houses? And what is lying, and laughter, and hope? I have spent the last three hundred years studying all of life, forging and reforging it to my own curiosity and whim. But I have never taken the time to study the minds of those that talk. Their societies, the things to them that are real, though they are not. Of pain and fear and longing. I must join you in this quest. I must go to the human city, and see and understand for myself.

It was clear there was absolutely no talking him out of his next self-imposed lesson.

They looked at each other.

'Well,' Allastassia offered, 'you shouldn't go looking like this. You will be attacked constantly by those who seek your knowledge and power. Even to simply pose your head on their walls.'

Oum nodded as if he'd already realised this. *A disguise then? As a chameleon to blend in? Hmm … no. I wish to converse.* He brightened up visibly. *Mimicry! I will make myself a new body, so as to appear as one of you! Yes! Then I can also experience walking, and sleeping … Oh, this is a very good idea. Thank you, Posk.*

Posk looked surprised at the compliment, but shrugged as if he meant it all along, as soon as Kialessa looked over at him.

Oum levitated up. *I am sorry to delay you further, but this process will only take a few hours.*

With a wave of his hands, the pieces of the stone egg floated up, their words glowing with meaning and power, new words forming on their surfaces.

You may need to entertain yourselves; I will likely not be able to talk to you much while I am undergoing the metamorphosis. He seemed to be busy calculating something on his glowing stone edges. But then he floated down to face them. *If I may, I would ask something of each of you?*

'Anything.' Allastassia grinned with a curtsey.

I need to obtain a sample of your life codes. I wish to make a new body to encase my true form, and I would like to style it after your own bodies. Will you take my hand?

'Take your hand?' Posk looked worried.

Well, Oum said with a grin, *the easiest way would be to lick your bone marrow, but I suspect that would not be a very agreeable option to you all. It is enough to simply touch your hand.*

'Eww,' Allastassia said, and everyone burst out laughing. It felt like Oum was trying to make some sort of light-hearted humour of the moment once more.

Posk shoved his way in first, and Oum looked very contemplative as he clutched Posk's big green hand in three of his. Oum shook all their hands, or at least held them. Kialessa didn't feel anything weird or uncomfortable. He must have been very gentle with whatever magic he was working.

Please, rest yourselves here. Oum muttered as he floated up and into his stone egg chrysalis. *You will be safe here; my forest will attend you.*

They looked at each other. Piex snatched up his book and began to draw some of the insects around, taking a few samples of what he must have thought were the most interesting leaves. Allastassia sighed, shrugged, and then started whispering to the trees. Darrix and Posk just sat down next to each other to admire it all.

Kialessa wasn't sure what to do; the entire place seemed just so sacred. But she couldn't really help herself, the trees were so gnarled and had such long, interesting branches.

So she started climbing the trees.

We live for only one reason: To learn how to love. Power is not important. Wealth, fame, all fade and die. Only love carries into forever.

Elven Queensage of the North – Sagesse L'aimé.

Long hours passed. Piex spent his time documenting lifeforms or gazing up at the egg. Allastassia went around talking to every single tree or plant and ignoring everyone. Darrix spent the time praying or meditating, and Posk took a nap. Once the half troll woke up, he took to throwing seeds into the tallest trees until Allastassia made him stop.

For her part, Kialessa just kept on exploring. The trees were strange; there just seemed to be too many branches, and they twisted so much this way and that. There always seemed to be a new branch on each tree to explore, or perhaps there really were. There was way too much space on each tree's branches to be explained when they were looked at from below.

Kialessa was just on her eighth tree, beginning to think it was time to explore another impossibly large and always growing tree, when she heard a strange rustle. She spun around and noticed the nearby foliage of some bush that grew up on the tree rustling around, as if something had just pushed its way in there.

It seemed exciting. Her weapons were not far away, and her friends close by, so she decided to explore.

She crept up on the bushes, finally noticing now how the shadows bent around her to help dim her outline in the dappled light of the forest. Carefully she parted the leaves, trying to see what had been there.

Beyond, she saw a small nest, made of curious things. And within, three baby dragons. They were staring back at her with a mix of curiosity and fear on their tiny little faces.

For a small moment Kialessa was so enchanted by her find she forgot how much danger she was in: to come between a mother dragon and her fledglings was to invite death. Carefully she crept away.

The first person she saw was Allastassia, humming to herself as she wove some flowers into a nice headpiece.

'Allastassia,' she whispered.

The enchantress looked over at her.

'I found baby dragons.'

Allastassia gasped. 'Dragons, really? Here?'

She nodded, grinning at the conspiracy of it all. No one knew, except her and Allastassia.

The enchantress looked concerned. 'How large?'

'Oh,' Kialessa replied with a "don't worry" wave of her hand, 'fledglings. Tiny. Not much bigger than my arm, really. Tiny.'

'Tiny, like a cat?'

She nodded.

'Brown?' Allastassia questioned her. She still looked concerned.

'Oh, no, not at all. Purple, and rainbow coloured. Very pretty. With large eyes and wings like a butterfly-'

'Excuse me?' Allastassia queried.

'Like a butterfly, with these big, wide eyes. They looked so cuuute!'

'There are no dragons the size of cats with butterfly wings, and especially not purple ones. Are you sure? How can this be? Well, it is a very magical forest, I suppose.'

Kialessa had to agree.

'I need to see them.'

Suddenly Kialessa was thinking this was not such a good idea after all.

'I did not see their mother. Do you think it will be safe? I don't think it will be safe. We should probably not go there.'

Allastassia was not to be dissuaded, and in her heart, Kialessa was too excited to care. Dragon chicks! What a treat! And she really did want to see them again.

'We need to be careful,' Kialessa repeated. 'I don't know where the mother is.'

Allastassia huffed. 'You can creep well enough for the both of us.'

'If only that was the way it worked,' Kialessa mumbled.

Quickly she climbed her way up. Allastassia daintily stepped up as the tree made little footholds for her, the twigs swaying out of her way.

They were on the bough in no time.

'Be silent,' Kialessa whispered.

Allastassia just grinned at her.

Carefully they stepped towards the branches and Kialessa parted them.

This time, there were only two dragon chicks there.

Kialessa wondered where the other one had gotten to. She carefully looked around.

'They are part fey, or have a touch of fey,' Allastassia whispered. It was a wonder they didn't flee right away. They did not seem at ease, but they were not frightened either.

'I wonder where the other one has gone,' Kialessa asked.

'Perhaps they can turn invisible?' Allastassia wondered.

Kialessa huffed. There was nothing they could do about that now.

Or was there? Had she not been studying with the wizards of late, and learnt their *mage sight* spell? It had not been easy, and she would need to know the position of Lumos in the sky. But the moon never moved, so it could not be too hard.

'I'm going to try *mage sight*,' Kialessa told her.

Allastassia nodded, stepping back. 'All right, but I didn't think the spell lets you see invisible creatures, only the presence of infornium magics?'

'Yup,' Kialessa agreed, and working a little mental mathematics, enacted the spell.

It took her a few moments to get used to the weird, sixth sense of seeing magical auras … They were so diverse, and always individual to the particular wizard. But the forest was rife with magic. It flowed in, and around, and all over. It was beautiful and amazing all at once.

She turned to look at Allastassia, and was impressed at the bright colours around her. Allastassia's eyes also glowed with magic; she could cast *mage sight* already.

'Ahh,' Allastassia said with some concern. 'There seems to be a large aura of illusion right on your chest area.'

Kialessa looked down, and sure enough, something was crawling up her chest. Instinctively she grabbed at it – something small and scaley and unseen.

It was the third dragon.

With an unintentional squeal, she tried to fling it off her, but instead it dug its teeny little claws into her clothes and armour. Before she could do anything about it, she found herself falling off the bough. She should have broken her neck, but the tree saved her, probably at Allastassia's request, and instead she simply bounced around a few times before she hit the soft earth with a loud scream.

The others came running.

Darrix looked terrified, and had his sword all but drawn. Posk was there, and Piex. They tried to help her up but she was a bit winded from the fall. Everything was still spilling magical colours in her eyes.

'Oh, you tried *mage sight*, well done,' Piex complimented her. 'Why would that make you fall out of the branches?'

Allastassia floated down in the arms of the tree. 'She found some strange fairy dragons … I'm not sure what kind. The siblings are up there.'

'Is the mother about?' Piex seemed very worried.

'I don't think they have one,' Allastassia replied.

Kialessa was scrambling to sit up in their arms. The enormous blob of light on her chest was still there, but she didn't dare touch it for fear of harming the little dragon. But she also really, really did not want a strange invisible creature sitting on her either.

Piex pulled some ground up stone mica from his many pockets and sprinkled it on her, intoning a simple invocation. The mica scattered around in the air, coming to rest on the ground, in her hair, on her skin, and in a cat sized dragon shaped pattern on her chest.

'Woah,' Posk stated.

'Curious,' Piex mused.

Kialessa was breathing heavily, really hoping the little dragon wasn't about to bite her, or breathe acid or something all over her face.

A moment later, the strange dragon fluttered from invisibility. It was gorgeous, and if she didn't know any better, it was smiling at her with sweet, childlike curiosity. It had large purple wings in shape and form like a butterfly, with pretty, glistening scales and a long neck. It also had a dangerous, scorpion pronged tail, but it didn't look like it was planning to use it any time soon. It started panting happily.

'Oh, hello, little one,' Kialessa said, hoping it meant her well.

It hopped up and down excitedly, and then it let her pat it.

'I think it likes you,' Posk said.

'What will you call it?' Darrix asked.

'What?' Kialessa asked. 'Call it? I'm not going to be keeping it, it belongs in the forest.'

It stopped panting, and looked upset.

She patted it again, 'Unless, of course, it wants a name.'

It smiled and jumped up and down again.

Allastassia and Posk laughed. It seemed to be an incredibly intelligent creature! Piex started studying it, and tried to measure it with a little string. It looked at him curiously, but didn't get off her chest at all.

'Buttercup?' Kialessa wondered.

The dragon did not look impressed.

'Mindsage?' she wondered.

It hated that even more.

'Wanderer,' Posk announced.

She looked at him.

'Because she wandered away from the nest to follow you.'

Kialessa looked at the little, happy dragon. 'Wanderer,' she pondered.

The dragon really liked that.

'All right, Wanderer it is!'

The little dragon popped up and licked her on the cheek. Its tongue was small and stringy and wet. She sat up and it jumped all around her, twisting this way and that under her arms and hair and legs like a long, sinuous snake. She continued to pat it and laugh, while the others watched on.

'Well, I suppose you'd better be going back to your mother,' Kialessa finally suggested.

Wanderer bit her.

It was such a surprise, and she was so fast Kialessa felt she could not have dodged if she'd wanted to.

'Ouch!' Kialessa said.

'No, bad dragon!' Allastassia chided her.

Wanderer cringed in regret, her ears back and her eyes sorry and sad.

Kialessa was about to join Allastassia in her chastisement, but the little dragon looked so sad. She put her hand up to her, and Wanderer cringed back. 'Oh, little one. It's all right. Please don't bite me. Not unless you really,

really have to, all right?'

That seemed to cheer her up.

Kialessa put her wounded finger up to the dragon, and it licked it, healing it in an instant. 'Oh, look at that,' Kialessa showed the others.

'I wonder how it seems to know Emerellian,' Piex queried out loud. It did seem the dragon chick understood them perfectly well.

'It's fey,' Allastassia said, as though that explained it all. 'We, well, they're often empathic, if not telepathic. Such magical creatures can understand almost any language well enough to get by.'

Piex nodded as if that did, indeed, explain everything.

Wanderer curled around Kialessa again, then, hopping up under her hair, puffed out a beautiful miniature cloud of glittering starlight. It was even prettier than the spell Piex sometimes used to put people to sleep.

'Do you think she wants to come with us?' Kialessa asked.

Wanderer ran around them, curling around each of their feet and squeaking excitedly.

'We're making a lot of new friends in this forest,' Darrix muttered.

'Don't we have to check with her mother?' Piex wondered.

Allastassia shook her head. 'She's a lot older than she looks, I'll gladly wager. And I suspect she does not have a mother, if she's a creation of the ancient. They made all humanoid life on this world, you know.'

Piex agreed, looking around. 'Perhaps Oum's stone egg has seen more use than it seems.' Though Kialessa did not know what he meant by that, she did not ask.

Kialessa had to admit, Wanderer was enchanting, and energetic. She spent a good hour chasing her around, her other little sisters joining in at one point. Not even Posk could keep up with Wanderer's swift and agile dashing around. She kept turning invisible.

Then Kialessa had an idea: she was in a very magical place, and she had a very rare and special talent, so she popped into the shadow realm.

Sure enough, Wanderer's soul was glowing brightly on the branches nearby, and so Kialessa grabbed her and popped back into the normal world. They were giggling with delight!

After an hour, it seemed the little dragon tired of the chase, and curled up by herself in the branches of a tree. Kialessa scootched closer, and patted the tiny creature. She was soft and scaled, and a delight to touch. Little sparkles of magical light flowed from under her fingertips, and Wanderer purred with content. Soon she yawned, climbed into her lap, and fell asleep again.

Darrix snuck closer to pat her himself. 'She's gorgeous,' he said.

Kialessa grinned.

'I don't think she can come with us,' he said.

Kialessa already knew that. This was a magical forest; the world outside could be cold and harsh. It was no place for a magical fey shoulder dragon.

***

The young boy that stepped out of the blue stone egg looked nothing like the ancient of legend that had floated into it. He was pale, with blond hair and heterochromia – one iris was a piercing blue, and the other iris a distracting green. His head seemed large and his lower jaw a little too small, though he didn't seem inconvenienced in any way. But he was wearing the same loincloth, which was not much. Posk dug into his pack and offered the boy his cloak.

'I am …' the boy began. 'Oh, that's so strange. New teeth. Um, well, I guess I should not be using my true name anymore. Have any of you a name you may give me.'

'Egg boy?' Posk suggested with innocent sincerity.

'Open-my-mind-to-wisdom?' Piex suggested, probably trying to

122

translate his true name into Emerellian.

'You are Toni,' Allastassia announced, and the discussion was over.

'You are quite tall,' Toni said to Darrix. Then he turned to Posk. 'Thank you, good man. I will fit seamlessly into your culture with appropriate attire.'

'But not if you keep speaking like that,' Allastassia informed him.

Darrix added, 'And I would not call Posk a man. He's a half troll.'

Toni, who was Oum, looked puzzled again. Except this time it was written by his facial expressions. They looked a little too puzzled, actually, as though this was some kind of new look Toni was trying on for the first time.

But then again, Kialessa wondered, what would it be like to be a soul in an entirely new body? His language and accent were excellent: polished Emerellian. She did not know how he'd learnt it all, and he wasn't speaking through their minds anymore. He seemed comfortable, and well poised. His bearing was quite noble.

'This I do not understand,' Toni asked them clearly. 'You are all of the human species, as I measure it.'

Now it was their turn to look puzzled.

Allastassia broke the mood with a laugh. 'Actually, Darrix is the only human here; it looks like you took most of your "life ribbon" – whatever that is – from him. I'm part fey, Piex is part dragon, while Posk here is half troll and Kialessa is, well, half demon.'

Toni looked them over. 'Even by the most lenient of definitions, the capacity to interbreed, you are all humans.'

Allastassia laughed like he was trying to tell another joke, but stopped when no one joined her.

'Now I do not understand,' Darrix said.

'When I combined your life ribbons to make my own, there was very little change required. I kept Kialessa's ability to access the shadowrealm, and Posk's superior regeneration and strength, Darrix's hardy resilience, and Allastassia's connection to the natural worlds. Gifts, from each of you. But I kept within the clearly observable species parameters. You are of one kind; I am sure of it.'

'Well, that blows several centuries worth of wizardry out the door,' Darrix grinned.

Piex lent forward. 'I still don't get it.' But this was not the old "whatever" that most people meant when they said such things. This was the Piex version, which meant, "I don't get it and I'm going to spend as long as it takes to understand it until I get it, or fall unconscious from trying, whichever comes first."

It took Allastassia to call halt to their academic chitchat sometime later. The sun was already low in the sky. 'Hate to break it up, scholars, but it's late and we promised the King we'd be there by now.'

Toni and Piex were sitting there, drawing glowing runes and twisting lines in the dirt and in the air. They looked up at her, and seemed to agree at the very same moment.

'Yes, that is true,' Piex said.

'Indeed. As you wish,' Toni said at the same time.

The two scholars stood.

Toni spoke: 'You will not make the forest edge in a day's time without help.' He began drawing runes in the air, forming a circle. Piex was watching, memorising them with deep intensity.

Toni huffed, and muttered almost as apology, 'It will take some time to get used to doing this the direct way. I will miss having two minds.' Intoning a single word, the lights in the air glowed, and then the space within the portal twisted exactly the way Kialessa had seen Daygon, her half-brother, high priest of her late father's fortress, often do.

Suddenly there was a thudding in the forest behind them. Kialessa turned in fright. High in the branches the red feathered bird glared at them, and from around the tree, the enormous plant-like creature walked. Then, slithering from chameleon camouflage as though he'd been there the whole time, was the stone brown dragon. A deep, quiet sorrow seemed to fill them all.

It was the dragon who spoke. 'Master, please. Please don't leave us.'

Toni sighed. The enormous creatures simply waited, seeming to drip with severity and, perhaps, fear.

'Take courage, guardians,' he told them. 'I will not be gone long, a decade or two at most.'

This displeased the dragon most visibly. 'They will corrupt you, Master, or they will try. You cannot hope to remain free of their greed, and avarice, and pride. If you leave … I fear for what you may become.'

Toni smiled at him, walking up, and the dragon moved closer. 'Do not fear for me, Power-of-the-Earth; I go to learn things I can know no other way.'

The tree monster growled, somehow.

Toni nodded. 'True, true, Heart-of-the-Trees. But if I do not go, then we will never know.'

They did not argue this.

Toni held up his hand, and it started to glow. 'Upon you I decree all my power, all my authority, and all my strength. You may stand as guardians of this sacred forest until I return, and the veil will not be lessened. Be of good cheer, and of good courage, and of good hope. You know I will return.'

The bird slunk down, and said something to his mind they did not hear.

'Thank you,' Toni smiled. 'Thank you, Strength-of-the-Beasts. Thank you.'

Without further notice, the enormous creatures retreated into the forest.

Toni stood a moment more, a small tear at the edge of his eye.

'You'll be all right,' Kialessa promised.

He shook his head, indicating she had not understood his sorrow. 'I only hope it will be worth it.' Saying no more, he stepped through the portal, and they quickly followed.

Death's Ally

Every character in a story, even a historical story, is now nothing more than a simple idea, a memory, a concept of all they were and a collection of the stories that surround them. You are a concept too, and will one day live on only in the memories of those whose lives you touched. Whether your life has a purpose or not really isn't the issue here. For even if life itself has no purpose, those who love you will miss you, when you are nothing more than a thought within their hearts ...

Tam, wildsage of the Goddess of the Waters Waaglah. In a personal communication with a deeply depressed student.

'You did *what*!?' Grudon shouted at them. The steward seemed upset about something, again. Kialessa emerged with her friends from the portal somewhere near the forest's edge, and sighted the lifeboat with the steward, the priestess, and two strong sailors rowing swiftly towards them. Allastassia and Darrix started a race, which Posk was winning, naturally, and Kialessa, Piex and Toni seemed to catch on to the end of their conversation with the blustering steward.

Allastassia spoke tersely to the King's first advisor. 'We did only what we were told – enter the veil and meet you here. And we are here, almost on time,' she pointed out.

Allastassia began to give him a brief report while they sorted out something on the boat. But Toni paused at the forest's edge, and Kialessa stopped by him.

The boy spoke, 'Kialessa, Wanderer has decided to join you.'

'She, what?' Kialessa was confused. Casting about with *mage sight* she soon saw the strange glow of the fey dragon hopping along on some branches nearby, that moved as though nothing more than a normal breeze touched them. 'Oh,' she thought out loud.

'I am not surprised. Such of her kind bond for life, as far as I can tell. Are you happy to have her accompany you?'

'Yes!' she quickly agreed. 'Though she need not hide.'

'I think it best,' Toni disagreed. 'Soul's such as hers are very self-sufficient, and independent. She can hide unimaginably well. She will, I suspect, come and go as she pleases, for I have given access to every realm I know if to her and her sisters – as was the project at the time. I am honoured that she chooses you, though I do not yet know what it means to have her life tied up in your own at this point.'

Kialessa watched the glowing dragon figure flutter out then, and hop onto the bow of the boat as if she already knew exactly that was what needed to happen. It made her smile. A friend, perhaps? Well, at least the rats on board would soon be less of a problem!

They stepped out together into the sunlight.

The steward was still flustered, but then he looked up, and noticed Toni. 'Oh … my …' the steward replied.

'And, we made a friend,' Kialessa informed him.

***

Toni stood in front of the Red King. The king was seated on the padded chair that served as his throne while they voyaged on the Dawn. His four most powerful advisers on either side, the Dawn's admiral grinning to himself as he leaned disrespectfully against the bulkhead as they all chatted. Kialessa and her friends flanked Toni.

No one had said anything when they'd brought a young, blond-haired boy onto the lifeboat. For a long moment the silence continued.

Then the King gave his steward leave to speak.

Lord Grudon looked embarrassed and hesitated somewhat. 'Well, ahem. Young knights of the realm … well done. I think-'

The King interrupted him. 'Amazing! Wonderful! How impressive! You not only fulfilled our request, but you found a friend as well. Simply wonderful!'

Allastassia curtsied. 'Am I to take it, then, my King, that you never actually expected us to enter the veil?'

The old King looked about at his senior staff, who glanced about guiltily. 'Well, actually, no.'

The priestess spoke up. 'No one has been able to enter that domain since the founding of our Kingdom. And yet you do. And who, are we to assume, is your new companion?'

Allastassia curtsied to her. 'My lords and lady, my King, may I present to you; young gentle Toni.'

The adults looked around at each other.

The King nodded at the young man. 'Welcome, young man. May I ask if you have a family name? You may speak freely.'

Toni bowed with impeccable skill. 'I am born of the forest, and take no family name as you measure it. I am pleased to travel with you, and wish to learn of your ways.'

'Are you a spirit, or a morphed dragon?' the steward demanded to know.

'Neither, though I am a friend to the King, and all who stand with him,' Toni replied with flawless grace.

They seemed to take him at his word, and relaxed visibly.

'Well, if you are to join with us,' the King wondered out loud, 'where are we to keep you? We have little room in my cabin here.'

'I am content to stay as a servant,' Toni replied.

The King looked thoughtful. 'As you wish. Be sure to let us know if you need anything.'

Toni nodded, 'Thank you, kind King.'

'And,' the sagemaster interjected, 'may we ask your purpose in travelling with us?'

'I wish to learn of your ways, if that is befitting.'

'We should warn you,' the priestess added, 'this is no light-hearted picnic we are on. We are hunted by a dread assassin.'

'I know,' Toni replied. 'He will make his second test this evening at midnight.'

***

All were awake at the appointed hour. The lookout called, and Kialessa rushed on deck with the others. Secretly, she was grateful for Toni's insight, and was looking forward to seeing how he would help out.

Dark mist was surrounding the boat in the waxing moonlight.

Sailors drew their weapons.

'What mischief is this?' the general demanded.

The priestess replied, 'Necromancy … anoint the weapons!'

Sailors knelt down to pour holy oil on their blades. Kialessa was mildly impressed at their preparation this time.

Dark shapes began to form in the haze, riding along the water behind them. The stench of death followed; an almost tangible sense of fear rode before it. The other two ships stayed well ahead, away from the danger.

'A terrible evil,' the priestess pronounced.

Kialessa looked at the gathering fog.

Toni stood beside her. 'This is … impossible …'

Sailors all around quailed with fear, making the ward evil sign over their hearts.

'*Metu liberabis!*' the wizard proclaimed, and the growing fear was swept away from them all.

'Stand all on deck!' the general announced. 'They will try to hamper the boats!'

From the mist, warriors formed. They looked and acted like brigands or thieves. They bared their teeth and snarled, but the fear was gone from Kialessa's heart.

Suddenly, a burning arrow sped from the general's bow and embedded itself into one of the ghost's chests. It dissipated with a long sigh, almost sounding like it was a relief to be rid of its own undeath.

Then, with a boat-trembling roar, the ghosts charged.

At least a hundred ghost bandits came at them from every angle. Allastassia granted several of them the mercy of dying again with a very impressive lightning bolt. Darrix and Aolith leapt up to the adult sized spirits without a trace of fear, or hint of being in any way inferior opponents. Dale managed to impale at least three of them at once with a blessed bolt. Natasha's hooves were deadly enough, but her curved blade slew all it touched.

And Kialessa's whip burst into white fire long before they touched the boat. With prescient power it brought down a dozen ghosts, the white fire of the unicorn's gift tearing their undead souls to shreds long before the hair of the whip even could.

The brigands died, this time forever, in barely a few heartbeats.

'Too easy,' the general complained.

The sound of sword hilts striking steel shields raced across the water towards them. They turned to looked starboard, and the general ordered the lookout to keep keen portward.

There, approaching them in full military formation, was a legion of tattered undead warriors, trained for and slain in battle.

'You asked for a challenge?' the admiral grinned at the general.

Choice, set free

'They bear the insignia of Emerel!' Aolith said, her voice choking and aghast.

'The traitor's legion,' Darrix explained. 'Sworn to defend the King of Nomer'el, then turned against him at a sorcerer's behest during the second demon war. What evil power commands such traitors!?'

Posk had visibly paled. 'An entire army of shiny ghosties!'

Even Darrix looked troubled. People held their weapons nervously. Everyone except Toni, who with a gently glowing golden halo had done nothing up to this point, but simply observe, standing alone at the prow of the ship. Kialessa watched his calm features. He seemed concerned, but unafraid.

The legion moved in full military formation. Dale managed to knock one down with his ballista, and the general finished it off with his blessed bow.

'Man the four quarters!' the admiral demanded, indicating he expected them to attack from all sides.

Then, as the legion got within striking distance, they charged. Sure enough, new ghosts appeared in the mist from all sides. The main force met the combined might of the general and the wizard, who with striking blows and glowing weapons held them all off.

As lucked seemed to have it, Kialessa and most of the other students appeared to be defending the starboard side. A traitor ghost met Aolith head on, and she parried his blow masterfully, yet ended up unbalanced from the sheer power of his strike. The ghost soldier's flailing blade cut a deep gash into the enchanted wood of the boat. Kialessa leapt around to try and trip him, but he dodged her whip easily. Then the whip itself leapt around unnaturally and encased his ankle, drawing him to one knee as he roared with unholy pain, losing his chance to impale Aolith. The soldier swept up his blade, intending to sever Kialessa's precious whip, but Aolith ran him through his ghostly steel breastplate and right into his unbeating heart. But before he had even fully dissipated into the mist, another two took his place.

Suddenly there was a thunderous drum, as if someone had struck the boat with a mighty power. Kialessa was almost thrown forwards as a blinding gale of white light swept passed her and into the ghosts. She turned around, and watched as the priestess struck the boat with her staff again. This time a few ghosts seemed prepared, but none could stand against the holy wind. They closed ranks and pulled back.

Again the staff struck, and this time it seemed to sunder both sword and shield as the ghosts began to dissolve.

But then Kialessa heard the dread ringing of some unholy bell. She looked at the stern, and saw a cloaked, translucent figure standing just above it in the air. Dark mist gathered around the ship, and within the baleful sound the undead soldiers stood tall once more. But the light prevailed on the boat, right up to the stern where the hooded figure seemed to swallow all light in the depths of his black cloak.

'It *can't be*,' Piex whispered in fear.

Blessing an arrow, the general fired at the apparition, but it flew right through the cloak and out the other side.

The shadow spoke, and its voice sounded like a man's. 'Seriously, Bon Sure'e?'

'Worth a shot,' the general replied with a casual shrug of his shoulders. The ghost warriors surrounded the boat from the very edges of the glowing light.

Suddenly, Kialessa realised she knew that shadow's voice. 'Uncle Tobiuus?' she asked.

Everyone turned to look at her.

'Well done, well done,' the evil wizard mocked her. 'Seems my nephew's favourite assistant has been keeping up with studies of her own. And, look, a headband of wizardry for you to keep! How fate has prospered you!'

'You're supposed to be rotting away the rest of your life in jail,' she informed him.

The cloaked apparition just laughed. 'And to what end? Would it not be a waste of my powerful life?' Then, just like him, he began to indulge in an uninvited philosophical diatribe. 'There is no meaning, no divine purpose in any one being's existence. So we must claim for ourselves the power to remake the world in our own image, according to our own desires.'

'And what of the gods who made us?' Federach demanded, as if to distract him with his own self-impressed monologue.

Tobiuus snarled. 'You are all so precious. There are no "gods", just those beings powerful enough to impose their wanton whims on others. You may say that we are a creation of the gods, but we are left to ourselves, occasionally getting their help when we amuse them enough. But life and fate are our own, at least for those who are willing to admit that truth.'

'Well,' the sagemaster, his arch nemesis, replied. 'I detect little inflornum hall of magic around you, meaning you are in some form actually here. But your body is insubstantial enough to allow even sacred arrows to pass though? I'm guessing you found some manner of crafting an ephemeral body of some kind. Impressive, I would very much like to know how you did that.'

Tobiuus seemed to glare at him from within his hood, but he did not remove it. 'You will die here like your stubborn, witless regent. Then let the true master's wishes be fulfilled!'

The sagemaster stretched out a hand, and raging fire leapt from it, almost consuming the entire forequarters of the ship. But the archmage negated the flames with bluish shards of light of his own. In the very same moment, the ghosts charged again.

'How does it feel to have your spells countered now, librarian!?'

Tobiuus mocked.

'Wizards, now!' the sagemaster replied.

From the edge of her vision, Kialessa noticed Marchan reading from a scroll. Green chains of ethereal light began to manifest around Tobiuus, and while he struggled to deal with the new threat the sagemaster presented, he was unable to stop the chains from embedding themselves in his spectral form. A great wind sprung up and tried to drag Tobiuus away, but now he was stuck to the ship.

Kialessa tried to see what was happening, but there was a lot of movement right now nearby. She wished she could help, her whip still burning white with righteous fury at the undead, its light seeming to bless and encourage everyone nearby. They were holding their own against the ghost soldiers who remained. Darrix's shield was starting to glow, and he moved so fast he was holding back two adult soldiers at once. Several fell to Federach's thundering flail, and another solider lost its undead head to Natasha's scything blow.

Kialessa turned, and noticed the sailor wizard thrusting a glowing gem into Tobiuus's incorporeal chest. It glowed brightly, burning him out from within. The archmage screamed.

Then the high priestess struck the floor again with the staff, white fire exploding from her. In its light, most of the remaining ghosts disintegrated, and the rest quickly fled.

The archmage evaporated, leaving nothing but ice and dust.

'Impressive,' sagemaster De'Feur stated, studying the remains.

The general stepped up, laughing. 'Seems the night is, again, ours!' and he slapped the old elven wizard so hard he almost fell over. The general apologised immediately.

The sagemaster stood, rolling his shoulder. 'Perhaps, but this is yet again a mere test. We have no doubt inconvenienced the archmage, but he will form a new body soon enough.'

'At least we know the depths of their depravity,' the high priestess stated. 'The undead legion … Unforgivable!'

The wizard shook his head. 'I doubt they will use undead again, now they have seen how effective you are at handling them.'

The steward bowed to the priestess as if in gratitude. 'At least, not while you are with us.'

Kialessa thought on that, and agreed. She turned to see Toni was safe, and he seemed lost in his own thoughts as he looked out at the dissipating mists. She wondered if he'd learnt what he was hoping to, for he'd done nothing to help.

She then felt movement behind her, and noticed both Posk and Darrix had flanked Piex, and were looking at him in great concern.

Piex's expression was dark and determined. 'He's supposed to be in *jail*,' he muttered, the fear, anger, and betrayal hanging heavily on his every word.

***

Later that afternoon, Kialessa was washing dishes in the gently rocking ship when an invisible, snakelike entity splashed into the dish water in front of her. She stifled her gasp, hoping it was Wanderer. But the gentle, cat-like footfalls and an almost playful dance reassured her. She was patting her little dragon head even before she'd finished casting *mage sight*.

'Where have you been?' Kialessa asked. Not a single other soul in the room appeared to have noticed them.

But the little dragon did not reply. It only waited for a brief pat, nuzzling her hand while purring. Then with a wet splash Wanderer leapt out of the sink and into some near dimension that probably didn't exist.

'I guess we gave you the right name,' she muttered, and went back to work.

The Visitor

*It can well be seen that the greatest single predictor of future life success amongst scholars is not intelligence, nor one's family wealth, nor even royal status of birth! I have trained humans for over three hundred years, and you know the ones who will always be happier and more successful? They have self-control, and exercise extraordinary patience and commendable self-restraint. Now, I do not advocate a life devoid of joy and simple pleasures, no. Yet those who succumb to transitory pleasures or look for immediate gratifications will always meet a bitter fate in the end. If I could offer you a single gold coin **now**, or a handful of such coins if you leave the first coin sitting along on the table for a day, would **you** wait?*

Sagemaster Coure De'Feur, in private conversation, 316CY.

Wizard studies were very muted that evening. The others were looking up spells and lore to deal with undead. Yet with uncharacteristic determination, Piex just sat there, fuming.

'It will do you no good to brood,' the sagemaster finally told him.

Piex sat up, and sighed. He wiped his face as if there had been tears, though there were none. 'Did we bring the *Reliquis*?' he asked the sagemaster.

The older mage nodded.

'Good,' Piex announced, and began to scribe out his latest attempts at the *fiery conflagration*. His quill scratched and shot about on the parchment in a messy, angry scrawl.

The sagemaster sighed.

Marchan looked like he wanted to cheer things up. 'Piex, aren't you a little bit curious about what we found in the ruins?' he asked with a broad grin.

Piex's pen paused.

Aolith sighed as though wearied by a poor story over-told, but smiled none the less. 'Oh, please,' she began.

Marchan fished something out of a pouch he had. It was a chunk of grey stone, embedded with a rod of steel or iron of some sort.

'These were all over the ruins,' he started.

'Yes,' Piex began, now clearly distracted from his brooding. 'This is not news. Steel embedded in stone. No one knows how the ancients did it. There is such all over Emerel, as you are well aware.'

'Yes, but let me tell you my theory,' Marchan began.

'Not this again!' Aolith protested, and the sailors laughed.

Marchan continued, unperturbed. 'You'll find this stone all the way from the ruins right up to the castle at Emerel. What if, and I know this sounds crazy, but what if Dae Montol wasn't a small city at the edge of a great nation. What if the ruins were actually *part* of the golden city?'

Now Kialessa found her interest piqued. 'You mean the city was so large it went from modern day Emerel right to the heart of Lenmer'el?'

Marchan nodded sincerely. Piex looked thoughtful. Aolith sighed again.

Marchan continued. 'It would explain several myths, such as the flooding of the city. What if the entire Shallowsea swallowed a whole third of it, like the legends say? What if there are more ruins than can be counted, just under the surface?'

'That would be a lot of gold,' Piex observed.

Aolith shook her head. 'We'd know by now. There's no way that much gold goes unnoticed at the bottom of a shallow sea.'

She then launched into an old debate with Marchan, who seemed to be enjoying her company more than he wanted to win a debate with her. Piex got out a few old maps and cited some legends from the time, which encouraged Marchan mightily. He had to put away his strange rock just to clear the table.

Kialessa was just beginning to wonder if they'd be getting into any actual wizardry tonight when there came an unexpected knock at the door.

Everyone looked at each other. No one had ever knocked at the door when the wizards were studying. With a wave of his hand, the sagemaster sent the two wizards pretending to be sailors – actually, to be fair, they were fully trained sailors with some respectable wizard training – to hide behind the wardrobes. And Aolith, to Kialessa's absolute amazement, turned herself invisible; the chair next to her creaked a little as she probably sat down on it.

Marchan opened the door.

It was Toni.

The young man smiled and walked in. He looked around, seeming a little curious. When his eyes fell on Aolith's chair he simply said, 'Oh.'

The sagemaster spoke. 'The mysterious boy of the forest, from within the veil of light by the fallen citadel! What missive brings you to honour us with your good presence this evening?'

Toni looked at him a moment; Kialessa wondered what he was thinking. Perhaps the wizard's educated words took some time to interpret, as was usual. But Kialessa guessed Toni was probably smart enough to know what they meant, so maybe he was wondering why the old elf felt the need to use so many large words to say, in effect. 'Hello. What do you want?' But then again, the room was full of magic, so perhaps it was just a lot for him to take in, having one mind right now and all.

Toni shook his head as if to clear his thoughts. 'I sensed magic. I trust you will not mind … I would like to know more, if I may ask?'

A tome floated down to the table from some bookshelves at the sagemaster's behest. It rested at the first page, open on the table in front of Toni. Kialessa recognised it immediately, the definitive treatise on all things magical: *Academicleas's guide to modern magic* – just about the first book any real wizard read in this world.

The wizard spoke. 'This is the beginnings of our craft, if you wish. May I ask if you have had much experience in the science of wizardry?'

Toni did not reply, but instead closed the book. Then, placing one hand on the cover, he shut his eyes. Soon his brow furrowed in concentration. Then he spoke. 'Oh, *this* book.' He sounded disappointed.

'You know of this?' the sagemaster asked.

'I have read the copy inside … I have read Piex's copy,' he said, looking sad. Piex, on his part, looked surprised. Toni continued, 'All is a confusion. A mess. I cannot imagine how you … make magic work at all using this.'

Marchan scoffed. 'We do well enough.'

But the sagemaster stopped him. It was not the student's place to speak while the master taught. The sagemaster looked at Toni thoughtfully. 'Perhaps you might like to elucidate a few errant theorems that displease you?'

Kialessa knew the wizard was cunning enough to ask for secrets. Did he know Toni was an ancient? They had told no one, nor mentioned it at all, for Toni's sake. But a blond boy with different coloured irises turning up from a place no one had entered in living memory? They probably suspected it, or at least thought him a dryad or travelling spirit of some kind.

Toni caressed the book, as if unsure of where to begin. He took a look at Piex's notes. He looked at him as if to say, "You seem upset," but instead asked, 'You understand the law that explains you cannot make something from nothing?'

Again the sagemaster replied, 'Yes, the law of transmutation. Academicleas hints at such in his seminal work here.'

Toni nodded, but looking again at Piex, simply stated, 'Then why are you applying the infinite divisions from an expected point of zero? You must begin with matter if you wish to transmute it into energy.'

That got their attention. Within moments, all the wizards in the room were poring over Piex's calculations, which were, it seemed, completely correct and flowed logically if you started from an incorrect assumption about time and matter and energy.

The sagemaster was able to create a floating glyph of energy, and then Toni audited it with his bare hands to form a complex calculation ring. The wizards were ecstatic, and even Aolith joined in the conversation, since Toni kept referring to her and answering questions she hadn't seemed to ask out loud. The kind of stuff Toni was saying was well out of Kialessa's reach, but it seemed to make the other wizards very happy. Everyone had forgotten about Marchan's pet theory by then, but perhaps it was for the best. As for their part, the two closet wizards never made a sound, and Kialessa forgot about them entirely until the next day, wondering if perhaps they'd gone somewhere else, or fallen asleep in there.

As the hours drew late, Toni spoke: 'This relates directly to a question I have most pressing on my mind at this time.'

'Say on,' the sagemaster honoured him.

Toni nodded with his immaculate politeness for a culture he was barely three days into knowing. 'How was the cloaked mage willing, let alone able, to harness those driven beyond death by using fear and remorse? This power, I have encountered it. But I would have never imagined any being would wield it willingly, even enthusiastically!'

They looked at the sagemaster. He cleared his throat, 'That, I suppose, is a question that goes beyond wizardry, to morality. The truth is I do not know.' He turned to Piex, who took it as his cue to speak.

'My uncle made the mistake, years ago, of turning to necromancy to gain his powers. He is deceived.'

Toni nodded, 'I fear continued contact with such "necrotic" forces would eventually corrupt one's body, and soul. If he is not slain by his own servants, he will surely find himself enslaved one day to those who gave him this power.'

The sagemaster nodded. 'On this, we are all agreed.'

'I tried to tell him,' Piex apologised.

Toni nodded. 'Such wilful acquisition of guilt and regret to manipulate those who cannot yet forgive themselves. It is …'

He seemed lost for words, so Kialessa helped him. 'Evil?'

Toni stared at her, but nodded. 'Why would he waste his mortal existence attaining such a debt?' He turned to Piex. 'Your uncle is making a terrible mistake.'

Piex did not reply, so the sagemaster took his place. 'We know.'

***

An hour later, as midnight arrived and with tired yawns she began to pack up her studies, a solemn shudder trembled through the entire boat. The alarm bell rang out, but only once or twice, and the sound was tremulous, as though the lookout had fallen to the deck. Then, bright and coloured lights began to shine through the cracks in the bulkhead, or through the wood itself as if it had become transparent. Kialessa's heart caught in her throat – were they under attack again? But then a gentle reassurance spoke peace to her heart and mind, though she was reminded of a sensation she'd known only twice before – a god had arrived.

Marchan and Aolith looked to be reading themselves to fight, but with a dismissive gesture from the sagemaster they both paused. The old elf stood swiftly, walked towards the door, and everyone followed him quickly. Toni, for his part, seemed neither surprised nor concerned.

As soon as the wizard opened the door, bright lights in a rainbow spectrum of pastel hues almost blinded her. There was music coming from somewhere, soft yet powerful. There was a sense of encouragement, but also enormous power.

In a moment, she saw the cause of the excitement. A giant leviathan was floating above the water in the air. It would have been a thousand times the size of Imagination's Dawn. The creature had hundreds of fins and tentacles of every colour and form wafting in the night breeze. It was glowing from within so brightly it seemed to her to be brighter than noonday. Kialessa knew it instantly from the pictures back at the college; it was one of the four chosen personal attendants to the goddess of the waters herself, Waaglah. And there was no mistaking it for a mere illusion; no one could imitate the sense of awe and power she felt in this god of the water's presence.

The sagemaster closed the door after them, and, opening it again, out walked the King and his steward. A regal power of light surrounded the King in the presence of the god, a gleaming fire of white and red. All knelt, except the King, who merely bowed.

'Da'hanaea, voice of the goddess of the waters,' the King spoke, not seeming at all cowered in this mighty being's presence.

For a long moment there was silence. Kialessa felt something press against her mind, something trying to read her thoughts. It was inobtrusive, but also incomprehensibly powerful. Then the deity spoke, with a soft voice that held such unimaginable strength she feared it alone could rip her entire country to shreds with a single angry word. Yet, by the grace of the goddess of the waters, none were harmed.

Good King of men, the enormous divine entity spoke, *my mistress bids you kindly reconsider your course. You have much trial this way, and she can no longer guarantee your safety.*

King Dunnkan seemed troubled, but not upset. 'I understand, eminent messenger of the Queen of the oceans. But I must know, can we succeed?'

The entity seemed to sigh before replying. *It is possible, we can foresee. But the trial will be difficult, and there will be much sacrifice.*

The King looked around at his people. 'And if we do not try? How much more will we lose?'

This time, the entity laughed. Not unkindly, but not in an amused manner either. It, or she, seemed genuinely … impressed? *If you succeed, millions will not know fear. If you fail, little will change. But this price is not your own to pay.*

This time, the King bowed. 'Then we go on.'

Again the entity chuckled, and began to circle the boat from a short distance. The other ships were so far away, but they held their distance. She was a huge, translucent form, filled with moving lights, like a mystical jellyfish from deep below the warm waves. She seemed to be studying them all in turn, one at a time. She seemed surprised to see Toni, but if they spoke, nothing was heard by any present.

At length the entity spoke again. *Let none fault you in your kindness, or determination, King of Lenmer'el. The wars of late have troubled my mistress. Seek communion with the King of the northern Shallowsea; he has a proposal that may assist. I will make a path for the merkin to follow. I cannot promise you safety, or success. But this journey will be profitable to you, either way.*

Kialessa was not sure what the being meant by that, and by the looks on the King and the steward's face, neither did they. But neither dared ask the deity for clarification – what was spoken was sure to be revealed in the time intended by the gods.

Again the entity chuckled, or sighed. She seemed to be moving away from them. *Life is breath, and breath is brief. From water you humans are borne, and without water you have no life. Can any of you speak aught of yourself? That you are less than the mud at the bottom of the Shallowsea; for at least the mud obeys the highest law it is given. But to you it is given to choose for yourselves. What does your life mean? Do five hundred million breaths make up a life?*

Kialessa was wondering what it meant. Was it, or she, upset, or perhaps annoyed, that the King had just chosen to directly disobey the council of the goddess of the waters? Or was it secretly impressed, as if he'd passed some test, that by choosing to go on he'd shown courage? Their lives, and breath, were all in his hands. Did it matter what he chose for them?

Suddenly, the entity breathed on the ship, and bright glowing lichen sprang to life all around it. Wood snapped together till there was no evidence of individual planks that made up the ship. The main mast twisted and swelled as if it had just become the trunk of a very tall, powerful tree.

The entity paused, and then Kialessa had the distinct impression that it was smiling at them. Subtle lights began to gather around the creature. It swung away, the ocean swelling in its wake and gently rocking the boat. Long, sorry sounds like a whale song filled the air, as if the leviathan was singing an arrhythmic, atonal song. It must have lasted several moments, but the sky fell dark again once more. No one spoke a word, not till many hours had passed and dawn began to light the sky once more.

4 Wanderer visits one night just before wizard training starts

Brandish

*"You waste too much time on being afraid of some god's judgement! Most are willing to forgive, and the other gods care so little about you that your witless deeds are simply ignored. So live a little; go to a party! Buy a new posk! Burn down your enemy's barn! Life is too brief to not have a little **fun**!"*

Brandish, just prior to his arrest in 202 CY.

'There's fighting on the deck of the Edge!' the lookout shouted.

The entire morning had passed without incident, but midmorning held an ill portent. Kialessa sensed it before she saw it; something was wrong.

Kialessa ran with everyone to the stern. Although it was midday, it was a dim, over clouded day, just like the admiral had told them it would be. He'd even gone so far as to predict a storm that night. The Edge and Gap were running a quarter league back, hoping to avoid most of the trouble the Dawn might face running point.

'Hard to port!' the admiral shouted, and the boat tiled to the right. The sails fell slack and then sprang back up as the Dawn changed direction with almost mystical haste and began to ride towards the beleaguered warship.

Kialessa looked out hard, finding she had to move position to see through the throngs of concerned onlookers.

Someone was on the foredeck of the Dawn with a huge axe. He was swinging it against the soldiers with prolific skill, cutting down every one of them that stood against him. He must have killed twenty or so of them already.

A bow sung out, and Kialessa did not need to turn to know it was the general's *Hera Lira*; with magical speed the arrow somehow managed to breach the distance between the two boats with its aim still true. Then, at the last instant, the axe swung about in his hand and deflected the arrow.

'It's a defending weapon,' Darrix announced, holding the hilt of his own sword all the tighter.

Toni was by her side, and seemed to decide it was time to state the obvious. 'The hunter's ally, who relishes murder.'

The man laughed and turned to face the Dawn, even as he punched an assailant in the mouth and knocked the poor soldier unconscious. He shouted at them all with another laugh, and it was very hard to hear what he was saying, but it sounded like, 'Hurry up!'

'What did he say?' the sagemaster muttered.

'He wants us to hurry,' the steward replied.

'Look lively!' the admiral shouted, as though the mere act of being loud might somehow speed up the wind and the waves. They were riding against the current now.

'Another test?' the general growled.

'Another,' the priestess announced. 'I did not expect an attack at midday.'

'Whatever,' Bon Sure'e replied, then without another word grabbed up a rope as though hoping his breath alone would help them ride at full pace towards the warship.

Kialessa watched on helplessly. The man, whoever he was, was tall – perhaps part-giant. He wielded an axe as large as any normal man with one hand, swinging it about with effortless prowess. He laughed as he continued his work of death amidst the soldiers. They were trying to fight defensively now; they knew they were no match for this part-human monster.

She dug her nails into the sideboard in frustration. Good soldiers were dying, and they were too far away to help. Maybe they should have never even taken trained soldiers on this trip? Only those wreathed in power and magic could hope to face the new friends of a master assassin.

Toni was next to her, looking on. He turned to watch her hands. 'Hmm, Kialessa, I would not-'

5 I would not ...

She never heard the rest of his words, as without any deliberate effort, she accidentally shadowstepped the entire distance between the two boats. The magic left her drained, and she knew she could not use her enchantress powers to magic her way back again. She found herself flung from the dim shadow of the mast into midday. For a moment she was surprised, then impressed, then terrified.

The boat she arrived on reeked of fear. To her right, a hundred soldiers quivered with dread, holding out a line with every good bit of determination that they possessed.

To her left, the giant human-monster stood.

It seemed she'd caught him off guard; he just

6 Brandish the Slayer

stood there, looking surprised. She took a moment to register his features. Knotted muscles hugged his bare chest, his arms coated in the blood of his enemies. He had tan skin and was entirely bald. His brow was thick, but his eyes held a held piercing wisdom. And in his right hand the giant axe seemed to hum with contentment at having tasted so much death.

'Ah!' the man announced with a satisfied grin. 'The King's pet demon!'

In that instant, Kialessa's magic whip turned white with righteous indignation, and its hilt leapt into her hand. It unfurled from around her waist, but hung, levitating, in the air around her.

The giant just grinned. 'Jerik will be *so pleased* to hear I did you the honourable service of removing your head from your shoulders today!'

The whip sizzled with raw anger. Kialessa did her very best to not look in any way as terrified as she now felt. She was not really equipped or cut out to take on a fully trained and prepared villain of his calibre. At best, all she felt she could do was hold him off from killing anyone else until the others arrived. But he was looking right at her, and she didn't want to even risk glancing away until the Dawn arrived. As if in answer, another arrow flew at his head and with a red spark he blocked it with his axe, not even bothering to look at it.

He grinned at her and took up a battle stance. 'I look forward to meeting Bon Sure'e again, and ripping his fingers off his hand one by one. So tell me, does he still prefer that whole axe routine?'

Kialessa just looked at the giant, wondering what his plan was. Perhaps he'd only killed twenty men simply for the chance to chat? Silence hung in the air.

'Very well, to death then,' and he charged.

Several dozen crossbow bolts flew from the wall of shields behind her. Most just bounced off his dark skin, one he deflected away from his face with the giant axe he wielded as though it weighed no more than a pencil. One struck true and lodged between his ribs, but shallowly.

But his attack was clumsy, she dodged it easily.

'Ow, who did that!' he demanded to know from the wall of soldiers.

A surge of power filled her. He made as if to advance on them, and Kialessa moved in closer. As she suspected he would, it was simply a feint, and at the last moment he swung his axe back toward her. Another clumsy attack; she dodged it easily as well.

He advanced on her swiftly then, he moved so fast! But she backflipped and avoided his grasping hand. Twisting her whip about, she struck him on the face.

Then he looked angry.

More bolts assaulted him, but he ignored them now. As he swung about with his mighty axe, she was put to her limit trying to dodge him. She jumped up on the stairs, and leapt off only at the last breath as he demolished them. She stood on the banister using her tail as balance, and almost dancing against the rope ladder that led up the mast, she pushed against it and towards him. She leaped off his bald head and tumbled toward the deck again. She didn't know how she was able to keep him at bay; she didn't feel tired at all, buoyed on by the thrill of battle or someone's prayers, she did not know.

He roared, and as she guessed, he advanced quickly once more. Someone threw a spear between his knees, and it might have tripped him, but he snapped it almost without noticing. She turned about to hit him in the face again, but noticed his right arm ready to grab the whip, and instead she held her attack. Wood splintered as he tried again and again to hit her. Rolling into another backflip, she found her way onto the other banister.

Again she tried to leap over him, using her dancing whip as a distraction. But this time he was ready for the tactic. He grabbed her mid-air and she hung from his fist by her ankle.

'You are a deft little dancer,' he said with a grin.

He swung his axe, and she had to put her foot against the hilt to stop it hitting her neck. She found herself almost standing upright in the air, he knee twisting almost unnaturally. Her leg hurt; his grip was impossibly powerful. He looked almost as annoyed as she felt surprised that she'd just dodged death again. He twisted her in the air, swinging again, but she curled up against his fist so tightly that he missed completely.

'Oh, bother this,' he muttered, and flung her away from him right into the air and away towards the sea.

She sailed towards the mast, towards the shadowed side.

She grinned, and her whip dimmed and tightened around her. Using more enchantments than she knew she had, she shadowstepped into the shadow of the mast and used it to catapult out of the shadows behind him. Without a sound, she tumbled into a somersault, and using both her heels and all the force she possessed, she kicked him in the side of his head.

His head barely moved a span. She back-flipped down to the ground and moved towards the shattered banister, hoping to trip him up and over the edge. Her leg hurt.

For a moment, silence reigned. No one moved. The giant looked over her, hatred and death in his eyes.

She wanted to grin, to laugh at him. But then again, she didn't want to die. Somehow, she'd just managed to keep alive for a few instants; she still had no idea how far away help was. The soldiers on the boat looked at her nervously, but she noticed several of them moving the ballistae into position to fire at the giant.

Then with a roar he charged at her.

She felt caught between death and the edge of the boat, fearing she didn't have the strength to step through the shadowrealm again, at least for today.

But she also knew he did not know that.

With a step back she managed to get her foot to partially dematerialise into the other dimension, and she ducked as if to move there.

Sure enough, the ruse worked. He turned around with soldier's grace to await her exit, but it never came. Instead, she unfurled her whip and it caught him on his heel at the exact moment he planned to put it down. He stumbled mightily, flailing about with both arms.

With a giant roar he fell over the side of the boat.

She was about to look over when there was a mighty thump followed by no splash – apparently, he'd embedded his axe into the side of the Edge and was now hanging there. Despite her fears, she moved and looked over. He was standing sideways on the side of the mighty warship, gripping on to his axe hilt as the only thing preventing him from falling into the sea. He looked down, and was about to try and haul himself up when a blue and gold fletched arrow embedded itself in his shoulder.

The arrow bit deep and he roared in pain. He hauled his axe out and began to fall into the water, when a portal opened up and swallowed him. She only had a brief glimpse of the world beyond – a dark cavern of some sort, apparently made of wood. There were other people in there, but she did not get a good look at them.

A moment later, the surviving soldiers began to cheer. Before she knew what was happening, a handful of them had picked her up onto their shoulders and begun celebrating.

'The wounded!' she tried to protest, but then noticed others were, indeed, attending to the dead and injured. But the soldiers around her were clearly frightened. Some of them had clearly just stared death in the face, and she alone had somehow stood between them and the end of their life. And, for a moment, they were probably feeling more grateful than words could adequately express. It was a sobering thought. Some of them looked like they were fighting back tears, and one of them was actually crying with joy. So she allowed them to pick her up on their shoulders, and helped them cheer.

7 Helped them cheer

The Dawn arrived only a few moments later, pulling up alongside as the ships rocked against the waves in the shallow seas. The instant they touched, the steward leapt up with more athleticism than she knew he had onto the deck of the Edge, the rod in hand, healing energy washing over the entire ship. She felt every nick and scratch, even the great bruise around her leg, fade and simply disappear. Six of the wounded stood, two of the slain rose to life again. People cheered and saluted, many offering prayers to various deities for deliverance.

'Baroness Winterhaven,' the steward addressed her with a smirk. 'You are not to go wandering off again like this, do you hear? Terribly irresponsible you are, at times. Terrible!'

She knew she was not in trouble, but she didn't know what to say, so she curtsied.

Soldiers began throwing their swords at her feet.

'Thank you, young baroness,' one said.

'My life is in your debt,' another told her.

They nodded and saluted her. It was so flattering she didn't know what to say. Like when everyone sings happy birthday to you and you just sit there, smiling. Only a thousand times more than that.

Soon the King and his other guards joined them. He was smiling at her. 'Report?' he asked the captain of the Edge.

'Brandish, the slayer, there can be no doubt,' the experienced sailor told the King. 'He had the best of us ousted with his fell and foul powers. If your … um, if Baroness Winterhaven had not intervened, well, a lot more blood would have flowed this day.'

Allastassia and some of the others were there now too, helping to care for injured soldiers and the slain, her new floral headband looking a little out of place in the bloodstained bulkheads. Kialessa looked around, and saw the others helping, while Toni stood on the Dawn, looking confused.

The enchantress looked at her with deep concern on her face, '*How* did you survive an attack from the Slayer?' she asked.

Kialessa wasn't sure. 'He didn't seem to be taking it very seriously,' she replied, but then noticed the steward tapping the rod of Lenmer'el meaningfully on his open hand. Then she remembered its powers, and the *Gratos*. It certainly would explain a few things.

He nodded silently to her, indicating she should keep this knowledge to herself.

So she just shrugged. 'The thrill of battle, I suppose …'

Allastassia clearly did not believe her.

'Thank you, honoured gentle,' the King replied to the captain, then turned to face the others. 'See to the injured.'

The captain saluted and went to work helping others. The King waited only until his closest guards, Aolith, and Kialessa were standing close by. With a nod to the priestess, she lowered her sanctuary over them.

The King nodded at her. 'Well done, Kialessa. You saved a lot of lives today.'

She curtsied, and went to say something diplomatic, like Allastassia would want her to say, something like, "Nothing more than anyone else would have done." Except that wasn't true; most would have died, and of those that wouldn't have, not all of them could cross between the boats in a single step. But she didn't want to say something trite, something like she was really feeling, something like, "That's all right, it was fun!" because that was rude and insulting. 'I, um …' she began.

The King saved her the trouble of deciding what to say by cutting her off. 'So, Brandish the slayer, Tobiuus the archmage. And someone who can command a giant squid. Seems our assassin has gotten himself a small team of his own of late.'

'It speaks of his desperation,' the high priestess scowled.

'Any ideas who might have summoned that beast?' the steward asked.

The wizard hummed, 'Given our assassin's unparalleled ability to both liberate and then employ masters of murder and destruction, I am at odds to say who it might be.'

'Truevine,' the priestess announced. The others looked surprised. 'She has not been caught in a century, and I find her growing powers over the seas, and not just the forest, deeply concerning. But I have that conviction within my soul; we face the elf.'

The general did not look pleased. 'I guess she was holding back then.'

'Then why all these tests?' the King mused.

'We passed every one of them!' the general blustered.

The sagemaster did not agree, 'Tobiuus, I am sure, did not expect us to anchor him and defeat his simulacrum form. The other attacks seem to have been diversions, to make us overconfident, or to make the soldiers afraid.'

'Then we wait?' the general growled, still holding his bow. 'I need to send that murderer back to the hells, soon!'

'We wait,' the steward agreed, looking afar off.

The general swore, spat on the deck, and stormed away.

The Storm

*Have faith, little one, and you shall see; that if you work hard,
and stay strong, there are gods enough in the heavens for at least **one**
of them to **eventually** take pity on you!*
San Glasstone, Blithling scholar, 219 CY.

'All hands-on deck!'

Rigging lashed against the bulkhead, torn free by the fierce winds. Torrents of water fell across the Dawn as though thrown from a giant's bucket. Kialessa gasped in the chilling, dark salt water that splashed against her face continually, driven by a howling, frenzied wind.

She had been waiting below deck, patting Piex as he groaned with renewed sea sickness. The admiral had sensed the storm three days out, and it hadn't let up yet. They had tied up all the sails and let the wind take them where it would. Now they were tossed without direction, probably somewhere towards the deeper centre of the Shallowsea.

Someone had hauled open the hatch, bringing again the briny scent of salt and sea, screaming the admiral's command. Like many of the sailors, Kialessa could only hope they had not offended the goddess of the waters and, if not, then perhaps there was some good in the storm, some danger kept at bay perhaps. But after two days of endless rain from a blackened sky, prayers were becoming exceedingly fervid.

She struggled to stand on the rocking boat in order to obey the command, but wisely, Piex decided to lie back down. Against the restless wind, she struggled up behind the others.

Darrix grabbed some flailing ropes and had them tied in moments.

Posk shouted a warning, and in a moment they were again drenched in a monstrous wave. Kialessa was thrown to the deck, the wave hitting with so much force it knocked the air out of her and pushed water in. She took in a mouthful of dark salt water.

Coughing and spluttering she tried to rise, finding herself washed right up the stairs and thrown to the deck at the rear edge of the ship. It was more than lucky that she wasn't thrown to the sea, she observed gratefully.

She looked up as lightning struck the sky in the endless war between the god of the sun and the goddess of the sea. In its flickering light, she was dismayed at the tattered and torn mainsail, and then noticed the sprit sail had been torn off and was swinging dangerously along one side of the ship. Sailors like ants struggled to cut loose or tie down everything the storm claimed as its own.

She tried to stand, but the ship was listing so much it was extremely difficult.

Someone grabbed her arm, and then hauled her over against the rails. 'Get back below little one, this battle is not for you!' It was Lord Grudon, the steward. His purple eyes seemed to blaze with an inner strength and fire as he fought the storm.

Kialessa knew he was right. This foe was far beyond her. She tried to start toward the hatch, when the ship suddenly lurched starboard. With a squeal she clutched on to the railing.

Suddenly there was a large crack that shuddered from the insides of the ship.

Everyone paused.

'That was the rudder!' the admiral shouted from the till, two other strong sailors helping him steer the now pointlessly spinning wheel. 'We need to face the storm!' he shouted, pointing. A large wave was rapidly rising up to their left.

'So if the assassin doesn't get us, the storm will,' the steward muttered with bitter ingratitude.

Sailors struggled to unfurl the remaining hind sail in an attempt to give them even a spirit of a chance at steering, when suddenly a wave of lively green magic flurried past their feet, bringing with it the scent of garden hills.

Kialessa looked over, and saw Allastassia summoning all the magic she could to her hand. Her new headband, forged in the enchanted forest, glittered brightly with fey lights. Then she stabbed her hands into the deck just behind the main sail. The wood there suddenly thickened and grew, as though roots were springing from the energy around her hands. The boat groaned and shifted as her power filled it.

Then the boat started turning, hard.

'She's fixed the rudder!' a sailor shouted.

'No,' Grudon grinned, 'just made a new one!'

The admiral and his men dashed to her side, trying to help her, coaching and counselling her on how to drive a boat using a wide swathe of wood she had probably only ever seen once or twice, and certainly couldn't look at right now.

'Hold fast!' the steward shouted, and men cried out in fear.

The ship turned to face the monstrous wave, which tilted them up, further and further. The Dawn groaned as the titanic forces struggled against and within her. Allastassia trembled and turned pale.

'She needs more power!' the admiral shouted.

Then the King walked out, time and fear seeming to slow in his presence, the armed royal guard at his side struggling against the wind and water. With a simple gesture, the King summoned the rod of Lenmer'el out of the steward's hand and into his own. Holding it out over the enchantress, her breathing steadied. A golden-green glow seemed to surround them both, and the water flowed away at their presence.

But how the boat listed! Kialessa found herself slipping against the deck as the boat rode up, almost horizontal. The steward gripped on to her.

'Take a good breath, little one. We're going *through*.'

Not a moment later the entire boat was inundated – no, submerged inside an enormous wave. Yet somehow in the silence it did not falter. A moment later it broke the surface of the wave and rode out the other side.

'That's amazing,' Kialessa admitted.

'That's magic,' the steward explained.

But perhaps it was something about their wonder, the fact that they were just a little distracted – a moment later the entire boat began to swing about, and it struck the riding surf behind the wave fiercely. Their fall was so violent, she had to wonder if the wave had been so large the seabed underneath was exposed. And in the resounding thud, the steward lost his grip and fell against her, tearing them both from the railing and plunging them down, down towards a fierce, churning sea.

Darkness surrounded her, and she struggled in wild panic for what she hoped was now upwards. With burning lungs she finally found the surface, splashes of water driving against her face so hard it stung. A bell was ringing. She looked about, and found the Dawn being driven quickly away. She tried to scream, to warn them. But as soon as she drew breath the salt water found its way into her lungs, and she coughed helplessly.

A dark shape loomed in the water nearby, but with a quick glance she realised it was the steward. He was floating, face down. Quickly she tried to swim over, finding the water completely unhelpful. She prayed in her heart, and then remembered how to swim. He was barely breathing, clutching to some piece of the boat that had probably torn away with him.

He looked at her, nodded, and clutched on to her tight.

'Where are your healing ointments?' she asked him.

He patted his vest pocket, but they were both dismayed to find only shattered glass within.

'Can you not call the King to us, with the rod?' she was sure it was possible somehow.

He glared at her. His sunken and weary face still carved with determination.

Her heart sank. She knew he would die before he ever tore the King's protection away from himself in order to save either of them.

Already, she was shivering. She swapped out her battle gear for the only outfit she had that was both light and resistant to the cold – the nightdress.

The steward held her close, and they waited to be rescued.

***

Not long after, the storm seemed satisfied that, having driven them from the boat, its task was done. The moon waxed brighter in the dark sky, but there was no sign of any of the other three boats, and the new morning seemed reluctant to reclaim the sky. She tried to stay warm against the steward, but he was weak and sluggish and could do little more than clutch numbly to the piece of wood he'd found. Her body trembled with the cold, and she lost all feeling in her fingers long before sunrise's grace finally lit the sky. Her guardian and companion looked even more pale in its glare, his hair now caked with purple blood. He looked very poorly.

'Why have they not found us yet?' she begged the semi-conscious steward.

'It is … a very big … sea,' he replied, and started slipping from his piece of wood one more.

Again she slipped between his arms and forced his fingers to hold to it. It was strange, precarious work, and the rough waves continued to pull them in all directions. She found she had to kick almost constantly against the water to keep them upright. Her arms ached and her body shivered.

Choice, set free

There had to be a better way to deal with this.

Suddenly she felt a surge of water against her legs. She cried out in fear, and it roused the steward.

'What was that?' she asked.

He mumbled.

Again the surge of water pushed against their legs. Kialessa decided there and then to at least stare death in its face. She removed one of the steward's arms from around her, and with a quick breath, she pushed her face under the water and looked around.

It was very hard to see; the water was all churned up and dark. But there was a form there, quite close. It seemed to have a large fish's tail, and a long body. Quite long, for a fish … and a neck too. Then, as it turned to face her, she could clearly see it hard arms and a head too. She stuttered for breath in surprise.

She put her head up and gasped for air. 'It's a mermaid … a merboy!'

The steward seemed surprised.

'I think it's the boy I saw the other week. Why is he out here?'

The steward seemed to have no answers.

She pondered out loud, 'Perhaps I should try to speak to him?'

'He can hear you well enough,' the steward promised her, 'even though he be under the water and you above it.'

She was impressed. It sounded like merkin had very good hearing, for all sounded like blankets and alleyways under the water to her.

So she spoke, 'Oh, good merkin … please, can you not help us?' She found her voice timid, and it shivered still with the chill. Kialessa began to wonder if she might not catch her death of cold with this breeze that flew constantly across the waters and pushed salt rain into her lungs again and again.

There was no answer. She looked again in the water, but there was nothing.

'Please?' she begged. It was cold.

Again the steward lost his grip, and with a squeal she clutched on to him, saving his life yet again. But it was not a battle she could keep up all day, and she dreaded the moment when she could hold on to him no longer.

Just as she was just beginning to despair of any deliverance, suddenly a young boy's head popped up over the water just in front of her. He had long, straight hair embedded with seaweed. His face was bright and young, or perhaps ageless. The energy around him was lively and curious, but also quite nervous and afraid. His eyes were a deep blue, almost purple. Small, dragon-like scales were imbedded deeply in his skin, but so gently they were almost impossible to see.

8 Anaesu, son of the Merking.

'Your keeper is dying,' the boy informed her. Apparently, he spoke very good Emerellian as well, with a strange, exotic accent Kialessa did not recognise.

'Please, can you help?'

The boy just floated there, looking on. It seemed to be very hard for him to make up his mind. Kialessa tried to recall every kind of lore, any skerrick or legend she'd heard regarding the merkin. Shy … affectionate … with enormous undersea cities she'd always wanted to see … They were very fiercely protective of their King. What should she say?

The boy spoke again. 'He's dying. You heard me, yes?'

'Yes!' Kialessa agreed, suddenly wondering if that was all he wanted – to make sure she understood him. 'Yes, indeed! Oh, if you can help in any way. We have lost our ship and–'

The boy interrupted her. 'Father said you should not have passed Megálo Dásos without the correct obeisance to Waaglah, or even the Tahum! Then you leave off late inside winter, and know not the prayers to stay the p'tum that *always* strives this time of year. What were you humans thinking!?'

The steward scoffed, and may have laughed. But he soon fell silent, and probably unconscious again.

'We weren't, I guess. Water is not our usual home.'

'That much is clear,' the merboy agreed. She liked his tone; it was not cruel or lecturesome. It seemed he only wanted to help someone who was clearly out of their depths and ignoring all the warning signs.

She had hopes for a rescue. 'Please, will you help us?'

He looked a little uncertain, as if there were rules. But he ducked down again, and a moment later returned with some red seaweed. He swam around to the other side of the steward and helped prop him up. The old man started as if he'd only just realised the merkin was there, helping them. The boy offered the steward the red fruits that grew along the weed.

'These will sustain you,' he told the older man.

With trembling fingers the steward tried to grab the berries, but it took Kialessa's strength to feed them to him. They bled deep red in his mouth, and he looked positively disgusted.

'Eat it all,' the merboy demanded.

The steward nodded, barely managing to chew and swallow the underwater berries, or whatever they were. 'Bitter,' he informed them. But at least he seemed a lot more awake now, and the colour returned to his fingers in moments.

The boy looked at Kialessa. 'We have no time to prepare them. This one was too close … Come, I will call us a turtle. Perhaps they will shelter you in the air you so love.'

Kialessa nodded.

The boy dove under the water again, and as Kialessa watched him, he blew a deep, stately note on a large shell he found there. She heard no note, but felt the vibrations in her feet.

He rose above the water to speak to her again. 'If they come, they come. What are you doing here?'

Kialessa coughed before replying: 'I suppose we'd rather not be. But we fell off our boat and would very much like to get back.'

The merboy looked away. 'She is a good distance now. I doubt they can return for you even if they would. We will have to find another way.'

'Thank you for your kindness,' she replied.

He blushed. Which was very cute.

She had to smile at him; did he like to hear a kind word so much? Perhaps they would find a way to make a new friend, floating and cold in an ocean that might otherwise kill them.

'I, um … We don't get to see the landmen often,' he said. Then he brightened. 'Is it true you ride beasts of fur and horn across stone walks at the bottom of the air? And that your cities are made of metal that does not rust, not in years? And, and, that your lands are full of pirates and murderers who trade lives as money?'

His face had lit up with enthusiasm. It seemed the merkin had legends of their own about the 'landmen'. How fierce they sounded! But perhaps, if all the merkin knew were pirates and castaways, it would make all humans sound quite a bit more … barbaric.

But the legends weren't untrue either. 'I come from a city, Lenmer'el. We-'

'Yes!' he interrupted in his enthusiasm again. 'The man nation sunsetward and south to ours. Why were you heading north toward Emerel?'

She needed his help too much to be bothered by the constant enthusiasm. 'Our King goes there every four years.'

'You brought a King!' He sounded ecstatic. 'Has he the rod that burns his enemies and shields him from all harm?'

'Yes,' the steward replied. 'That's the one.' His voice was a little gruff and he glared at Kialessa as if to warn her to keep silence. Either this was private information, or it was "his" topic, being the King's protector and all. Kialessa let it be, which was easy, because the merboy was still speaking.

'And apparently you use metal as money and not shells. Why do men do that? Metal does not grow like shells do; how can it have any value? And … Oh no…'

His voice trailed off, and Kialessa looked to where his nervous eyes were now fixed. There, gliding toward them, were two large shell spears. Whatever was carrying those spears had no trouble cutting through the water – they came so quickly!

Kialessa looked at the steward in alarm, but he seemed quite composed and calm now, though the red berries still dribbled down his unkempt face. Either they faced no threat, or he was so used to staring down death that he no longer feared it.

Just as the spears came into reach distance, a large form rose up out of the water. It was a huge merman, muscular and handsome. He was a mountain of a man, with no beard but long hair. He wore seashell armour about his arms and shoulders, but none at his ribs. It was there that Kialessa really could see clearly the dim red patterns of his gills as they hid behind his ribs, the water clearly dripping from them as he prepared to speak.

'Anaesu! We are not pleased to see you so far away from the people again! The rumours are true, you have been following them, have you not?'

'I … yes.' He said a few words in his own language, but then slipped back into the common tongue. 'I'm sorry, landmen, this is Captain Darissius, of the local legion. And he is, um, my larger brother, um, big brother, sorry.'

Captain Darissius nodded, and then saluted with his spear.

Kialessa sighed with relief; it seemed he would be no threat to them at this time.

Darissius swam up, 'This one is near to death,' he informed them, looking at the steward.

Anaesu shook his head, as if this was old news. He tried to say something in his own language, but his brother stopped him. The boy repeated his words in their common language. 'I call a sea turtle. She can shelter them in the air for as long as they need.'

'Oh little one, this is why we do not send children like you to care for the lost landmen! They will die in this cold air. See, the little red one shivers all over. No, if they are to survive, we must take them to our barracks.'

Anaesu nodded. 'I would never have assumed such an honour,' he said, with quite a bit of tact.

Darissius splashed his brother. 'Anaesu, you are trouble!' he mocked him. And the younger boy protested, but didn't dare splash his brother back. Perhaps it was something in their culture where you don't splash your older brother, or a military officer. Or a captain. Who could tell!?

Darissius pulled a soft bottle from his belt, perhaps made of cured leather. The other officer, a dark-haired male with an actual beard, joined them and offered his bottle too.

'You are fortunate,' Darissius informed them, 'that the goddess smiles on your misfortune this day. Few carry this elixir but the captains and their men-at-arms. Come, drink this, and you will be made a merfolk till the next dusk, at least. Or till you breathe the air again, whichever is soonest.'

Kialessa almost squealed with delight, and the steward scoffed at her enthusiasm. All her life she'd wondered what it might be like to fly through the sea, to talk to fish and live like a mermaid so unafraid of the water, and now that wish was about to come true!

The steward was removing his shirt.

She looked at him in confusion.

'You want to be able to breathe, don't you?' he asked her.

Then she noticed all the merfolk had bare chests. Their gills were quite visible between the gaps in their ribs.

'Oh,' she said.

At Darissius' command, the males swam to face away, giving her … well, it was some privacy. Her face was blazing elven more red than usual; they could probably feel her burning embarrassment from where they were floating.

For a moment she had to consider if it was really worth it.

She did not have to think for long. She removed the sash from her waist and all her clothing went with it. Then she tied the sash around her chest as high as she could, at least, so it was still functional as some shred of modesty.

Then she took the offered drink, and drained it quickly. She'd expected it to be quite bitter, but it was really very sweet. Golden lights erupted in the water around her, and she felt her legs snap together and start changing shape. Their motion dragged her head under the water, and she started to panic.

She felt young hands on her shoulders, and opened her eyes to see

9 Kia of the Sea

Anaesu there, swimming in front of her. He was smiling broadly, swishing his tail. She looked down, and with almost a squeal of delight she noticed her own scaled, lava red tail twitching in the water.

He smiled at her, and then, slowly, took an open breath through his mouth.

That was when she realised she was still holding her breath.

It was hard, *really hard*, to reprogram all her innate fears and do something so unnatural as breathe water. But she knew she had to.

She opened her mouth. Instead of being salty, the water now tasted … well, there were tastes she had no words for, actually. Washable? No. Fluid? Well, that was obvious. It tasted wet. Not unpleasant. A bit dusty perhaps.

Anaesu was waiting.

All right, she said to herself. *Just breath it in.*

She didn't give herself time to panic, and just sucked in the water. This time, there was no choking, no coughing fits or panic. The water just flowed in, and then, weirdly enough, flowed out again through her rib cage. She could feel the water moving through her … gills.

Now she could taste the salt, but it was not overwhelming; it was the flavour against which all others were measured. She had to wonder if air tasted like this to merkin.

She looked over, and was surprised to see the steward, mertail and all, swimming around with practiced skill. The soldiers had bandaged his head nicely and held his clothing in a strange sea net. He seemed far healthier now, and was grinning at her.

'Kick,' he told her. 'Both legs, same time, same direction.'

She noticed how she was slowly sinking in the water. She tried to kick, realising she was used to alternating legs, and found with a tail she went nowhere. So she kicked together.

'Further,' he told her. 'You don't have knees now, so you can bend all the way forward.'

She watched as her legs bent unnaturally forwards, right past where they should have been able to go. She bent her merkin tail backwards and found she swished up towards the fading sunlight.

'This is amazing!' she admitted, thrilled to find it every bit the miracle she'd hoped it would be, and pushed and pushed against the water until she collided straight into the mud underneath.

Anaesu laughed, but helped her right herself up.

She had a very hard time steering, even with webbed hands, and was grateful Anaesu was happy to hold her hand and help her along. They were soon swimming along at an impressive pace, though the two professional soldiers seemed to be barely put out by the effort at all.

Soon her eyes adjusted to the strange darkness of the ocean. Little lights turned out to be flocks of glistening fish, and almost invisible lines in the water were actually giant hovering jellyfish. She realised she could see far further than with her usual eyes. Yet the others left little time to sightsee as they travelled along, the steward chatting business with the soldiers the entire way.

The water was getting deeper and deeper all the time. Soon she spotted some whales, far off in the distance. Shortly after, they came to a great fortress in the ocean. The ocean currents swam powerfully in an endless circle around it, and they had to fight them to carry on.

They were almost immediately greeted by a dozen armed soldiers, who floated to attention and saluted Anaesu's big brother as soon as they saw him. One of them talked to the grownups, and then Darissius turned to speak to her – she still held his little brother's hand. 'Fortune indeed; the high priest of the northern sea King is here to see you.'

Anaesu let go of her hand right away. When he spoke, it was with clear concern in his voice. 'What is that creature doing here?'

Darissius grinned. 'Not you, son of my father's second wife. Our guests.'

Anaesu's anxiety was catchy, and Kialessa offered him her hand again. He took it, and helped steer her on. She did not know who this "high priest" was, but she believed she would not need to fear anyone while the soldiers and steward swam nearby.

As they swam, she watched the bold merkin manning the battlements, mermen and merwomen pretending not to watch them as they swam between coral cliffs, between the watchful sites of enormous ballistae armed with sharp obsidian-tipped bolts.

She could not help but note that, should anyone wish harm upon the merkin, they would surely meet their deaths at this strong and well-defended fortress.

The Northern Sea King

The purpose of life is not to be happy, it's to feel like it has made a difference that we have lived at all.

Gundren Oakfellow, dwarven prince of the Eisenhügel.

They were led through the fortress, guards everywhere. It looked to Kialessa just like the barracks in the castle back home, only much larger. It was a small city, a citadel dedicated to defence from some foe. There were kitchens, and workshops. There were a few youths but no children, and she wondered to herself if perhaps they were being kept safe further down?

Darissius led them toward a large undersea hall, which might perhaps have served as a throne room should the King ever visit. It was large, far larger than any structure above the waters could dare support.

There was a simple yet intimidating throne, and beside it a creature. It looked like a cross between a merman and an octopus. Dark miasma surrounded the being, and Kialessa wasn't sure if it was her own misgivings or if a palpable sense of evil surrounded it; Anaesu was certainly very nervous.

The creature, which did have a face like a merman at least, swam closer. 'Don't worry, princeling, I won't hurt our visitors.' Its voice set her on edge. It sounded sincere, but she did not want to trust it. So, this was the sea King's high priest? Her previous confidence gave way to a tangible misgiving in the presence of this slimy, powerful creature, and the room fell completely silent when it spoke.

To her surprise, it was the steward who spoke next. 'Karnissis the wise, it is an honour to speak to you at last!'

The entity swam slowly toward them. It regarded the steward closely. 'You were but a boy when last we met, Grudon. And under such ironically similar circumstances!'

The steward bowed, and might have spoken, but it interrupted him. 'What a pity you changed so much!'

10 Karnissis, divinely chosen protector of the Merking

That might have bothered the steward, or alarmed him a little, but he bowed again. 'Your reputation for discernment and insight is truly well deserved, mighty Karnissis.'

The being laughed, not cruelly, but not kindly either. It sighed. 'I won't bore you with the details, Grudon. My King has long sought alliance with

174

the humans, this I am sure you already know. There have been some developments of late, however, that alarm him greatly. The goddess foresaw your arrival here and told me it would be a chance to speak you … *dust muckers*. I told my King, and he so kindly, ever so *thankfully*,' here the creature's voice was full of mockery, 'begged my indulgence to come and invite you personally to seek an audience with the only rightful King under the sea.'

The steward grinned. 'You were tasked the job of fetching us yourself.'

The being hissed.

The steward continued, 'And after prophesying our arrival too? Such a thankless task. I don't know how we will repay you, mighty Karnissis.'

The creature seemed amused, and swirled around the steward, 'Oh, there are often opportunities. And this!' Suddenly he swam right up to Kialessa, and it took her breath away. Which wasn't a very accurate statement – it was more like he smelt like old winterberries and the stench made the water in her gills hold still a moment, which was not nearly as poetic an expression. She decided to not get hung up on it.

The creature spoke, 'The halfling! Why Grudon, she has your mark written all over her. Does she know yet?'

The steward nodded.

'Two protectors for one King … not a good sign, not good at all.' He spoke now, right to her. 'Did you know, little one, that I am Mya's chosen to protect *my* King? Can you see it? No? I didn't think so. One must have the sight of a priest to see such trivial things. Mya is always so careful about who she chooses to stabilise governments and such. Your talents clearly lie elsewhere, I suspect.' Here he glared meaningfully at her hand, clutched tightly in Anaesu's hand, which still trembled. 'You know, you don't have to like the person you protect, little halfling,' he said to her, and she assumed by halfling he meant tae'anaryn. 'You don't have to like them at all. But you do have to *protect* them. And you do have to *obey* them.'

Suddenly Darissius lunged forward, spear drawn. When he spoke his voice was dangerous, but polite. 'Karnissis, were you not so vital to my father's life, I would end your bitter whinings this instant.'

'Easy, easy now, young prince.' The creature backed away. He seemed old, perhaps lame. 'I speak only the truth; you know I can do nothing else! I do not share his tastes; it is fair to say. I may not like the man, but I do *love* him. I can do nothing else.' He seemed contrite. Almost defeated. She had to wonder what strange history this creature held. Would he claim the King's throne in a heartbeat if given the chance? Or had he tried and failed so many times he'd given up? Or did he simply enjoy being wise and creepy?

Karnissis backed away, glancing at her as he did. She had the distinct impression that this was all some perverse test, just a monster observing the lives and emotions of the higher creatures he was made to serve. He did not want her pity, or kindness. He wanted everyone to fear him. It was as if he looked to create shadows and darkness in bright places just to find somewhere to hide in plain sight. His wilful unkindness puzzled her.

The "octo-kin" Karnissis spoke again, 'I have prepared the carriage. Grudon, my King would see you now, if that is convenient?'

The steward thought for a moment. 'I think it but three hours journey to the palace here, if I am right? Surely a half day to prepare ourselves would be wise?'

Karnissis scowled, but looked like he didn't care. 'Well said, dust mucker. Half a day to prepare yourself and the half-breed to meet the King. I will come for you when the sun's face is at its zenith; you can meet the King as the sun and moon stand aside each other in the sky. A precipitous moment for a precipitous beginning, don't you think?'

'Again, the mighty Karnissis speaks with unquenchable wisdom,' the steward bowed.

The creature seemed to approve of the steward's politeness, or fawning. 'So be it,' and it swam out the window in an instant.

The roomed seemed fairer without it.

Darissius snarled, 'Is it just me or does everyone else just want to hold their breath near that creature?' he remarked.

She wanted to agree, but decided it wiser to keep silent. Anaesu was holding her hand a lot less tightly now.

Darissius gestured to some guards near the door that Kialessa hadn't noticed, and two of them left quickly. 'Well, your clever keeper has won you a good half day to prepare. I suppose you have a plan, yes?' He turned to the steward.

Half a day was not long enough to absorb the rapid information dump the steward tried to unload on her in the next few hours. It seemed he knew an awful lot about merkin traditions and culture, some of which could have easily been shared at the college if they'd known about it. How to bow, how to sit. How to eat food that floated. There was a lot. They were taken to a large guest room, where some merladies tried to help her dress appropriately, which involved choosing some lovely clamshell bras that really deserved a lot more time.

The steward then began to launch into a comparative discourse of the seventeen nations northward, though she could only guess why. There were scores of names she needed to know from each of the powerful Kingdoms. How was she supposed to cram it all in in only a few hours, even with a magical headband!?

But she did her best. It seemed important to him.

Soon, two royal guards arrived with Anaesu, and they escorted them through the city. Outside they rode a royal carriage pulled by dolphins that whisked them through the water at incredible speed. The steward tried to continue his lecture but it was a loss now – there was so much to see! Her mind bubbled over with questions for Anaesu; what were those lights? How did the great sea whales breathe? There were houses and houses of

Choice, set free

merkin dwellings, all built within strong walls of stone and glass. Their culture was impressive, and would have to take up at least a quarter of the entire Shallowsea by her reckoning.

Too soon they found themselves entering the deeper, darker realms of the sea King's domain. Gold gilded buildings glittered in the pale light that filtered down to this level. Hulking guards and half-merkin, half-whale men greeted them with raised tridents and noble salutes. The entire ocean teemed with wonder and life and light.

They rode past an ancient amphitheatre with a golden throne, perhaps where the King would hold court for his entire nation? They headed instead toward a giant floating undersea barge, glittering with pearls and opalescent light. It was magnificent.

Karnissis soon joined them, holding a giant trident of pure gold. It was a wonder that he could lift it, and he seemed to be struggling. But no one dared help him. She recognised it as the token of the entire nation, the King's most prized possession. She could feel the raw power radiating from the trident, and dared not touch it for fear of her own life.

Within the giant floating barge were several large rooms, but she had no time to admire them. They headed straight for the largest at the front – a glass covered window in a pearl studded room, seashells and starfish encrusted in such organic patterns they must have been grown there.

And floating there, looking out the window, was a huge, muscular merman in the prime of life. He had a golden, floating beard and very long hair. He wore braces of gold and a girdle of red along his teal tail.

He regarded them only a moment before he swam up; his deep voice trembled the water all round her. 'Visitors from the surface world, I see!' He swam closer, and without effort took the trident from a bowing Karnissis and slung it over his shoulder. 'It's been too long! You must be Grudon, the steward of fair Lenmer'el, of which I have heard so much!'

The steward gave a very graceful underwater bow, 'Mighty King, I am honoured beyond words to finally meet you in person.'

The King nodded. Then he turned towards her. She had been quietly hoping he might just ignore her, but now his fierce, regal gaze was focused directly at her. 'And the halfling, as they have said. Greetings, little one. I trust you have found our cities pleasant to your eyes?'

'Y- yes, honoured King,' she stuttered, trying for an underwater curtsey. Despite practicing it successfully a dozen times already, she went too far over and struggled to right herself. She ignored the angry and frustrated glare the steward was no doubt giving her.

The sea King was grinning. 'Such a little one. Anaesu; son of my second wife, and you will speak for her?'

Anaesu replied with more fear in his voice than she expected a boy might have toward his father. 'I know her but one day, father, but her heart is pure as the daylight, I p- promise.'

The King gave him the same laugh, the kind of laugh he probably reserved for children. He looked at her a moment, as though thinking, then glanced at the steward. Then he swam away towards his window. 'Join me,' he commanded.

They swam up, which was tricky. The soldiers were very strong and tended to use all the water for themselves. But soon she and the steward floated next to the sea King, admiring his royal city within the ancient caldera that was buried deep in the Shallowsea. Outside the window, hundreds … no, thousands of soldiers paraded in silence. It was the royal army, yet not a hundredth the size of the entire sea King's forces, or so she had been told.

'It is fair, is it not?' he asked them.

'Such glory rivals even the glittering jewels of the High King's crown,' the steward fawned, with such sincerity in his voice she had to believe he actually meant it, though it surely was not the right thing to say if the High King himself had been in the room.

The sea King gave a gentle laugh. 'Indeed it is! Beauty and worth, each merkin a warrior of great skill and experience to set at odds the wiles of Pikal, and wisdom to read the mood of Waaglah herself.'

Again she thought it daring to compare himself to the gods, but she'd been told the merkin royalty were expected to speak like that. They had … different legends to attend to.

The sea King continued his speech: 'We are a mighty Kingdom, are we not, with treasures beyond your reckoning, land dwellers.' With a wave of his hand a wall fell down to reveal a room, a large room, filled to the roof with glittering treasures. Some were clearly from the troves of sunken ships, others the twisting metal sculptures of the merkin themselves. It easily rivalled all the treasures in all the land of Lenmer'el twice over.

He did not give them more than a few moments to admire it, but Kialessa was astonished. Such a show of force, of wealth and of power. 'But why do you show us these things, good King?' she asked.

She only barely caught a glimpse of the panicked and frightened face of the steward. Only then did she remember that she was supposed to wait on a King, to only speak as he gave her leave. But perhaps it was his friendliness, and the comfort she felt in his presence. Or perhaps the wiles of an unnamed god that gave her heart leave to speak for itself. Even so, her hands covered her mouth in fright.

He laughed, as she felt he would. 'No, I don't mind. It is an astute question from a clever mind, is it not?'

His guards agreed.

The steward visibly relaxed, as did Anaesu.

The King swam around so she could see better out the window, and his demeanour drew grim. His face was at her level now, and he put his arm over her shoulder when he spoke. His touch was warm, warmer than the sea, but gentle. 'Because we need allies, halfling. All this, our might, our wealth, our beauty, is threatened by the Twarnae; the shark men.'

At their name, the mood in the room became severe. The guard's faces tensed up as if with bitter memories.

The King continued: 'They are savage barbarians. Monsters. Monsters taming monsters, and hunting our people for brutality and sport. We slay any we find in our seas on sight, but they keep encroaching. Once, it was only in spring. Now, I hear, they have the audacity to hunt us in winter as well! We need to destroy their people from under the waves, and as Waaglah gives us this missive, I live to see it done.'

She gasped. She didn't mean to. To defend themselves was one thing, but to wipe out another sentient race? It was just like what the trolls were talking of doing last winter to all the humans. It did not seem to her like the right thing to do.

But then again, she had never met a sharkman, the Twarnae. Were they as wretched as the sea King felt? His Kingdom certainly was … glittery.

'Father,' Anaesu began.

'No son, I will hear no more of it. We have tried speaking to them, giving them gifts. They hear nothing of diplomacy, and certainly nothing of reason. We must force them from under the sea forever. Only then can we know the safety and peace the goddess intends for us.'

Kialessa was wise enough not to answer, for how could she counsel a King on an issue she knew nothing about, and for which his people had died? So she waited.

The King swirled up again in the water suddenly, his trident starting to glow. She swam backwards, its light somehow hurting her undersea skin with a power that felt a little like fire. The guards did not move, but the King took his trident away so it didn't hurt her anymore. 'And so, Grudon of Lenmer'el. You are here in answer to my people's most fervent prayer! I beg you to bear our message to the High King, and this document. We seek to open discourse with our far northern neighbours. Let us discuss trade, and diplomacy, and war!'

He held out a pearl scroll case which the steward took with great ceremony. 'I will make sure this reaches the King of Kings, personally,' the steward promised, his voice trembling.

The sea King nodded. 'Too long we have dwelt in our shallows. We seek to know the mind of the Kingdoms of men. Let us hear from them.'

The steward bowed again, 'And I, for my Kingdom, will send ambassadors to your seas before the season's end! This is a momentous day! A propitious day! A wonderful–'

He stopped at Karnissis's snarl.

The sea King laughed. 'We are all aware of your doubts, *protector*. This alliance will free us all in time, you will see.'

Karnissis slunk forwards, but still trembled on the floor. He spoke as if his words, though sincere, could get him in very big trouble. 'The men poison their waters, they snare our game … treachery and betrayal are their catchwords. We will not profit from this.'

The King glared at him, more puzzled than infuriated. 'And what would you have me do, Karnissis? Two towns razed. Seven more abandoned. We are at war, protector. Each must do his part.'

The abomination glanced at her once the sea King had said his piece. 'Yes, my King.'

The King gestured, and a guard brought up a small chest. 'Treasures. The smallest trinkets from our mighty treasuries. Let the High King consider my alliance. Our need … is great.'

The steward bowed gracefully, and spoke with devotion, 'I will do the utmost in my power to ensure the High King sides with your people against this injustice!'

Then the King looked down at her again, and a wry smile played at the corner of his lips. 'And, should your need prove great …' a merman brought him an ornate, jewelled seashell horn, adorned with ageless brass and pretty gems. 'Should your path be dire beyond all hope, and you need our deliverance to ensure this message and this treasure makes its way into the right hands, I give you this. It is one of our culture's most sacred treasures.'

Karnissis was glaring at them, a cunning look in his treacherous eyes.

The sea King continued. 'Simply activate this magical horn. It takes but a kiss, and the sound will summon to your aid an entire legion of my fiercest troops. We may help you but for one hour only. But if any impede your progress, I will be honoured to send my sons to assist you.'

The steward was gushing gratitude, while Kialessa stole a look at Anaesu's bigger brother and his mermen-at-arms. They both looked very serious, as though this was a solemn promise between nations. She smiled at Anaesu, and he snuck a little grin back at her. She sighed with relief – at least their tragic accident was going to be a blessing as well. To have the merkin by their side? What an advantage to enjoy while a dread assassin pursued them on the sea!

She held the horn; it was light in the water. She knew its power was great, but all power had limits. There seemed to be a special limit with this, and she knew it would only work once. She had to be very careful about using it at all. If she used it lightly it would offend the powerful sea King, or, worse, perhaps even put the merkin soldiers in danger. She decided there and then to not use it at all unless King Dunnkan or the steward told her to. It was simply too important.

Carefully she placed it back in her chest, via the shadow realm, grateful to see it still worked even though she was underwater, and the ship was so far away by now that she had no way to get there. She wondered if she could perhaps step all the way into the shadowrealm and back on board, but she knew she did not have enough power to do that yet, or maybe ever. It was just little trinkets from a little pocket dimension hidden somewhere in the nation far away. It would take an eclipse, or some very skilled wizardry, to give her that kind of power again.

The sea King nodded, and then turned away. 'Anaesu, come. Talk with me,' and with a flick of his hand he dismissed them all. Anaesu looked worried, and floated to his father's side. The sea King turned to look out his window, saying nothing more.

The steward hurried her outside. No one spoke until they were back at the carriages. All but two guards left them, and the wicked high priest.

Karnissis snarled at them. 'Well done, halfling. You played right into his story, didn't you? Left a nice, wide opening for his self-serving monologue.'

'You seemed impressed enough by it,' the steward spoke for her.

Karnissis pulled back, and grinned. 'What my liege says is true, we are at war. Have you had no inclination? No signs? You wanted to travel these waters, after all. You might as well know who owns them.'

The steward looked to argue, but held his tongue. It was probably something about who owns the air above the waters, which is where the boats predominantly travelled. But that was not the kind of argument to get into surrounded by merkin threatened by war.

Karnissis chuckled unkindly at the Steward, but grew serious again. 'What my King says is true. And the sharkmen are too dug into their waters to the north. Hidden in … shoals and crevices. We lose too much trying to dig them out. But I do believe that the King seeks to dissuade them more than annihilate them, and he hopes the magic and warriors of the High Kingdom will do just that. But I have no hope. We are too far away, and the sharkmen's waters lie between ours and the High Kingdom. It is not a convenient alliance for the High King to consider.'

The steward was silent as they alighted the carriage and prepared to move on. She tried to put as much distance between herself and whatever black goo Karnissis constantly emitted, but kept finding his tentacles winding their way around her tail fins as though he meant it. His touch was cold, like the sea.

She listened as the steward and protector engaged in a fairly in-depth discussion of politics and alliances, though she began to lose interest around the second hour. Their carriage raced along at impressive speed, and the soldiers must have been the elite of their kin to keep up.

Suddenly the carriage lurched. She almost fell right on top of Karnissis but one of his tentacles held her away. 'You'd best brace yourself, little one,' he said with a disconcerting, knowing smile. 'We are under attack.'

11 Imagination's Dawn, side view

Truevine

*If all I could hope for was to die with a good conscience that I had
done the humanly best I could just to help my fellow humanity, even
if I died on a dread assassin's blade, I would die peacefully.*
King Dunnkan, 314CY.

The water around them suddenly spun in a strange vortex. A moment later, the carriage struck the bottom of the sea, and Kialessa felt her gills burning painfully. Something unnatural was forcing itself into her body, and it was dry and hot and prickly. She gasped in the assault, when suddenly she realised she was breathing air again. She looked down, and sure enough, her legs were slowly forming from her tail.

She stood up, her leather armour forming around her body and legs, ready to get to the work on whatever had attacked them. The carriage was smashed and lay on its side on the wet stones, the dolphins long gone. Then she noticed the rushing sounds, like a waterfall, and gasped for fear as the water rushed around her, leaving a space of about twenty paces around. It looked like an arena, and the evening stars were clearly visible above.

She then heard a noise, and turned to see one of the mermen soldiers gasping for water. He was trying to edge himself toward the maelstrom wall. She dashed over to try to help him reach the lifesaving waters, but he was very heavy when surrounded by air.

Then she noticed the steward standing up, his official clothing forming around him from a magical ring. He looked grim.

'Help me!' she cried.

The steward looked around carefully, then leaped to her side. Together they started shoving the confused and suffocating soldier toward the wall.

'What about the other one?' the steward asked.

She looked up, and saw him almost in the middle of the arena. She was about to rush to his side, when a figure emerged from the far wall. It was a female, tall and pretty. She had antlers, and wore what looked like nothing more than leather, vines and leaves. The water parted before her as she drew twin scimitars from her back.

12 Truevine

Kialessa didn't have the chance to take another step when the woman waved her hand. In that instant, all the water drained from the struggling soldier's body, and he died pitifully right in front of her.

Choice, set free

Kialessa gasped. She turned around and found the steward shoving the remaining merman into the waters. He whispered something to the soldier that she could not hear in the thundering waters, and the merman fled at full pace. Then, wiping his hands, he walked back to stand in front of Kialessa. 'Well, well, well, Lady Truevine, we meet at last.' And he bowed.

She just stood there. Her eyes were dark and her features sharp; a pure blood elf, that was clear. She held herself high, bold and unafraid in the least. She folded her arms. 'Grudon. I cannot allow you to get that message to the High King at this time. And just for the tae'anaryn, I'm sorry, but I cannot allow either of you to get back to your King at all.'

The steward pulled his sharp, thin blade from its sheath. It was glowing blue, but soon adapted to a dire red shade.

Truevine looked a little worried now.

Kialessa took it as her cue to draw her weapon from the shadowrealm as well. The acid dagger was a small comfort in her hand, but she still doubted she'd get to use it against someone capable of controlling water like this. Her heart thundered in her ears, and she was afraid. But she had to do something.

The steward glared at the waters to the side. 'Well!' he roared.

Karnissis' snide voice echoed against the walls of roaring water around them. 'And interfere in Waaglah's test of the righteousness of my King's decree? Not a chance.'

'You'll tell him you barely escaped with your life,' the steward accused him.

Karnissis just laughed and drifted away into the water, presumably to watch the outcome of the battle from there.

The steward then turned, and whispered something to her: 'Not your knife, the whip,' he replied, but held out his hand as if to hide her behind him.

Kialessa nodded, and waited. If the whip was something that could stall or surprise Truevine, she thought she'd best keep it till the last moment.

The steward took the chance to step twice toward their adversary. 'So, we see you are working with the Dog now? Is that who holds the chain around the neck of the most powerful druidess this land has seen in a generation?'

Incredibly, she spat. 'I answer to no man.' The water whipped around them, sharp spats of water flying against her face and stinging Kialessa's.

The steward stepped again. 'And yet you serve the will of a rising tyrant. What did he promise you? The freedom you so claim to crave?'

Truevine looked angry now, and took a step toward them. 'I am always free! And I do not answer to him, or any man!' she threw her arms down, and the water and mud at the edges of their arena shot up into the air.

Kialessa had no idea what they were going to do against such power. The steward could probably best her if they were in a city. And if he had the rod.

As if on cue, in a glimmer of sparkle and hope, the rod of Lenmer'el appeared in his hand.

For a moment she was thrilled. Then panic filled her heart as she realised he had just drawn away the King's greatest protection. If the enemy was planning to strike, now would be the time.

'*Et num manus,*' the steward intoned, allowing the rod to touch Kialessa's shoulder. She understood in that moment that calling the rod to hand was a power that it possessed. And that power was named *Et num manus.*

She showed him her fear, but he seemed unconcerned. And, she reasoned, if he was the King's chosen protector, then he would know when to hold that rod, and when it was safer in the King's hand.

Or, at last, perhaps the others might finally know where they were and come to pick them up.

Grudon pushed against the wind and driving rain. 'You don't have to do this, Truevine! Those men deserved what they got from you, but you can still clear your name! Come with us to the court of the High King!'

'Nice try, Grudon,' she lectured him. 'But life, all life, is too fleeting for me to care. What are we, but a single drop in the ocean of destiny? Too soon we are gone, sunken back into the endless miasma of fate. People like you struggle, thinking you find happiness in simple pleasures or great works. But life, any life, was never about being *happy*. It is about making sure it *mattered* that you lived at all. And no one will ever forget the lesson I taught those men. I made a difference in the world, and even though people will forever curse my name, the world is a better place because of what I did.'

Grudon looked a bit shocked, and … pitiful, at what she had said.

Truevine continued: 'Such a brief chance to make a difference in the world, before fate requires you present yourself before your immortal judges.' She sighed, seeming devout, almost sincere. 'And for you, little child, that time is today.'

Suddenly a column of water struck the steward, and he fell to his knee. But the water sprayed up all around them, deflected against an impenetrable sphere that surrounded them.

'What?' shrieked Truevine, but it only took her a moment to recover.

Seaweed and lichen suddenly swelled around their feet, threatening to entangle them. But with a swift gesture, Grudon the steward dismissed the magic. Kialessa was impressed; she did not know he could do that. And it wasn't wizardry either; it was clearly an enchantment, which meant the part fey councillor was an enchanter as well, and she had never known it.

Then he charged Truevine in a smear of light in a way she'd never seen before. Great tusks like bone shot up from the ground to protect her, and the steward smashed them to dust with the rod. She lashed out against the steward with her scimitars, who fought against her with rod and sword.

Their fierce battle sent shockwaves through the ground. Grudon was moving fast, faster than she knew he could, backflipping and teleporting, or whatever it was. Truevine had no trouble keeping up, nature itself lashing against the steward and hampering his attacks. A moment later he had maneuvered her so that her back was turned to Kialessa. This was her moment.

Then he slipped to one knee on the mud.

Just as Truevine was about to leap forwards with a killing blow, Kialessa called the whip to her, and lashed out. It wrapped around Truevine's ankle at just the right point to trip her, but instead it felt to Kialessa as though she'd just caught hold of a tree trunk firmly stuck into the ground. The elf's leg didn't move at all, and Kialessa noticed how the mud rose up to make sure she was in contact with the ground at all times.

But the whip sizzled as powerful justice itself burnt the wicked druidess.

She glared at the whip, then at Kialessa. 'He gave this to *you!*' She seemed incensed. Faster than thought she struck out her hand at Kialessa, and a bright orange flame raced toward her.

She tried to dodge it, knowing she was immune to most kinds of fire, but not willing to test her limits, when a fist of water intervened and saved her. From deep within the water Karnissis laughed.

The whip unwound before Truevine could strike it, and the steward was on his feet in a moment. They stood to face her.

Then, with a sinister word, Truevine suppressed the powers of the whip and it fell to the ground, limp.

Kialessa was aghast, and reeled it in as fast as she could. How she hoped this was but a temporary setback!

'Enough,' Truevine shouted. Raising her hands, thunder rumbled in the sky. A white bolt of lightning raced down, but the steward magically deflected it entirely with his sword. He charged the druidess, but a moment later lightning tried to hit Kialessa as well. She barely dodged it, but was only mildly harmed by its power.

Truevine was really going hard at the steward, and he was struggling to keep dodging lightning. But the rod of the King was in its full power, bending space and raising an impenetrable shield to protect him.

But he stood alone, surrounded by a wall of thundering water. In the end it was not the lightning or Truevine's fevered attacks that stalled him, but a sinuous strand of seaweed that tripped him at her command. Truevine leaped forward and tried to cut off his hand, but her aim was poor. Even so, the rod fell from his grasp as her blade bit deep into his wrist, and he fell to the ground.

Kialessa screamed. There was nothing she could do now. Covered in mud and gasping for breath, she wondered if there was *anything* she could do against the powers a true master of nature.

Thunder rumbled in an unnatural storm as Truevine held out her sword point at his neck. She breathed heavily. 'You fought well, steward, but the line of your King will end with this generation. Now-'

Kialessa stared at the scene. Dark water thundered about them. The steward looked injured, and barely breathing, holding his partly severed hand in his other, both his weapons on the ground and out of reach.

Of reach …

Kialessa never gave Truevine the chance to finish. She reached out, and called the rod to her own hand with a whispered *Et num manus* drowned out by the thundering water. As the rod appeared in her hand, she felt its powers and prayers flow through her. Without knowing how, she smeared through the light and clobbered the druidess as hard as she possibly could on the side of her head.

The steward Lord Grudon stood, drawing healing from a healing stone and casting its dust aside. Then he grabbed the rod from Kialessa and picked up Truevine by her hair.

She was barely conscious. 'What? How?'

The steward pressed the rod against her forehead. 'You will leave off the pursuit of our King, and present yourself to the elf Queen for justice immediately.'

Kialessa recognised the power of the *Veridictus* immediately. It was a promise, and a curse. A powerful command she had to obey or suffer continuously until she did. The elf screamed, trying to force away the power. But the burning energy seared the symbol of the nation right into her forehead. The steward threw her on the ground, then moved to stand between Kialessa and the druidess.

Truevine laughed, but her power was gone. The waters fell silent, but still swung around them over the muddy ground like an unnatural wall. She glared at them. 'You think you've silenced me, and brought reprieve to yourself? You are a fool, Grudon.'

The steward smirked at her, raising the rod.

Truevine grunted as the symbol glowed in her forehead. He spoke: 'I grant you your life, for now. Begone.'

She glared at him, then glanced at Kialessa. Her face looked sad, betrayed. As though she'd been fighting all her life, and now faced an inevitable judgement. Then she disintegrated into autumn leaves.

Swiftly the waters gathered around their ankles.

'Let's go,' Lord Grudon told her, grabbing her hand. A moment later she felt the magic gathering around her as the King finally summoned his rod, and them, to his side. She only had a moment to look out and see Karnissis smirking at them through the water. He bowed, but said nothing, and she was gone before she could say a thing.

Destiny's Maw

*The courageous know no fear? No, that is a lie. To be courageous
is to feel that fear, and to do the right thing anyway!*
General Bon Sure'e, 314 CY.

The moment they arrived back on the deck of the Imagination's Dawn, the enormous ship rocked fiercely. Sailors ran about, trying to hold down rigging in the heaving waves.

'They're here!' the admiral shouted. 'Full about, NOW!'

Kialessa had to steady herself as the boat listed dangerously sideways. People ran to and fro in the gale. She felt a small nip at her elbow, and looked to see the easily recognisable shimmer of Wanderer. She was glad. 'So you've been waiting here for me too?' The dragon circled around her arm, then disappeared away somewhere. Kialessa was not concerned, she knew she would be safe. But she wasn't so sure about everyone else.

The general glared at Grudon, and spoke with wild disbelief. 'You're *alive!'*

'Apparently so,' the steward said grimly, and went to help.

Darrix cheered, and Kialessa turned to see him tying down rigging with Posk's help. Piex was there, drenched with sea water, magically hardening damaged balustrade. Toni was there too, pondering the entire scene with a detached curiosity, as if he was clueless as to how to help, or busy helping in ways no one could see. He had not tried to rescue her when she'd fallen overboard, but perhaps he was too far seeing for that.

The next moment Allastassia grabbed her hands. She looked worried, and had she been crying? There was no time to ask. The sky was dark but stars shone clearly, so why was the sea so rough?

'What's happening?' Kialessa shouted in the driving wind.

'Look!' Allastassia said, pointing in the direction in which they were now turning.

What Kialessa saw filled her heart with clear, present dread. It was a dark ship, proudly flying the red flag of the pirates. A certain, very real fear followed along with it. The boat was long, very long, with a single sail. It drove along behind them swiftly, honing in on the Dawn with predator-like passion. There looked to be oars, manned by at least a hundred rowers at each side. It was more than a pirate ship; it was a ship of war. The Edge and the Bounty raced to the left and right of the Dawn, both struggling in the strange winds that tore at the sea and kept the sky empty.

A sailor shouted, and Allastassia leapt to help her tie taught the mizzenmast with swiftly growing vines.

'It is the Destiny's Maw!' Aolith shouted to her.

For a moment the words made no sense to her.

But Piex knew. 'How? That pirate ship has not been sighted off the coast of Sanmar'el in a generation!'

'Well, she's here now!' Dale replied. He looked tired, but less afraid than the others. Kialessa did not know how long they'd been fighting the sea while she discussed politics over tea with a merking. The steward appeared to be conferring with the King, who was pausing from tying down rigging himself.

'The sea is troubled by her,' Natasha told them.

'A dire omen,' Federach said, not even clutching on to the banister as the boat rocked and rigging moaned.

'But she's supposed to be on the other side of the continent, a memory of children's tales!' Marchan confirmed.

Darrix nodded as the ship turned directly towards the Destiny's Maw and opened full sails to steer directly toward her. 'Yet here she is, in the hand of our mortal enemy.'

Kialessa turned to face the rapidly approaching pirate ship, and a dread rage filled her. She knew that feeling only in the presence of one being, one creature. It was the assassin.

They were a good half league away, but they watched the Edge turn sail as well. Kialessa grinned. This was going to be it. This was the moment they'd set sail for. Sailors cheered, though it might be their death today. This was the day they had prayed for: a chance to free their nation from the threat of a master assassin.

Suddenly a deadened fear settled on Kialessa's heart. Something was … wrong.

'Man your stations!' the high priestess shouted, the concern in her voice indicating the same misgiving had found its way to her heart as well.

Kialessa stared hard at the Destiny's Maw. The oars were retreating.

'She's pulling up oars!' the lookout shouted. Kialessa was momentarily impressed that anyone had the courage to weather this gale in the crow's nest.

The silence only lasted a moment. 'Full sails!' the King shouted, though they were running so already.

The steward sneered. 'What new devilry is this!'

Kialessa glared with the others. Destiny's Maw was changing. The oars were taken up; the mast was … shrinking? She warned the others, though they surely must have already known. Then the mighty pirate ship of legend turned east, towards the merchant hulk, the Bounty.

The Edge wasted no time, all thirty of its oars pressed against the water in double time. The priestess prayed, and while the sails did not slacken, no divine hand doubled their own progress. The Dawn was struggling upwind.

And the Maw was now pointed directly at the Bounty. It listed neither left, nor right. No sail it bore, nor oars touched the water. Yet it sped on, and seemed to be gaining speed. Then, unless her eyes deceived her, the Destiny's Maw's left and right banisters pulled up from the water and began to circle towards each other. Kialessa felt she could hear the creaking of the wood from here. But the Maw simply kept on changing shape.

'What's going on?' she wondered.

'I knew she was magical, but this is new,' Aolith muttered.

Then the banisters closed together above the boat, forming her into a strange, cylindrical …

'… Serpent!' Darrix realised. 'It's a giant sea serpent! The Destiny's Maw is a giant magical wooden sea serpent!'

Sailors doubled their efforts again, and the pace of the Edge picked up, though there was little they could do this far out but watch.

A moment later the transmuted Destiny's Maw dipped underneath the surface of the Bounteous Shallowsea.

The Bounty must have noticed the danger she was in. She had almost turned fully around.

But it was never going to be fast enough. Half a breath later, the entire Destiny's Maw emerged from the sea to block her retreat, a gargantuan serpent of wood and fear. Somehow, the boat put its head back, and roared as lightning danced in the starlit sky.

Suddenly, as though reminded of its own purpose by the magical noise, the Dawn leapt forwards. The sails fell numb as the Imagination's Dawn torn through the sea at mystical haste, driven as though pushed by some unseen god's hand.

But they were still too far out. Kialessa could only watch in horror as the giant sea serpent began to wrap itself around the other boat. Sailors and merchants risked nothing more, but threw themselves bodily overboard to the mercy of a churning sea.

Then the howling wind died, the echoing thunder ceased. In the appalling silence the creaking, grinding, dying echoes of the Bounty were clearly audible. People were screaming, and there was nothing they could do to help.

Desperately she looked over to her King, the concern and pain evident on his face. She begged him with her eyes for leave to go over there. But he shook his head fiercely. There was no safety in a tactic their enemy could have prepared for.

Again the Dawn surged forwards, and she almost fell over backwards. But the pace then slowed. There was nothing they could do now.

Within only a moment the Maw had entirely encased the Bounty in a triple twist of its hardwood coils. There was a gentle creaking, followed by a violent crack as the serpent split an entire ship in two.

Ballista bolts from the Edge fell short, but the serpent did not wait to test that threat. Nor did it stop to finish its work of death, but with another impossible screech that tore at Kialessa's compassion and made her heart hurt, the wooden monstrosity slunk under the waters.

'Full pace towards the survivors!' the King called.

'She's heading this way!' the lookout cried in alarm.

Kialessa armed herself again. So this was it? What were they going to do? Surely the King had planned for every threat imaginable, but for this? A legendary boat lost to time that should not even be on this side of the continent?

He looked worried, as though this was not the kind of threat he had been expecting.

Sailors had thrown themselves to the deck, drawing weapons and praying fervently. The ship suddenly swayed to one side, and Kialessa got a clear view of the oncoming unnatural monster. The sea bulged as the Destiny's Maw, the greatest sea serpent of legend, ploughed on toward them.

People screamed.

'Enough! Stay your fears for the pirates you send unprepared to meet their gods today,' the steward's voice held a magic of its own, clearly a powerful enchantment. 'On your feet. To arms, to arms!' It seemed few sailors needed convincing to fight, but they all needed the power to do so courageously, and the steward held that power. An enchanter – Kialessa would never have guessed.

The sea slackened as the beast swam about. She ran to the edge of the Dawn and looked out. The sea moved about, tilting the deck. The Destiny's Maw swam about them slowly, from half an arrow's flight out. Kialessa was horrified at its sheer size. It seemed simply unimpeded by the water in away way, though it should have been a boat full of air. They could have shot at it, but there was little they could do effectively while it hid under the water.

Then the submerged monstrosity turned slowly, and swam towards the Dawn. Kialessa prepared herself with all the others for a jarring collision, but, instead, the Destiny's Maw collided with an *Impenetrabilis* that the King conjured to protect the ship. There was a dim ringing sound.

Oddly, the strange blend of boat and monster chose not to contest that power further, and began to swim away.

'Come back, you coward!' the general screamed.

Sailors jeered the serpent. But it did not heed any of them. Turning quickly from the path of the Edge, it disappeared into the depths of the sea. Her heart sank, as battle today felt far better than several more weeks of waiting. Why had the enemy been driven off so quickly?

A sudden slithering took place around her arm, but her momentary shock was displaced as she realised it was the invisible Wanderer, who started purring almost immediately. She knew they were safe now.

She looked for Toni, but he seemed to be stuck in his distant thoughts. Then he spoke: 'Why couldn't the pirate play cards?'

'Oh no,' she feared another joke was percolating.

'Because the captain was standing on the *deck.*'

Despite herself, and all the threat, she had to chuckle about that. 'Why didn't you help us?' she asked.

He seemed lost for words. 'I did. I mean, I wanted to …'

She left him to his confused thoughts as they raced to help the survivors.

'At least we didn't seem to lose anyone here,' she muttered to herself, wishing the boat was a lot faster just right now. But the survivors had plenty of flotsam to hold on to, and they were helping each other.

'Ah, about that,' the admiral grinned before replying. 'Seems Ginger doesn't like the Dawn any more, he jumped overboard! We fished him out, but I think we'll put him on the Edge as now.' He sighed. 'We still got Socks, but I'm at a loss to explain where all the ship's rats seem to have gotten to.'

Kialessa thought she might have an idea, but no one asked her about it. Soon they arrived to help the struggling passengers in the water.

'Divide the survivors fairly amongst the surviving ships!' the King shouted.

Rope ladders were lowered, sailors helping people onto the boats while soldiers stood with weapons drawn. The Edge soon drew alongside the Dawn, and Kialessa was impressed at the military boat's height. Its double hull was twice the strength and thickness of that of the Dawn, its great ram glistening in the water.

'Hey, hey, little one!' a vaguely familiar voice called. 'Let down a ladder, will you kindly please?'

Kialessa looked down with a start, for there, waving his hand up towards her from the water, was Darrix's father.

To The Shallows

The wizard sighed, 'Sadly, we have not found that to be the case.
*Some must **make** their mistakes before they learn from them.'*
Recollections of the tae'anaryl.

Kialessa handed out hot mugs of steaming stew to the shivering survivors on deck. They thanked her, and smiled.

Soon she came to the man by whom Darrix stood like a soldier on guard. Harrobar Minerson, his father, was talking. The older man's deep voice carried far across the deck. 'We thought we'd escaped their notice when Destiny's Maw came between us and the Edge and headed straight towards the Dawn here.' He coughed; Darrix rubbed his father's back. The older man shrugged him off. 'Can't have every prayer answered at once.' He spoke an old saying, pushing his son's helping hand away again. 'Guess something happened, and they decided to take out the Bounty instead.'

'That happening was the return of my chosen protector and his apprentice, I hasten to add,' the King informed him. No one interrupted.

Darrix's father nodded, 'And fortune it was, since I suppose none might have survived at all had you not put to flight such demonry. We owe you our lives, my King.'

The King did not reply, and Kialessa wasn't sure if he was bothered by Darrix's father's quick attempt at flattery, or if he actually agreed.

Allastassia was checking on the injured, and spoke to Darrix's father. 'I'm sure we will recover the merchandise, my lord,' Allastassia said. No one was sure of Harrobar Minerson's proper title. Technically, it was 'gentle', as for any of the common folk. But he was perhaps the richest merchant in Lenmer'el since the fall of the Djinn, and his youngest son a paladin's squire. He seemed rising nobility to most, and certainly spoke like one. Their nation was still not sure of what to make of the rising merchant lords.

Darrix's father waved her aside. 'Never fear, little dryad. They are but trinkets. The value of our lives far exceeds the fine furs and dainty trinkets of Lenmer'el, I can assure you.' He shivered in the night cold, 'Here,' he said, raising the mug of stew she gave him. 'To the health of our King!'

'To the King!' many shouted, raising their improvised toast.

King Dunnkan smiled, and nodded. Without another word he left for his cabin, hidden somewhere on the boat.

'We have dishonoured him, failing to destroy the Maw,' Piex worried.

Harrobar, who seemed to command most of the attention that night, disagreed. 'We weren't ready. We are now. I am sure the assassin is growing impatient; attacking a helpless merchant caravel is poor compensation when you pursue a King.'

Darrix agreed. 'Still, we'd best be on guard.'

His dad looked around with a grin. 'Plenty on guard here, it seems.'

'You will be crowded,' Natasha told Darrix's father. 'There is no room in the servant's quarters, and you may have to sleep in shifts.'

Harrobar smiled at her, and rising, gave Kialessa a pat on the shoulder. 'And what of it, when we have such fine company to keep!'

Kialessa wasn't so sure. Much food had perished on the Bounty, and many more mouths to feed had arrived here.

He looked at her. 'We have far greater treasures to keep safe, right here,' he said, patting his chest pocket, and for just a moment she had to wonder if he meant the hearts of his friends, or something he held inside his pocket.

***

The new dawn came swiftly. They rode close to the shallows now. It meant their way was slower against the curve of the shore and endless shore breezes, which sometimes did not help. But they knew the nature of their enemy, the boat the Dog was using: a pirate ship of legend.

Kialessa had given the King and his councillors her full report that morning, and now her best friends, and new friend Toni, insisted on hearing it all again. All while Wanderer curled around her ankle's unseen and unnoticed by anyone else.

'Gills? Understandable,' Toni reported of his own experience, 'but why not take live air directly from the water, thus maintain the integrity of a hardened skin without the burden of exposing organs to the outside environment? Eyes, I can understand. But the breathing apparatus? Curious.'

She did not ask him what he meant.

Two more weeks slid quickly by without incident. The crews worked together as best they could, some of the merchants taking to fishing all day from the rear of the Dawn. Food was not running low, but variety was. And the sagemaster refused the general's repeated requests to teleport him back to anywhere for supplies. No one would seriously risk leaving the King so undefended during this dangerous journey, and the King refused to leave everyone else to danger by leaving without them.

But their enemy seemed content to wait. A storm came and went; a large pod of whales was seen heading out towards the south. Piex set fire to the rigging twice, trying to master his legendary *conflagration*, to no avail. Toni went about asking everyone what they were doing, and why, interspaced with some genuinely witty attempts at humour, as well as some genuinely… not so witty attempts.

Wanderer turned up twice more, always invisible, simply to keep her company it would seem. Kialessa had to wonder if the dragon wasn't there all the time, so she left out little morsels of food, which occasionally disappeared – thought it might have been Socks. But Wanderer never came when called, or if she did, Kialessa could not see her. Socks did seem a little more nervous, now that she thought about it. It made her wonder if they were getting along, or not.

She went to find Piex, and found him repairing some ropes with magic. 'Hey, there,' she said. 'I have a question.'

'Ask on,' he replied.

'Who do you think would win in a battle between a fey shoulder dragon and a cat?'

He paused, but it was the admiral who replied. Kialessa hadn't even noticed him nearby. 'You think a dragon, hands down, wouldn't ya? Cat's can't fly or breath fire, right? But those cats is lucky as the gods themselves, else why they always land on their feet? And it is said,' he whispered, 'they guard the lands of the dead, walk'n' as easy into other realms as effortlessly as you walk through a doorway …'

That, Kialessa could readily believe. Especially of Socks.

The admiral continued, 'So I reckon a cat'd take a dragon, 'specially if it was one of those li'l ones.'

'How about one the same size or so?' Kialessa indicated with her hands.

'Cats is more patient too, and tough as any human ever was … I'd give Socks here a 50/50. Be smarter to make them friends though, no?'

'Yes, I think I would prefer that tactic,' Kialessa agreed. If she had not felt the niggling threat of a master assassin every waking hour, Kialessa would be having a simply delightful voyage.

She began to wonder if the master assassin hadn't lost his best and perhaps only chance.

***

The night was late, and Kialessa was grateful her tasks at wizard studies were almost done. Toni did not often come to wizard studies, but seemed to prefer to sit in the front of the boat, staring away into the distance as if trying to read the minds of everyone in the nation or something. He was often silent, and isolated. He tried a new joke at least once a day, but his questions grew steadily more complex, though there were less of them.

Still, she knew it was him again as soon as he knocked on the door to the wizard's room.

The sagemaster's face brightened, and she could not help but smile at him.

A sailor went to open the door for the pale boy.

He walked in and gave a graceful bow. 'If I may, honoured gentle, I have another question I am quite lost at answering?'

'Say on,' the wizard said, getting comfortable. Most of the room carried on with their tasks.

'What is it that you teach your children about death in this world?'

And that was when all the other tasks in the room stopped.

The wizard paused as if to gather his thoughts a moment. Then he sighed, and asked, 'What have you learnt?'

Toni gave them a gentle smile. 'You are taught that when you die, your spirit leaves your body and must travel through the afterlife. You teach that there are seven different heavens preserved by the seven elder gods. You teach that if a spirit is strong in faith and goodness, they may journey to the various homes of the seven Elder gods, and present themselves there as servants for eternity. It is there that they are happy, and may rest.'

He paused, then continued: 'However, if a soul is evil, still bound by the addictions of this life, then they must travel through the hells. You teach that there are nine levels to the hells, each more dangerous and addictive than the last. Should any soul pass beyond the ninth door in the afterlife,

into the proverbial tenth hell, their spirits are never heard from again –
presumably, lost for all eternity.'

'You speak the truth,' the sagemaster nodded.

Toni continued: 'You believe that, when a soul dies, its spirit is
separated from its physical, corporeal form. Yet if that soul is strong
enough, it may return to that body and bring it back to life. It has three days
to achieve this, as no soul known is to return to life beyond dawn on the
third day without the most exquisite of sacrifice. Yet death is not, of
necessity, a permanent thing in this world.'

'Excellent,' the sage returned, 'but may I add one thought? We have
learned that those who die before their time; of old age, often find
themselves in the hells, whether they belong there or not. And we have
often found that those who are eviller, or who die a more painful or tragic
death, find themselves further and further into the afterlife of the dammed.
It makes the journey back to the mortal realm to reclaim their body, or even
to ascend to the thrones of the gods, just that much more difficult.'

'Hence,' Toni agreed, 'upon your worst foes you wish the most cruel
and painful of deaths.'

'Yes, indeed,' the wizard said, his face severe. 'Hanging, for instance,
almost always sends one to the fourth layer of the hells. Thus, such a fate
awaits all found guilty of murder in this world.'

Toni nodded. 'Yet even those so slain may return to life.'

The sagemaster agreed. 'And we take such to mean they were innocent
of their crime, in some manner. Or at least that they have obtained a partial
if not complete forgiveness by the gods of such a sin, for only they can
rightly judge such.'

Then Toni looked confused. 'Then why slay such at all? Does it not
make more sense to converse with them, to try and talk them out of their
course of action? Surely such would-be murderers can be reasoned with!
Have they no insight into the value of even a simple life?'

The wizard sighed. 'Sadly, we have not found that to be the case. Some must make their mistakes before they learn from them.'

Toni looked confused. 'Truevine hunted for vengeance, Brandish for sport. Tobiuus to establish his superiority. Yet the assassin seeks some prize I do not fully understand. It is as though he seeks to serve one who strives for power by silencing voices that do not agree with his own convictions. Yet it is clear that death will not achieve this for him. It is a paradox I do not, as yet understand.' And he sat there, being sad Toni, for the rest of wizard studies that night and the next.

***

Kialessa shuddered in the cold that evening as she went to retire, swiftly changing out for her eternally warm night dress. The night was dark, which meant Kialessa could see everything perfectly, while the humans stumbled about and lit extra lanterns on deck. Thick, low clouds hung in the sky between the moon and the sea, while a stiff breeze hurried them along. She made for the hessian sheets that were her bed, three bunks high in the overcrowded hull. Dust floated down from the sailor who had the bunk above, but Kialessa was careful to not sneeze. For if she did, she might just lurch her head forward enough to poke the sailor with her horns, and she was not willing to do that – at least, not any more than once in the journey.

The headband was in downtime, but still she found her mind wide awake. She tried to remember the times tables Piex taught her, because that always seemed to put her to sleep. But it didn't work. She hummed the songs from Allastassia's play last year, since the boat was so noisy all the time it was impossible to be bothered by a little extra noise. But it didn't seem to work either.

So she put her hands behind her head, sighed, and stretched out.

Perhaps she would go for a walk? But that was dangerous. The humans were already nervous, and the deck didn't need any more dark shadows for them to fear.

Then she heard a noise. It was a scratching. But it was coming from outside the boat. Had that been what was keeping her awake? Was it coming from the hull, or above? She could not tell.

It came again. She sighed.

Then louder.

She shook her head. Was she supposed to go out and find what was bothering her? What if it was something dangerous? What if it woke up someone else?

Then it tapped a strange, deliberate tapping.

That was weird, Kialessa thought. She looked around. No one else seemed to have noticed. Wanderer, perhaps?

Then it tapped, again. Almost a rhythm. *Definitely not Wanderer.* Something was trying to get her attention.

Quickly, she slid out of bed in almost perfect silence. No one seemed to notice.

She was near the fore hatch, which meant the sound was coming from somewhere at the front of the boat. They kept her and the others near the hatch in case there was trouble. But Kialessa had ways of getting around that others didn't. Shadowstepping wasn't exactly silent work, but she'd never been deliberately silent about it.

Then she stopped. What if it was something that wanted to harm her? But there were guards on deck, and she could alert them.

Then she felt a bit silly about it. Things scratched about the boat a lot, from the rats that hid in the bilge deck, to the beaked fish that fed on the barnacles. There was no sense in waking anyone up for a nothing.

But then again …

As silently as she could, she shadowstepped up onto the deck. The breeze was cool and unpleasant. She did not want to spend long here.

The lanterns swung in the night wind, the sails thumped in the breeze.

She looked toward where the sound was coming from, and noticed a sailor lying down. Then another one, unmoving and unconscious.

And there, crouched on the stern as though he didn't have a care in the world, was Jerik, would be "assassin of Kings".

Just as she was about to move, he hushed her.

She froze. There, chained to the deck, was Darrix. He was sweating and struggling, but could not move against the taught ropes that held him. She'd never even heard him somehow capture Darrix from below deck. 'Put up a good struggle, you know. Can't waste talent like this.' A moment later Jerik's knife appeared in his hand, and he dangled it down towards Darrix's throat. The young man pulled away.

Kialessa stood at ease, yet her breath caught in her throat. She desperately wanted to scream, to warn them all. But then the assassin would just stab Darrix and fade away in sand like he always did. How had he overcome the night watch so easily? Where were the King's guard when she needed them?

Jerik chuckled. 'They're not making this very easy, are they little one? Traveling in their might and power with only a glimmer of vulnerability, hoping to draw us out.' He sighed. 'I'm beginning to fear I may fail my dread master a second time.'

She glared at him, hoping very much that was exactly what would happen. Should she talk to him? Would there be some alarm or misgiving that might warn one of the others? Might she reveal some tactic he held?

'I bet everyone assumed the steward was going to die when fate took you both to meet the mermaids,' Jerik chuckled. 'Shows how stupid they all are.'

She glared at him, desperate to be holding the pommel of her whip. If she needed to use it, she would have to be very, very quick.

Choice, set free

'You're very tense, you know that?' Jerik said, standing up with precision balance on the gently heaving balustrade. 'Slows your reaction time. You gotta … loosen up a bit.'

Darrix said nothing, but kept working his bonds.

Jerik grinned, as if he was still waiting for her to actually say something. 'So who's your new friend, Kia? The blond boy with freaky eyes. A missing prophet perhaps? That was Tobiuus's theory. Truevine preferred the morphed silver dragon theory. I must say how very *angry* I am at Grudon for dismissing her. But Brandish, he's still the smartest, I say; wanted to withhold judgement until he cuts the boy in half.' Jerik chuckled.

'What are you here for?' she asked the assassin.

He grinned. 'Just, catching some night air, I suppose!' he leapt down in front of Darrix, his feet making almost no sound as he touched the deck, and then leant up on the rigging. 'But I suppose if I can take out the King's royal – albeit backup – protector, it might do me some good. So I suppose this is goodbye, little Kialessa. It has been a disappointment knowing you.'

He toyed with his knife, as if waiting.

Kialessa turned and looked at Darrix. He was struggling, his hands making their way to his belt. He was reaching for his father's knife.

Yet it all seemed a little wrong. Darrix wasn't the kind to stab an assassin in the back. He was patient. He was prayerful. He would usually be calmly praying right now.

Then she saw it – the glimmer in the night, the fake twisting of the ropes. This was just an illusion. Jerik was just waiting for her to act so he could find an opening, and an excuse, to cut her down.

The instant Kialessa realised that she summoned her armour and her whip. It burst into white flame around her, lighting up the deck fairly well, melting away the illusion the assassin had created. Then she shrieked, something she was very good at. Every living creature on both boats would be awake by now. Voices could be heard. Then the sailor in the nest rang the alarm bell.

Jerik put his palm up to his forehead and sighed. 'I was hoping-'

He was cut off by an authoritative voice, 'Fall to your knees, assassin!'

Kialessa turned, and saw the high priestess standing, unnoticed, by the port rigging. Had she been there this whole time?

Then Kialessa staggered as the force of the priestess's will swept past her.

Jerik never stood a chance. He fell to both knees and his hands hit the deck.

The priestess stepped forwards, golden manacles in her hands ready to bind him.

But the assassin was fast, inhumanly fast. In the next moment, he shapeshifted into a dog – the large greyhound he was the first time he'd tried to kill her.

Two sailors, whom Kialessa had no idea were hiding nearby, were on him in a moment. The priestess threw them the manacles, and they struggled to bind him.

Yet it seemed he was even better at fighting as a dog than as a human. They grappled with him a moment, but, becoming sand, he escaped their clutches.

'Hold!' the priestess demanded, and for a moment it looked like she had succeeded.

But then the mini sandstorm broke free, and in an instant he was a dog again. He charged toward Kialessa, but she brandished her dagger, and Jerik looked unwilling to face it again. So, instead, he charged the priestess herself.

The old dwarven lady swiped at him with her mace, but he narrowly dodged it and lunged at her. She cried out as the dog clamped his teeth down on her armoured forearm. It could not have penetrated the chainmail, but the priestess cried out as if it had.

Several bolts imbedded themselves in the deck as sailors on watch had finally been made aware of the situation. Someone launched a *magus spherae*, and Jerik yelped as the magical energies discharged into his flank.

The priestess threw him loose and clobbered him with her mace. It should have broken several ribs but he leapt away as though it was merely a painful scratch.

Armed sailors poured on deck.

The dog stepped backwards and the entire deck lit up by some magical command. Then he backflipped towards the foredeck by the mizzenmast, turning back into a human as he did. 'Well,' Jerik admitted with a grin, 'this isn't going as planned!' He laughed.

For a moment the attackers paused.

Then, with a bow, he floated away in a sandy mist. Several people tried to stop him, but arrows were useless.

The next thing Kialessa knew, Piex was standing beside her. He looked like he was concentrating, '$4\pi r$ ... carry the three ... Serros at 70 degrees below the horizon ... Oh, it's just too complicated!' He looked apologetic.

Allastassia threw lightning at the retreating sandstorm, but it merely cringed, then disappeared from their view.

'Good work, everyone!' the King said with a broad grin. 'We drove him off the ship!'

Everyone cheered, but then Kialessa noticed Darrix seemed preoccupied. She ran to his side; he was helping the old dwarven high priestess from the deck. Her face was pale.

'What is it, what's wrong?' Kialessa asked, perhaps a little too loudly. Everyone stopped.

'It burns, like fire,' the priestess confessed.

Everyone gathered around. The bite had torn clean through her steel chainmail, and red and sore skin was clearly apparent.

She held out her arm for Darrix to bless it, and the swelling died back.

But he did not look pleased. 'I fear my faith has failed you, my mentor,' he whispered.

The King and the steward pushed their way to the front, studying the wound with great intention.

'Could it really be a toxin of such potency that even the Eternal's light cannot right it?' the steward muttered.

'Maybe there is some devilry in the wound?' the King suggested, as people circled their hearts at the suggestion.

'No,' Toni informed them. His word seemed to carry a kind of mental power and authority, if it were possible. Everyone stopped.

He walked calmly through the crowd and stepped up to the wound. 'Darrix, your prayer was highly effective, but the cause of the toxins remains. They're animals, too small to see. Single units. I have witnessed this before, but never at this steep an exponential rate. Also, they do not necrotise the flesh, but repurpose it. Fascinating, simply intriguing,' Toni mused, glaring at the wound in rapt attention, while moving his hands as though feeling the air around the wound in some mystical manner.

'And?' the steward demanded.

'And,' Toni stated with the most detached curiosity, 'I would say you have three days to live, honoured priestess.'

People gasped; several sailors swore.

'A *disease*,' the priestess explained.

Then people stood back.

She shook her head. 'We now know at least one thing for certain.'

'The assassin is, indeed, a were-dog?' the steward finished for her.

Now everyone stood well back, except the King and the steward. Darrix pulled Kialessa away, and dragged Toni with them.

The priestess did not look concerned, not at all. 'Lycanthropy. Curious how it spreads so quickly!'

The King gestured to the wizard, who it seemed had only just been awoken. 'Get her home.'

'No,' the priestess disagreed. Then, apologising to the King, she stated, 'This is beyond our skill. I will need to be taken to the Medicarium at Emerel to appeal to Lumos herself. There is no other way to assure my healing.'

The King looked at her with a deep frown, but nodded.

The wizard took the priestess's uninjured arm, and the steward looked meaningfully at the King.

So the King spoke: 'Well, let us hope the assassin sees this as his chance to attack again tonight!' Sailors took it as their chance to cheer. They armed weapons and looked ready.

Again, the wizard, sagemaster Coure De'Feur, wove his teleportation incantation. In a small thud of air and twingle of magic, they were gone.

Toni looked at the place they once stood with intense fascination. He turned to grin at her, 'When is a sailor not a sailor?'

She realised it was about time for his daily joke.

'When he's aboard.'

She couldn't help but snicker. That was actually fairly witty.

'Keep alert, you two,' Darrix told them, looking more than a little annoyed. 'If the assassin returns, we need to be ready for him.'

'Right,' Kialessa agreed, and went to give her report to the steward and the King. 'We'll be ready for him when he comes back.'

But, naturally, the cowardly assassin did not return that night, or the next day, as the Imagination's Dawn slipped quietly across the heedless waves.

The Sharkmen

When all seems grim, remember, look for allies in the most unlikely of places.

Nemon, 3rd Sage of Lumos, keeper of Times.

The lookout sounded the alarm. It was late on the second day after the attack. Armed soldiers' thundering footprints headed up to the deck, the merchants and travellers heading below.

'What is it?' the steward shouted.

'Merkin, and they surround us at a distance!' the lookout replied.

Kialessa studied the far waters with great intensity, but it was impossible to see that far.

The priestess then held up and orb, and it floated above her hand. In a moment it had projected a glowing image of the water far away. Perhaps one of them sensed the sensor, or perhaps they were just very lucky, but suddenly an individual lurched itself out of the water and gazed intently toward the Dawn. The creature had legs and arms like a human man, but the head and skin of a great, grey shark. His hundreds of teeth were bared, and he carried a pair of sharp, hooked spears.

The image sent a shockwave of concern and fear through the assembled soldiers. They ran to man the ballistae, loading deadly bolts of iron. The others took up their bows, while the admiral had to organise several others to arm themselves with spears and head below deck, in case the sharkmen attacked from that way.

The admiral scowled. 'Trust that cowardly assassin to side with the sharkmen monsters!'

Kialessa wasn't sure which way to head, there was such a panic on deck, so she just tried to keep out of the way against the balustrade. Then she noticed the King, standing calmly next to the steward. They didn't seem bothered at all.

Lord Grudon tapped the rod on the deck, so very gently, yet it brought everyone to a standstill. 'Let us first see what they want.' He seemed to be talking just to the King.

King Dunnkan paused. 'You know the legends as well as I, of the bestiality of the sharkmen. But perhaps these are, indeed, the idle tales of sailors?'

They looked over at the admiral, who was manning the till, trying desperately to find a way out of the circling sharkmen. 'Ain't naught but tales of death and savagery to all who pass their waters,' he told them.

'As I understand,' the steward told them, loud enough for all to hear his calm and steady voice, 'they and the merkin measure their territories by the temperature of the water, more or less. As winter ends, the merkin press against their borders, forcing them back beyond this point and nearer Emerel. I would be surprised if they would send a force to attack anyone this far east so near springtime.'

Most did not seem convinced, and few seemed to understand what he was talking about.

'Then why do they send so many?' the admiral retorted.

'They are far from their waters,' the steward replied with casual grace, standing towards the prow of the boat. 'They seek protection in numbers in waters that are not theirs this time of year. If they've only come to talk, I imagine they will send a messenger over shortly.'

Everyone looked out, Piex sending his sensor widely abreast. Soon the lookout called, and it was possible to see two wake lines heading gently toward the Dawn.

The steward grinned at the admiral, who with a derisive snort ordered, 'At ease ... but stay alert!'

***

Soon the two individuals came up along the side of the boat, on the side where the Edge wasn't anchored. Kialessa and the other young ones were told to hold back, and she couldn't see. A strange voice shouted in a thick accented version of Emerellian that Kialessa had not heard before, requesting permission to come aboard.

The King granted the permission.

There was a moment of silence, then a loud splash as two sharkmen somehow propelled themselves out of the water and onto the deck of the ship.

Kialessa was amazed. They were men, but sharks. Their heads were sharklike, their eyes dark, threatening orbs. Their bodies were muscular, their hands and feet webbed. They stood a little uneasily, as though standing upright was unfamiliar or uncomfortable for them. The first was huge, even for a man, with dark markings like tattoos across his arms, face and chest. The second was smaller, with a gleaming golden shell necklace and subtle golden crown, and he bore within himself a princely importance that made her suspect he was royalty.

The two sharkmen stared back at the humans and their allies for a good moment.

The steward stepped forward, brushing away the drips of water that had landed on his clothes from the sharkmen's rather impressive entrance. 'Ambassadors of the King of sharks, we welcome you to the Imagination's Dawn, vessel of honour of King Dunnkan, King of Lenmer'el and–'

'Your vessel smells of burnt olthar and tears,' the giant complained. He coughed, and took a swig of water from the vessel he carried, allowing the water to flow out over his gills and down his body. 'Urgh!'

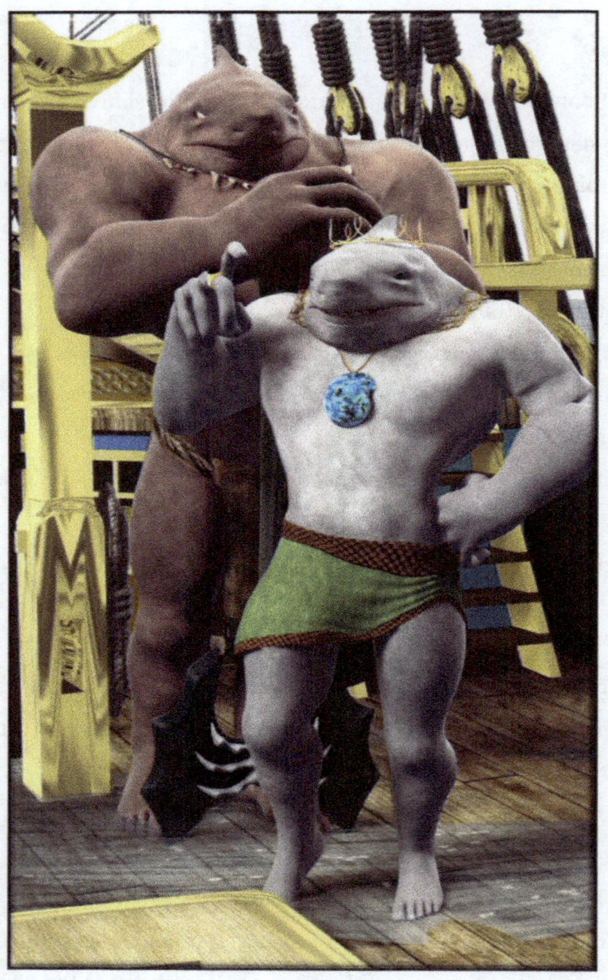

13 Prince of the Northern Waters

The younger sharkman stepped forwards, but his steps came uneasily, as though the wood itself were sharp rocks to his flippers, feet, things. 'Forgive my bodyguard's rudeness,' he said, with a polite bow and a far more polished accent. 'Oversea is not a place we are comfortable with, at least not until after many nights.'

The steward did not seem bothered, but King Dunnkan didn't look impressed.

The steward continued the introductions, and the younger sharkman soon waved him to silence. 'I am Prince Anaxarides, of the Raizen tribe, second to my father's throne. You have too many names and I cannot hope to remember them all! Please, our missive is just to your King.'

Again the steward smiled, the picture of diplomacy itself. 'As you wish, wise Prince Anaxarides. You may speak to the King through me. What missive is so important that the King of all sharks would send messages to our humble trading vessel, so far from your sacred waters at this time of year?'

Kialessa knew the steward was just pointing out that they weren't in the sharkmen's waters, probably hoping to ensure no conflict was brewing.

Prince Anaxarides took a swig of the sea water himself. It seemed the effort of talking outside the water was very taxing to them. 'My King bids you safe travels, and notes a dark entity is pursuing you. If you wish, we could drive it away for you?'

The steward almost replied, but fell silent as King Dunnkan spoke: 'I do not advise it. This dark entity is the Destiny's Maw, and it bears a master assassin who seeks my very life. This is not a conflict the gentle sharkmen should concern themselves with.'

The sharkmen looked offended. Kialessa realised that "gentle" was a title of great respect amidst her people. But perhaps these two muscle-bound sharks thought of being gentle as an insult. Even if they did, they bore it with a measure of practiced grace.

The prince bowed. 'If you insist, for no Kopis may be interfered with amidst our own people.'

The admiral must have looked confused, as the prince turned to him to explain, 'A sacred ritual of battle. When a challenge is given, someone must surely die. And none may interfere; it is amongst our most sacred laws.'

The general nodded, but the steward barely concealed his disdain. So was "kill or be killed" truly their law? They were more barbaric than the trolls, he would be thinking for sure.

The prince seemed unsteady; his feet were not made to stand on solid land. His bodyguard moved to steady him, and he held the far larger sharkman's forearm. 'Please, good King of men. If you will hear out our petition this day?'

The King nodded.

Kialessa looked around. The soldiers were armed, and wary. The lookout bore three at this time. They would be scanning the waters for signs of treachery, but the surrounding small army of sharkmen seemed to be content to swim a long way off.

The prince took yet another quick swig of his water, the liquid spilling out of his gills and onto the deck where it lay. 'I am sent by my father, all-King of the waters under the white moon, including all that you call the "Bounteous Shallowsea".'

Kialessa almost scoffed; it was a rude thing to say about the merkin who lived there too.

The prince continued: 'He wishes you a safe journey, and offers you a gift.'

The larger sharkman pulled out a rod and what might have been a large sack of sand. He emptied the sand onto the deck, and drew a large rectangle in it with the rod. A moment later the sand became silver-golden with magic, and a strange chest made out of what appeared to be a single giant clam rose up.

The sailors were impressed.

The bodyguard threw back the lid, and within, the entire clam was filled to overflowing with gems, pearls, and objects of such pure gold that the sea could never taint it at all.

Now the sailors were *really* impressed.

The steward spoke: 'Beautiful, without comparison! But, pray tell if you may, for why does your good King offer us such priceless treasures?'

'Is it so hard to believe, good servant, that the King of all-waters does seek good relationships with those that walk on dry land? This is a mighty gift; can you not see that?'

Things became tense. The treasure was inviting; some of the sailors looked as though they wanted nothing more than to run their hands through the cool golden coins and treasures. But without the King's leave, they did not dare.

The steward nodded. 'Son of the all-King,' he used a rather flattering title, 'we are honoured beyond words at the King's magnanimity. So tell us all, please, we beg of you – how may we repay such great kindness?'

Allastassia smirked, and even Kialessa could see how the steward was very tactfully asking exactly the same question he'd just asked.

But the prince seemed taken by the words; he stood, and smiled to himself with his toothful, sharkish grin. 'A wise request! And I shall grant it. For years now, our father has battled in vain against an implacable, slippery, malicious foe – the merkin. He is growing weary of their constant rebellions, and seeks an alliance with the human sailors and their boats of wood against this vicious, murderous foe.'

Oh, thought Kialessa, *it's blood money.*

What do you mean? Toni's voice asked her inside her mind. She was momentarily surprised, since he'd stopped doing that since he came aboard. But apparently it was something he still could do.

They're trying to pay us to kill their enemies.

Intriguing! Toni mused. Which was, Kialessa though, rather unhelpful. Did he think it right, or wrong? Surely there was nothing wrong with seeking help against an adversary, else why have the city guard and judges and such? But to be paid as a common mercenary to slay and plunder for the prize of gold? It would be deeply insulting to King Dunnkan, and any right-thinking human of all the lands.

Allastassia reached over, and held her hand.

'What?' Kialessa asked her.

'Nothing,' she whispered in her incredibly tiny voice. 'It's just that you have a tendency to … you know …'

She did not know.

Allastassia continued as if it was an apology: 'Speak your mind when it is not you place to do so, you know?'

Kialessa huffed, and folded her arms. The dryad was right, of course, but Kialessa didn't want to admit that now. Her 'speaking out of place' had allowed her to meet the King in the first place, and helped save his life. She glanced at the King, but his expression was unreadable.

The steward continued with infuriating tact. 'An alliance, what kindness! What grand magnanimity! But, please, we cannot take these treasures, for we are unworthy-'

'Indeed,' the prince swiftly agreed, 'but take this missive to the King of Kings at Emerel. We would have him consider our invitation.'

For a moment they were silent.

Kialessa was *fuming*. What was her King to them: a mercenary and a messenger boy!?

Few seemed to share her indignation, or they hid their feelings very well, which was rather proper.

The steward grinned. 'We shall indeed, and thank your father for his great generosity!'

But Kialessa could no longer keep silent. A divine indignation boiled out of her, and she fairly yelled the accusation: 'Fine of you to speak of "Kopis", then offer us gold to fight your battles for *you*!'

Everyone stared at her.

Her heartbeat raced.

'Who said that?' the bodyguard roared. With inhuman speed and strength he hefted his weapon, and looked to charge in her direction.

Kialessa felt soldiers gather protectively around her, and steel swords were drawn. For a moment she was speechless in the incredibly show of loyalty – almost enough to drown out the burning shame she felt for, once again, speaking out of turn, and speaking for her King.

Allastassia buried her forehead in her hands.

The young prince was fast. 'Leonidis! Down, now! Back! Get underneath the waters. Go, now!'

The bodyguard was fuming; trembling with rage he leapt off the boat and into the waves with such force it set the Dawn rocking.

The prince watched to make sure he left. Then he turned. The steward began to apologise, but was cut short as the prince laughed, 'Who was that? I must know. I am impressed, for we have heard only of the cowardice and fear of those who walk in dry lands. Please, let me know!'

The steward beckoned, and the wall of protectors stood away from her. There she stood, right in front of the sharkman prince. His scent was appalling, like sea salt and fish guts.

He looked at her, and immediately she recognised surprise in his eyes. The steward saw it too. The prince spoke: 'So, the red-skinned dry-walker of fable is not only a female, but a *child?*'

Immediately the steward grabbed her shoulders and pushed her forwards till she stood right at the prince's feet.

Was this punishment, or praise? she wondered.

The prince knelt down, and she noticed how his knee took poorly to the floor, as though it had little or no bones therein. 'You're smaller than I would have thought,' he informed her.

She had nothing to say in reply.

The prince spoke: 'Stories over three hundred years ago spoke of the red-skinned dry-walker who would come if we ever tried to make an alliance with their King. It is said she would have the power to make, or break, that alliance. So, little one, what do you think of my gift? Are you so unimpressed?'

Everyone looked at her. *Everyone.*

Kialessa just prayed. Years of diplomatic training and all of Allastassia's advice on courtly manners slipped from her mind in their most needed hour. What was she to say? Was she the focus of yet another prophecy, three hundred years ago?

'So now you have nothing to say?' The prince grinned.

She looked around. The steward nodded at her. It was clear he wanted to hear her speak – which was rather unfathomable at this moment. Her King was nowhere to be seen, and she really wanted to know what he thought. Such diplomatic transactions as this were the work of Kings, not servants. Was she supposed to decide for herself? Or maybe she could drag the experienced steward into the conversation.

The prince gestured at the treasures, and she stepped forwards.

He stood painfully, and gulped his water again.

There were crowns, and gems polished pure by Waaglah's hand. It looked to be more wealth than the entire nation, though it was curiously about the same as the Merking's offering. But could it really be worth their lives? Gems and cups and crowns sparkled in the daylight.

There was a moment, and she looked up to see the wizard glaring at her with concern in his face. She stepped back; perhaps the treasure was cursed somehow? The priestess would be best to deal with it, and she was not available right now.

And what would happen to them all if they refused to help? Would it cost them their lives anyway?

She turned to face the prince. 'We can take your request to the High King, gladly. But you needn't bribe him so. We are unworthy of such treasures,' she tried to say, being diplomatic like the steward.

The prince looked annoyed. 'Among our people, it is sacrilege to expect any to do service without just recompense.'

'Then you're not really looking for an alliance, are you.' The words popped out of her mouth before she'd realised they were in her heart.

He looked surprised, then confused. Then he nodded. 'No, I suppose you are correct.' With a wave of his hand the treasure box folded up, and sunk below the sand, where it disappeared in a glittering shower of silver sparkles.

The prince folded his arms, and looked out at the waves. 'You have judged wisely, red child of destiny. I am impressed!' He paced the deck. 'I must admit, your ways are strange to us, and your words are confusing. And this air! Oh, how it stings me!' He growled, and shook like a dog. An incredibly tall and muscular dog with hundreds of razorblade teeth. 'The King will not be pleased with our failure … though perhaps we are wiser to take it to Emerel ourselves? Hmm….'

Kialessa realised the problem right away. 'The waters are cooler near Emerel, aren't they? They run down from the Feuderach Mountains in the dwarven lands, covered all year with snow and ice.'

He looked down at her. 'We thought you creatures mad for liking such saltless water, but have since learnt that it serves you. It makes no sense, see, since your blood is full of salt like the sea before us! But yes, we avoid such waters at all times, though the treacherous merkin seem to prefer it! Thus to pass these waters ourselves is … inconvenient. Yet to send you on our errand is perhaps … condescending. Hmm … I will need to consider your words.'

He didn't even nod, didn't turn to say goodbye or bid the King good health, but in the strange manner of the sharkmen simply leapt overboard. It was rude, and it was wrong.

She turned around. Some seemed angry, others afraid. No one spoke.

'Well,' the steward summarized, 'that was the rudest creature I have ever met!'

Some laughed, and most got back to work. The King was by her side in a moment. 'Well done, well done!' he said, but he was always being nice to her. Her young friends gathered in, since proper protocol was not really being observed during the voyage – they weren't supposed to touch the King, but he allowed it here. 'That was a very dangerous situation we were in Kialessa. I think you may have bought us some valuable time.'

'What do you mean?' she asked.

The King sighed. 'I do not like this situation we find ourselves in, not at all. For a hundred generations the merkin and sharkmen have been at war, and we have been avoiding them both. Now, in one week, both their Kings offer us a king's ransom to take sides against their enemies?'

'It means complete control over the entire Shallowsea,' Darrix guessed.

The King nodded. 'And that's not a decision I have the authority to make.'

'But if they both seek entrance into the Great Kingdom,' Allastassia asked, probably already well aware of the answer, 'they will never work together; would they rather die than be part of the Great Kingdom together? The merkin are so powerful, and the sharkmen mighty warriors. Yet they will kill each other and any who stand by them on sight!'

'I think,' the King paused a moment, 'that is *exactly* the predicament we find ourselves in.'

There was a gentle tug on her mind, and as one they all turned to see Toni glaring at them. He shuffled his feet a moment as if he couldn't decide where to go. Then he marched up to the them and stated his favourite phrase: 'This I do not understand.'

As the King was beside them, it was tradition to not answer till he gave them leave. So they waited.

'What is it you want, young man?' King Dunnkan finally asked.

226

Toni paced, backwards and forwards. 'How is it that you so soon receive the gifts of the merkin, but shun the gifts of the sharkmen? Is it that they are so ugly to your eyes?'

The steward joined them, for he was never far from the King. 'I think it far more than a matter of appearance. It was their manners.'

Toni seemed to interrupt him. 'But they wanted the same thing!'

The steward shook his head. 'Of this I am convinced; in the end, the merkin will simply chase the sharkmen from their waters to protect their people. The sharkmen have sought the complete annihilation of those they consider their ancestral foes, they always have. And once they are done, they will look for new slaughter to entertain themselves.'

It was Toni's turn to disagree. 'I do not believe this. They are hunters, it is true. But they tire of the sport soon enough. Do you really think they would simply hunt their foe to extinction? Life exists for a greater purpose! If they really are so vile, then will they not turn against each other soon enough? Are any, truly, so cruel?'

Allastassia seemed sympathetic. 'It's not like a hunt. Living, um ... *aware* beings such as ourselves can fight over so much more than territory or mates or food. You know yourself that we are hunted by an assassin that seeks for none of those things.'

Toni pondered, and nodded, seeming sad, as though weighed down by a great responsibly. 'I sensed as much when I spoke to him.'

That was a surprise for Kialessa to hear. When had Toni spoken to the assassin? Recently? On the night of his attack? And what had they talked about? Had he told no one else of what he'd learnt?

'We need to know what you talked about,' Darrix said to Toni.

Toni shook his head. 'Nothing you do not already know. I wanted to know why he was attacking you, and he would give me no useful answer. His mind is powerful; it was difficult to gather, and neither he, nor the powers he serves, would allow it. This I do not understand ... how can one justify a hunt for no other prize than the death of their quarry? It is … wrong …'

'We fight for much more than our next dinner, young boy of the forest,' the steward explained.

Toni sighed. 'In four days, we will be beyond the veil that marks the end of your national territory. In two days, a storm will arrive. I am sure he will make his final attempt at your life then, King Dunnkan.'

Kialessa did not know what Toni meant; their nation had no visible 'veil' that she was aware of. But they were getting close to the end of their national waters and were soon to enter the waters of Emerel.

So that could well mean the assassin had one … last … chance.

The Tempest

*Does life have a purpose? I think it does; to become – to recognise that the divine already lives within you. To experience, yes, but to **become**. To learn, yes, but to discover things you **couldn't know**. To approach perfection, to love beyond what mortals alone can ever understand! … The purpose of life is to touch the divine.*

Lumos herself, as written by Taup Elfkin, 2nd Sage of Lumos.

Thunder rumbled in the distant sky. All day the Dawn had been towed behind the Edge as a hundred soldiers pushed against the waters in the windless calm before the storm.

'This is no normal storm,' Federach whispered. 'I sense we have not done enough to placate the goddess. She sends a tempest, to remind us to be humble.'

And now that giant storm visibly approached. It was angry with lightning. Everyone was on edge, and no-one spoke. Kialessa did not doubt that they all felt the oppressive hammer of fate strike them against the anvil of luck and the sea. No hand strayed far from a weapon.

When the wind finally arrived, it struck with passion. Every unfurled sail snapped taught in a moment.

'Fifteen degrees starboard!' the admiral shouted from the till. 'Raise the mizzenmast!'

Toni stood by her.

'The assassin is there, in the storm, isn't he?' she asked.

'He rides in the wooden serpent under the air-water interface. But his poise is leisurely; he will not attack as yet.'

Kialessa nodded. Everyone on the Dawn sensed it.

The admiral ordered the ships untethered and the oars pulled up. He quickly sailed the Dawn till the two ships were almost touching side to side. Their large underwater capable ballistae fully loaded and pointing down.

'Are you sure the boats are at a safe distance?' the steward demanded.

'Aye!' the admiral boasted, 'Without their druid, they have little control over the winds and waters, thanks to you and the young baroness!'

The steward nodded, and glanced at her. He looked worried, as if he'd not slept well of late.

A thunderous boom swept across the water. Kialessa couldn't tell if it was distant lightning, or some unnatural force.

'Full sails, let's outride this storm!' the admiral shouted.

For a full two hours they sped along, trying desperately to outrun the storm. But it was heading westward, and though they drove closer and closer to the shoreline, they soon could go no further. Huge wet drips begun to fall against the ships.

Suddenly there was a gut-wrenching scream. Kialessa turned to see a sailor dragged off the boat and into the waters by some kind of kelp rope. Ballistae fired. Kialessa ran to the starboard side, even as the admiral demanded against the driving wind, 'Hold back! Keep away from the edges of the ships! They're using lassos!'

Despite his advice, she crept carefully up, hiding beside a huge ballista. The water there was red with churning blood. A moment later, the sailor surfaced, and they threw her a rope. Dark shapes moved under the water, but fled as more ballista bolts with wide, scything blades rocketed down to the water. The sailor was dragged up, battling bravely with her one dagger.

A creature leapt out of the water, trying to drag her down again. She'd stabbed it in the gills even before it had laid hold on her. It was clear to any who watched: it was an armoured sharkman. It fell, dead, into the waters again.

'And thus we see the monsters have already allied themselves with the forces of evil,' Natasha condemned them.

They dragged the sailor quickly aboard. She was bleeding heavily from a deep wound in her shoulder. She collapsed on the deck, apologising. They were trying to dress her wound.

Then the water on deck was suddenly swept away in a driving spiral. Toni stood by her, standing above her, and held out his hand, palm down. A blue-green light visibly emitted from his hand; blood flowed back to its place, her skin resealed, and her wound was healed in instants.

Kialessa heard her saying something to Toni, probably thanking him, but she had no time to listen. Sailors shouted in alarm. Kialessa turned to see hundreds of kelp ropes being thrown around the ballistae themselves. There was chaos on deck. They tried to cut away the ropes, but the sharkmen had so many! Axes were drawn, sailors hewed with their might, but there were several large cracking sounds as most of the ballistae were pulled away or damaged beyond repair.

'Look to the Edge!' someone shouted.

Kialessa looked, and noticed that the sharkmen were not trying to pull away its ballistae, since it was too high. They were simply trying to climb aboard. They used thick ropes, and some climbed with hooked claws on the ends of their muscular arms. But they clearly struggled to fight in the air, and the soldiers were holding their own. They rushed to pull alongside.

The Edge listed sideways as the admiral drove the Dawn flat against the side of the much larger boat, crushing several climbing sharkmen. Crossbow bolts were cutting them down quickly, but there would be dozens more climbing over the other side. And within a breath they had begun to climb aboard the Dawn as well.

But they fought poorly in the air, and could barely hold their ground.

Battle was breaking out all around her, and Kialessa wondered what she should do to help. Her whip was, curiously, a natural tan, which meant the unicorn's gift would not help her – for now, it was just a normal whip.

Lightning lit up the sky as Allastassia battled. Darrix was leading a handful of soldiers to keep the sharkmen away from the foremast, and they obeyed his orders with exactness, like he was a general already as well. Piex held back with a handful of wizards, protecting the King while he held the rod that gave them the skill and prayers of an entire nation. She looked for Posk, and was amazed to see him ripping apart ropes with his gauntlets and teeth while he clung single handed to the side of the Edge.

And Toni stood there, looking confused, right beside her. He did nothing.

'You could help us,' Kialessa asked, trying to be polite. If he could ward an entire forest for three centuries, she knew he'd have a few tricks up his four sleeves, somewhere.

He looked over in the scattered rain. 'Death, and life … with no purpose …'

She shook her head. He was useless without answers.

The water to the starboard roared, and in a spout of sea spray, a giant sharkman landed on the deck.

It was the prince's personal bodyguard, Leonidis.

Without wasting a moment, the King held out the rod and encased the giant in a glowing shield of energy. He looked around as if expecting the assassin any moment, but nothing new happened.

Battle continued around them.

'See to the battle,' King Dunnkan told them. 'This is simply a distraction.'

The bodyguard struggled, but soon realised there was no escape. Knowing the ruse had failed, he stopped struggling and grinned. 'Not that this knowledge will do you any good.'

Soldiers were fighting on all sides as sharkmen continued to climb aboard and be cut down. But Leonidis looked about, seeming concerned.

'So much more death than you were promised,' the King told him.

Kialessa realised she had a chance for information, and she marched up to him, invoking what subtle permission she had as the King's backup protector. 'Why did you side with our enemy?'

The steward guessed what was she was thinking: 'They promised you victory, but the cost is far greater than you anticipated.'

The Leonidis glared at the steward. 'A King has many protectors, but who are you?'

Grudon did not answer.

Kialessa's head was spinning, trying to understand what was happening. 'You sided with the assassin … He told you to fight us … He probably told you the battle would be easy, yet only now you see our resolve.'

The bodyguard glared at her.

The steward spoke: 'Don't you see what he's doing? As so many of your brothers die, the cost of it will be laid on us. He seeks to make you hate us all the more. He seeks to have you lay to us a debt that belongs only to him!'

Kialessa realised what he meant. 'He wants you to hate us for the death of the slain. But he knew so many of your kind would die. This is not a trap for us, but for you!'

Her words struck true, but then the sharkman grinned. 'Oh, I would not be so sure of your victory today …'

The Dawn suddenly jolted to one side, pressed away from the Edge.

With a flick of his wrist, the King sent the bodyguard flying away into the troubled sea.

There was the screech of tearing wood, and a moment later an enormous maw of some creature rose up between the boats. Within a moment, it lifted up as high as the tops of the sails. It glared at them a moment, seeming to bore its dire will into her soul. Then it pulled its face back and opened its mouth to the sky; it wailed a deathly, shrilling screech that shook her bones and stole all conviction from her limbs. Several sailors fell trembling to the deck.

Archers tried to shoot at it, but it ignored them. It turned around to begin a deathly embrace of the Edge. One of the disguised wizards caused a large chunk of it to begin to rot, but it simply flinched. Rigging snapped and wood splintered as it began its slow death hug.

'Axes!' the general roared.

Before most of them could stand, a muscular figure jumped down onto the deck. 'You called?' Brandish, the slayer, grinned at the general.

'Back for your long overdue execution?' the general grinned.

'Fate has kept me alive too long to die at the hand of a rank incompetent such as yourself,' the Slayer chuckled.

'Brandish!' a voice shouted on the wind, sounding a lot like the archmage Tobiuus. 'This is no time for your games!'

'Silence, archmage,' Brandish said with a grin, licking his axe. 'This will take but a moment. But just in case … Sharkmen, now!'

A hundred seaweed ropes with grappling hooks attached themselves to both the boats. Brandish saluted the general, and drawing two hand axes each they charged.

A hundred sharkmen were climbing aboard, and the giant sea serpent continued to wrap around the Edge, despite the spears and swords of the sailors. The sharkmen closed in with a hundred bared teeth each.

'Grudon, so let it be!' the King shouted a command as he and the royal guard swept down every sharkman in reach.

The steward nodded at her.

She looked up at him, not understanding.

'The horn, use it now!' he hurried her, and she wondered why no one had felt to mention this rather important detail previously.

Kialessa reached down and pulled the Merking's horn from the shadowrealm. She pressed it to her lips even as a dozen sharkmen died on the swords of Lenmer'el while trying to stop her. The note was uncertain, and weak, but the magic soon swelled and lifted, bright lights of pink and green swirling in the air.

'The merkin!' a sharkman shouted.

'The Merking is coming!' another roared.

'We are not prepared!' a third shouted.

The sharkmen began to run back into the sea.

'Get back here, you tools!' Brandish shouted. He stepped away from his battle with General Bon Sure'e, turning his back on his adversary.

But Kialessa knew it was just a ruse.

The general, however, did not. He lunged at the barbarian, and at the last moment, Brandish's axe swung about his, as he seemed to know it would. Bon Sure'e might have guessed it too, as he moved to block the twisting axe, but it was simply too fast. There was a sickening crunch as his right hand was stuck between his own armour and the sharp edge of the barbarian's axe.

Brandish threw him away, and Kialessa was horrified to see the general's blood-soaked hand lying on the ground.

'Looks like …' Brandish begun, but then with a groan feel to his knees.

The general covered the stump of his hand and struggled to his knees as well. He took the barbarian by the hair of his head, but didn't seem to have the strength to bring him down.

With a confused look on his face, Brandish drew a long, thin blade from his chest.

'Worth every price,' the general told him. It was clear he'd scarified his own hand just to pierce the barbarian's heart. It was a killing move, a death sentence. Those who died with a wound to the heart were not known to come back to life ever again.

Brandish drew back the blade to strike the general down, but the older man punched him in the face, and they both fell over. Brandish, the slayer, lay on the ground, his eyes open even in death. For an instant the world seemed to hold its breath.

Then there was a lurch followed by a crack as the serpent tightened its grip around the Edge. Without the sharkmen to protect it, dozens of axes and spears hacked away at its wooden scales. There was a deep groaning from the Edge as the giant sea serpent began to wind its third and final coil around the ship.

'Kialessa,' she heard Darrix shout. 'Come near!'

Kialessa turned, and noticed the general now lay on his back, pale in the lamplight of the stormy night. Darrix was by his side, another sailor uttering prayers.

She threw herself kneeling at the general's side, his breathing ragged. She looked at his course beard and white skin – he was wounded, but he had lived through worse. He would live …

… but not his hand.

Curiously, Darrix now held the disembodied hand up, and gently took the general's arm. Dark blood still oozed from the stump.

Darrix looked at her, and begged, 'The unicorn's gift.'

She held out the hilt of her whip, blazing white in the dark night.

Darrix touched the hilt and held the hand against the stump of the general's arm, and then the young man prayed. His face seemed to become very calm, as it often did when he blessed others. But then it started to glow gently.

Her whip started to grow warm, then uncomfortably hot. She was sure it would be a scorching pain if her heart were any more impure at this point, but by the Eternal's grace, it was apparently good enough.

Kialessa watched as the blood flowed back into the general's arm, the skin sealing around the wound, his hand setting back into place immediately.

There was a crack, and a mighty creaking. The Edge was about to be destroyed.

'Stop it!' the King was shouting to the soldiers.

'We cannot! A dark magic prevails around it!' a sailor shouted from the higher decks edge. Great wounds were welting what looked like sap along the serpent's flanks, but it turned and twisted, making it difficult for anyone to strike a telling blow.

Kialessa heard the general muttering something. She jumped down again to hear him.

'Use fire,' he muttered.

'Use fire!' Darrix shouted.

Kialessa feared no one would hear him over the noise. So she breathed in deeply, and threw her growing enchantress powers once more into her voice. When she screamed, all nearby fell back at the strength of her noise: 'USE **FIRE!!**'

Crude oil was thrown over the beast as they tried to light it in the driving rain.

Kialessa looked around for Piex. He seemed to be helping the sagemaster protect the King, though there were no sharkmen now. She ran to him.

'Now might be a good time to use your *fiery conflagration*,' she told him.

He looked like he already knew that. 'Lion rising, the star of the King in declination … nineteen by fifteen seven hundred ….'

Again the Edge creaked. The serpent gave a mighty heave. There was a deep crack, yet the Edge did not sunder. The serpent screamed as if in frustration.

'Light it, light it!' the steward was screaming.

Allastassia threw lightning at it, but it barely singed it. The serpent screamed and gave another mighty heave, but again it did not prevail.

Kialessa felt a twingling of dark magic, the voice of Tobiuus echoing through a near dimension somewhere. It was as if it were blessing the serpent somehow.

There was a roar as Posk tore a lantern from the mast and smashed it against the wooden monster. With inexplicable power a fire burst out along it. The serpent screamed and immediately let go. Within a breath it was fleeing out to sea once more.

'Kill it, before it gets away,' the general muttered.

Swords conjured from the air by the sagemaster impaled the beast as it fled, but nothing could destroy it.

A moment later, the area was filled with an almost surreal calm.

'She's taking water!' a sailor shouted from the Edge.

Kialessa looked, and noticed how low the battle frigate was in the water now, listing to starboard.

She heard a shout, as several sailors threw the body of the Slayer into the waters. With what felt like a hateful and angry glare, the spirit of Tobiuus departed.

With the war now over, another battle took place. It took an hour to patch the enormous damage the Edge had taken, yet still she would leak. Both ships had been damaged, yet the storm continued to rage against them. Rain drove continuously on, hampering every effort to keep the boat afloat. More than fifty sailors were slain, a hundred more injured. It seemed no one had escaped unscathed.

Dawn began to light up the sky as the rain continued on. The admiral approached the King. 'She's of no use to you now, my liege,' he stated.

King Dunnkan looked concerned.

'We cannot take the injured on,' the steward argued, 'they will surely die in the next attack.' He was pointing at the general who still refused to rest, though he needed help now even to stand, even as he barked out orders to the soldiers under his command.

Finally the King nodded as though he agreed. 'Divide the hale among both boats. Have the Edge head for shore with all haste, make repairs, and re-join us at Emerel before spring. The rest of us will press on to the borders by tomorrow night, should the goddess so will.'

Tired sailors stomped away to do what needed to be done.

The King looked at his general. 'Coure De'Feur, my sagemaster – get this man to Emerel immediately.'

'But sire,' the sagemaster began to complain, 'that will remove me for the entire day! I will not be back until you have crossed the border, and that may not be soon enough.'

The King nodded. 'I know, Master De'Feur. But the life of my general is forfeit if you don't. They will use it against us, if only in retribution for the death of the Slayer.'

The general looked like he might have argued, but he was too pale now, and his eyes did not focus properly. 'They will use this as their final opportunity,' he muttered to the King in the thin rain.

'So be it, I tire of these games,' the King commanded, and then saluted them as the sagemaster teleported the general and several of the most injured far, far away from the safety of the Dawn.

A voice spoke at her shoulder. 'He sends them away?' It was Toni.

Kialessa was suddenly struck by a sense of injustice. 'Why didn't you help? You could have helped us tonight!'

Toni looked sad, and a little perplexed. 'But I still don't understand what they want.'

But she was too tired to be angry. She was just sad, and hoped they would let her rest soon. There was one day, one more day till they hit the waters of Emerel, where the sharkmen would not dare follow them.

Yet in all that night, no merkin had arrived to help them as they'd promised. The note was magical, why did they not come?

And Toni, possibly the most powerful creature in the entire world, had just stood there, looking up at the slowly brightening grey sky, so entirely lost in thoughts so deep, or questions so unanswerable, that he had done nothing.

But someone needed her to hold some soaking rope while they rewound it. So she did.

Figure 14 The King's Four bodyguards

Waaglah's Rage

*Why live? To make a difference; your difference. To win a war,
to speak honestly to your father. You are here for a job only you can
do. So be yourself, your own true, powerful self.*

Words of the goddess of the waters. Spoken by Drou
Negerthaal, half-twarnae priestess

Again the waters heaved against the hull of the ship, pushing her about
as if the sea herself did not know whether to speed them on, or drown them
now and be done with all the violence. Kialessa realised how grateful she
was that Wanderer was not here right now.

If she had slept, it had been in fitful moments while trying to keep the
damaged ship racing ahead. Everyone was exhausted, even the wizards'
powers so spent they had to repair the hull the old way. Even then she was
still taking on too much water, and they had to bail it out. The lower deck
was entirely drowned by the treachery of sharkmen spears, everything
soiled or cast out of the ship to lighten her – the extra rigging, the food, even
the bright and coloured curtains for the parade that awaited their arrival at
Emerel. The Edge was gone, and with her most of the wounded and many
of the best soldiers.

'We shall look all amuck,' Allastassia complained. Her hand was
bandaged where a sharkman had bit it trying to prevent her using magic,
but it hadn't stopped her.

'At least we won't be dead,' Posk replied. He was covered in abrasions
where he'd brushed against the sharkmen's sandpaper skin. But he still
looked the healthiest of them all.

Piex was no longer pale, but had not eaten well that morning. 'One more day … that storm has given us such speed! If we can just hold out for today, we should cross into the waters of Emerel by tomorrow dawn, and the sharkmen won't follow us there.'

'But what of the assassin?' Kialessa asked. She hoped he would not follow them there, but he probably would.

'The King has lost all but his protectors, as chosen by the gods,' Darrix explained. 'You, and the steward. If you cannot keep him safe, none can.'

She knew he meant it to be inspiring, but with his ashen face and tired features, it just came off like a threat. No one spoke for a long time.

Posk huffed.

'Why would you complain, son of a troll princess?' Allastassia glared at him.

He huffed again, and took a moment before speaking. 'Maybe this isn't the right way to go about this?'

'Say on,' Allastassia glared at him.

Posk huffed again, looking at his knuckles. He seemed to bear a great weight, as if he knew he was about to say something that might upset everyone. 'I mean, this trouble. Why pick a fight here, above the waters? We would do much better above land, among our own people.'

Remarkably, Allastassia seemed to take her time before replying. 'To give the enemy a false sense of security. Don't you think the King prayed for days and days to know what to do? We would not be here if we couldn't win.'

'Tell that to the dead guys,' Posk challenged her. Many sailors had died.

Allastassia just glared at him.

Kialessa looked over at Darrix. He looked concerned, but said nothing. He'd told her long ago it was better to let them argue it out.

'I don't think-' Kialessa began, but Posk cut her off.

'Whatever, *I* don't even need to be here,' he said, and walked off.

'How dare you-' Allastassia begun, hair flaring with static.

'I'm gett'n' a bucket!' Posk shouted over his shoulder with a wave of his hand, not even looking at her.

Allastassia huffed with annoyance, and went away to mend some ropes.

'Everyone's exhausted,' Darrix explained.

'Almost everyone,' Piex said, and pointed over at the foremast.

Toni was standing there, unmoving even in the fierce breeze. He seemed immune to the sea spray and he never shut his eyes. Their ship was dying, their strength almost spent. But still, the only surviving member of the first race of all humanity did nothing.

Kialessa could not help the burning rage that surged up inside her, and she looked away hoping he would not notice.

But he did, and staring towards her, opened up his thoughts just a touch.

Kialessa felt blinded by the sudden torrent of wisdom and information that rushed by her. It was as if Toni was trying to understand a million equations all at once, and none of them had any solid answers. Why was the hunter pursuing them? Why had he tried to command the undead? How were they using such imperfect words to create within reality events that led only to their own destruction, and then embracing it? Why did they think to spend their brief mortal lives for a prize none of them would ever obtain?

Tears slipped down his pale face, and he looked at her, and through her.

Deep guilt gripped at her heart, and she feared she had hurt Toni somehow. She looked at him, and wondered if, perhaps, he really was trying. In his own confused and awesome way, he was already doing everything he felt he could do. And now he was tired, and afraid, and more than just a little lost.

Perhaps you should rest? she told him in her heart.

He nodded, turning, and stumbled to the deck. They rushed to him, Darrix helping him up. Toni's skin was as cold as the ocean herself, and she wondered how he was even alive right now.

Casting aside the worries of a sinking ship, they took him below deck, wrapping him in warm blankets and putting him by the stove in the hope it might warm him a little.

'A rest will do you good,' she told him.

But he was already asleep.

***

The night came all too soon. Kialessa took what sleep she could, but found again she slept fitfully, if she even slept at all. Eventually she decided further attempts would do her no good, so she arose and climbed silently to the deck.

The rain had slackened, but the wind had not.

She turned, and found the King standing by the till. To his left the admiral, to his right the steward. And behind him the nine members of the King's guard, those who legends told and history had shown, "Did not fear dragons."

No one stopped her as she approached, nor showed even a hint of disdain or fear, as she forgot to bow, and simply held out her hand for him to hold.

'Are you afraid to die, my King?'

He looked at her, a gentle kindness in his eyes. 'I have already lived longer than most men can ever hope to. I lived to bring peace and prosperity to my people, and to protect them from harm, and from their own stupidity at times. I have nothing to fear from death. Dying, perhaps, but not death. If all I could hope for was to die with a good conscience that I had done the best I humanly could just to help my fellow beings, even if I died on a dread assassin's blade, I would die peacefully.'

Kialessa nodded, but really hoped it would not come to that.

Suddenly there was a cry of alarm from the lookout: 'The serpent!'

The steward waved the rod, and Allastassia's lens folded out from light itself. There, deep in the darkness far away, the red sails of the ship could clearly be seen.

'Sound the a-' the steward begun, but the King cut him off.

'Not yet, my faithful steward,' the King told him.

The steward looked at the King as if he were a fool.

King Dunnkan explained: 'Let them take what rest they can while this monstrosity pursues us. It will be time to fight soon enough.'

The steward whispered to the King, but still she heard it clearly: 'They will not allow us to reach Emerel.'

King Dunnkan nodded.

Kialessa ran to see. There was nothing she could spot in the darkness. She turned to look at the steward and the King.

The protector Grudon seemed to read her thoughts. 'An hour, even with their impressive pace. And how long till we reach the border?' he asked the Admiral.

The older man looked grim before replying, 'Slightly more.'

'Full sail, onwards!' the King commanded. But his voice was tired. He had not slept in days.

Kialessa looked again toward the horror that pursued them in the darkness, then down at the faithful ship that held them above Waaglah's cold embrace. It made her think of the priestess who had held down the staff at their launching, and truly it had been a portent most accurate.

There was a shifting of slithered scales, and Wanderer made herself visible as she moved along the Dawn's rigging and rear balustrade.

'So you're here still with me?' Kialessa asked.

The dragon poked her with her nose, and looked very sad, and tired. Kialessa wasn't sure what it meant, but she knew that whatever bond the dragon shared with her, it was very well aware of what she was feeling too. It wrapped around her arm, and snuggling down with a little whine, fell quickly off to sleep. Soon, she disappeared into nothing once more.

Kialessa sighed. Comforted by the dragon's presence, she felt both energetic and exhausted.

'Swiftly on, Imagination's Dawn!' she begged.

***

An hour raced past, silence on board as sailors slowly roused. Kialessa sat at the stern, warming her fingers with her breath as she and all the King's guard watched the slow pursuit of the serpent. Yet the King and the steward kept their eyes determinedly on their invisible goal in the gathering dawn.

Suddenly the wind pushed harshly from the wrong direction, pulling the sails askew.

The admiral started shouting orders to get things happening, when suddenly the steward's voice thundered to all aboard, 'Awake, they are here!'

Sailors, armed yet weary, burst from below deck as others soon followed.

The Dawn pitched sideways in the wind, confusion reigning as she lost a lot of her speed.

Yet the serpent seemed to have no such disadvantage.

'This is it,' the King seemed to grin at her, and drew his sword.

Now the serpent drew rapidly on.

But she didn't feel like now was a good time to fight. They were at too much of disadvantage. They were not far from the border now, a stark break in the cloud-lines clearly demarcating the border between the magic of the assassin, and the safety of the capital nation. 'Come on, come on, brave one!' Kialessa begged the ship, but she seemed to be struggling, unsure, confused, and afraid.

The King looked at her, and seemed to make up his mind about something. 'ON!' the King roared.

Suddenly the sails seemed to catch some form of mystical breeze that wasn't there, others rolling up of their own magic. The Dawn surged on. Within moments they were pulling away from the serpent.

Kialessa wondered why they had not tried that before, but one look at the King assured her that was not an option. Golden sparkles floated from the rod, beads of sweat dripping from the King's face. She had the distinct impression that he was trying, no, was determined to push the Dawn the last remaining leagues in person, if he had to.

There was a demonic screech from behind them, and she turned to see the serpent struggling to keep up.

Sailors dared grin, a few cheered.

Then there was an enormous shockwave that blasted out from the serpent and through the water. As it hit the Dawn it seemed to ignore her, but then the entire ship pitched dangerously forward.

Then the Dawn plummeted downwards on the retreating sea.

It looked to Kialessa as if the sea was opening up her mouth to swallow them. But then that mouth gaped wide open and with a sickening crunch the entire Imagination's Dawn stuck in the mud and stones at the bottom of the Bounteous Shallowsea. For a moment it seemed everyone was too stunned to say anything, but then the boat listed dangerously sideways, and sailors screamed out in panic and fear.

Kialessa was so surprised she barely had a moment to realise what had happened. They were stranded, landlocked, on the bottom of what should have been the sea. There was no thunderous whirlpool of water, so she wondered what had happened.

A moment later, there was a roar unlike any she had ever heard before. It was as if the voice of a hundred thousand rivers cried out in rage. She looked up, and there, silhouetted by the pale light of a growing dawn, rose up a mountain made of the sea herself. She had no name for what it was, and neither did it seem anyone else did. Was it a god? Or an elder abomination none had ever spoken of before?

Perhaps because no mortal had ever survived an encounter with the god-like being before them.

Sailors fell to the floor, begging for their lives.

She looked to the King, his guard standing strong and brave. But his face looked confused, bewildered, and … awestruck.

Again the primal monstrosity roared, and it seemed the very ground shook around them.

It looked like a giant wave, standing up at least a league into the sky, drawing all the water away from them and all the entire ocean nearby. It raised two fists of rage, and formed a face made of colossal waterfalls. And, without mistake, it glared right at them. It was as if the rage of the goddess of the waters herself had taken physical form, and was prepared to destroy them for some trespass they had inadvertently committed.

Yet the King stood defiant. He stood firm, and shouting his denial, struck the Dawn with his sceptre. The glistening golden field shone out, engulfing the entire boat.

Yet it must have looked like nothing more than a single golden pearl before the elder abomination in front of them.

It roared again, closing in, and the sky shook.

Kialessa turned, and noticed the serpent keeping well its distance now at the top of a hill of water, far away.

The abomination glared at them, contemplating them with fierce

248

anger, and she had to wonder; was it angry at them for something? Or angry at whatever force compelled it to strike out at them now? She feared then that, for as powerful as her Kingdom was, it was surely to be measured as nothing before this god-like abomination.

Then, she heard singing.

It was such a strange event she had to look around to see if others had noticed. It seemed to take them a moment, but soon it was clear they all heard the chorus. The music was strange and sweet, a special kind of lonely. It was a sound she'd heard before ...

'The mermaids!' she squealed. 'They heard us!'

Instantly the chorus arose, and the waters around them calmed and stilled. She looked about – there were hundreds of merkin, thousands. They swam about in the water, singing as if nothing in the world could bother them. They brought lights of green and pink and the brightest silver.

And the abomination seemed mesmerized by them.

Sleep in the sea, under the waves,
Silence your storm, now dreamtime plays.
Stars in the sky, sand at your feet,
Sleep in the sea, resting complete.

She was glad the powerful lullaby was not directed at them, or their entire nation might have fallen asleep. She looked at the serpent, grinning mischievously. How their enemy would be annoyed by this!

The mermaids swam on, calmly climbing up the troubled mountain of seawater. It shuddered and sank, slowing losing all form and gently releasing all its hate. Within moments the waters touched the edges of the Dawn again, lifting her to her place above the waters.

Sailors wept and cheered. They saluted the merkin. Kialessa looked out, when suddenly a spout of water carried Anaesu and his brother to stand in the water, eye to eye with the King.

'The promise is kept, and the alliance of men and merkin stands,' Darissius pronounced.

'And will be honoured again,' the steward spoke for the King.

Anaesu grinned at Kialessa, but said nothing. His brother nodded at the King, and then with a wave he too fled into the waters where they belonged.

The magical song soon ended, and the merkin disappeared without a trace.

The Purpose

'We might not get to choose the day we die, but we do get to choose the kind of life we live today.'

Darrix, cited in 'The year in jail', by the Tae'anaryn.

'Onward!' roared the admiral.

The sails snapped taught, and the Dawn surged forwards. A handful of breaths later they touched the light between nations.

Sailors wept anew and cheered. They hugged and celebrated.

Kialessa grinned – they had reached the borders of the capital of Emerel. She glared at the serpent, knowing it would not dare cross into these waters.

But her glow soon faded as the dreaded serpent immediately did just that.

'How!?' the admiral gasped.

But there was no denying it. The dreaded pirate ship of legend ploughed on without pause.

'To arms, fools!' the steward roared.

It took the soldiers too long to realise what was happening.

'On, onwards, now!' the King shouted.

'How is it possible?' the steward asked.

The King looked down at Kialessa before replying, 'I wish I knew.'

Again, the wind seemed to work against them, and yet it worked well enough for the serpent; she was catching up fast.

Kialessa clutched the bannisters with whitened knuckles. This was hope denied; their last prayer, unanswered. To have the assassin chase them into the waters of the capital nation should have been impossible. But, somehow, the depraved monster rode on. She looked, desperately hoping that perhaps some mighty warship of Emerel might be heading to their salvation, but there were none.

She looked around. Her friends were not here on the rear tower, but then she remembered she was not supposed to be here either. This place was for the King and his royal guards only, or else how could they have enough room to protect him?

But she was here, and she wanted to protect him too. Not just him, but everything he meant – kindness, the entire Kingdom, and freedom from cruelty.

And she was not going to let the assassin take that away from her, not ever. Not till her last breath, and not even then.

'Look aft!' the lookout shouted.

She looked, and it seemed an enormous grappling hook, trailing a glistening chain, had been launched from the serpent and was now flying towards them.

'Hard aft!' the admiral warned them.

The Dawn pulled hard, but it was not enough. The bolt spun in the air, twisting towards them, edging closer each moment.

Then, incredibly, a heavy bolt from their own ship sung out and hit the grappling hook mid-air. It did not stop its flight, but it fell short.

Sailors turned, and to her surprise saw it was Dale who had saved them. With a grin he saluted them all.

'Shot, Dale!' Posk congratulated him.

Even though she liked to hate Dale, Kialessa could not help but admit that she was impressed.

'Enough!' the King shouted. Sailors stopped. His voice had a dread finality to it. 'We do not run; we do not flee. Come, cowardly assassin! This day you end your hunt, as either I or thee will perish!'

The Dawn responded immediately, furling her own sails and turning about.

No one cheered, and all grew serious.

There were no merkin to save them, for this was beyond their waters. There was nowhere to run, for the King had chosen to make his stand. Here, they fought and prevailed, or died.

They stood there, weapons drawn, as the pirate ship closed in. She watched them all, her good friends and brave companions. They looked afraid, but faced death with calm determination. Facing death, together, in foreign waters. 'For the King!' she shouted, and they cheered.

'For Lenmer'el!' he replied, and they cheered even louder.

'For the right to live without fear!' Posk shouted, and others shared their convictions.

'For my family!'

'For my children!.'

Kialessa noticed Darrix's dad, and wondered if he'd said anything. But he held his scroll close to his chest.

She drew her dagger and grinned, almost snarled. They might not win this fight, but they would surely put up a fight worthy of all remembrance.

A stench of undeath and seawater flowed against them, cheering their enemies on.

Sure enough, the serpent began to change just as it reached bowshot. The pirates on its deck ducked down as the edges of their enormous longboat closed over them. If it wasn't for the impending doom of terror, Kialessa felt it might have been quite fascinating.

Dark clouds struggled against the waxing sunlight as the first ballista bolts struck against the serpent. Kialessa was amazed at their speed and accuracy as the artillerists gave it their all. But in moments the serpent was deep under the ocean.

It did not circle them, but drove straight for the kill.

Suddenly dark lightning curled up on deck, a ball of black energy coalescing into the form of a man. In his hands, he held two huge axes.

'Back from the dead so soon, Brandish?' the steward asked, hiding well any fear in his voice.

The half giant said nothing, but grinned. Yet within that grin, Kialessa saw a dark hatred, a deep loathing driven by pain. Something had happened to him, something … not good.

Without saying a word, he began to lay about him, death dealt quickly at his hands. The tide of death was stemmed only as the honour guard rushed down to meet him.

Thus the King stood, alone, with the steward, the admiral, and herself.

Quickly she wove the protection of her whip around them all. It glowed brightly, just as it had on the day she denied the Khozmoh Djinn.

Brandish was being pushed back, fighting four honour guard at once. Suddenly white lightning struck at them all, felling two of them. The remaining guard took their place without pause, but neither did Brandish allow any quarter.

Kialessa looked to see the archmage Tobiuus, or what remained of him, battling from the fore of the ship. He seemed to be made of shadows tied together cruelly by shadow weave. It looked like he might be about to unleash some other horror, but Natasha the cervitaur charged him. She lay about with her magical hooves, driving away the undeath around him. It seemed the senior students would hold him there, at least for a time.

Kialessa waited. The serpent was rising up beside them. It twisted its back to them and split apart, raining down pirates with skins of wood. Battle broke out all over the Dawn, and she shook as the Maw curled the very end of its tail right around the foremast of the ship, right behind the area the archmage was using. But she knew the assassin had another friend – the druidess. Was she next? Had she kept the command to see the elf Queen, or was she free?

Or was the next threat to be the assassin of Kings himself?

The serpent screeched, and Kialessa knew she should not look. She knew it was too dangerous. But she could not help herself.

There was a flash of motion, and she turned around to see Jerik emerging from his whirlwind of sand, his beloved dagger in hand. He had lunged out at the King, but the admiral had gotten in his way. He'd probably tried to block the blow with his sword.

But Jerik was a master assassin, and death his ally. The admiral had only managed to block the dagger with his own heart.

He fell against the King, already dead.

She could only watch as the men only a few paces away fought with magical haste. The steward swung with such speed he cut Jerik on his shoulder, the other blade blocked by his own. Then the King swung out with the rod. An enormous glistening barrier of light blasted against Jerik, but instead of dying, or at least being flung off and into the water, he reached out behind him and seemed to place his hand into some kind of enormous glove of pure stone; he held it out just as the golden light was about to hit him. It looked for an instant as if the King had tried to hit a mountain. Neither man moved.

Again the steward struck, Jerik forced back by the fervid blows. The assassin feinted left, lashed out, and stabbed the steward right in the chest.

Kialessa almost screamed, but then in the next instant the steward disappeared from the knife's edge and appeared to the assassin's left. He lashed at the assassin, who managed to block one sword at his throat, but was stabbed right through his abdomen with the other.

Incredibly, Jerik, the dog, assassin of Kings, seemed only mildly annoyed. With a lurching punch of the stone fist, he rocked the entire Dawn, blasting all three of them – herself, the King, and the steward, off the hindcastle and down onto the deck below.

Kialessa rushed to help the King up, finding the steward had landed, somehow, on his feet. Without even looking, he loosed a pretty, ornate dagger no bigger than his thumb out at Brandish. The giant grunted as it sunk deep into his right arm, where the nerves were, and the arm struggled to hold its axe.

The King held out the golden shield against the assassin, but the cruel man did not move. Kialessa could hear fighting amongst the injured below deck, but there was nothing she could do about that now.

'Little help, goodman Jerik?' Brandish seemed to smile with a touch of his old humour.

Kialessa kept her eyes on the assassin, but from the sounds of things Brandish did not have long to live against the King's guard, and all who died again fell ever deeper into the unrelenting embrace of the afterlife.

And at the back of the boat, bright lightning fizzled to a disappointed pop. 'Your assistance would be most precipitous, assassin,' Tobiuus grunted.

Jerik just glared at her, and snarled at them. Then he spoke, a voice of inexplicable command as a dim halo of golden light momentarily surrounded his scalp: 'Stop!'

Battle ground to a sudden halt, a few scuffling feet indicating that, perhaps, a life or two had indeed been spared as they fled to safety. The wooden pirates fled into the sea, guarding their living serpent.

'As you can already see,' King Dunnkan spoke, 'this day will not be yours.'

Jerik glared at him. 'Lower your protections, King, and I will gladly spare these human lives, even this little half-soul you so treasure. All their lives, at the cost of your own.'

There was a moment of silence, then the steward laughed, soon joined by the bravest of the soldiers. 'Assassin, please, do not think to invoke a fey oath to secure your cause today!'

Jerik grinned back. 'Worth a shot. All right then, you all die. Remember to thank your kind King for sending you all to the deepest layers of the abyss this day.'

Soldiers and sailors shouted their hatred and denial at him, but without a pause he turned into sand and began to drift away.

'Aolith, now!' the King shouted.

Kialessa turned, and it looked like whatever Aolith was about to do was something she was already ready for. Holding out great loadstones, she and Marchan raced to the hind deck even as the giant serpent began curling around the ship, their path made all the clearer. Shouting enchantments Kialessa could not hear, massive waves of magic like the heatwaves above a fire emitted from the stones, and in their power, the whirlwind of sand shook. The steward and some of the King's guard were racing towards the hindcastle even as Jerik formed his face and torso from the cloud of dust.

'No!' the assassin cursed.

Kialessa did not miss her chance, but loosed one stone after another from her sling, sacred to the goddess of the hunt, at him. They blasted into him with a radiant damage that shook the sand all through; the sling dancing into her hand with prescient wisdom, it allowed her to strike far faster than was natural. Then a dozen arrows, tipped with gold and fire, blasted against the semi-corporeal assassin from the soldiers down on deck. Those looked like they *really* hurt.

The steward approached quickly, even as Kialessa protected the King again, levitating whip and acid dagger in hand. It seemed Tobiuus's image was defeated too, as she was soon joined by the other students, forming a ring, protecting him with their own lives.

Jerik threw his head back, and screamed. With two fists of sand he punched the deck, and a deadening magic flowed past them all. Kialessa and the others were protected by the faith of the rod, but all others were swept into unconsciousness by the powerful magic. Even the steward.

For a moment there was silence, broken only by the slow, deep groaning of wood against wood as the serpent completed its final circuit.

Jerik looked taxed, wounded. Slowly he took physical form again, but it seemed to take all his strength to stand. The boat jarred, but there were no sailors or soldiers now to fight the Maw's deadly embrace.

Jerik stood, but leant on the balustrade as he walked slowly and painfully toward them. 'I like this knife,' he said, as it appeared once more in his hand. Kialessa could see it was a dim metal now, and short, no longer than his fist. But it was also thick, almost two widths at the hilt, but cruelly curved and hooked. 'It is a good knife. Simple, fast. You'd be amazed at what you can do with just a little knife.'

As one, Natasha and Aolith shot at him with arrows, Marchan with a trio of *magus spherae*. Somehow, he managed to dodge or deflect each one, though the spheres bursting near his face still charred him.

Kialessa's heart pounded in her chest. The honour guard were all down, the sailors scattered, slain, or asleep. It was nothing but a wall of pre-adults guarding their King. It was all she could do to spiral her whip around them, and allow its magic and faith to protect them all once again.

To her relief, she felt Wanderer brush past her, and, unbelievably, Socks was somehow safe amidst their feet. She watched as the two little creatures curled up nervously together for protection under a broken jib in the centre of their circle around the King. She wished there was some way she could whisk him, and them all, to safety. But she could not just hop dimensions like a little cat and fey dragon seemed to find so easy to do. She had to believe in fairy tales right now, because they'd need a little more than luck to save their Kingdom.

Jerik stood on deck, and nodded to them, indicating with his hand. 'Come, children, send me your best. I'll make it quick. You won't even know you're dead till you hit the grey veil.'

No one moved from the circle of protection, the circle around the King.

'Come on, then,'

'No, thanks,' Dale replied.

Jerik scoffed, then coughed blood. Wiping it, he indicated to the circle with a careless, casual wave of his hand that belied just how inhumanly fast he could move. 'Yes, yes, Kialessa's circle of goodness, born of the sacrifice of a prince of unicorns, or whatever. It will not save you, and you will all die so painfully this way.'

There was a gasp, and Kialessa turned. Right against the balustrade, directly on the opposite side to them, was Brandish. He looked grim and miserable, the dagger still embedded in his twitching, axeless arm. 'Death's not fun, kids,' he lectured them, standing painfully. 'Just get out of the way.'

Again the Dawn jolted as the serpent rose up in the air to glare at them, death in its eyes.

'Time to be unhappy again then,' Aolith mocked the assassin with immeasurable courage.

But Jerik interjected. 'Brandish went third layer, mind you. That's a long way to dig into the afterlife. I needed some … help. But this knife, my little knife. She's a fifth knife. So I just want you to know that none of you have to come back, because it hurts. It's *hard* – or so they tell me.'

Brandish grunted his agreement, and it seemed to Kialessa that he really meant it.

'Never,' Darrix told them, and they all agreed.

Jerik sighed. 'Brandish, kill them.'

Instantly, the King added the forcefield of the rod to her glowing white barrier – but it was weak … tired.

With a roar, the barbarian swung his axe against the golden field. Again and again he bashed against it, while they followed the King's command to hold back. Sinister power seemed to grow within him, and suddenly he hit the barrier with such mighty power that great cracks appeared in the air, reflected in the diamond sphere at the end of the rod in the King's hand.

Kialessa knew they had only moments to act. If they left the radius of the sphere, they would leave the circle of protection. But if they stayed, they might have to face that axe. And if, by some fell power, he sundered the power of the rod? Then they all definitely died. She didn't have the strength to escape via the shadowrealm; where were they to flee?

Suddenly there was a hissing at her feet. She looked down in alarm to see Socks emerging, threatening the assassin. He looked afraid, and took a step back. Then Wanderer joined him, spitting at the assassin.

'Well, that's brave,' thought Darrix out loud.

As one, they somehow ran through the forcefield, attacking the assassin with magic and, as far as she could tell, raw luck. He looked confused and struggled to lash out at them, stumbling away.

'This is our chance,' she whispered to the King.

He smiled grimly. 'Federach!' the King shouted.

The stout dwarven priestess nodded. Just as the King dismissed the field, she raised a stone club against the giant. The entire boat suddenly stood firm as if it were sitting on land. Brown and red light surrounded the young dwarf, and before Brandish could swing again, the light blasted him in the chest. Almost instantly his axe moved to protect him, but he was pushed a pace or two backwards with a roar of pain and frustration.

'Earth and stone defy thee this hour,' Federach muttered curses against him, 'and the Earth Mother deny you, murderer and *traitor*!'

Everyone cheered her on, laying their hands upon her shoulders to give her their courage and strength. Brandish took a pace forwards, but was pushed back again. Federach tried to manoeuvre him to fall off the broken banister, but he was very powerful. Again he grunted deeply as he took a step forward, and the light from Federach intensified.

Kialessa glanced back to see Jerik just watching with curious amusement. It was as if he didn't care at all if his ally died and was cast so deep into the hells he might never return again. Again she pondered who the cruel man was, and why he did what he did.

A movement caught her eye. It was Toni. He was levitating, calmly, just in the air at forequarters. His form was translucent, as if he were hiding in some nearby dimension perhaps. He was watching the conflict with rapt attention, his brow knit as if in concentration.

Again, she found herself getting angry at the young ancient. Again he did nothing while they fought for their very lives. Was this all some kind of perverse joke to him? Would he ever step up and make a difference to those he called his friends? Or were they just animals, to be studied by his vast alien intellect?

Suddenly she heard Marchan shouting arcane words. Kialessa turned to see a scroll disintegrating in the young wizard's hand. The glistening shards of light it formed then blasted into Brandish's chest, and he grunted. Jerik looked a little surprised at that.

Then the half giant's feet turned to stone.

'A gift, from the sagemaster,' Marchan smiled, the lingering sparkles of the scroll drifting away on the salty sea breeze.

'No, no!' the Slaughterer roared. He breathed in deeply, trying to fight back the inexorable paralysis that was overtaking him. But his soul was impure, and his strength spent in battling a priestess, and in battling death itself by trying to deny its claim on his soul. With a roar of frustration and betrayal, he turned entirely to stone.

Posk did not waste a breath but leapt forward and punched the statue of the Slayer with such force it turned almost entirely to dust, and with a wave of his hand Piex blew the remaining shards of stone and sand overboard instantly.

As one, they all turned to face the assassin. Socks and Wanderer looked exhausted and injured, but not fatally, and scurried back to the safety of their arms.

Jerik tried for one of his carefree grins, but it looked too pained. 'Well, that was actually pretty impressive.'

The boat gave a solid crunch, and tilted sideways.

No one could stop Jerik as he resumed his sand form and floated up to stand on the serpent's head. 'So let the sea take you all! For none return to life who die within her embrace; but that was always your gamble, wasn't it, King of Lenmer'el?'

The Dawn tilted further, and Kialessa could not help but scream. They clung on to each other and the rigging. Yet as the boat twisted almost sideways, Kialessa saw their danger. The wooden pirates now floated, menacingly, in the sea. With blades drawn, they awaited them. They swum in circles, a deadly whirlpool springing up among them. It was clear that if they touched that water, they would be drawn quickly under, and the pirates would make sure they stayed there.

Lightning struck in the dawn sky as the serpent roared. The entire boat lunged, the front section drawn out of the water by the power of Destiny's Maw. The others were trying to keep from being swept into the water below.

'Time for something new!' Darrix shouted.

Kialessa looked at her King, and suddenly he didn't really seem like the bold, indestructible man she had seen so many times in the throne room. He was an old human man, with weathered features. His breathing was hard, his eyes tired. He had not slept in days; he had been fighting assassins and those that sought him ill all the days of his life, from the shadows, in his dreams, and now even on the ocean deep. She knew he had a plan for death, and that the Kingdom would be more secure than she'd ever realised without him. But even so, without another miracle, they would all die.

The boat surged and heaved, creaking under the impossible strain of the serpent's embrace. And yet, for it all, she did not shatter. Somehow the Dawn held on. Just like all of them, in the darkest dawn, as the billowing surge conspired against them. They had to hold on to the hope that life was worth living just a little bit more.

Desperately she grabbed his royal red lapels and shook him, pleading with her eyes for him to somehow find deliverance for them all.

He looked at her, his eyes taking far too long to focus on her face. Then he seemed to snap out of whatever oppressive spirit might have been trying to cloud his judgement. 'Ah, indeed, Piex. Now is the time for that *fiery conflagration.'*

'What?' Piex, forgetting all manners, stumbled into his favourite phrase.

'Do it!' Aolith demanded. 'Get that serpent to let us go or we all drown!'

'Target its mouth!' Dale instructed.

'I don't think …' Piex stuttered as Darrix grabbed him in his arm to try to keep him from falling away. 'Um, indeed, now would be a most precipitous time for such a course of action; however, it is yet untried that I have mastered a sufficient level-'

'Shut up and do it!' Allastassia shouted.

There was a scream as Natasha's hooves slipped and she fell, held on at only the last moment by Marchan's hands. Pirates tugged at her, but seemed only to be taunting her; none held on.

'Just do the burning, now!' Posk shouted, sliding down to help the far weaker wizard. A pirate leapt out of the water and Posk shattered his wooden face with his enchanted gauntlet.

Piex's brow furrowed in concentration, but he shook his head. 'I can't! I just can't … I'm going to burn you all!'

'Little can stop that now,' Aolith smiled, clutching the rigging that held many of them on.

'Death to fire, or death by water. Would I gladly die at the hand of one who was only trying to help me,' Natasha shouted, struggling against the balustrade as she stood away from the pirate's clutching hands.

King Dunnkan put his hand on Piex's shoulder. 'It is time,' he said.

It was an order, and a prayer.

Piex nodded, whispering calculations to himself. Magical lights twingled about his headband as he worked.

Again the boat shifted, and groaned. The serpent heaved once more, and the bow began to bend dangerously. Any instant now and Kialessa knew the entire ship would split, and they would be thrown into the churning, death filled waters.

Suddenly the sky was lit up with bright, orange, welcomed fire. It burst directly into the Destiny Maw's face, right inside its serpentine mouth. Instantly the press against the Dawn slackened, and a moment later the sky was rent with the Maw's agonised cry. Flames leapt up from her mouth as if the entire entity had caught fire. The coils began to loosen.

Everyone cheered once more.

'No!' Jerik cried from her head, patting the fire away from his own clothes. 'No, keep fighting! Destroy the Imagination's Dawn! Now, do it now!'

But the serpent was injured, and with a terrified cry pulled away. The entire Dawn shook violently as the Maw released her back onto the sea. Pirates struggled to catch a hold of her as she fled, her mouth burning with fire and pain for several dozen paces till she began to dive under the waves.

Jerik's voice could be heard shouting against the wind as he clutched on to the Maw's burning skull. 'No! Go back, destroy it now, or I'll kill you as well!' He beat her, but she acted as though she could not feel it at all against the agony in her skull.

They cheered as she fled.

Safe Harbour

We are not of this world. Every heart yearns for the place where it belongs, where it came from before this mortal frame. We wander in life, at times so terribly lost, for a place we cannot find. Cast out on a dangerous sea, all we seek is a safe harbour. The purpose in life …
is to return back home.

Nemon, 3rd Sage of Lumos, keeper of times

They hastened to the rigging, while Darrix and Natasha tried to minister to the injured and sleeping, those who by mere luck had not been cast into the waters. There was little that could be done, so dread had been the enchantment.

'Darrix, hasten!' Aolith commanded.

He stumbled toward the lower deck. His hand was bandaged, crushed by some pirate. It would be dawn before they could do anything proper about it. She looked about – they were well and truly spent. Everyone had multiple wounds, including herself, the other youth, and the brave animals who had stood with them. Amidst the soldiers and sailors there were almost none now who could even stand. It did not look good. She shook the fear from her heart and hurried to try to help Darrix.

There, within the lower deck, it appeared as though eight or so more sailors and soldiers had managed to survive. They looked as though they had been batting for their very lives below deck, where the wooden pirates had tried to break through the hull.

Darrix struggled down immediately, near a tall human man who lay bleeding, propped up by some broken rigging and what little remained of their blankets. It was his father.

Kialessa hurried down as well.

'He fought like a dragon,' a wounded soldier stated with reverent awe. It looked like he'd lost his entire arm in the battle. 'Never seen anything like it. That one gem merchant kept every last pirate from ever setting more than a single foot on this hull without dying for it.'

Darrix checked his father, who, gaining some consciousness, smiled at his boy. 'Good fight, well worth it.' He grinned.

Darrix checked his wounds. 'Serious, but it should not claim your life.'

'You got some of those prayers for me, my boy?'

Darrix put his hands on his father's head, and was about to begin a healer's prayer when the old man shuffled, tucking his ever-precious scroll case deeper into the folds of his vest.

'Something is wrong,' Darrix stated. 'Father?'

His old man looked wary, and perhaps ashamed. He drew out the case. His fingers were blue and stiff but he handed it to her, so with a wary heart Kialessa held it. It felt cold, and strangely heavy.

'Go on,' he told his son.

Darrix did not continue, nor seem pleased in the least. 'Father, what is in that case.'

Harrobar Minerson sighed wearily. 'A promise. Something not just for you and your mother, mind you. But for the whole Kingdom. You know, King Dunnkan knows all about it. He had me bring it on board.'

Darrix simply waited.

Harrobar sighed. 'It's not important right now. Go on, my son. You'll find no trouble praying over this man's soul now.'

It seemed he was right; the blessing was unimpeded. Darrix's father fell straight to sleep.

Darrix took the scroll case from her, and looked like he might even open it. But then he seemed to decide against it, and tucked it into his old man's vest again. He shook his head, and sighed. The rigging creaked ominously from outside. Darrix hurried past her to help save the ship.

She looked again at the older man's face. He was still young, seeming younger than her father. He was tall, with impressive features that made him quite handsome. But whatever it was in that scroll case that he valued so much would have to wait.

Kialessa raced on deck and looked around as they struggled, ten students and one old King trying to drive an entire sailing ship. It would take more than their best efforts to get going again.

'Come on, old girl,' Kialessa begged the Dawn. 'Just once more.'

The boat suddenly lurched forwards and began to propel herself against the wind, with tattered sails and broken masts. Miraculously, she somehow ploughed on.

'How is she doing it?' Piex marvelled.

'It's the Imagination's Dawn,' Allastassia smiled.

The ship moved on; not quickly, but her pace never did slacken. A dozen soldiers soon joined them, but it seemed they struggled to fight off the magical sleep, or the grim hopelessness that tugged at every heart.

Soon the bosun set all their feelings to a sad soliloquy.

Oh Jenny, don't be sad,
Your sons are dead at sea.
Called over wave and tide,
They heard the goddess's plea.

But light a little candle,
And keep it for your boys
They heard the Kingdom's call,
And picked up swords, not toys.

So Jenny, don't be said,
Your sons are dead at sea.
But light a little candle,
Then light one more for me …

Soon Posk climbed up to the crow's nest. 'The giant sea snake is still following.'

They ran to the aft, looking hard at the horizon. Sure enough, the Destiny's Maw still ran after them.

'We've seven days to make the ports at Emerel,' Aolith told them. 'We can't afford another battle before then.'

'Neither will the sagemaster be back till later,' Marchan added. 'If he can find us at all beyond the archmage's wizardry.'

They looked at the King. He seemed battered and bruised, but as determined as ever.

'Do we stand, and fight?' Dale asked. It seemed a bold but stupid thing to do. Kialessa did not think they could win another battle.

The King looked at his steward.

'Our foe is far better equipped than we could have ever guessed,' the part fey councillor thought out loud. 'That power used to defy the rod was the magic of the giants, and that sleep enchantment reminded me of the southern elves. Who sponsors this assassin and would have access to such diverse and wonderous tools must be powerful indeed. An ancient evil, perhaps?'

'You suspect the Dybbuk?' Aolith asked, referring to the legendary famine dragon of the Blithling lands, who was credited with starting the second demon war.

The steward shook his head. 'I do not know.'

The King looked out at the horizon. 'I am not keen to battle that creature again without the sagemaster's help. Tobiuus, or his projection, however weak, is still a problem.'

'Unlikely,' the steward insisted.

The King raised a questioning brow at him.

'I instructed the sagemaster, when taking the general to the capital, to send guards to the prison where Tobiuus remains. They are to bring him out, bound, and enfeebled. If Tobiuus really is the cause of this trouble, he will have been dealt with by now. And I doubt we will see Brandish ever again.'

The King nodded. 'Then we outrun her till the wizard or the high priestess returns?'

The steward was grim in his reply: 'Unlikely. The Maw is simply too fast, even with her great injuries. With the powers of the assassin driving her on, it is unquestionable that she will catch us by nightfall, and all but Baroness Winterhaven will be disadvantaged in that fight.'

The King sighed, and then suddenly the entire boat lurched to a stop.

'What is this?' the King asked.

People looked about, but only Allastassia had an answer. 'She's … upset.'

'Who?' the steward asked.

Allastassia's face took on a dreamy look, as it did when working her mighty magic, or when talking to trees. 'The Dawn. She's … upset … Upset and … angry. Very, very angry.' She ran her hand along the balustrade, the rich mosses glowing at her touch.

There was a gentle shudder in the waters that made Kialessa believe her friend's words were very, very accurate.

'Angry?' the steward asked – he had seen greater wonders, yet seemed to question this.

'Oh no.' Allastassia sounded worried.

And then, ignoring the wind, the entire boat began to swing about to face the Maw.

'How?' the steward asked.

What remained of the sails slackened and flumped about in the confused breeze. Every breath was held. The dark outline of the Maw was clearly visible on the far horizon.

King Dunnkan was the first to speak. 'Then she demands we make our last stand, here, now, while the light of the sun still beckons us to rise, and fight, and win.'

It felt like it was their cue to cheer, but no one spoke. It was little wonder; the steward had just outlined how this was a battle they could not win.

'For Lenmer'el!' the King affirmed.

Then they cheered. Sailors worked the sails till they caught the breeze, and the Dawn moved on till it rode against the fierce gale and directly towards their foe.

Kialessa gulped, and did not feel like facing that dark serpent and the master assassin again today. She had just seen him move mountains … This was not the chance they'd hoped it would be.

In the next instant, Toni appeared in a glittering shower of what sounded like shattering glass, levitating in the air in front of the King. 'No,' he stated, and suddenly all the wind died. The Dawn stopped as if held by an invisible god's hand.

'If you have another suggestion, boy of the Forbidden Forest, I would dearly love to hear it,' King Dunnkan said with great tact.

Toni nodded, gazing out at the far horizon. 'I still don't understand … but he hunts without quarter for a prize he simply cannot keep. This offends the natural order of all things, yet they willingly do so without regard for the value of their own lives, in absence of the alarm in their own conscience. This is abomination, this is evil. This is unnatural … and it must be stopped.'

Kialessa gasped as if she'd been holding a breath she didn't know she had. Toni was going to *help* them!

Toni began to glow deeply from within. The glow brightened until it lit the entire sea. Within, a cocoon of light seemed to spread around him, and in a moment it shattered. And there, still glowing with deep blue radiance, was a tall being with four long arms.

Sailors threw themselves to the deck in awe and fear.

Toni spoke to all their minds: *Stand down, good King. I will deal with this assassin personally, once and for all.*

King Dunnkan looked up at him, seemingly in awe. 'I advise against it, young one. We know too little of this assassin and his powers.'

Then I am sure to bring you news, Toni replied. With that, his four arms swung about as if twisting space itself somehow; he formed a neat portal with well defined, glass-like edges. Clearly visible on the deck of the Maw, a hundred wounded and panicked pirates made of wood gazed back.

Then, in an instant, Toni and his portal disappeared.

Of her own will the Dawn swung to one side so they could all see.

A moment later, a huge plume of red and black smoke, riddled with lighting, rose up from the Maw. It took several breaths for the sound to reach them, but it sounded like the raw strength of nature roared in its might.

'That sounds like a volcano,' Piex informed them all.

Black lightning streaked from the dot on the horizon, then red. A huge wave of magical power shook the ocean, followed by a supernal pulse of fey energy that caused moss and lichen to glow with a thousand hues, and triple in their size. Then a great white light shone down from the heights of the sky above, followed by a pulse of destruction that sent debris high into the air. The shockwave that followed almost knocked them all down.

For a long time there was silence.

Then the lookout shouted, 'The Maw retreats!'

Toni, as Oum, takes a stand.

Sailors and soldiers cheered.

But then there was only silence. Toni did not return. Socks the cat appeared at her feet, gazing intently at the battle scene. It did not bode well. A sad fear welled inside.

'On,' the King whispered. 'On! Find the ancient! On, on now!'

The Dawn surged forward with mystical haste, but even then she feared it would be too late by the time they arrived. The sea was strewn with the broken and torn bodies of pirates made of wood. It looked as if none had survived.

'Over here!' a voice called, and Kialessa was relieved to see it was Anaesu, the green haired merboy, who had surfaced to call them over. His older brother waited not too far away, saying nothing.

'The merboy,' Allastassia seemed impressed.

Toni lay half submerged on a strange load of wood, as if it had somehow been a part of the Maw's heart. He was cut and bleeding from a dozen little wounds. Swiftly they carried him aboard, Piex's levitation magic being put to gentle use.

The wounded ancient lay dying on the deck of the Imagination's Dawn, a creature of legend who was once so powerful they could bring peace to warring gods. He looked at them all with trembling eyes. *He escaped, I know not where*, he confessed. Pale grey blood oozed from his wounds, turning the deck a pearlesque white with its touch.

Natasha spoke the obvious: 'He's dying.'

'Toni!' Kialessa shouted, daring to touch his face and try to hold open his closing eyelids. She spoke his true name: 'Oum! Awake, and get up! You cannot die today!'

Toni coughed, *You place too much emphasis on the importance of life*, he told her weakly. *For what better death is this, than to die for those you care about?*

His words touched her mind and heart, and she found herself crying. He had been very brave, risking his own immortal life for their temporary

Choice, set free

safety. He could have outlived the entire lifetime of the world if he'd wanted to. But, instead, he'd willingly spent it all for the life of his friends.

A moment later, Wanderer tugged at her shoulder, slipping from invisibility and startling everyone nearby. The little dragon limped down, and tapped her nose to his, and Kialessa knew she offered her life in exchange of his own.

No, little one, he told her. *You are so brave, but you are simply not enough.*

Her friends clustered around her, tears in every eye.

'You did it, Toni,' Posk told him. 'You chased away the assassin, and you saved our lives.'

That is good, he replied. *Then perhaps today is a good day to finally meet my mother and father?*

Kialessa could not bear the thought of holding her friend until he passed away. She looked at the circle of concerned faces around them. Her gaze settled on Darrix. 'Is there nothing you can do?'

Toni seemed to smile. *The disease is no match for my own immune system; however, the neurotoxins have set off a cascade of chemical reactions I fear I will never stay in time. This is perhaps my last moment upon this world …*

Darrix immediately pressed his way to Toni's head. 'If there is anything that can be done, I am willing to try.' Immediately the young squire recited the healing prayer against poisons that he'd been taught many times.

The King held out the rod, glowing a soft golden glow, and he spoke: 'Not yet, brave young Ancient, councillor to the gods. I think your time upon this world has not yet come.'

Darrix's hands and face glowed brightly, the way the high priestesses did when she worked her mighty acts of faith and healing, and when she'd helped cure a boy paralysed from snakebite, or recalled a mother who had died during childbirth.

The light settled around Toni, healing all the injury and hurt.

Toni looked surprised, and filled with wonder. Soon his own light began to glow, and he levitated up off the deck of the ship, his arms forming strange patterns in the air that brought a deep and lasting sense of peace and healing.

I did not know that was possible, Toni said. *You have taught me much today. I thought my death inevitable!*

Darrix smiled, seeming drained and still kneeling. 'We might not get to choose the day we die, but we do get to choose the kind of life we live today. Thank you, Toni, you have saved our lives.'

And you all have saved mine! he smiled, with a broad grin. He threw his arms out and the area filled with light and healing. Even the Dawn righted herself, seeming blessed by his gratitude. *I live, another day! It is a good day!*

He began to laugh, and seemed to invoke a swirling dance in the air. She could not help but join him, it was such fun! Someone grabbed a fiddle, and it soon seemed an entire orchestra joined them, dancing in the air.

All too soon, the music ceased. Clasping each and every one of them with his arms, Toni thanked them all personally for believing he could live. He then went downstairs and healed everyone there too. At some point, Kialessa was never sure when, he turned back into the little white-haired boy with one green eye, and one blue. If anybody else noticed, they didn't seem to mind.

The rest of the day fled by with magical haste, the dim lights of the far harbour of Emerel coming soon into view.

'That journey should have taken a week,' the steward mused.

A moment later the King stood by her side. He looked old, but strong. Already his friendly, fatherly demeanour was slowly slipping away, as the image of King who ruled a nation took its place. He bore a simple nobility underneath his tattered royal attire. He smiled at her. 'Kialessa ... thank you for all you did on this voyage. It would not have been the same without you.'

Suddenly her heart caught in her throat. It would not have been the same voyage if he'd died! But it was worse than that; she had failed him. They had all failed. Her chin quivered and, as she knew he would, he held her before she even had a chance to ask.

'Don't cry, little one. We gave it our best, what more could we have given? If the Eternal had expected more, He would have made it possible.'

She tried to push away the childish tears from her eyes. 'We will get him, next time,' she promised them both.

'If it comes to that. But for now I have a special mission for you.' The King began to look quite serious. Within the High Kingdom I feel I will be as safe, if not safer, than in my own Kingdom. You need not worry about me anymore.' He held her at arm's length, and bent down to look at her eye to eye. 'The High King has a college, with the best students from all the world. Go, and study, and learn all you can. Make new friends, and experience all those things I could never hope to teach you. Will you do this, for me?'

She nodded.

'There will be a new college, and entirely new friends. I will check in on you as often as I can.'

She nodded. This seemed an easy task for her to do.

But he looked quite sincere, 'Entirely new folks to meet. You will be all right, won't you?'

She nodded fiercely. If she didn't have the chance to free him from an assassin on this voyage, she could at least go to college for them all!

The steward approached. 'There is also the parade to attend, and whatever function or event the High King whims to have us sit through.'

The King laughed. 'Admit it, Grudon, you like the socials! So many interesting people and their *secrets*.'

The steward grinned. 'True, true.' Then he looked down at her. 'I suspect next year will be very busy for us all. We may not have much chance to speak, Baroness Winterhaven. But I suspect you will find ways to speak to us, should the need arise.'

She was just beginning to think that was more Allastassia's role, when she suddenly sensed the presence of the steward near her mind. It was a curious sensation. Then she realised he was using the powers of the rod of Lenmer'el.

And she grinned too. Yes, indeed, she had ways to communicate to them all, if needed.

'Go,' the King commanded her, looking as if he had more to say to the steward. 'You'd best help with the packing below deck!'

For a moment, she was just happy. A new college? New challenges? 'I will give it my best!' she replied. If she could not succeed in this quest, perhaps she could do all the better at the next one.

'You always do,' the King replied with a believing smile.

***

The evening fell to peace, and soldiers and sailors finished their preparations to disembark. The Dawn rode in steadily, but she was a mess: sails ripped, seaweed still clung to her rigging and sides.

Toni was sitting, calmly, near the forecastle, when she felt he wanted to speak to her.

She approached, and heard her four closest friends approaching as well. It seemed no one else was invited. Socks was already there, looking content.

She walked to stand beside Toni; she put her arms around him and gave him a great big hug. He looked surprised, then unsure, then hugged her back.

She looked at him, and somehow knew his thoughts. He was sad, but resolute. 'You are not coming with us?'

'You are correct,' he replied, with a long sigh. 'There is great danger here, even to me. I would not wish that danger to follow you as well.'

She nodded, and patted his arm. 'Where will you go?'

He did not reply, but said instead, 'I must see more, and understand deeply the minds of people. There are great forces at work, trying to tear far more than just your one nation into shreds. Great evil runs deep throughout all this land, and your one King cannot hope to stem it alone. But as I now understand, there are those who seek willingly to concur and destroy, and would call all such a virtue … There is much I still must learn. I will be gone for some time I think, and it would be safer for you all to forget me.'

Her heart leapt into her throat. She knew he had every power and authority necessary to do just that.

She looked at her friends, and they seemed to share her thoughts. 'Please don't, Toni. I'm not willing to forget you, or what you did for us.'

He looked at her, and then at the others. 'Just the others then. So be it,' and with a wave of his hand, she imagined he did just that. 'Let them remember in dreams or flashes of insight, and wonder forever what really was, and what was just a dream.'

She thanked him with another hug. The next thing she knew, Posk's huge arms wrapped around them both, and then Allastassia's and Darrix's, though far more gently. If Piex joined in, and she had to guess he did, he was so gentle she felt nothing.

Toni stood back, and his eyes were filling with tears. He touched his face, seeming surprised, but then explained, 'Oh, this is nice.' He looked out at them all with a look of supreme gratitude. 'Thank you, my friends. And remember, you don't only live once; you live *every day*. So choose life.' He smiled, nodded, and then in the blink of an eyelid, he disappeared.

'I would so much like to know how he does that,' Piex said.

Allastassia gave a shuddering sigh. 'I think I will miss him.'

Posk nodded. 'Good. Very good.'

***

'I suppose we must prepare to disembark,' Darrix stated.

The stench of the docks lifted up in the air towards Kialessa, and she listened to the sounds of sailors working in the evening glow. The scene in the twilight was startling to her eyes; the docks alone were larger than the entire castle, than the entire city of Lenmer'el. Merchant caravels came and went, yet they were so large as to make their distance deceptive – the smallest of them was still larger than the Edge.

There was a nip at her elbow. It was Wanderer again. Her friends watched in silence as the little dragon turned visible again.

'Hello, little stranger,' Kialessa grinned. 'I'm glad you are safe.' She patted the little dragon, but it soon moved away.

They looked at her, closely. Her ears were back, her eyes afraid. Wanderer looked out at the ships and dirty harbour, and she mewed nervously.

'This is not her place,' Posk concluded.

Kialessa had already sensed that, though the thought pricked at her heart. Already, she felt she'd lost too much on this voyage. So many new friends who were now memories. Would they ever see each other again?

Allastassia hugged her, and Darrix stood close. Piex put his hand on hers.

But it still made her cry. 'Well, go on then,' she ordered. 'Off with you, little dragon. Go to where you know you will be safe!'

Wanderer waited only a breath more, and flew away, cautious eyes on the busy docks. It was not until she turned completely invisible again that Kialessa felt her longing gaze watching her from in the sky somewhere.

'Dragons have a strong will,' Allastassia said. 'I am sure you will see her again.'

'I know,' she replied. But it didn't ease the passing.

Within the hour they were pulling into the main dock. Smaller ships had cleared the way, a military vessel escorting the beleaguered Dawn into the welcomed embrace of the harbour's arm. Kialessa watched as they drew only a few paces away from one of the medium sized warships of the capital city of Emerel. It was huge, with ten times the number of soldiers that she'd ever seen on their own boats. The bright purple and gold banners floated clean and proud in the sea breeze, the fires at the forecastle beaming out similar colours. Some sailors looked down at the Dawn as she crawled limply past, and pointed. And Kialessa realised they were pointing at her.

She stood at the banister, but then stood away. This was another nation; one leagues away from her home. They'd failed to defeat the assassin, but they'd driven him away. Would he leave off his hunt for good now? Would his fear of Toni keep him away?

And what of the people, this mighty, impressive nation that ruled over them? Their King had sent a small, *small* portion of his army to their land last year, and they had overturned everything.

And they had not learnt to trust a tae'anaryn on their own merits, as her own nation had.

Cautiously, she held out Allastassia's scarf, the one she'd been given at her birthday at the end of last year. Allastassia had told her it would make her look human, if she covered her horns with it. So she did. She watched in wonder as her skin lost her usual red hue and took on a colour like a human's. She had no wings to hide, but her tail was well used to curling up in the small of her back. She would look just like one of them now.

No one said a word to her as she took to the banister beside her four closest friends. Then Posk took to admiring the large cranes they used to load the enormous sailing ships, while Piex described their mechanics. No one in Emerel need ever know who she really was.

15 Just like one of them …

But then she wondered what they would know about her. Would they look for the tae'anaryn that had overcome so much to be with them today? Would they respect other tae'anaryl, like her many tragic siblings, if she pretended she was someone she was not just to fit in?

Or was it the price she must pay to stand out?

'Check out how they're all getting to work!' Posk admired.

She did not know what challenges awaited them within. A new college with hundreds, rather than dozens, of students? A council of the seventeen Kings of the entire Great Kingdom? Would she get to meet the High King and his entire court of the most powerful and wondrous individuals in the entire world? And the assassin had not been defeated, but would he hunt then now, even with all that had happened?

'Yes,' she said with a grin. 'I suppose it's time to get to work now.' And without a second thought, she removed the scarf, and set her face toward the future.

Punishment

Jerik, the dog, assassin of Kings, stumbled toward the Tyrant's chambers. He was well and truly drunk by now, all the better to deal with the cruel beating he knew he was about to receive from his angry sovereign. But he could also feel the eyes of the Wytch of the Wayst upon him, even right now, spying on him from the dreamworld. But this time he just didn't care.

He pushed open the double doors to the flawlessly manicured palatial room before him. The others were already here, which meant he was late. It would make no difference to his fate. 'Sorry … traffic,' he lied.

'Bring him,' the tyrant ordered.

The armed guards gripped him painfully by his forearms and dragged him to the reagent. He could have fled, become a dog, or floated away on the gift of the Blithlings if he'd wanted. But, in all truth, he feared his tyrant's justice far more than what was about to happen.

They threw him at the older man's feet, his Kingly powers throbbing away in the air around him. But they did not stop the tyrant from kicking him in his mouth. He fell to the floor, and counted at least a dozen other boot falls before the tyrant was done. The last blow crushed his face between boot and stone, leaving him spitting blood in a dizzying world.

As duty bade him, he yelped, then whimpered.

The tyrant stood proud, caught somewhere between the indignity of kicking his favourite servant, and the fact he would have genuinely enjoyed it. 'You promised me victory this time, *Jerik*.'

He took a moment to reply, not because he wanted to, but because it was apparent he'd just broken some ribs recently, somehow … 'Yeah, no, deserved that, I did.'

Unexpectedly, the tyrant kicked him again, this time a non-life-threatening boot to his thigh. For a brief moment, the blinding pain was the only sensation he knew.

No one spoke. And no one dared speak for him.

Eventually Jerik spoke for himself. 'I am a worm. I am less than mud. I don't deserve another chance and I won't ask for one. But if you spare my life, I will kill them the next time.'

His voice caught in his throat as the tyrant scoffed. 'You have lost your best chance, servant, and the largest portion of respect that I ever had for anyone. I am of mind to cast you out from my presence entirely.'

That cut him to his canine heart. It hurt, more than anything else had. He lost his humour, his self-depreciation, and wept, 'Please …'

The tyrant snarled, somehow touched yet again by his unquestioning loyalty. 'You still have your uses, *dog*. Dunnkan has made it to our Kingdom at last, and she will no doubt leave his side to study at the college. They are too well protected there; their allies are strong! And any attempt at their lives will likely tarnish the reputation of my favourite city. So, no; you do not have a second chance, not at this time. The regents have gathered, and there is much to do for our wider plans to come into fruition. Leave them alone, for now. It will make the humiliation of their defeat all the sweeter when fate eventually sides with me.'

He looked at his cruel master, momentarily impressed at the patience with which he destroyed those he considered his enemies. So there were more important things now? Perhaps. None would ever forgive him the fact that the troubling monarch of the little southern nation was at the council of the Kings – always looking for concessions and dignity and caring for the less fortunate. It was a trouble they did not need in the world that was becoming. 'Master … I will make this up to you.'

The tyrant scoffed. 'Perhaps. But those wounds are unsightly, and we can't have them festering, can we?'

Choice, set free

'No, not at all, my master.' He winced, fearing what would come next.

And with that, the tyrant poured an entire vessel of concentrated vinegar over his face.

To his credit, the dog did not scream all the while the acid burned his skin. Nor did he weep, till he'd found his own place among his kin that evening. There, they bandaged his wounds and licked his skin. There, in the dark sewers under Emerel, they stood by him, and for him, and with him. No, his tyrannical master had his priorities. But his family would watch the girl, who had somehow defied him again by befriending the mermen, striking down Truevine, and even somehow allying herself with an actual living Ancient of legend.

'Watch yourself, Kialessa Winterhaven,' he promised his reflection. 'For the dogs have caught your scent…'

Appendix

Teacher notes

This book asks perhaps the hardest, and yet most important existential question that everyone at one point or another must answer for themselves – what is the purpose of life?

Every Day

This short chapter sets out the villains' main quest. Who are they, what do they want, and what challenges must they face?

Setting Out

Kialessa is looking forward to another adventure. Who goes with her? What are their goals?

Kialessa asks another important question here – what is the purpose of life? This is not life in specific, that is, what is your individual purpose for being here, but life in *general*. And as Jerik said in Chapter 1 of Book 1 – everyone has a right to disagree, so don't feel you have to all come up with the same answer. So how would you answer this question at this moment?

Three Days

Piex is not doing so well with his travel sickness, is he? What can he do? And Kialessa has to face another challenge she is not built or prepared for – learning how to swim. Can you swim? And how might you react if you found a mermaid while you were out swimming?

The chapter quote is derived from a saying by American playwright Mark Twain. What do you think of the saying, 'The two most important days of your life are the day you are born, and the day you find out why'? Does your life *need* a purpose for you to exist?

Wizards

Again, Kialessa's talent and the privilege of her friends allows her experiences few others ever have. And I hope you'll forgive me if I use this as another excuse to give Kialessa a new outfit!

The chapter quote by Tomin is worth more than a casual glance. How many of us act as if we are made a certain way, whether we like it or not, and so that's how we have to be? Are we born to be unhappy, poor, or a failure, or do we have freedom to rise above our own creation?

The final paragraph is meant to be food for thought as well. Can a night-time prayer of gratitude really make a big difference on tomorrow?

The Squid

This chapter just gives me a chance to explore the heroes' strengths, weaknesses, and relationships. Plus it's an excuse for another song, and that's always a great idea!

What about the chapter quote, "… The meaning of life is to give your gift away" (From 'Finding Your Strength in Difficult Times: A Book of Meditations' by David Viscott, published in 1993, though it may have been influenced, derived, or inspired by William Shakespeare or Pablo Picasso? Perhaps such a thought is timeless?) It relates to a similarly powerful expression by Ralph Waldo Emerson in an 1843 essay entitled 'Gifts':

> *Rings and jewels are not gifts, but apologies for gifts. The only gift is a portion of thyself. Thou must bleed for me. Therefore the poet brings his poem; the shepherd, his lamb; the farmer, corn; the miner, a stone; the painter, his picture; the girl, a handkerchief of her own sewing.*

The idea here, of course, is not that only gifts born of pain have meaning, but that gifts have different values dependent upon the compassion, thought and concern of the gift giver. So to give hours to studying dance, science, or football is **good**. But then to use the gift of those hard-earned skills to bless other people's lives is **better** – to inspire, to teach, and even to earn a living and support one's family. What are your thoughts on this matter?

Every Hope, Every Prayer

Did Kialessa make a tactical error in failing to watch out for herself while protecting others? The steward certainly thought so! Do you think he dealt with confronting her and his King with his concerns appropriately?

What does it take to overcome a great challenge? Why does it feel sometimes like it's all too much, as if life is trying to rip out our hearts and watch us die in the most pitiful, painful manner possible? Is it because we are strong, and made of something different, something special? Could it be life trying to teach us to trust, and to value things of eternal worth? Could it be that no other battle will test us more, and that no other battle will make us stronger? We may have to face it alone, with all the love and prayers of those who care for us, but alone nonetheless. For if pain must be a part of life, mustn't there be some purpose to it?

The Peninsula

Ever since I thought of writing this book, I've thought it would be cute to have our heroes sent on an impossible quest they're not supposed to begin; yet somehow, they complete it and exceed all expectations. Is this an analogy for life's challenges? I do not say ... but since life is made up of a large number of usually very simple things, perhaps part of life's meaning is to find purpose and perhaps even joy in the little achievements.

Of the quote, what can we say? Does life need a meaning to be joyful, happy, and satisfying? Can you find significance in even simple moments, bringing joy to life, whatever its meaning? It reminds me of a cute comic on finding joy in life, regardless of its meaning:

(Cited 27 June 2021 from https://xkcd.com/167/)

The Master of the Forest

In finding a purpose for life, how much depends on what we choose to be? 'But life and fate are our own … at least, for those who are willing to admit that truth.' What does it mean to embrace the forging of one's own fate? Are we driven by our primal urges to simply seek pleasure and avoid pain? Are we nothing more than the programming our history and society have taught us? And when that society is taken away, beds and prepared food and even comfortable toilets, and we find ourselves in an untamed jungle, are we more, or less, than what we truly are?

The Toad

Atheists have some of the most wonderful and enduring philosophical arguments I've ever heard – and some of the most compelling reasons to do good that I've ever known. For example: "It's a strange myth that atheists have nothing to live for. It's the opposite. We have nothing to die for. We have everything to live for" (Ricky Gervais, American actor).

Along this line of philosophical reasoning, it can well be asked if only metaphysical answers can be found to such an existential question as 'is there a meaning to life?' Or, can profoundly simple, deeply rational, soul consoling logic be found without recourse to the supernatural? Such a thought is what drives today's quote – regardless of what kind of life you live, you are one day food for other beings – 'So if you can find any **joy** in your life,' presumably without destroying other people's hope and joy as well, then, 'I think you have found a good thing.' What do you think?

I really wanted the magical words for meeting the great Master of the Forest to be simple – polite. You just need to ask. And sometimes in life, you really, really, really only need to know that. Sometimes, just ask. Just like in Book 1, "Life won't change unless you ask it to." But that doesn't mean you need to be impolite about it! What do you think?

Stone Words

The quote, 'The more we care for the happiness of others, the greater our own sense of well-being becomes,' is attributed to the 14th Dali Lama Tenzin Gyatso, and perhaps should be written on stone. The full quote is well worth a good read:

'I believe that the very purpose of life is to be happy. From the very core of our being, we desire contentment. In my own limited experience I have found that the more we care for the happiness of others, the greater is our own sense of well-being. Cultivating a close, warm-hearted feeling for others automatically puts the mind at ease. It helps remove whatever fears or insecurities we may have and gives us the strength to cope with any obstacles we encounter. It is the principal source of success in life. Since we are not solely material creatures, it is a mistake to place all our hopes for happiness on external development alone. The key is to develop inner peace.'

In this chapter, we also meet Toni, who is sure to be seen again. Who is he, and what do you think he wants?

Wanderer

What do you think of the thought that we live only to learn how to love? Love seems to me to be a somewhat paradoxical thing; it is rare, and precious, but also so very common as to influence every event of every day. You can get swept off your feet in a moment, yet we must also battle to keep love alive constantly. There are many different kinds of love: romantic love, brotherly love, and divine love. But perhaps also practical love. Love can take more than one lifetime, it seems, to believe, trust, understand and apply. Perhaps it is worth a lifetime getting to know how to love?

Wanderer turns up here; in a narrative sense I see the fey dragon as symbolic of the ending of Kialessa's childhood, and the path through the magic forest a rite of passage beyond fantasy, into the harsh, and yet rewarding, realities of adulthood. Wanderer is the life-long reminder of the preciousness, innocence, and honesty of youth, and will serve when a reminder of this innocence is needed. Things have been fairly simple for the tae'anaryn up to this point – obvious bad guys, difficult challenges that are still dealt with directly. It is quite deliberate that no matter what cruel truths are uncovered, and what harsh changes are wrought within her closest circle of friends, they will always have this precious memory of a three-day wilderness campout where they faced great challenges together, and won the friendship of a demi-god himself.

Death's Ally

In a world of magic, where anyone's thoughts can manifest as things in reality, might there be some kinds of magic that are dishonest, taboo, and wrong? Tobiuus is supposed to be one person who has crossed this line and done terribly immoral things in the quest for power. He is an offset to Piex, his brother's grandson, who is also destined to become a wizard of great power. And when you are the one in power, do you ever find it tricky to know how to wield this authority? Where do we draw the line between what is good for the ruler, and good for the ruled? Is uncle Tobiuus "right"?

All must die; it is one of the two things Benjamin Franklin felt he could guarantee about being alive in this world. Who will miss you when you die? And even if, for now, the answer for you is 'nobody', how can you live a life so that you might be missed when your time is up? Keep in mind that "being missed" is certainly not the only reason to live or to die, but can perhaps help inform such deep and compelling questions.

The New Student

The quote today has reference to the Stanford Marshmallow Experiment, a study on delayed gratification in 1972, led by psychologist Walter Mischel (who, like Einstein, was incidentally a Jewish scientist fleeing Nazi supremacists). Michel and his colleges concluded that self-control at even the age of 4 was a great predictor of future success in life. What would you do if presented with one marshmallow now, or two if you could wait out 15 moments of just sitting there? Is self-control, or the "principle of delayed gratification", such an important indicator of future success in life?

Toni is helping the wizards to study. What would you do if a demigod of knowledge turned up to your science class? Would you listen, or be bored with all the seemingly useless trivia? But while I'm at it, does it require a demigod to teach important truths, or can you learn useful things from seemingly incompetent teachers, or even wilfully malicious ones?

A messenger from the goddess of the oceans turns up here to suggest they reconsider their course. What does King Dunnkan decide, and why?

Brandish

Brandish, the Slayer, is a figure that definitely struggles with delaying his personal, immediate gratification. The idea is that while it has led to power, it has also led to a reckless, hedonistic, selfish life. Does he have a point though, that life is brief so you might as well enjoy what you can? It's the kind of sentiment summed up by "YOLO" – You Only Live Once. Is it that our actions can be chosen, but consequences, not so much? Besides, Toni disagrees with YOLO – you live every day, you only die once …

Somehow Kialessa is able to hold off his slaughter until sufficient help arrives, making her again a national hero. How does she hold her own in a battle against the Slayer?

The Storm

The next book could almost start here, but I put them together anyway.

Kialessa is driven from the boat and forced to survive in an environment very dangerous and unfamiliar to her. What does she have to do to survive?

Will you give me a moment to rant? In storytelling, the trope 'Deus Ex Machina' refers to a character who hasn't been mentioned at all in the story suddenly turning up and fixing everything at the last moment, which is considered bad storytelling. It refers to ancient Greek plays where an actor playing a god (i.e., the 'deus') is lowered into the environment using a mechanical crane (i.e., the 'machina') to solve someone's problem. However, I am concerned this trope misses something important in a polytheistic society as evidenced in the Greek plays – the idea actually is that if you have faith, work hard, and do your best, then there are enough gods in heaven that at least *one of them* will eventually take pity on you and help you out. What do you think?

The Northern Sea King

Today's quote is from Ralph Waldo Emerson: "The purpose of life is not to be happy. It is to be useful, to be honourable, to be compassionate, to have it make some difference that you have lived and lived well." Your thoughts? While it can be inspiring to know you made a difference, is it possible to make the world a better place doing nothing at all? I think of Lorenzo from Lorenzo's Oil, whose parents' determination and commitment to helping him confront his debilitating sickness, and his own tenacity and courage, resulted in life-saving changes and a powerful confrontation of entrenched power systems in society.

How have you made a difference in the world, deliberately or accidentally? Intentionally, or simply by being in the right place at the right time?

Here, Kialessa meets the mermaids, including some of the most powerful individuals in their fiercely military culture: the King, and his divinely appointed protector. This is very meaningful to the story, as Kialessa learns a protector does not need to like their protectee at all, but they still must protect them. How could this affect her actions in the future?

Truevine

Truevine the elf suffered a terrible crime many years ago, and wrought an unspeakable vengeance on her perpetrators *and* their families. Now, for reasons not revealed here, she is willing to work with the Dog to slay King Dunnkan and his protectors – and she almost succeeds.

But what do you think of her words, and her justifications for killing guilty people? Does it really matter if you change the world, and trade your own immortal soul for that privilege? Is *anything* worth the price of knowing you changed the world?

Do you think Kialessa will meet Truevine again?

Destiny's Maw

In this chapter, we learn that the assassin is pursuing them from a ship of legend, the Destiny's Maw, a boat with the ability to transform into a giant sea serpent that can crush other ships to splinters. We also learn that Darrix's father is on the voyage as well, hiding a secret he will not share here. But the assassin does not choose to attack the Dawn, even though there are hundreds of passengers thrown into the sea nearby. Why not? Did the assassin miss his first opportunity? Or could the fear of their situation, and inevitable over-crowdedness and food shortages, weaken the heroes' resolve even more? Will fear lead to exhaustion? Is the assassin simply trying to make his victims afraid?

To The Shallows

There is a lull in action as the assassin contemplates his next move and tries subtly to weaken the heroes' forces. Then, getting impatient, Jerik teleports over there to try and remove Kialessa again, just in case it helps his cause. Again, however, he finds his foes too well prepared and too ready to meet any threat he can, thus far, present.

However, he does manage to remove the high priestess from among their forces, and she is particularly good at dealing with the undead … On the other hand, the heroes had removed Truevine from his forces, and she was very good at manipulating nature and the creatures of the sea. So, a stalemate again, as yet?

We touch on the current cultural perceptions of the afterlife in this magical world. Imagine having a choice if you wanted to come back to life or not? Or, sometimes, do you already? There have been countless stories amongst thousands of human cultures, and what do all these 'gods' need these souls for? In either event, if your consciousness did live on after your death, what would you do? Where would you go?

The Sharkmen

It seems the war in the Shallowsea is reaching new heights, as both the great powers of the sea seek alliance with the humans against their great ancestral foe. Is it wise for King Dunnkan to take sides, especially seeing as they are one small boat on a sea filled with potential enemies?

This event makes me ponder some old questions – is it *possible* to be friends with everyone? Are some people really not good friends, and you maintain a better relationship as only acquaintances? And is it *wise* to be *everyone's* friend? Is it possible to please all of the people, all of the time, and what do you do if you can't?

The Tempest

Sometimes, life is hard. Sometimes it is unimaginably, unrelentingly, unapologetically difficult! Those times either crush us, or bring out our best – but either way, they define us.

The journey is going poorly for Kialessa, but still Jerik does not seem to find the chance he seeks to destroy the King. And why do you think the sharkmen have sided with Kialessa's enemy? There's actually a very practical reason, but you will not be told until much later …

Waaglah's Rage

So, has the assassin missed his final chance?

The ocean abomination is a great, primal entity summoned by the sharkmen at the bidding of the assassin. But this is also why the merkin are able to quell the monster, as they, too, are masters of the ocean magics. The idea is that they heard the horn when Kialessa sounded it, but were unable to come until they "came in great numbers", and arrived only just as the monster was summoned by the sharkmen – a very lucky circumstance indeed.

What of Toni? Do you think he should be doing more to help? Or is this all he can do?

What do you think Kialessa and the other heroes should be doing with their time right now, as the Destiny's Maw closes in on them?

The Purpose

Kialessa is trying to be very brave in a very, very difficult situation here. What motivates her and her friends to push on during hard times?

Piex has to be especially courageous, as in the face of multiple failures he is called upon to save everyone. He probably had divine help, with a magical world and a powerful King and all, but still, I hope you thought it brave of him to face a challenge he had failed at many times before.

Here we meet the idea that humans, in this world, sort of have nine lives as well. What would you do if you had three days after dying to decide if you'd like to return? This helps to place a limit on resurrections, as if you lived in a world where death was not permanent, who would fear it? And we need death to feel like a very dangerous challenge if we're going to use it to make a story compelling.

Safe harbour

What does Toni finally learn here? Are there some questions that really have no logical answer, but must be dealt with as we feel is the best course of action anyway? Does that include the question, "What is the purpose of life?" I hope I've inspired you to consider some meaningful answers to this question. But I also hope that, like Toni, not having an answer doesn't paralyse you into eternal indecision and existential ennui. And lest you ever become too overburdened with this question, I leave you with one of the most sage pieces of advice I have ever known:

(Taken 27th June 2021 from https://xkcd.com/220/)

The sins (Emerellian afterlife)
By sagemaster Coure De'Feur, 314 CY

Young Gentle Toni,

Perhaps you may find the following treatise of some use. It was given by Hard Gmore, the late high priest of Serros. Please keep in mind the priests of Serros are deeply strict and notoriously uncompromising, their priesthood structure organised under an entirely militaristic order. And yet their faith is the predominant of all in Emerel, indeed, the entire Great Kingdom. You will find their teachings instructive, at times even inspiring, but you must, as I know you always do, think for yourself, and weigh the virtues of their at times perplexing and paradoxical doctrines for yourself.

Eight sins make us impure, yea, in nine sins there is death. To commit any one of them is to commit all of them, for the least of the sins is enough to make us unworthy to live in the light of Serros's perfection. Death is the reward of every sin. In death those who are pure enter into purity. The residue must remain in sin until the times of redemptions, as Lumos' will attests.

In these eight sins there is suffering, yea, in nine sins there is death, and in death the impure must walk in death. For lying, and sloth. For lust, and greed, which is also the greed of power. Pride is the fifth sin, and cowardice is a deeper sin. For in these six sins there is death, and for the remaining three a greater death. Beware, for in these there is woe pronounced upon a deeper woe. Yea, for hatred is a burning pain, and envy an undying rot. But beyond all these there is the treachery of a broken oath. Beware, beware, beware.

The previous treatise is generally taken as the definitive in terms of describing the nine levels of the afterlife. It is a matter of ancient conjecture how much of this speech remains, or was perhaps even perverted by the *Sacrimony*. It is, however, treated as canon by the faiths of both Serros and Lumos. But not, paradoxically, the god of the dead himself: Ik'skuretza.

How deep a sinful soul is cast into the afterlife is believed to be a matter of their sins, and the deeper one is cast, the harder it becomes to return to the lands of the living, and from there to a better afterlife. Each soul is given till the third sunrise after their mortal death to return to their physical form, otherwise they remain dead forever after. Good souls, it is believed, are claimed by their god's servants immediately.

Thus the afterlife here upon Mya acts as a place of continuing trial and teaching until 'the times of Lumos', which is taken to mean the eventual forgiving of most souls, and their transportation to a peaceful afterlife upon one of the other six planetary bodies of the local system. Souls who commit the three deepest sins risk an eternity in the hells, possibly more.

Here are my current conjectures on the sins, and the possible refining virtues that may free a soul, living or dead, from this vice.

1.   **Dishonesty and hypocrisy** are the first of all the sins, often acting as a precursor to any and all deeper sins. While honesty and truth are seen as the antithesis, failure to be tactful is seen as a subtle yet pervasive version of this sin. It is considered that all sentient souls are dishonest in some way; thus, without the imposition of the divine, none can expect to find their way to a heaven without help.

2.   **Sloth and laziness** are the second worst sins, again, to which all fall prey in one way or another. Deliberate sloth is not to be confused with the 'rest of the righteous' or 'peace of the productive', as the teachings attest. Sloth is overcome with industry, while a subtle version of this sin, as per the priests of the Pantheon, is the worship of idols or deity not approved by their faith – considered an act of indulgent laziness, denying the 'true work' of worshiping aright.

3.   The third sin to which all are beholden is **Pride**. Generally taken to mean hubris or arrogance, some consider any attempt to live outside the station of their upbringing a form of this sin, though it is noted most who ascribe to this harsh view are quick to excuse either themselves or any to whom the hand of the divine is revealed. I, for one, am not convinced. The antithesis of pride is considered humility, service, kindness. The giving of charitable wealth is seen as a sure means of overcoming this unavoidable sin. A curious yet subtle version of this sin is the claim to powerlessness; that the Gods have not provided a way to prevail or die trying.

4.   Few consider **Envy** an unavoidable sin, but as I study humanity, I must admit that I, for one, am not convinced. This sin includes covertness, or wanting more of what others have. It is considered that looking after oneself

appropriately is the antithesis of this sin, as it is taught: 'take care of yourself, there is unseen trouble enough in every life to cure all envy.' A subtle version includes not only the envy of those with more wealth and power, but the envy of those with simpler, happier lives. It appears to include greed, that is keeping goodness intended for others to yourself. It includes such deeds as hoarding, as opposed to wise provision for the future.

5. **Cowardice** is given as very serious sin, which includes abandoning a post, failing to 'go down with the ship', and other such acts of fear. The antithesis of fear is taught to be trust; trusting in the purposes of the divine for a life, and death, of any mortal.

6. The next sin is **Ingratitude**, including wanton, erratic, and selfish behaviour. It includes a capricious or child-like demand for more good than that which you have already received. A subtle version involves giving away precious things for a thing of no worth. It includes carelessness, or not taking proper stewardship of those things in your care, including children, the aged, the injured, and the innocent. It is often considered a gateway sin to the three greatest sins now following.

7. Perhaps the sin third to worst is that of mortal **Lusts**, not just of the sexual, but also of all kinds of over indulgence and megalomania. It is perhaps subsumed in a willingness to take without regard to the consequences. The antithesis of Lust, according to Lumos, is kindness, and according to Serros, self-denial. A subtle version includes all abuses of power, those who use their authority to manipulate and control others without righteous ways, or who attempt to use their power to

hide their other sins and crimes.

8.   **Hatred** even to death (taken to mean murder); it is noted that those who hate even to death may not receive forgiveness of this sin in this life, or in forever. Priests of Lumos teach that it is a great virtue to forgive a murderer, guaranteeing transit of the saint to a heaven. Love is seen as the healing antithesis of hate.

9.   The greatest sin is almost universally considered to be that of **Breaking an Oath**, for obvious reasons. While it appears all natural forms of life and matter obey the laws given them without flaw or fault, sentient life seems uniquely able to rise above such: choosing their own career, and perhaps even fate. In so doing, they can betray the expectations of others, friend, foe, or god, and knowingly and willingly do that which they have sworn not to do. It is not sure if any such can ever be forgiven, for it is not heard of that any who are put to death for such crimes are ever brought back to life.

How to overcome death

Most who die do so at their appointed time, and do not return. And while some have returned to life of their own volition within the three sunrise limit, most souls who pass into the afterlife must seek the interposition of a priest or priestess, known as a 'calling priest'. The soul seeking to return is generally referred to as the 'petitioner'.

The calling priest must have travelled to the level of the afterlife the soul currently resides at. Few priests can call beyond the third layer, and only the greatest living ever achieve the sixth. Beyond that are the truest legends of resurrective faith, Nemon, 3rd Sage of Lumos, known as an 8th priest, having returned even repentant murderers to life on at least two known occasions. However, most accidental or sudden deaths leave the soul in the first layer of the afterlife, coterminous with the mortal world, and it is easy to return to life – relatively speaking.

Please note, however, that the calling priest takes a terrible risk – their life may be required in exchange; they may find themselves drawn into the afterlife with the petitioner and find themselves unable or unwilling to return. Their health, or physical qualities such as speech or sight, may be sacrificed. In addition, some other price or quest may be laid upon the petitioner by the gods.

Most petitioners face further complications, depending on the nature of the death. A cursed knife may steal a soul for a particular deity, which complicates returning. Evil souls are usually claimed by their dark masters for eternal torment, and must be wrested from their suffering. Also, properly consecrating an evil doer's grave may make it harder, if not impossible, to bring their soul and body back together again.

Finally, the general populace deeply believes that if it is 'your time', and you still insist on returning, life will be much worse for such. Stories abound of petitioners whose life deteriorated meteorically after their inability to accept the god's judgement on their appointed time to die.

Guides

Diary of Allastassia Greens'holm, Enchantress in honour of Lenmer'el.

Since successfully navigating my chrysalis last Autumn, thanks be to the moon goddess, I am ever more aware of the bright red star that she has sent to guide me through my life, set at about 150 declinations to her shining face.

Kialessa's new friend visits her often, and though it seems the tae'anaryn is rarely aware of Wanderer's presence, both seem very content at the nature of their relationship. It is this topic that I wish to address this night, that perhaps these words may give some wisdom to my future children, and perhaps their descendants. It is the topic of our <u>life guides</u>, those seven spirits sent by the greater gods to protect us through life, above all from the demons of Neth (benighted his name), though it would seem topical to discuss the minions of the god of monsters — Oodria'a. My own monster, a horrid thing with far too many spiney fingernails and a face most abhorrent, was sent away by my father when I was about four, and I admit I have never feared what might have lurked under my bed ever since then. But all this is beside the point.

As I was saying, as there are seven Elder Gods, each sends a spirit being to protect and guide us in our lives. As such, we believe:

Serros — an **angel** in the heavens who watches us. The priests at Emerel teach that the angels do not judge us, but faithfully write of all our deeds so that the god of the Sun may judge us. While it seems this might make them dispassionate towards us fickle, flawed mortals, the priests teach that the angels are almost all very nice and kind. Stories are told of angels visiting various petitioners and saints, though I have never met mine. Kialessa and Piex saw one once, but I'm not sure she is either of their angel guides, but rather one filled with the particular task of leading us to the Far Keep and, most importantly, warning us of the dangers we would face there.

Lumos the Moon — as mentioned, all have a **star** to guide them. Some have met their stars; Flower apparently swallowed hers, and I have no idea what that means. I sometimes feel mine calling to me to be patient, or to give me some clever idea, such as when I invented my lens. I'm sure he/she is a very talented and interesting fellow, and I look forward to thanking them when I die, if not sooner.

Annas, goddess of beasts — the goddess of love and war sends an interdimensional **spirit animal**. I will not speak of mine here, but I truly believe Kialessa just encountered hers as a physical entity known as Wanderer. It is not uncommon that Kings and great rulers have such powerful entities as dragons to be their beast guide, so I'm not surprised the King's protector has one as well. You can see images of the golden lion that is said to protect King Dunnkan all over his throne room.

Plannas, god of plants — while other gods seek for spiritual entities, Planas is unique in that his is always devotedly physical — an actual **plant** that is supposed to be very healthy for the particular individual for whom it is assigned. Aunt Mayblossom always complains that hers is radishes, but they do her much more good than the pastries she seems to consume in great quantity! Like most dryads, I am in life a part of my plant; though unlike most, I am not tied to a single plant, but may choose from among them freely. If you must know, it is the lavender blossom climbing vine, which grows in wild abundance in lands such as Emerel. A stout bloom from midspring all through late winter, it is, as I am, influential to life and important in many magical spells. I will place some here when next I acquire it, as when I summon it, it will not last, as you know!

Mya the world — it is held that a certain **crystal** is for each soul upon this world. I thought mine the red ruby the King gave me last year, but lost it all too soon. I fear I shall never find it again, because I was unworthy, but perhaps the Moon goddess shall be kind. I fear I have offended her deeply, actually ...

Waaglah, goddess of the Waters — unlike other guides, the goddess chooses for each soul a **body of knowledge** though which they can 'know the divine', or, at least, have gainful employment. It is said that once such is found, there is a free flowing of wisdom and understanding, a delightful, joyful spirit that entirely takes hold of one's soul, but that never remains and should never be forced to do so. I always have assumed mine to be the art of enchantments, though I have not had a servant of the goddess confirm so. I do like music, though, and if I weren't so gifted in magic would pursue music as my only love!

Pumos of death — the god of shadows, who seems to like Kialessa very much, places at the feet of each soul in this life their **shadow** as a constant reminder of their inevitable death, though I think it also reminds us to beware of sin, for nothing hidden from Serros the Sun is hidden from the God of Shadows. I am not fond of my shadow, though she seems to do nothing against, nor particularly for me. We travel together, and for now, that is enough.

Would that might be the end of it; however, both Neth, Oodri'aa, and possibly most if not all other gods have apparently set a servant or two to watch over every mortal life. It seems to be a lot of attention, but we mortals seem to manage it — perhaps due to the intervention of the Elder? Perhaps we are unaware of our own retched and crowded state? Others claim our sometimes-random thoughts are simply the promptings of our guides.

Some teach that it is the guides that we pay the most attention to that have the greater ability to influence our life, so I suppose that cuts down on the noise.

As for me, I am not sure. I simply write these things for your information.

Allastassia Greens'holm

Regarding Waaglah

By Coure De'Feur, sagemaster of Lenmer'el

The goddess of the oceans is generally considered a powerful, ancient, inscrutable force of nature. Her priesthood, almost exclusively priestesses, are like the oceans that they worship; they follow no set dogma, just as water takes any form it is given. What little they have written down gives scant and confusing insight into the nature of the goddess. To them she is inspiring, powerful, and deeply passionate, the weight of her wisdom compelling her to a measure of isolation amongst the other Elder gods. Yet she also provides countless practical insights into even everyday necessities.

One common theme amidst the writings of even disparate servants of the goddess of the waters is the apparent theme of coming to know the 'goddess within'. Unlike the priests of the sun or moon, who strive through law and ritual to become closer to the divine, the goddess of the waters appears to teach that divinity is already the right of every living creature. Pain and suffering, as much as joy and success, are given as one of the great ways to come to know the divine as **<u>an aspect of what one already is</u>**.

*The shrines of the goddess of water are readily available at most major cities and ports, and frequently found in water or riverside monuments. Waaglah likes men (a **lot**), but she is staunchly supportive of females, overtly preferring to protect them on the water – yet still more men are sailors. And while her priesthood is almost exclusively female, this is not always the case.*

The faithful of Waaglah range from mystical witches hidden in dark bogs, to human commoner storm-summoning maidens living full-time upon the waters. They are silent city scholars who touch water but once a year from their sacred font, to fish-like beings who are forbidden to rise above the surface of their lake. They all seek wisdom and knowledge and understanding, and are generally kind but stoic individuals who care little for the turmoils of the world about them.

Teachings of the goddess of the waters include, but are not exclusive to:

'She is the sea.
She is the raging storm, the silent quell.
She is the wind and the waves.
She is the depths, and she is the sky.
She is the goddess;
Wayglah.

Let not the fears of others concern you – you are the raging storm; you are the gentle sea.
You have permission to rest. You are not responsible for every broken thing.
Yours is the sacred house, let none defile who do not answer for this crime.
You are the indignant rage of the storm.
At times, rest upon the shore. At times, dive deep within the hallowed depths.
Within the hallowed depths lies the sacred history we hide from ourselves. Only when one swims in the depths does she learn not to fear that darkness.
Let those who answer to a husband do so, for honoured is your bondage. That a new soul may enter this life through the gift of men, yet only do they live by the power of woman. Yield each new young man to his kind at the door of his adulthood – let his way be strength, and his honour is his glory. Ever in each man's heart lies a sacred chamber that opens only to one whom he calls "mother".'

Book 8

The assassin must leave off his quest in preparation for the great council of the Kings, and Kialessa is left to her own devices in the most threatening and dangerous situations of all – high school.

But what sinister forces are gathering against her and all who embrace the freedom to choose? Will old friendships sunder as new friendships are forged? And will they find compassion in their hearts for the famous half demon in the most powerful nation on earth? Will she finally stop the assassin and his tyrant, or will she finally find she's been nothing but a pawn in a much larger game all along …

Place the date and your personal mark here each time you read this book – libraries included!

Why not share your experiences and thoughts with the fandom? Get a grownup's permission and visit

www.DrJoe.id.au

for fan art, sequels, competitions and more!